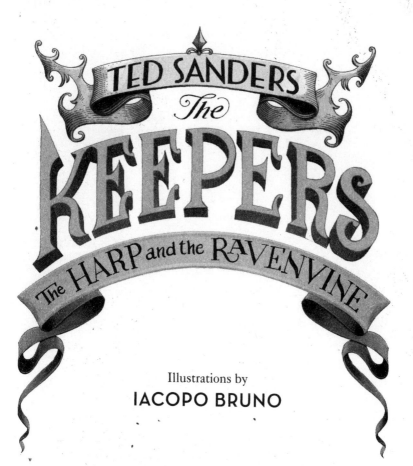

TED SANDERS

The

KEEPERS

The HARP and the RAVENVINE

Illustrations by
IACOPO BRUNO

HARPER
An Imprint of HarperCollinsPublishers

ISBN 978-0-06-227585-1

Typography by Carla Weise
16 17 18 19 20 CG/RRDH 10 9 8 7 6 5 4 3 2 1
❖
First Edition

Little Bo Peep

The Departed

For Dad,
for teaching me how to have adventures

"Some people talk to animals. Not many listen though.
That's the problem."
— A. A. MILNE, *WINNIE-THE-POOH*

CONTENTS

Leaving Home

The Sundered Bloom

PART ONE

Leaving Home

CHAPTER ONE

April

APRIL WOKE IN DARKNESS TO THE SOUND OF BARON GROWLING. Not that she could hear the dog, exactly. He was far out in the backyard at the edge of the woods. It was impossible to hear anything outside, not with the window closed and Uncle Harrison's ancient air conditioner wheeze-rattling from the next room over. No, it wasn't the *sound* of growling that woke April from her troubled sleep. It was the . . . what? April didn't quite have the word for the way the dog's warning bloomed inside her mind.

She wasn't sure there was a word.

She lay in her bed and focused on Baron's anger, vibrating like a wasp's nest in her head, until she swore she could almost feel a rumble in her throat and chest. It made her heart pound. Baron was a farm dog, sturdy and wise, not the type of dog to get riled up in the middle of the night without reason. For a moment April was sure the stranger she'd seen yesterday had returned, the woman with fiery red hair, watching the house from the trees. But no—yesterday, Baron had barely bothered to notice the red-haired stranger before she slipped away. Whatever he'd caught wind of tonight was something . . . different.

April waited for the dog to settle down. Instead his growling grew deeper. April's arms and legs began to tingle, aching to act. She kicked the blankets back and sat up, reaching for her temple. She couldn't hear Baron growling, no, but she didn't have to hear.

She just knew.

She knew because of this: the mysterious object she'd found at the flea market two weeks before. Flat, and about the size of her open hand, it was a delicately crafted golden vine, curling and beautiful, with tiny gold and silver leaves. April wore it wrapped around the back of her left ear, where it hugged her tight, as if made for her. It lay snug against the side of her head, the only jewelry she had ever even tried to wear. But of course the vine was more than mere jewelry. Much more. April wasn't willing to say that the vine was magic—she didn't believe in magic, and felt only a little bit bad about it. But there was no denying that what the vine did was . . . phenomenal. Yes, that was a good word. Phenomenal.

Downstairs, the ancient grandfather clock in the hallway began to chime. It was three in the morning. After it fell silent, she pressed the vine against her temple, listening hard.

Through the vine, a part of Baron's mind was alive inside her own. He was a brave dog, a good dog, protecting the farmhouse, protecting April and her older brother, Derek, and fat Uncle Harrison. Just as she'd known that Baron hadn't felt threatened by yesterday's red-haired stranger, April knew how badly he yearned to bark at whatever was out there now; her own throat itched with the urge. Even more, though, she knew that a terrible stench drifted out from the midnight woods, digging deep into Baron's sensitive nose, stinging and foreign and troubling.

April couldn't actually smell this stink. Nonetheless, a huge part of Baron's brain—and therefore April's as well—roiled with disgust. Disgust and anger and fear. Underneath all his bravery, Baron was afraid of this smell. And therefore April was too.

She lay there, worrying but trying not to fret. April always tried to stay calm on the outside, no matter what was going on inside. If only the vine was working as well as it was supposed to, she thought. If it were, maybe then she could stay here and discover what had Baron so spooked. Maybe she could know *everything* Baron knew—hear what he could hear, smell what he could smell, discover the truth about the invader in the woods—if only the vine were whole.

But the vine wasn't whole. It was broken.

She ran her thumb across the broken stem of the vine, a single rough nub that hung down just in front of her ear. The vine had been like this when she found it. A piece had been

5

amputated, a nauseating thought. She preferred to believe that the missing piece was out there somewhere in the world—she *had* to believe—but without it, the vine was incomplete. *She* was incomplete. She didn't know how she knew this, but she knew this with every fiber of her being. Without the missing piece, she couldn't hear as clearly as she was supposed to, even when she concentrated her very hardest. And sometimes, when she pushed *too* hard . . .

April shoved the thought down. It wasn't good to dwell on things you couldn't do anything about. Instead, she would do something about Baron. She stood and went to the window, rocking the crooked sash open gingerly. Though it was the middle of June, a startling and unsummerish slap of cool air pushed in, toppling the delicate pyramid of cicada shells on her nightstand. The brittle amber husks skittered across the hardwood floor. Outside, April could now hear Baron's agitated whine for real. He gave a round little half bark. In her head, his unease rose and fell with the sound of his voice.

She climbed out onto the roof below, the gritty shingles digging into her bare knees. She clambered to her feet, her toes gripping the steep slope with the ease of long practice. She squeezed past Uncle Harrison's old air conditioner, careful not to bump against the window. Her dim shadow spilled across the roof in front of her, drawn by the hazy half-moon behind. The black bodies of the trees rose all around the yard, breathing softly in the wind. The air prickled her arms. There was a storm coming—she could feel it not only in her own bones, but in Baron's as well.

It was because of Baron that she'd learned what the vine could do. She'd come home with the vine that first day, not knowing what it was or what it did, but bursting with an exhilarated confidence she'd never felt before. The vine was hers and no one else's, a secret garden of wonders to which *she herself* was the only key. She'd sat on the back porch with Baron by her side, and after an hour of fussing, she had experimentally snugged the vine around her left ear. It fit perfectly. A few curling branches jutted out below her ear, while over the top a longer meandering arm stretched delicately toward her temple, splitting and looping like the ivy that grew across the garage.

She'd felt warmth against her skin, and a comforting pressure, and then . . . it was almost impossible to describe. An entirely separate consciousness had opened up miraculously inside her own, a sea of emotion that wasn't hers—comfort, affection, contentment. All of it both totally foreign and completely familiar. She'd forgotten to breathe, forgotten even to see. "Who are you?" she'd said aloud, and as soon as she spoke, the new mind within her mind trembled attentively, almost as if it had heard her.

At the same instant, Baron had lifted his head and perked his ears at the sound of her voice. April met his gaze, and his tail began to thump, and a slow jolt of simple joy flooded her, coming not from within but without. She took the vine off, just to see, and everything went gray and blank. All that bright joy disappeared. When she slipped the vine back on, it came flooding back.

That was when she knew. She was reading Baron's mind—or no, it was more like the vine allowed Baron's mind to overlap her own, like she was both herself and the dog at the same time. She could feel his love for her, really *feel* it, as big and as simple and as pure as love could be, and because Baron loved her, in the strangest way it was like loving herself too, and . . .

Suffice it to say that there had been crying. Tears of astonished joy—quite a few, actually. And April firmly believed there was no shame in that.

Afterward, she'd learned that the vine worked on every animal, not just Baron. Or to be more specific, it worked on every *nonhuman* animal—the vine didn't work on people, thank goodness. April much preferred the company of animals to the company of humans anyway. She always spent her summers wandering the woods and meadows around the house, climbing trees and wading Boone Creek and quietly watching animals live their lives.

And now with the vine, those activities were magnificently transformed. In the last two weeks she'd opened herself to the minds of nesting robins and foraging raccoons and thirsty leeches and once, at Doc Durbin's vet clinic just through the woods, a wounded badger. Deer, toads, squirrels, snakes, red-tailed hawks—almost every animal one could hope to find here in northern Illinois. And in each encounter, a part of each animal's consciousness—fear, excitement, boredom, pain, hunger—became a temporary part of her own.

It was a miracle made just for her, she sometimes felt, and the vine was without question her most prized possession. More than a possession, actually. She was so connected to it that on the rare occasions when she took it off, usually just to shower, she could feel the vine pulling at her, an ever-present tug of longing and belonging. The vine was not just hers, but *her*.

Yet because of the missing piece, that deep burn of ownership came with a constant, ragged ache. She was defective. She was incomplete. Wondrous as it was, using the broken vine was like trying to read a book that was barely cracked open. With each animal she listened to, she knew there was a deeper immersion to be had, a fuller story. It was as if she could hear a far-off hum but couldn't quite make it out. Twice she'd pushed hard to get that fuller story—once with Baron, once with the wounded badger—and things had gone . . . badly. But she couldn't worry about that now. Right now, she had to keep herself within the limits of the vine as it was, not as she wished it to be. April rubbed the broken nub one last time and kept moving.

She stepped over the sticky line of tar at the ridge where the roof bent around the back of the house. Here, outside Derek's room, the breeze hit her hard, shrinking her skin across her bones and throwing her long hair across her face.

9

Down in the yard, Baron stood stiff-legged, the yellow fur on his broad shoulders bristling, his head pointed alertly toward the woods out back. He shimmied and growled, then froze again, ears pricked. April didn't smell anything on the air, but she knew Baron still did. Foul. Bitter. Burning.

April couldn't see anything in the jagged jumble of moonlit shadows. She couldn't sense anything with the vine, either, aside from buzzing insects and the slumbering family of sparrows that lived in a nest beneath the gutters. That meant one of two things: either the mysterious intruder was beyond the range of the vine, or it wasn't an animal. She called softly to the dog. "Baron! What is it?"

That familiar wave of affection pulsed through the vine at the sound of her voice. Baron whined and fidgeted, giving her a half glance and two quick tail wags.

An instant later, the air was split by the sharp *crack* of a stick breaking underfoot, somewhere out among the trees.

Baron charged toward the noise, stopping at the edge of the lawn. He began to bark ferociously. Panic and rage exploded in April's chest. She steeled herself against her own dread—and Baron's fury—and inched closer to the edge of the roof, trying to spot movement between the towering slender shadows of the trees.

And then, suddenly and unmistakably, one of those shadows walked.

A towering silhouette, impossibly tall and impossibly thin, ghosting swiftly through the trees. Ten feet tall or more, arms

10

the size of saplings, strides long enough to cross Boone Creek in a single step.

Gasping, April lurched back. She toppled over, banging her head against the wall beside Derek's half-open window. Baron continued to bark and charge as the shadow slid away. What was it? Before April could stop herself, she let the outside world fade and flung herself open to the vine, needing to know what Baron knew. The dog's rage, his fear, his disgust flooded through her. The vine quivered with intensity, resisting her, the broken stem aching like a snapped bone. She reached for more, urging the dog's mind to spread through her own.

And then the vine started to scream. A silent scream that filled her head. "No, not now," April whispered as everything went white and loud and hot, blinding and deafening and burning. The very cells in her brain seemed to be on fire, the pain unbearable, but she held on. Baron's barks sounded like the thunder of the gods, shaking her ribs. Each of the stars overhead glowed as bright as the sun. And above all she smelled something stinging and bitter and rotten—the foul stench Baron had been smelling. April clung to it, trying to make sense of it, but the vine's screaming whiteness grew and grew, stabbing at the backs of her eyes until at last she couldn't take it anymore. She tore the vine from her head and collapsed back against the house again, gasping.

Swiftly, her senses came back to her. Baron was still barking. The stars were distant and tiny again. She thought she could still smell that foul smell, faint but unmistakable—like rotten eggs. The shadow in the woods was gone.

Meanwhile her head pounded, and in her hand the vine, with its ever-broken stem, seemed to shudder with pain, quivering and electric. "I'm sorry," she told it. "I'm sorry."

From the window beside her, a trapezoid of light fell across the roof. A moment later, Derek heaved the window open with a single impatient thrust and stuck his head through, curtains billowing out and around his sleepy, stubbled face.

"First Baron!" he bellowed, using the dog's full name. "Shut up!"

The dog quieted at once. "I'm sleeping," Derek called out, as though he needed to explain himself. "People are sleeping." He ran a hand through his rumpled brown hair. He looked into the sky skeptically for a moment, still not noticing April, and then pulled his head back in. April tried to calm her pounding heart, to ease the knife of pain in her head. She slipped the vine back around her ear, hiding it under her hair. Before Derek could close the window, April swung around to face him, still so breathless she could hardly speak.

Derek leapt back, a choked cry popping out of him— "Jah!" He fell against his dresser. "Pill, what are you doing out there?"

"Sorry," she said, puffing hard. "Do you smell that?"

"You scared me to death." Derek held out a strong hand. "What are you doing out there? Come on—inside." April glanced back into the trees one last time. Whatever they'd seen was gone now. The stench still lingered in Baron's nose, but his alarm was dwindling, replaced by a rising swell of vigilant pride.

April took Derek's hand, not needing it but not wanting to seem stubborn. "You seriously didn't smell that?" she said as she climbed inside. "It was like . . . acid. Terrible." Derek slid the window closed, and her nose began to fill with the odors permeating his room, ordinary eighteen-year-old-boy smells—sweaty sheets, manky clothes, empty soda cans, musky products.

"Is that what Baron was barking at?" Derek asked. "A stink?"

"There was something out in the woods."

"Something," Derek said.

"Something crazy tall. But like a human."

Derek glanced sharply at the window. His chest seemed to swell. "Someone's out there?"

"I didn't say some*one*."

"Right," he said slowly. He nodded at her, feigning seriousness. "Crazy tall, but like a human. Plus a bad smell. Maybe it's Bigfoot."

He was teasing her. As always, she waited a beat, letting her irritation drift away so that it wouldn't show. Derek wasn't going to take her seriously. And why should he? She hardly knew what to think herself. Almost automatically, she slipped into the easy rhythm of their usual banter. "I don't believe in Bigfoot," she said.

Derek smiled and scratched the scraggly beard he'd been trying to grow out. "Right, I know. But what if Bigfoot believes in you?"

"In that case, I appreciate his imaginary support." April replayed the vision of the shadow she'd seen, reminding herself how firmly she did not believe in Bigfoot, or the Loch Ness monster, or any ridiculous creatures like that. The problem was, she could not think of anything else she *did* believe in that would explain what she and Baron had seen, and smelled. Not an animal. Not a man.

Suddenly she remembered the woman with the red hair. She couldn't possibly have anything to do with this, could she? Surely not, and yet there was something in the way the woman had looked at April from across the yard. Not threatening, exactly, but . . . fierce. Penetrating.

April shivered, and caught sight of herself in Derek's bureau mirror. To her surprise, she didn't look frightened at all. She looked . . . alive. Not pretty, exactly, despite her thick auburn hair. Her face and her body were stringy and plain. Her nose was slightly crooked, a family trait. Her hair covered the vine, keeping it hidden, but the golden tip of it glinted at her temple, and her hazel eyes were bright and brave. For a moment, watching those eyes, she almost forgot she was looking at herself.

Derek said, "Pill, what were you even doing out there this time of night?"

"The barking. It woke me up."

14

"You sure got out there fast."

"I'm a light sleeper," April said, tugging her hair over the tip of the vine. "You know that."

"Only when there's something on your mind."

April had to resist rubbing her aching forehead. There was plenty on her mind. The shadow. The stench. The searing pain and the blinding light that came whenever she tried to push the broken vine beyond its limits—what she'd come to think of as a whiteout. It was the missing piece, of course. She was only trying to do what the vine wanted to do, what it was supposed to do, but she couldn't. Not without the missing piece.

The vine was calm now, no longer white-hot with agony, but the pain of the missing piece remained. It would never go away. Sometimes she imagined that missing piece, distant and adrift, like a fallen leaf that had been blown far from its tree. Sometimes a sensation came to her through dreams, as if someone had cried out in a voice only she could hear, and the vine seemed to cry out in response. But it never came to more than that. And maybe she was better off assuming that it never would. Not everything that was lost could be found.

"I do have a lot on my mind," she told Derek. "But I never understood that expression. Shouldn't it be 'in my mind'?"

Derek sighed. Wind rattled his window. The first few drops of rain began to chatter against the glass and onto the sill. Outside, Baron noticed the rain but didn't bother to take shelter, still determined to stand guard. Derek closed the window and then crossed the room, opening his door.

"Back to bed," he said. "Whatever's in your mind, try to get it out."

"You don't seem that concerned about what I saw," April said.

"I'm more concerned about you falling off the roof."

April stepped past him into the hallway, lowering her voice so as not to wake Uncle Harrison. "What I saw was so tall it could have *dragged* me off the roof," she whispered, trying in some strange way to be funny. But once the words were out, she realized they weren't funny at all.

Derek just stared at her for a moment, one hand on his door. "Shut your window, and stay inside," he said. "There's a storm coming."

AT BREAKFAST THE next day, a Tuesday, April softened three frozen waffles in the microwave before crisping them up in the noisy toaster oven. Derek, who was working construction with Uncle Harrison this summer, came clomping down the stairs in his work boots. April's head rang faintly, still tender from the whiteout the night before.

"Morning," Derek said.

"Morning."

"Bacon?"

"Yes, please."

Derek threw half a slab of bacon into a skillet. "I heard you go outside earlier. Did you go looking for footprints?"

April hid her frown. Sometimes it wasn't so great having a brother who knew you so well. April *had* gone looking, taking Baron with her to search the rain-soaked patch of woods for traces of the tall man. Last night's storm had knocked a few new limbs down. Baron had sniffed around intently and growled to himself once or twice, picking up faint remnants of the terrible stink, but there'd been nothing to see.

"I did," April said, skewering a slice of waffle on her fork and letting the syrup dribble off. "No luck."

Derek poked at the bacon with a spatula. "So the tall man . . . tall thing. Just your imagination?"

April pictured the shadow she'd seen. "No. Baron saw it too. And we—he—smelled it." She tipped her head forward, making sure her hair still covered the vine. She wasn't going to pretend she hadn't seen what she'd seen, but the vine had to remain a secret. "Anyway," she said, "I think I'll tell Doc Durbin about it."

Derek laughed and stabbed at the bacon. It sputtered and hissed. "It was probably Doc you saw in the first place. She's always stomping around out there."

April didn't bother to inform him that the figure she'd seen in the woods was at least twice as tall as Doc Durbin, and not nearly so round. He'd only tease her more. "Well, if it *was* her, then I guess she'd be the best person to ask, wouldn't she?" she said lightly.

"Or the worst," Derek intoned, trying to sound sinister.

April ignored him. Derek liked to make fun of their

quirky neighbor, but Doc Durbin was a sensible person who always treated April seriously. Doc was a veterinarian, a job April imagined having herself one day. April frequently stopped by Doc's for a visit in the late afternoon, as much to see the hodgepodge of wild animals Doc rescued as to see Doc herself. April always learned something new with each visit—especially now, with the vine.

April's current favorite rescue was a young raven with a broken wing, a survivor of an apparent cat attack. He was due to be released back into the wild any day now. Arthur—that was the name Doc had taken to calling him—was rather remarkable. His intelligence burned more brightly than any animal April had encountered, before or after she found the vine. Unlike Baron, who saw the world as a simple landscape of friends and foes and food, Arthur seemed to view his environment as a series of problems to be solved. He had figured out how to unlock two different cage doors with his beak before Doc rigged up a third with a steel latch too heavy for him to open. He played with toys—sticks, twisty ties, balls of aluminum foil—with a distinct sense of mischief and experimentation.

Arthur was also extremely talkative. In addition to his throaty crowlike call, he was able to make several other sounds, from a froggy croak to a gentle cluck—*tok tok tok*—to a passable imitation of his own name, as if he were a parrot. April had taken to feeding Arthur by hand, which was not strictly encouraged, but she liked the way he took the meat or baby carrots or chunks of dry dog food—his favorite—delicately into his thick beak. She admired the way he measured her intent, and his surprising patience with the process. It wasn't at all like Baron's desperate, gluttonous joy at dinnertime.

Thanks to the vine, April also knew that Arthur's wing had been fully healed and without pain for the last few days. He was desperately ready to be set free. There was no way she could share this info with Doc, of course, and besides—somewhat selfishly—April wasn't quite ready to say good-bye to the bird yet. But soon she would have to. Doc had promised her she could be there for his release, probably tomorrow.

"It makes me nervous when you're on that roof," Derek said suddenly.

"What?" April asked, lost in her thoughts.

"The roof. I wish you would stay off of there."

"Okay, Mom." She bit her lip as soon as the words left her.

Derek started flipping the bacon, two slices at a time. Dots of grease leapt from the pan. "Don't call me that," he said quietly.

A few minutes later Uncle Harrison came down, the stairs creaking under his enormous bulk, and the three of them ate in silence. Afterward, Derek and Uncle Harrison left for work. April's headache faded at last, and she cleaned up the dishes, feeling that strange mix of happy and sad she always felt when she was left alone in the house. But after last night, there was an extra thread in her mood. She tried to tell herself it wasn't fear.

Dishes done, she wandered out onto the back steps. She

didn't need to scan the sunlit trees to know that nothing unusual was there; Baron's relaxed state of mind told her so. The dog slouched across the yard and lay down beside her, looking much older than he had last night. And he was old. April and Baron had been alive the same number of years— thirteen—but while that was young for a human, it was mighty old for a big dog like Baron.

April rubbed the dog's thick yellow head and wondered, not for the first time, if Baron himself felt old, if he even had a concept of what "old" meant. It was the sort of thing April had spent her whole life wondering, and now, thanks to the vine, she was maddeningly close to knowing the answer. Animals didn't really have language the way humans did—the vine made that very clear. But the vine also suggested something beyond language, a connection she couldn't quite wrap her brain around, a kinship just beyond her reach. She rubbed the severed stem of the vine with her thumb. The missing piece again. Always the missing piece.

Sometimes April imagined that if she sat quietly enough and focused hard enough, she could think the vine into repairing itself. She tried it now, pretending that whatever tendril had been snapped off could somehow regrow itself, that the vine could become whole again—that *she* could become whole. Her thoughts wound through the coils of the vine and streamed out the broken end, pouring into the air. She kept at it even as her headache began to return, followed by a sick swimming sensation in her gut, as if she were waiting for a roller coaster car to drop.

A voice cut through the air. "You'll want to stop that."

April startled, wrenching her thoughts away from the vine. Baron lurched sleepily to his feet, coughing out a single gruff bark. The red-haired stranger from the other day stood at the bottom of the porch steps, gazing up at them with a smile. Her bushy, apple-colored hair shone in the sun. A large pendant hung from her neck, a brown wicker sphere the size of a tennis ball.

"Stop what?" April asked calmly, trying to ignore her racing heart.

The woman cocked her head, a wild glint in her dark eyes. Her gaze slid to April's left ear, where the vine lay hidden. "Don't poke at the wound. You're like an injured fish, bloodying the water. We don't want that." She glanced over her shoulder toward the woods. "Sharks have been circling."

Immediately April understood—this woman knew about the vine. Whoever she was, she *knew*. And not just about the vine, but apparently about last night's shadow too. *Sharks have been circling.* April reached out and laid a hand on Baron's neck. He was calm, untroubled, snuffling at the stranger amiably. April said, "I saw you the other day, watching the house."

"Yes. And I saw you. You're the reason I came."

"But you're not a . . . shark?"

"No," the woman said with a laugh. "I'm a Keeper. Just like you." The woman didn't bother explaining the word, but instead held out her wicker pendant. April watched in wonder as the tangled sphere swelled ever so slightly, creaking softly as it expanded and shrank like a balloon. "Not *exactly* like you, of course," the woman said. "Everyone's talents are different."

Breathless, April eyed the pendant, an absurd surge of hope blooming in her now. Here, it seemed—out of the blue morning sunshine—was someone like her. Here, perhaps, was someone who might be able to help. That broken bit of the vine ached at the thought, but April willed herself to stay steady. People, like all animals, were best when you treated them with quiet patience. You couldn't go throwing around your own hopes, your own worries, your own confusion. It was better not to push, not to grab, not to run. It wasn't that you had to bottle yourself up, exactly, but you did have to keep . . . still.

April eyed the pendant. "I see," she said evenly. "And what are your talents?"

The pendant swelled again. "For starters, I can see things most others can't. That's how I found you—I felt you bleeding." Her brow furrowed with uncertainty. "Tell me, is the wound very bad? May I see it?"

Be steady. Be true. Slowly, April drew back her long hair, exposing the vine. It was the first time she'd shown it to anyone, and her heart rose again in her chest. The woman gasped and leaned in for a closer look. April forced herself to stay still as a deer. The wicker pendant dangled just a foot away. The woman clasped it with her right hand, where she wore a wooden ring on her pinkie. The wicker sphere pulsed in her palm, and April swore she saw a faint shimmer of light inside.

When at last the woman leaned back, her eyes seemed to trace an invisible line in the air between April and Baron. "It suits you," she said.

April let her hair fall back over the vine, blushing. "Thank you."

"I'm Isabel," the woman said.

"I'm April. April Simon."

"April the empath."

"Empath?"

Isabel gestured toward Baron. "That's your talent—you can listen to animals. My own talent lets me see that plain enough. I can also see why I felt you from five miles away. You're strong for an empath, and your instrument is badly broken."

Her instrument. The vine. "How badly?" April managed.

"I can only guess. The true answer has to come from you."

"A piece is missing."

"Amputated, yes," said Isabel curtly, not a trace of sympathy in her voice. "And you don't have the piece, do you?"

"No. The vine was like this when I found it."

"Do you know where it is?"

"No. I don't even know if . . ." April hesitated, swallowing. "No. I don't."

Isabel tugged thoughtfully on a curl of her fiery red hair. Her face seemed alight, as if some delicious thought had just occurred to her. "You haven't had the vine for long, I think. How did you find it? Who introduced you to it?"

"I found it on my own," April explained firmly, puzzled by the strange phrasing. "No one introduced me."

"No one's told you anything about your instrument, then. About who you are and what it is."

April shook her head. "Actually, this is the first conversation I've ever had about it." Isabel turned away, muttering to herself. April thought she heard her say "Duck town," which didn't make any sense, but then she very clearly heard a name: "Warren." Who was Warren?

Abruptly Isabel spun back. "Listen," she said. "Most new Keepers aren't given the information I'm about to share, but I need to explain. When I said I can see things that others can't, I was talking about something called the Medium."

"Okay," April said slowly, baffled.

"The Medium flows all around us, unseen. It powers our instruments—yours and mine alike. The veins of the Medium are invisible to you, but not me. I can feel those veins, and I can pinch them and pull them too. That's my talent." She grasped her wicker ball again. "And when I looked at your instrument just now, I . . . learned something. Something you might not know." She leaned in again, her gaze deep and fierce. "Are you aware that your missing piece . . . *survives*?"

April swallowed the word, blinking back the sudden water that rose in her eyes. She had believed that the missing piece survived, yes—she had to believe it—but she didn't actually *know.*

"Your missing piece exists," Isabel insisted. "It lives on."

April clutched at Baron's fur. He turned his head and licked her hand, worry and discomfort bubbling softly. "Where?" she asked thickly.

"Again, I can't answer that. I can only see so much. It's up to you to find it again."

"Me? But I wouldn't have the first idea where to look."

"You're a Keeper. Surely you recognize the call of your own instrument."

"I can sense the vine when I take it off, even through walls and things. I'm sort of pulled toward it, like . . . like a flower toward the sun. Is that what you mean?"

Isabel nodded, fussing with her wooden ring. "Yes. We're all bound to our instruments. The vine is a part of you, and the missing piece is a part of the vine. Reach out for now. Try to feel it. The call won't be quite the same, but it'll be there, faint and far—like a star you can barely see."

April stood and took a deep breath, hesitating. She thought of the phantom late-night cries she sometimes imagined, and realized she was scared. If she failed to feel the missing piece now, what would that mean? Wasn't it true that certain answers were worse than no answer at all? Not everything that was lost could be found.

"What's the matter?" Isabel said.

"Nothing, I . . ."

Isabel studied her face. "You're afraid to try," she said gently. "You're afraid you won't feel it."

"Yes."

Leaning back, Isabel crossed her arms knowingly. "Maybe that's why you haven't felt it yet."

That had the undeniable jolt of truth. April, who prided herself on not ignoring wisdom when she heard it, nodded and took another deep breath. She closed her eyes. She probed questingly at the presence of the vine. She was a Keeper, a word that made no sense to her and yet made all the sense in the world. The vine was her instrument. It was her. A gentle river of power flowed from the vine to her and back again, a current pulsing in time to her own heartbeat. She opened herself to the possibility that another strand of that current might be out there, faint and far—the missing piece. She wouldn't be afraid. She would approach this encounter like any other. Truth, patience, stillness. Morning cicadas pulsed buzzily in the summer trees. The sun warmed the back of her head. "What will it feel like?" she asked softly.

"I can't describe that," Isabel said. "No more than I can describe the smell of rain."

April was just thinking what a lovely notion that was— how *would* you describe the smell of rain?—when abruptly, dimly, she felt something. Something both far away and immediately present. A quiet plea, a faint magnetic pull, a tiny distant beacon of hurt and absence and need.

"Oh!" she cried. The missing piece—it was out there,

broken and alone and taken from her. *Taken.* The thought filled her with a startling, breathtaking surge of rage.

She turned toward it, toward the sun, anticipation growing. She could barely feel it, just a trickle, but it was unmistakable. "It's there," she said, brimming with wonder and anger. "I feel it."

She opened her eyes. She found Isabel standing very close, her face savagely intense, the wicker ball clasped firmly in her hand. April took a step back, and on the instant the call of the missing piece vanished.

"Which way?" Isabel demanded.

"It's gone now," April said blankly.

"No need to worry. If you felt it once, you'll feel it again. Which way?"

April pointed to the southeast, trying to feel the missing piece again. To her great relief, she felt the trickling call once more. This time it clung to her, weak still, but perhaps a hair stronger. April fought to stay calm.

Isabel straightened, staring off into the distance. "It's in the city," she said.

"Chicago?" April said. The city was indeed southeast of here, an hour and a half away by car. "But how do you know it's there?"

Isabel hesitated, seeming to measure her words. When she spoke, her voice was tight. "There's a place in the city, a secret place that doesn't want to be found. I'd bet my life your missing piece will be there."

"What kind of place?"

"A fortress. There are people there, people like us, hoarding and hiding and—" She stopped. Her expression had grown fierce, but now she smoothed her face. "It doesn't matter. What matters is that we find your missing piece. We need to make you whole again." She laid a friendly hand on April's shoulder and smiled. "We need to go."

Isabel said this so matter-of-factly that for a second April didn't know whether to laugh or pack her bags. "*Whole again . . . We need to go.*" She backed away, sinking onto the steps beside Baron. "But I can't just . . . *leave.*" The thought was ridiculous, of course. She was barely a teenager. Derek would never let her.

Isabel shook her head solemnly. "You don't understand," she said. "You don't have a choice. You are Tan'ji."

Another unfamiliar word, the strangest yet. *Tan'ji*. And for some reason, this word made April so weak in the knees that she was glad she was sitting down. "Wait," April said, trying desperately to find her bearings. "Wait. You keep using words like I know what they mean. Instrument. Keeper. Tan'ji. And it's almost like I know what you're talking about, but I don't."

"You don't know the words yet, but you already know the bond." Isabel pointed two fingers at the vine and said, "This is Tan'ji." She pointed to April. "You are Tan'ji. Your instrument belongs to you, and you belong to it. It and you both—together—are Tan'ji."

Together. April understood that, at least. She understood

28

bonds. "And you are Tan'ji too? You and your instrument?"

Isabel clasped the wicker sphere, her face hardening. "That's right. This is Miradel. I'm her Keeper. I'm Tan'ji just like you."

April noted the woman's peculiar possessiveness, and was surprised that the wicker ball had a name, but she didn't respond. She tried to straighten her thoughts. She was Tan'ji. She was the Keeper of the vine, apparently. And while a part of her knew absolutely what that meant—the vine was *hers*—another part of her struggled to comprehend.

"You'll learn the words in time," Isabel said, as if she understood. "Right now, only the bond matters. If a piece of Miradel was missing, I'd do anything—go anywhere—to find it. Because I'm Tan'ji. You'll do the same for your instrument."

April couldn't bring herself to deny it. "And you're sure that my missing piece is going to be in this . . . secret place."

"I could be wrong," Isabel said lightly, "but it doesn't matter. We'll follow the call of the missing piece and see where it takes us. If I am wrong, you will know. Besides, you can't stay here. It's not safe for a young Keeper unprotected, especially one with a broken Tan'ji. Blood in the water. I told you."

The shadow in the trees. "I saw something in the woods last night, right back there. It moved, and it was really tall, like . . ." She looked up, gesturing into the air overhead.

"Impossibly tall," the woman finished.

"Yes."

"And there was a smell."

April nodded, her heart pounding. "What was it?"

29

"One of the Riven," Isabel said. Then she added ominously, "They've come for you. They've come for the vine."

April's anger flared up at those final words, but her confusion and fear wouldn't let her sustain it. "Who are the Riven?"

"Their hunters have found you," Isabel said, not really answering the question. "They've found you just like I did. I told you, you're bleeding everywhere."

"But what I saw wasn't human."

"No," the woman said simply. Her eyes said she would explain no more.

April swallowed. "What do they want with the vine?"

"They want your power."

"They can't have it."

"Then you can't stay. You're unprotected here. You have to come with me." The wicker ball swelled again. "Come with me, and I'll keep you safe."

From the southeast, the call of the missing piece—that lonely and kidnapped part of herself—seemed to flicker and grow another fraction stronger. "I'm only thirteen," April said lamely.

"I was only nine when I . . . began." Isabel's face turned dark. "And some are even younger."

"But I can't leave my brother. I can't just *go*."

Isabel squatted down and peered up into April's face. "Keeper, listen to me. For the time being, your brother is safer with you gone."

April searched for something to say, something sensible,

something that would clip the wings of this absurdity that had exploded out of nowhere. But she found nothing. Nothing that could erase the pull of that distant beacon. And with that, she knew she would go. She would leave with this woman, would go searching for her missing piece, go far from whoever—or whatever—these Riven were. She would keep her brother safe. Leaving with Isabel would be, in a way, the most sensible thing April had ever done.

Isabel knew it too. The sad, intense smile returned to her face as she searched April's eyes. "You don't have a choice. We Keepers often don't."

April nodded decisively.

"I've seen your brother, you know," Isabel said. "And your dad."

Briefly April wondered just how long Isabel had been watching her, waiting for the right moment to approach. "That's my uncle, not my dad. My parents are dead." She emphasized the word "dead" deliberately, as she always did, but Isabel didn't flinch. "They've been dead most of my life."

Instead of saying she was sorry, as most people did, Isabel asked earnestly, "And how has that been?"

Thrown once again, April searched for the most truthful answer she could. "I . . . guess I don't know. I don't have much to compare it to." She sighed and looked up at the house she had lived in for the last six years, the house she still thought of as Uncle Harrison's. "Will I be able to come back here?" she asked, not quite able to look at Isabel.

"You can't come back without protection," Isabel said. Another nonanswer. "But you're not safe here now. We have to follow the call and find the missing piece. Then we'll do what we can, and I'll tell you what you want to know."

"I need until tonight. I have to get some things together."

Isabel beamed, clearly pleased. "Bring a backpack, nothing more. Pack a blanket. And food."

"Okay," April said. "But also I have to . . . Derek. My brother."

"What will you tell him?"

April thought. "I stay at my friend Maggie's sometimes. Sometimes for a few days."

"That'll do."

"And if I'm not back in a few days?" April kept her words as light as she could, but they felt heavy coming out of her mouth.

Isabel locked eyes with her, that wild glint back in her gaze. "You are Tan'ji now, April," she said, her voice steely and sad at the same time. She reached out for a moment as if to take April's hand, but then let it fall. "Things can't be the way they were."

CHAPTER TWO

Nine Days

HORACE ANDREWS THOUGHT HE MIGHT NEVER STOP BEING tired.

He lay on his bed, with Loki the cat slumbering enviably at his side. It was a Tuesday afternoon in mid-June, nine days after the raid on the Riven's nest and the rescue of Chloe's father. Nine days since the escape from Dr. Jericho and the rest of the Riven in that dark, underground labyrinth. Or at least, the calendar claimed it was nine days. Horace sometimes felt like only hours had passed, and that his exhaustion had not yet left him. At other times, though, the rescue seemed like a distant thing, years old, and his memories of it seemed like nothing more than visions from the Fel'Daera—promises made, but not yet fulfilled.

The last nine days had been confusing. Confusing and lonely. Summer days were often lonely, but this was a new kind of emptiness. He hadn't seen Chloe since the night of the rescue, hadn't been back to the Warren, hadn't received word from Mr. Meister or Gabriel or Neptune or Mrs. Hapstead. In a way, not hearing from the Wardens was a relief. No more missions, no heavy expectations. Most of all, no more secrets. No more lies.

But of course, he was still a Keeper. And not just a Keeper. He was a Warden, charged with protecting the Tan'ji from the Riven. Being a Warden meant new secrets around every corner, deep and surprising secrets—secrets which, when revealed, could knock you off your feet. And nine days ago, Horace had learned a secret so surprising that he still hadn't found his feet again.

As if on cue, he heard the front door open. It was 4:04; his mother was home from work. She called hello up to him, and he hollered back. This was a change from their normal routine—or maybe it was the new normal, her calling out instead of coming up in person to chat. He wasn't sure who to blame for that, but wondered if it might be himself. His relationship with his mother had changed ever since the nest—or rather, ever since the talk they'd had just afterward, a talk that felt as much like a dream as the nest itself. Yes, secrets had been revealed that night—deep and surprising—but what scared him was that he hadn't even glimpsed the bottom. His mother was keeping deeper secrets still, secrets he wasn't sure he wanted to learn.

Horace preferred not to think about it. As a result, of

course, he thought about it all the time.

He lay there for another ten minutes, wondering if he could fall asleep again, maybe sleep until dinnertime came. Loki, stretched out lazily on the bed beside him and purring agreeably, certainly seemed willing to try. But Horace couldn't sleep. Instead he took the Fel'Daera from the pouch at his side—a small oval box about the size of his hand. He swung the lid slightly open, the two halves swiveling smoothly apart like wings, but he didn't look inside. He hadn't looked inside the box since the nest. Every day was the same anyway, especially without Chloe around. Why bother?

He closed the box, slipping it back into its pouch. From a small pool of marbles on his covers, he plucked out a shooter and dropped it into the thick fur on Loki's flank. The cat didn't stir. Horace kept going, seeing how many he could get to stay. With each new marble, he chanted softly to the cat: "Three little marbles on you. Four little marbles on you . . ." These were the sorts of mindless activities he busied himself with these days, keeping his brain distracted. He was up to eleven marbles when a sharp, familiar voice rang out.

"God, Horace, need a new hobby much?"

Loki leapt up, scattering the marbles. Chloe—Horace's good friend Chloe, so brave and fierce and pretty and true—stood at the foot of the bed. She was tiny, but her presence was huge, her dark eyes as full of keen mischief as ever. Her black hair had grown out a little. The Alvalaithen, a bone-white pendant in the shape of a dragonfly, hung around her

35

neck. Its wings were a blur, fluttering madly. Chloe grinned. "Sorry for not knocking," she said.

Horace grinned back, reveling in the sight of her, the sound of her surly voice. "I'm pretty sure you've never knocked," he said. "Why start now?"

The dragonfly's wings went still. The Alvalaithen—the Earthwing—was the reason she never knocked, of course. She didn't have to knock. When the dragonfly's wings were moving, she was incorporeal, her body still visible but formless like a ghost. This was her talent. Going thin, she called it, and while she was thin she could walk through walls, through trees, through fire—through anything.

Chloe looked around the room, and up at the glowing, precisely plotted stars on Horace's ceiling. She went to the window and bent down in front of the tiny message she'd written on the wall the very first time she'd come here.

> Dear Horace,
>
> I hope this doesn't get you in trouble.
>
> Your friend,
>
> Chloe

She peered at it for a moment and then announced flatly, "Being here again makes me feel sentimental."

Horace laughed. "I missed you too," he said.

Chloe licked her thumb and rubbed at the word "trouble," but it didn't budge. She grunted, apparently satisfied.

Horace couldn't help but notice her arm. Two wide, fresh scars slashed down her right forearm, one on the inside and one on the outside, running from wrist nearly to the elbow. Eight inches long, they were shaped like the flames of giant candles. She'd gotten these scars—far from her first, but possibly the worst—on the night of the rescue. She'd gone thin and plunged her arm into the mesmerizing green fire of the crucible, deep in the Riven's nest. Extinguishing the crucible's light had effectively destroyed the nest and freed her captive father, but these scars were the price. Mocha colored and smooth as ivory, they drew Horace's gaze like the flame that had created them.

Chloe noticed and held out her arm, showing them off. "What do you think? I sort of like them."

"They're . . . kind of cool looking," Horace said, surprising himself by admitting it. He'd been horrified the first time he'd seen any of her scars—the slashes in the hollow of her throat, the forest of textured skin that covered the bottom half of her legs. But these new scars were different—dark instead of light. Burns left by a flame that was not a flame.

"They're good reminders," said Chloe. "That was a heck of a night—or a night and a day . . . and another night, I guess. Have you recovered?"

"Probably not."

"You had it the worst," said Chloe.

Horace wasn't sure how true that was, but it had certainly been bad—horrible, actually. Sometimes he woke up in the night thinking he was still trapped in the great iron boiler Dr. Jericho had locked him in, the lightless coffin where he'd spent nearly twenty-four hours. He'd spent that terrible day not only facing his crippling fear of small spaces, but also knowing that his escape depended on a future he alone had foreseen—the future he had promised to his friends, the same future they too had risked everything on.

Sometimes Horace still couldn't believe it had all worked out. Yes, he was the Keeper of the Fel'Daera, the Box of Promises. And yes, he could see the future. By opening the box and looking through the blue glass bottom, he could see what was happening a single day forward in time. But there was no guarantee that the future the Box of Promises revealed would come to pass exactly as he had seen. Promises could be broken, after all. On that night, however, everything he'd seen through the box had come to pass, even when it seemed impossible. Inside the nest, he had sent Chloe's dragonfly forward through time twenty-four hours—another power of the box—and she had been there to receive it, exactly as the box had foreseen. Thanks to the box, and with Gabriel's help, they'd destroyed the crucible, freed Chloe's father, and escaped from the terrible clutches of Dr. Jericho.

Chloe sank onto the bed, giving Loki a scritch and fussing with the marbles. Horace now noticed that the scar on the inside of her forearm reached all the way down into her palm, where it branched jaggedly, like a stubby winter tree. She sighed and said, "I feel a little bad. I snuck in past your mom just now. I wasn't sure what you told her after the nest—how you explained being gone for so long. I thought maybe she might be blaming me."

"No," Horace said quickly, and found himself wanting to say more. But he had no idea where to begin. "No."

Chloe searched his face. "You okay? Everything going all right?"

"It's cool," Horace said. "Totally cool. I've been sleeping a lot."

"Me too. My dad and I are still staying at the academy." The Mazzoleni Academy was a boarding school downtown. Chloe and her father, Matthew, had been staying there ever since their house had been burned down by the Riven. Chloe wasn't a student at the academy—and it was summer anyway—but the academy was more than it seemed. Deep beneath its walls lay the Warren, the secret underground headquarters of the Wardens.

"My dad and I have been playing a lot of chess," Chloe continued. "I'm getting pretty good, so you better watch out."

Horace nodded, expressionless. He and his mother had not played chess once since that night. "Your dad's doing better, huh?"

"*Much* better. He's like . . ." Chloe's face glowed, and Horace understood. She had her father back again. "The only bad thing is, I haven't seen Madeline much. She's still staying with Aunt Lou." Horace had only met Chloe's little sister once, a girl with serious eyes and copper-colored hair, but he knew she and Chloe were very close. Chloe had practically raised her. Chloe's mom was not in the picture, having abandoned her family when Chloe was little. She'd simply taken off one day, never to return. "Anyway," Chloe continued, "what about your folks? How's your mom?"

Horace shifted uneasily, knowing how much Chloe liked and trusted his mom. "They're fine. My mom is . . . you know. She's good. Fine. The same."

Chloe peered at him suspiciously. "She's good, fine, the same. Super convincing. Are you in trouble? Grounded or something? Whatever lie you told her about the nest, I'm guessing she didn't believe you."

But that was just it. He hadn't lied. Unbelievably—unthinkably, even now—he hadn't *needed* to lie. "Not grounded," he said. "Everything's fine."

"Fine," Chloe repeatedly dubiously. "Well, that's good news, Horace. Because you've got to come with me."

Horace frowned. "Mr. Meister wants us?"

"Yes. He was going to send Neptune to come get you, but I volunteered. Heavily." She smiled. "Beck's waiting for us down the street."

Beck was the Warden's enigmatic chauffeur, a driver who ferried the Wardens around the city in a run-down cab. Horace felt a brief surge of excitement at the thought of seeing Beck, of returning once more to the Warren with Chloe, but almost as soon as his excitement appeared, it faded. Going to the Warren meant seeing Mr. Meister again, and Horace wasn't ready for that. Not after what he'd learned.

"Why do they want me?" he asked. "What's happening?"

"I'm not sure. Mr. Meister was in full cryptic mode. He said, and I quote, 'Something long asleep has been awakened.'" She imitated Mr. Meister's crisp German accent.

It was impossible for Horace's sizable curiosity not to be stirred by those words, just for a second. But only a second. "Great," he complained. "More secrets. Very helpful."

"Horace, what is going on?"

"Nothing."

"Ah," she said wryly. "More secrets. Very helpful."

Horace sighed. He spoke lightly, but his heart pounded. "I found out something about my mom, okay?"

Chloe frowned warily. "You say that like it's bad. Are you about to tell me something bad about your mom? Because as someone who doesn't have a mom of her own, I sort of rely on yours to be ongoingly awesome."

"Yeah, well, you tell me how bad it is. It turns out she knows who Mr. Meister is. It turns out she knows about the Fel'Daera—she's known all along."

The wings of the Alvalaithen fluttered, just for an instant, as Chloe's eyes went wide. Horace knew just how she felt. Mr. Meister was the leader of the Wardens—technically the Chief Taxonomer, overseeing the collection, cataloging, and safekeeping of all the instruments the Wardens could find, trying to keep them out of the hands of the Riven. And the old man was a recruiter, too. It was Mr. Meister—and his partner, Mrs.

Hapsteade—who had made it possible for Horace to find the Fel'Daera in the first place, to become Tan'ji. But neither of Horace's parents knew anything about all that.

Or so he'd thought.

"Explain, please," Chloe said quietly.

Horace told her the whole story, how he had come home before dawn after the escape from the nest, only to find his mother waiting for him. How she'd spoken of people and things she had no business knowing—Mr. Meister, Mrs. Hapsteade, leestones, Keepers, Tan'ji, the Box of Promises. "She knows about me," Horace explained. "And you. She always has."

To his surprise, Chloe seemed to be suppressing a smile. When he finished his tale, she threw her arms wide. "Well, that explains everything," she said, beaming. "That explains why your mom is so chill. She's a Keeper, like us."

As usual, Chloe was adapting more quickly than he had. But Horace shook his head. "She told me she's not a Keeper. She's not Tan'ji."

"Then what is she?"

"I don't know," Horace admitted.

"She didn't tell you?"

"I was pretty exhausted that night. She said we could talk about it after I recovered. She said I could ask her whatever I wanted, whenever I was ready. But . . ." He trailed off, shrugging.

Chloe scowled, mimicking his shrug. "But what?"

42

"But I never asked."

Now she reared back and shook her head. "Wait, your mom drops the bomb that she knows all about the box, and the dragonfly, and the Wardens and everything, and two weeks later, you still haven't brought it up again?"

"Nine days. Not two weeks."

"I mean seriously, what is wrong with you? You're Captain Curious. You ask more questions than a five-year-old. You not asking questions is like me not . . ." She fished around for an example.

"Hassling me?" Horace offered.

"Very funny. But yeah, actually."

"It's not so easy to ask about this. This is different."

"How is this possibly different?"

"Because my mom says she knew the Maker of the Fel'Daera."

Chloe stared at him for a long time. As was his habit, Horace counted automatically while he waited. *Five, six.* Chloe's eyes flicked to the box in its pouch at Horace's belt, then back to his face. *Eight, nine.* She said softly, "But the Makers are the . . ."

"Yeah," Horace said, knowing they were both thinking the same thing.

The Riven.

Chloe squirmed. "Okay, but Mr. Meister said that the Riven of today aren't really the Makers. They're like the sad, scary leftovers of the original Makers."

43

Horace remembered the story. The Makers in question were the creators of the Tanu, wondrous and seemingly magical devices that operated outside the known laws of physics. Tanu came in all shapes and sizes, from simple Tan'kindi that could be used by anyone to powerful Tan'ji that would only bond to certain individuals. All the Tanu, both grand and humble, had been made by a mysterious race living quietly on the fringes of humanity, long ago.

"The Altari," Horace murmured. According to Mr. Meister, a few Altari had been friendly with humans from the start, even giving them gifts of Tan'kindi. Back then, it was assumed that only Altari could bond with and use the more potent Tan'ji. But at some point it was discovered that some humans had the ability to become Tan'ji as well. A rift then grew among the Makers. Some embraced the idea of human Keepers, but others rebelled. This rebellious group renamed themselves the Kesh'kiri, the Riven. They lurked in the shadows and dedicated themselves to reclaiming all the Tanu for themselves, to hunting down every last human Keeper. The rest of the Altari, meanwhile, went even deeper into hiding, all but vanishing from the face of the earth.

Now, it turned out, Horace's mother claimed to have met one of them—and not just any Altari, but the Maker of Horace's own instrument. The very thought left him completely unmoored, full of doubts and an angry confusion that he couldn't seem to tame.

"Well," said Chloe, "whether we say Riven or Altari, the

Maker of the Fel'Daera must be terribly old."

"I guess so."

"Where is he now? Is he even still alive?"

"I don't know," Horace mumbled.

"Why would your mother have met him? And when did that even happen?"

"I have no idea. It doesn't matter. Let's just go to the Warren."

Chloe shot up and planted her fists on her hips, fuming. "I see. So this is what happens when I'm not around. Wallowing. Throwing yourself a pity party."

"I'm not wallowing."

"You are. You feel sorry for yourself because somebody knew something you thought was private. And now you're afraid to ask your mom about it. You're afraid of the answers."

"I'm not afraid. I'm just not ready to talk to her. What's there to be afraid of?"

"Betrayal," Chloe said simply. "Jealousy." She held out the dragonfly. "I know what the bond is like, Horace. My claim on the Alvalaithen is way beyond ownership—my instrument *is* me, completely and privately and forever. And if someone came along with some older claim to it, even a tiny one, it would drive me completely nuts. I would want to send that person packing, because who the hell are *they* to presume to know something about *my* Tan'ji? Heck, I didn't even like having to ask Mr. Meister what the dragonfly's name was."

It was true, of course. So true that there was nothing more

to discuss. "Fine," he said. "You're right. I don't want to ask my mom what she knows about the Fel'Daera, or its Maker. Not at all. So let's go. Something's going on at the Warren, right? Mr. Meister says someone woke up, or something."

Chloe snatched a pillow off Horace's bed. The wings of the Alvalaithen began to whir, and she swung the pillow mightily, right at Horace's face. He flinched, but the pillow passed clean through his head like a ghost, cool and shocking.

"You're the one who needs to wake up," Chloe snapped. "I'm not taking you anywhere until you get your answers."

"I'll get my answers when I'm ready."

Chloe swung the pillow again, and Horace forced himself not to flinch, but this time the pillow smacked him hard, right in the face.

"Gah!" he cried.

Chloe dropped the pillow. The dragonfly had gone still again. From the other end of the bed, Loki watched them with wide golden eyes. "You're not fine," Chloe said. "You're distracted. Half your brain is curled up in the corner, worrying about what you don't know. And the Keeper of the Fel'Daera can't use his Tan'ji properly with only half a brain."

Now it was Horace's turn to scowl. He picked up a marble and chucked it back into the pile with a *clack*. "If my mom wanted me to know, how come *she* hasn't brought it up again?"

"Probably because she's a good mom—unlike mine. She's here. She's not pushing. It's your Tan'ji, Horace, and she's waiting for you to bring it up—waiting for you to be you, as usual. And instead of doing that, you've been pouting."

Another marble. Another *clack*. "Ah, crap," he said. She was right. She was right, and he'd been stupid—a pity party indeed.

Chloe grabbed him by the hand and hauled him to his feet. "Let's go. Right now. Beck can wait."

His mother wasn't in her room. They went downstairs, past the empty living room. As they entered the kitchen, Horace started to have second thoughts. "Chloe," he began, "Maybe right now isn't—"

Chloe came to a sudden halt. "Too late," she said.

Horace's mother sat at the kitchen table, smiling tentatively, clearly expecting them. A vase of freshly cut daisies sat on the windowsill beside her, white petals vibrantly aglow in the afternoon sunlight. But Horace's eyes fell immediately upon the strange, delicate object in his mother's hands. About the size of a football, it was obviously Tanu. Horace had never seen anything quite like it—four curved pieces of wood bent together, outlining a shape kind of like a fish. The open space within seemed to glimmer faintly.

"Hi," said Horace's mother.

Horace was rooted to the spot. He looked over at Chloe, sure she had planned this whole encounter from the start. But Chloe just stared at the strange Tanu, clearly as stunned as he was.

His mother said, "I hope I haven't guessed wrong, Horace, but I think maybe you're ready to finish the conversation

I started when you came home that night." Smoothly she unfolded the Tanu in her hands, unfolding the four curving arms one by one until it became a bowl-shaped letter X. From each arm a rising ribwork of shimmering strings ran toward the center. The device looked like two sailboats crisscrossed at right angles, each with glinting strands of light for sails. Horace couldn't quite pin those strands down, though. The moment he focused on one, it vanished, twinkling. Counting them was an impossibility.

"What is that thing?" Horace breathed.

"Sit and let me tell you," his mother said kindly. "You too, Chloe. Both of you, please—sit and let me tell you everything I can."

CHAPTER THREE

Wild Now

LATE TUESDAY AFTERNOON, WHILE DEREK AND UNCLE HARRI-son were still at work, April headed over to Doc Durbin's. She wore her most practical hiking dress—simple and sturdy—and the rugged old boots she'd inherited from Derek. She walked the path through the woods to the clinic with her eyes closed, finding the way by memory and feel, and also with the help of the vine. She could sense the presence of the forest all around her, especially the trees. Plants didn't truly have consciousness, and didn't really think, but they were alive and had a presence she could feel, like the faintest mist of rain. Especially trees. Especially forests. She walked slowly beneath the peaceful, outstretched boughs now, headed for the veterinarian's house.

April was hoping not to run into Doc. Not only did Doc have a way of reading April's moods, but she wasn't shy about asking questions, and April didn't feel very equipped to handle many questions right now. She was risking the visit only because there was someone else she had to say good-bye to. Someone she knew for a fact she would never see again. Not after today.

April and Isabel had arranged to meet after dinner, at the old abandoned barn, fifteen minutes away on foot. That, apparently, was where Isabel had been staying. April knew the barn well, having discovered it years ago when exploring the far side of Moraine Lake. It was the kind of abandoned barn people might stop to take pictures of, collapsing elegantly into a picturesque meadow. It was a dramatic place to hide out, a dramatic setting for a secret rendezvous. April hadn't yet decided whether that was a good sign or a bad one.

After Isabel's departure that morning, April had immediately marched inside and packed her things. She'd already decided to go searching for the missing piece, so there was no reason to delay getting ready. Plus, there was something about getting ready to leave that made the leaving more certain. Not that she was uncertain, not at all. She had actually never been so certain in her life.

So certain it scared her.

What she was about to do should have been unthinkable. Not only was she going to leave home, but she'd have to lie to Derek about it. She'd never lied to her brother before—well, not until recently, and certainly not about something so big. Her determination to leave should have been wilting under mounds of guilt and love and loyalty. Or at the very least, she should have been keeping her determination alive by reminding herself that she was doing this partly for Derek's sake. Staying here was dangerous. The Riven were coming for her. Though she didn't know what they were, exactly, she knew they were bad. Very bad. By leaving, she was keeping Derek out of harm's way.

But that wasn't why she was leaving. As far as the Riven went, she'd only seen shadows, only heard Isabel's stories. Frightening shadows, frightening stories, yes—but it wasn't fear or nobility or sacrifice that fueled April now. It was selfishness. All day long, the call of the mysterious missing piece had grown stronger, more true. By late morning it had begun to tingle tenaciously in her brain and her spine, an itch she could neither scratch nor ignore. And now it beckoned to her with a voice so powerful that she suspected—but could not quite admit—that she would go looking for it even if it meant putting Derek in *more* danger. The thought wasn't a happy one, but it didn't matter. She had to go. She had to become whole again. And after that, well . . .

It was hard to imagine past that.

She'd packed her school backpack with two more hiking dresses, an extra pair of shorts, two shirts, and plenty of underwear. Also toothpaste, her toothbrush, her retainer— which felt more than ever like a burden, but at least a familiar one—a small blanket, two favorite issues of *National Geographic*, and a can of bug spray. After a moment's thought, she'd also pinned her armadillo brooch to the inside of her bag. The brooch, which she hadn't worn since she was eight, was the only piece of her mother's jewelry she still held on to.

Isabel had told April to bring food and money as well, which to be honest wasn't very encouraging, but it didn't matter. She'd scrounged up all her savings, seventeen dollars and forty-seven cents. Then she'd gone to the kitchen and grabbed a few apples, four bottles of water, a half-empty bag of rippled potato chips, and five packages of beef jerky from Uncle Harrison's massive jerky supply. Beef jerky was not April's favorite—partly because ever since he quit smoking, Uncle Harrison always had a stick of it hanging out of his chubby mouth—but it still seemed like a very adventury sort of food.

Now, with the backpack stashed safely in her closet at home and the call of the missing piece coursing through her bones, she walked the well-worn trail to Doc Durbin's, eager to see Arthur the raven one last time. Doc was keeping the raven far out back, in one of the big pens she used for larger animals. That was good, because with the vine it could be overwhelming getting too close to the vet clinic itself. Being around so many animals at once—especially domesticated animals like cats and dogs—was like having a dozen people talking inside her brain all at once. Even now, just walking through the trees, she was bombarded by the presence of hidden creatures in the forest all around her, most of them alert to and alarmed by her passing.

It was a strange existence, living with the vine. She had always been attuned to animals, but now a walk through the woods or around the lake was a whole new experience, a whole new plane of awareness. More often than not, she never saw the wild creatures she sensed. She could guess some of their identities by location—birds or squirrels overhead, mice or toads or salamanders down on the ground. Usually she could identify them vaguely by their temperaments too: smaller creatures tended to be more neurotic; mammals tended to be keener and more conflicted; reptiles and amphibians were sludgy and torpid. Birds were often as sharp and complicated as mammals, but definitely more foreign—their brains felt older, somehow.

Insects were largely unnoticeable, thank goodness, unless she really focused. Bigger insects were easier to tune in to than small ones like flies and mosquitoes, but she'd learned to avoid insect brains whenever possible. Last week she'd been watching the hummingbirds dart around the feeder outside Doc's house, feeling their hyperkinetic and surprisingly ill-tempered minds tumbling about inside her own. Suddenly she'd become aware of an alien presence in the mix, predatory and hungry. No—worse than that. Murderous. A mind that had no trace of consciousness or self-awareness, as cold and as dark as the underside of an iceberg.

Fighting off the savage thoughts, she'd circled around the feeder and was horrified to spot an enormous praying mantis, almost as long as her hand. Unbelievably, it was trying to catch one of the hummingbirds, lashing out with its hooked forelimbs whenever one of the tiny birds hovered too close. She'd reached up and flicked the bug away in a spurt of panic. It briefly took flight and then dropped heavily into the weeds. Even as it fell, she perceived nothing from it but an unwavering desire to kill and devour. The memory made her shudder.

But of course the vine could do more. Right now April could pick up only certain kinds of thoughts from the animals she listened to—moods, intentions, emotions. Things like hunger, fear, contentment. But she knew in her bones that the vine was meant to dig deeper. Brains were more complicated than that. April had told Isabel about her whiteouts, how when she tried to open herself wider to the vine—to access an animal's mind more fully—the searing pain and blinding whiteness came. Isabel had peered closely at the broken nub of the vine, and made April promise never to push so hard, but she wouldn't say any more than that.

April passed the little pasture where Doc kept her two goats, Moo and Shwoo. She liked the goats fine, but thought of them as apathetic, unintelligent dogs—greedy for food and not much else. Just beyond was the little shelter where Arthur lived. She felt him before she saw him, brooding grouchily about his captivity. But as soon as the raven spotted her, he began to gurgle musically, cooing and clucking as he bobbed his sleek black head. Happiness blossomed in April's mind, a friendly vibe of belonging. She also caught a bit of anticipation mingled with mild hunger. Arthur, of course, had learned to associate April's visits with food. If there was one thing the vine had taught her, it was that animals—especially wild ones—thought about food almost all the time.

"You probably think I brought you some treats, don't you?" April said.

"*Dontchoo,*" Arthur squawked loudly, trying to imitate her. "*Dontchoo dontchooo.*" He stuck his thick beak through the wire and snapped at her in a sociable way.

She did have food for him, of course. A plastic bag full of dog food was stuffed into each of her front pockets. "Guilty as charged," April said. She pulled out a chunk of kibble now and offered it to him. Arthur examined it for a moment, then snatched it deftly from her palm and swallowed it whole. A surge of eager pleasure roiled through April's head.

"I'm leaving soon," she said. "I guess you are too." She offered him more dog food. He took it, and a few more after that, but his enthusiasm quickly began to wane. Now that the excitement of April's visit was wearing off, and his hunger fading, his earlier mood was returning to him. Frustration. No—anger. When she offered him a sixth chunk of dog food, he plucked it impatiently from her hand and tossed it on the ground. He didn't want food. He wanted out—no, "want" wasn't nearly strong enough a word. His imprisonment was maddening, bewildering, and if he'd at first felt a strange kind of safety in the cage because of his broken wing, all shreds of that were gone now. He was better. Ready.

Watching him, reaching out for him as far as the broken

vine would safely allow, April became aware of a deep yearning that flowered in the young bird's mind, a yearning that
seemed now to fill the muscles of her shoulders and chest
with an unbearable itch, a primitive need.

The need to fly.

Arthur shuffled down the cage and took the heavy iron
bolt of the cage door in his beak, shaking it hard. He wanted
it open, now, and suddenly—inevitably—so did April. Freedom. Flight. Wildness. An urge so powerful and right that
April couldn't possibly have denied it. She glanced up at Doc's
house and crouched down in front of the cage.

"Here," she told the still-struggling bird. "Let me."
Arthur reared back, uncertain, and watched keenly as she slid
back the heavy bolt. The cage door swung open wide. "It's
time now," April said, stepping away. "You're all better."

Arthur hopped up onto the sill, cocking his head at her.
She could feel his curious mind at work, trying to make sense
of this new development. Although the door was open just as
he'd wanted, he struggled for a moment to fully embrace what
that meant. But then other emotions began to grow like a new
fire: caution, hope, excitement.

Arthur chirruped softly and dropped heavily onto the
ground. He took a couple of questing hops across the dirt and
then stretched his startlingly large wings, beating at the air.
His broken wing was weak, but working. Joy. Confidence.
Or at least, again, those were the best names April had for
what the bird was feeling. She wasn't even sure they could

be called emotions, but they were strong and pure and full of life.

"That's right," said April. "You're wild now."

Arthur strutted over to April's feet. He cooed at her and plucked at her shoelaces, then looked up at her with his bright black eyes. A flood of gratitude, a warm pulse just an arm's length away from affection—pure and simple and shockingly human—washed over her, sprouting goose bumps along her arms.

"You're welcome," she said, water rising in her eyes.

No sooner had she spoken the words than Arthur squawked loudly and launched himself upward, his wings beating the air so powerfully that the breeze lifted the ends of April's hair. Although she couldn't actually feel what it was like to fly, the thrill of the bird's first flight in weeks hammered her, a surge of adrenaline that made her gasp. Arthur sailed over the yard, still calling, drifting out of sight over a line of dogwoods, headed into the woods. He flew out of range of the vine, and abruptly his presence in her mind winked out completely.

April clutched the front of her dress, feeling empty and breathless, alone with her thoughts. Moo and Shwoo were watching her blandly, vaguely hoping she had food for them too. They felt like rocks. She glanced up at the house again, but apparently no one had seen what she'd done. Not that it mattered. Arthur was gone. Wild now. She stood there for a moment, her eyes locked on the spot in the trees where Arthur had disappeared, hoping he might return, knowing he wouldn't. "Wild now," April murmured to herself. "And I guess I'm next."

WHEN DEREK AND Uncle Harrison got home from work, April started getting dinner ready. Derek came down to help her after showering and changing, but she didn't get up the nerve to ask about staying at Maggie's house until they were all seated at the table. The truth was, she and Maggie hadn't been hanging out much lately, and not at all since the vine. She hoped Derek hadn't noticed.

"So," she said, trying not to sound like she'd rehearsed the lie a thousand times, "Maggie invited me to stay at her house for a few nights. Her mom can pick me up after dinner, if that's okay."

Uncle Harrison grunted and waved a fork to indicate it didn't matter to him, an unnecessary gesture. He had never shown much interest in April, seeming to regard her as a strange flower best left untended. He left all the parenting decisions to Derek, which was fine with April. If she was a strange flower, Uncle Harrison was like a lonely, cud-chewing beast—too self-absorbed to be either unusually cruel or especially kind.

"A few nights?" Derek asked. "So when would you be back?"

"Friday evening." That would give her three full days to find the missing piece.

Uncle Harrison looked at her through his squinty little

eyes, an entire breast of chicken dangling from his fork. "Need some girl talk?" he said. "Too manly in this house, I guess."

"Um . . . sure. Yes. Way too manly," April said. "Girl talk is what I need."

Uncle Harrison chuckled and tore off a great bite of chicken, then turned his attention back to his plate. Conversations with Uncle Harrison never lasted much longer than that.

Derek gave April a doubtful look. "I thought Maggie talked *too* much," he said. "Last time you stayed there, you came home and demanded a day of silence."

"Well," April said, keeping her voice steady, "maybe I'm maturing. Maybe I'm becoming more community minded."

"Uh-huh," Derek said skeptically. "You know, sometimes I think if you mature any more, you'll be ninety."

"Thank you," April said.

Derek seemed unsure whether to laugh or frown. "Okay," he said. "Just . . . call me from Maggie's when you get a chance. Let me know you're still alive."

April dropped her eyes and nodded. For some reason those words—*still alive*—made her stomach sway.

"Promise me, Pill," Derek said softly.

She looked up at him. He made an O with his left hand and held it up to his eye, peering at her keenly through the ring. April swallowed. This was a private sign she and her brother had invented long ago, when things were bad. The orphans' oath. This was their vow to each other—a promise to shed every secret, abandon every lie, put each other first forever. The orphans' oath was their reminder that whatever else failed or fell apart, the two of them never would. And here Derek was, invoking it now.

April couldn't even remember the last time either of them had asked for the oath. She lifted a heavy hand and copied the gesture now, somehow managing to meet Derek eye to eye. "Promise," she said.

After a beat, Derek flashed her a brilliant smile and winked through the O. He dropped his hand and went back to his food.

"That's what I like to see," Uncle Harrison said loudly, as if he had any idea what had just occurred. "Families being families."

"Well," Derek said, fussing with his mashed potatoes. But he never finished the sentence. They spent the rest of the meal in silence, and the only way April could keep herself from crying was to latch all her thoughts onto that missing piece, so far away and so desperately lost, and to remind herself that the only thing worse than leaving would be to never go at all.

AFTER DINNER, APRIL left home.

And it *was* home, she thought, as she stood on the porch with her backpack, watching the sun sink into the treetops. Even if this house had never fully felt like it was hers, it was the only home she had. But now she was leaving it behind, and First Baron, and even dull Uncle Harrison, who hardly said ten words a week to her. All because of the vine. Two weeks with the vine, and then the sudden arrival of a stranger, and here she was ready to head out alone, not knowing when she'd come back. It was madness, really. The only thing that kept her nerves together was the constant presence of the vine, and the belief that it belonged to her far more than she belonged to this house.

Derek, of course, was another story.

She'd not been able to give Derek the good-bye he deserved, for fear of drawing too much attention to herself—possibly by collapsing. "See ya," she'd said casually, and Derek had replied, "Yup. Have fun." Uncle Harrison had only grunted, which in all honesty was probably what he would've done even if he'd known the truth.

April bent and peeled a crisp flake of gray paint from the dilapidated porch floor. She rubbed it between her fingertips until it crumbled into dust, and then she started down the long gravel driveway, keeping her spine straight and not looking back. But she'd barely gone around the first bend in the drive before her spine went weak. Baron. He was following far behind, curious and eager. A moment after she felt him, she heard his collar jangling. She stopped and turned.

"No following," she told him, but the dog didn't slow. She held out her hand before he could get close. "Stop. Sit."

Baron sat, confused and concerned and slightly hurt, but happy as always to please. April didn't go back to him.

There had been too many hard good-byes already, and while April wasn't opposed to being sentimental, she felt in danger of overflowing. She reached up and rubbed the broken stem of the vine, letting the jagged edge prick her thumb softly. "You stay here," she told Baron, her voice wavering. "You stay good." And then she turned and walked away from him.

Baron stayed, but his confusion lingered, tugging at her. He let out a little bark of worry. April kept moving, trying not to notice that she was crying openly now, until at last she was beyond the vine's range. Baron's worry winked out like a candle. Knowing him, she felt sure that he hadn't yet moved, still listening to her leave, still wondering where she was going and when she would be back.

She wondered much the same.

She walked on, letting the tears flow freely and silently, probing at her sadness and deciding that it was warranted . . . of course it was warranted. But beneath the sadness, there was that same bedrock of sureness, an absence of doubt. She was doing the right thing. She was doing the *only* thing. She was Tan'ji now, Isabel had said. She might not yet know everything that meant, but she felt it was the truth. She felt her missing piece out there, waiting for her up ahead as surely as Baron was still waiting behind.

At last she reached the trail she was looking for. It led past Moraine Lake and on to the abandoned barn where Isabel would be waiting. It was a walk she knew well. But the trail through the trees would get dark long before the road, and after what she'd seen last night . . . well, it only made sense to hurry. She slipped between the shrubby buckthorns along the driveway and into the woods beyond.

She kept walking. All around her, forest life was either going to sleep or just waking up. She tried not to think about Derek, or Baron, or Arthur, or Doc. She kept her focus on the missing piece, somewhere far ahead. It grew darker, the sinking sun tangled in the trees. Her tears finally began to dwindle.

Suddenly she stopped dead. Something was wrong. A still and trembling fear had wormed its way into her mind. She focused on the source. Two small mammals—chipmunks?— low against the ground off to the right. A young raccoon up above, just ahead. All three were as tense and motionless as she was, frozen and hoping not to be seen. But not by her . . . by something else.

And then a footstep. Just one, off to her left, crisp and unmistakable—the crunch of last year's leaves beneath a cautiously placed foot. She stared out into the trees. A frantic crowd of sparrows flickered past her, fleeing. She couldn't feel any new presence through the vine. Even the trees seemed to still themselves. April's heart began to hammer.

"Hello?" she started to say, but as she took a breath to speak, a stinging stench filled her mouth, her nose, her mind. She recognized it at once—the smell from the night before. A single word came to her, emerging from her memory of Isabel's fierce face.

Riven.

April ran. Instantly a pursuit broke out, as something large began to crash through the woods after her. And now it was joined by another—or was it two others?—off to her right, shadowing her, keeping pace with her easily. She peeked over and saw a towering shape far back among the trees, striding swiftly on two long legs.

She ran as fast as she could. Not for herself, but for the vine. If that's what they wanted, they couldn't have it. Her footsteps pounded desperately against the dirt. Before long, though, she realized she could not escape. Her pursuers were keeping up with ease—barely strolling!—and the barn where Isabel waited was still far off. So April did the only thing she could think of.

She stopped.

She stood there breathing heavily for a moment. She had no idea if the Riven spoke English, but she couldn't flee and she couldn't fight, which only left talking. She found her breath—and her nerve—and called out into the woods, "Come on, then! Let's talk!"

Silence, six heartbeats long. And then off to her left, a shadow detached itself from a tree and stood there staring at her. It was a man—but no, not a man—a thin, looming figure twice as tall as a human being and as skinny as a poplar. He was dressed in black and had a dense mop of black hair atop his pale, skeletal head. His eyes, tiny and dark, bored into her like needles.

April wrestled with her fear, determined not to let it show. "What do you want?" she called out.

The figure shrugged silently and spread his long arms. His ghostly white hands were as big as April's torso.

April stood strong. "I know you can understand me."

The tall figure smiled then, his mouth wide and cruel and full of tiny teeth—so many teeth. His massive hand was wrapped around a full-grown maple as if it were a sapling. She could swear he had an extra knuckle on each hideously long finger. When he spoke, his voice was somehow both musical and sinister at the same time. "Yes, you're quite right, my dear Tinker," he sang. "I can."

No sooner had he spoken than a sudden clamor broke out far behind her—the throaty shriek of a large bird. April turned—a crow, or a raven? The bird was too far away for the vine, but the calls echoed brazenly through the woods, a raucous challenge. She listened hard and stared even harder down the trail. Another series of calls tore through the evening air, and when April looked back at the tall man in the woods, he had vanished. From the other side of the trail, she glimpsed two other tall figures retreating swiftly through the trees. Soon there was no trace of the Riven but that terrible lingering smell.

A large black bird dropped out of a tree and glided toward her. A raven. When it was twenty yards away, April felt the bird's consciousness explode inside her own—a fading aggression, a blooming excitement, a steady trickle of familiarity.

Arthur.

The bird vanished into the gloom of an oak tree, croaked twice, and then swooped closer. He dropped to the ground just a few feet away. Turning to face the spot where the tall man had been standing, Arthur puffed out his throat feathers and belted out three more emphatic warning calls. He burned momentarily with an anger April had never felt from him before. When he was done, he strutted over to her, feeling pleased with himself. He gurgled at her amiably and then bent and tugged at her shoelace.

It seemed the bird had chased off the Riven, those impossible creatures. But how? And why? April heaved the bird's thoughts into her own, opening the gates wide, needing to understand. From the bird flowed fading strings of anger. No, not just anger. Hatred, deep and instinctual.

Suddenly, a shout. Isabel herself was striding fiercely down the trail, barking out orders. "Stop that!"

Arthur, startled, briefly took wing but didn't go far.

Isabel marched right up. Miradel was swollen and swinging. "Quit it with the vine already," Isabel said. "I know you're broken, but you've got to learn control." She brushed past April and peered out into the trees. "Blood in the water, remember?"

April fumbled to obey. She hauled her thoughts away from Arthur, from the other signals of nearby animal life. She even tried to quell the quiet hum of the trees, focusing instead on her own thoughts, her own emotions, her own senses.

Gradually the awareness flowing through the vine subsided into the background.

"I told you not to use the vine," Isabel said, still scanning the trees.

She hadn't, though. She'd only told her not to push too hard. "I'm sorry," April said, "but are you saying every time I use the vine, the Riven will feel it?"

"I'm saying it's a possibility."

"So what am I supposed to do?"

"Be smarter," Isabel said curtly. "Remember that you're being hunted."

Hunted. By ten-foot-tall monstrosities who wanted the vine. "One of them spoke to me," April said. "A very tall one."

"I know. I heard him."

"He called me a Tinker."

"Yes," said Isabel. "That's what they call us."

"And then Arthur scared him off."

"Who?"

"Arthur," said April, pointing. "The raven."

Isabel looked over at the bird with surprise. Encouraged, Arthur hopped closer. "If you say so," Isabel said cryptically, and went back to scanning the woods. What was that supposed to mean? Arthur walked over to April, patiently wondering about a snack. He was still feeling proud and angry, but starting to wonder why no treat had been delivered.

April reached for the dog food in her pocket, admiring how Arthur's keen intellect perked up as he recognized the gesture—not with a doggish greed, but with a puzzle solver's curiosity about where the food actually came from. Without thinking, April opened a space in her mind for Arthur.

On the instant, Isabel rounded on her with ferocious speed.

"I said *stop*," the woman spat icily, flashing her teeth, and the world itself became ice. Cold bit into April's bones. Arthur's presence vanished from her head, and a beat later she realized it wasn't just Arthur that was gone.

The vine itself was nowhere. For the past two weeks the vine had been a part of her, as present as her hands, her mouth, her heart. Its power had become as constant and expected as sight. But now she couldn't feel the vine at all, couldn't summon up its power. She reached up to touch it, and her fingers found the curling metal, but it was no relief at all because the vine was . . . gone.

There but not there.

Horrified, April stood frozen. She gaped at Isabel. The woman's own heart seemed to be glowing, a tangle of green light pulsing from her chest—but no, not her heart. What was it? And who was Isabel? Lost in the yawning absence of the vine, unable to even allow her knees to buckle beneath her, April struggled to speak, unaware who she was talking to or if she could even be heard. Green light. Red hair. So cold. The vine was lost. April opened her mouth—what mouth?—and tried to make words: *What did you do?*

CHAPTER FOUR

Revelations

Horace couldn't take his eyes off the puzzling Tanu in his mother's hands, with its sails of shimmering thread. He couldn't imagine what it might be. A twisted knot in his belly tried to insist that he didn't want to know what it was, but for the first time in nine days, he refused to turn away. He reached for the comforting sensation of the Fel'Daera, snug in its pouch at his side. He was Tan'ji. He was the Keeper of the Box of Promises. Whatever his mother knew about the box, or its Maker, nothing could diminish that. He angrily crushed his doubts flat. He had a right to know . . . everything.

His mother watched him for a moment, then turned to Chloe. "I sensed you up in Horace's room," she said. "I suspected he might tell you about me. And Horace, I figured that once you two talked about it, you might decide . . ."

"Yes," Horace said. "I'm ready now." All the grumbling,

caged-up questions of the last nine days now practically tripped over themselves to get in line in his head, including a brand-new one—what did his mother mean when she said she had sensed Chloe?

"Good," his mother said, clearly relieved. "But first I want to apologize. Not for this, but for that night. I'm sorry I told you what I did, when I did. My timing could have been better. I just . . . I get tired of the secrets."

She sounded weary, and that weariness felt so familiar. "It's okay," he said stiffly. "I'm sorry, too. I've been . . . pouting."

Chloe stirred at Horace's side. "I should go," she said, though her eyes too were glued to the Tanu on the table. "I can wait outside."

"Please stay," said Horace's mother. "There's nothing I'm about to say that you shouldn't hear too."

Chloe glanced at Horace. He nodded, and she sat. Horace joined her. Chloe fiddled with the dragonfly, clearly nervous.

His mother set her Tanu on the table. It rocked slightly, like an alien boat at sea. "I can only imagine how many questions you must have, but we need to start here. This is called a harp." She ran a finger down one face of the shimmering strings. They made no sound but quivered with prismatic light—red, gold, green, violet. "Every harp looks different, but they all contain these threads. Can you see them?"

"Sort of," replied Horace, while Chloe said, "Yes."

"I thought you would. Most people can't see them at all,

but Tan'ji often can." She plucked idly at the strings, making them quiver and gleam. "I guess I don't need to explain why we call them harps."

Horace cocked his head, watching the strange threads flicker in and out of sight. "But what does it do? It's not Tan'ji—you're not Tan'ji."

"No. I never went through the Find like the two of you did, and I never will. Harps don't take the bond."

The Find, that period of searching when a new Keeper struggled alone to discover the powers of his or her instrument, was a mandatory rite of passage for every Tan'ji. "Why not?" Horace asked.

"Well, first of all, there's nothing super special about this harp. You could hand me almost any old harp, and I'd be able to use it."

"So harps are Tan'kindi," Horace said.

"Not exactly. Harps won't work for just anybody." His mother sighed and frowned, running her fingers up and down the shimmering strings, spilling a silent kaleidoscope of color across her palms, across the table. "I'm not really sure how much to tell you."

"Tell me everything," he said.

"I can't do that. There are some things I don't know. Some things I don't care to share, even with you. Plus there are certain other things I've sworn not to reveal. To anyone."

"Great," Horace said. "So much for no more secrets."

Chloe said, "I'm sorry, Mrs. Andrews, are you saying you

71

took an oath not to talk?"

"'Oath' sounds awfully culty. Let's say I took a vow—a vow I believe in. I can't and won't tell you everything."

"No offense," Chloe said, "but you sound like Mr. Meister."

Horace's mother frowned. "That's probably fair. I haven't seen him in twenty years, but even back then he could be maddeningly mysterious."

"Twenty years," Horace said, doing the math. "Since you were a teenager?"

"Yes. I was sixteen when I left—"

"Does he know I'm your son?" Horace interrupted. This was one of the questions that had been nagging at him.

"The Wardens tend to keep tabs on things when they can, so yes, I assume he does. Mrs. Hapsteade too."

"Why didn't they ever say anything to me?" Horace insisted.

"Possibly they thought it wasn't their place to say."

Or maybe it was yet another secret the old man hoarded for himself. Horace leaned forward hungrily. "Why would they keep tabs on you? Did something happen twenty years ago? Is that why you left the Wardens? Or wait—were you ever really with them?"

Chloe held up her hands. "Okay, Horace, we get it. Floodgates are open. This is why you shouldn't fret in silence for nine days. I'm pretty sure your mom has lots to tell us, so maybe we just let her talk. Okay?"

Horace sat back, trying to tame his seething mind. "Fine. Okay."

Chloe looked at Horace's mom. "I have a place for you to start. If you're not Tan'ji, *what are you?*"

Horace's mother laughed. "Good question. Easy answer. I'm a Tuner."

"What's a Tuner?" Horace asked.

"First, a little background." His mother bent her head for a moment, clearly gathering her thoughts, and then spoke. "You see, all the Tanu—Tan'ji and Tan'kindi—need power to function. Energy. This energy is called the Medium, and it's all around us, all the time. As a Tuner, I can sense the Medium. I can tweak it. I can alter its flow in small ways."

"That's what you meant when you said you could feel me upstairs," Chloe said.

"Yes. Because you were nearby, I felt a change in the Medium when you used the dragonfly." She smiled. "A very familiar change."

"But this Medium," Horace said. "What kind of energy is it? Where does it come from?"

"I don't know where it comes from originally, but I do know that before it reaches your instruments—and you—it flows through the Mothergates. Have you heard that name?"

"No," Horace said, feeling at once exhilarated at all this new information, and frustrated—no, infuriated—that he hadn't heard it before. "What are the Mothergates?"

"Again, I don't fully know. I've never seen them. I can

feel them, though." She dropped her hand and pointed at the floor beneath the kitchen table, off to her right. "There's one in that direction, on the other side of the world—several thousand miles away." With her left hand, she pointed at the floor again, beneath Chloe's chair. "And one that way, not quite so far." Then she straightened and pointed out through the corner of the kitchen. "The last one is that way, much closer than the others."

Horace and Chloe exchanged a glance. Chloe lifted her feet and looked straight down under her chair. Horace tried to imagine what was on the other side of the world in the directions his mother had pointed. Australia? The Pacific Ocean? Egypt?

"So there are three of these Mothergates," he said slowly. "Scattered around the world, but one of them is closer by. Is that right?"

"That's right. The third one is very close, relatively speaking. Just a couple hundred miles away, I think. It's hard to say—the gates are kept hidden by a powerful Tanu called the Veil. That's all I know."

Every sentence his mother uttered was filled with new knowledge. Horace felt so silly now, remembering all his efforts to keep her in the dark about the Fel'Daera and the Wardens—*he* was the newbie here, not her. He forced himself to remember there was no shame in that.

"This is killing you," his mother said, watching him. "Your brain is going to explode."

"If my brain was going to explode, it would have happened before now."

"It's true," said Chloe. "My brain has nearly exploded just *hearing* about what's happening inside Horace's brain."

Horace's mother laughed. "The point is, the Medium flows from the Mothergates and into your instruments—into you, too. And my harp gives me some access to those flows. Let me show you. Take out the Fel'Daera, and hold it in your hands."

Somewhat warily, Horace pulled out the box and held it out. Chloe leaned forward eagerly.

"Higher. Good. Just like that." His mother reached for the harp. "I'm rusty," she said, grimacing. "Don't laugh."

"I am so far away from laughing," said Horace.

His mother laid her fingers against the strings and began to . . . what? At first it looked like she was playing an actual harp, plucking at the strange threads. But as he watched her fingers move deftly, he saw that sometimes she pushed instead of plucking. Or sometimes she grasped a string between her thumb and forefinger, or between the pinkies of opposite hands, and drew down the length of the thread. Her fingers worked like the legs of weaving spiders.

A girlish laugh of pure joy popped out of her. She covered her mouth, embarrassed. Horace was startled to see shiny wetness in her eyes. "Sorry," she said. "It's been so long. I think I've been craving this more than I knew."

"But haven't you had the harp for years and years?" he asked.

"Yes, but a harp alone does nothing. A Tuner needs a Tanu to work on. Without a Tanu, I'm like a painter without a canvas, or a mechanic without a car. And until quite recently, Tanu have been in short supply around here."

She took a deep breath and went back to the harp, pressing and plucking. She tipped her head slightly, and her eyes faded into the distance. All her motions were precise and arcane and beautiful in a way, and her face became a chiseled slab of calm concentration, and Horace knew that even if she wasn't Tan'ji, still she was tapping into the same pools of thought that he swam in when he used the Fel'Daera. What a secret to have kept from him all these years. He remembered how she'd caught him with the raven's eye—the small, round Tan'kindi that provided a bit of temporary protection from the Riven. Or better yet, when she'd first spotted the Fel'Daera in his room. What must she have thought?

"God, Horace," his mother said suddenly. "I would not want to be you."

"Who would?" said Chloe.

"Why?" he said. "What's wrong?"

"Nothing," his mother said hastily. "I don't mean that in a bad way. It's just . . . I'd forgotten how crazy the Fel'Daera is. But I think I've got it now—or some of it, at least." She gave him a mischievous look, her fingers still stretched crookedly across the threads of the harp. "Feel this?" she said, pushing the thumb of her left hand forward, bending one of those strands.

Abruptly, Horace felt the Fel'Daera slipping from his grip. He clutched at it instinctively before his eyes told him that the box wasn't actually moving. But her thumb nudged the string again—and again he sensed that the box was sliding, toppling. Except it wasn't.

"What are you doing?"

"Messing with you," she admitted. "With a harp, I can take hold of the Medium that flows between your consciousness and the Fel'Daera. I can manipulate those flows—between a Tan'ji and the Mothergates, or between the instrument and its Keeper, or within the instrument itself. I can interfere with the Medium, or assist it. I've got hold of it now. The part I'm messing with is a kind of proprioception."

"A what?" Chloe asked.

Horace had the answer to that one. "Proprioception. It's a sense. There are more than just five senses, you know. Proprioception is the one that lets you touch your fingertip to your nose even with your eyes closed."

Chloe frowned and then tried it, seeming surprised by her own success.

"See?" said Horace's mother. "It's knowing where all the parts of yourself are. And when you're a Keeper, that proprioception extends to your Tan'ji, too. It explains why Tan'ji like you always know where their instruments are. And it's what I'm messing with now." She wiggled her thumb back and forth, and again Horace felt—but did not *see*—the box sliding back and forth in his hand. He sat staring for a moment,

77

letting the strange war between his senses rage on.

"That is . . . insane," he managed.

"So I hear. But that's just a parlor trick. I'm a Tuner, so the main thing I do is . . . tune."

"Tune what?" Chloe asked.

"Instruments," she replied, indicating the box and the dragonfly. "You see, over time, every Tan'ji becomes attuned to its Keeper—the Keeper's strengths, weaknesses, tendencies. The very will of the Keeper, in fact, becomes embedded in his or her instrument. The instrument, though, almost always outlives the Keeper. When that happens, the bond is broken, but the imprint of the last Keeper still remains within the instrument itself."

Horace set the box down on the table, concentrating on the bond. He already knew that there had been other Keepers of the Fel'Daera before him, but he didn't like the reminder—particularly because Dr. Jericho had hinted, more than once, that the Fel'Daera's last Keeper had met with an unpleasant end. Horace tried not to imagine what kind of an imprint might have been left behind within the box.

His mother continued. "Instruments that have no Keeper are called Tan'layn—the unclaimed. Tan'layn are always in search of a new Keeper, usually with the help of someone like Mr. Meister. The Wardens have warehouses full of Tan'layn, as you probably know. But before the search for a new Keeper can begin, each Tan'layn, ideally, should be cleansed of its last Keeper's imprint. That's where we Tuners come in. We take hold of the Medium within the instrument and remove whatever residue we find. It's somewhere between a house cleaning and an exorcism, I suppose. We eliminate the presence of anything unwanted, returning the Tan'layn to its original state. Tuning makes it much easier and safer when—if—a new Keeper comes along to claim the instrument."

"Safer how?" Chloe said. "What happens if a Tan'layn doesn't get tuned?"

"At best, nothing. At worst, the new Keeper finds that the instrument doesn't always do as asked—that the shadow of the previous Keeper's will hasn't gone away." She screwed up her face, thinking. "From what I understand, it's sort of like getting a dog that used to belong to someone else. The old influences linger, sometimes dangerously so. Tuners remove those influences."

Quietly, cautiously, Horace asked, "So were you the one who tuned the Fel'Daera, after . . . after its last Keeper?"

"No," his mother said firmly, gently. "Not me. And I don't know anything about the last Keeper, or how that Keeper lost their claim."

"But you've felt the Fel'Daera before. And you said you knew . . ." Horace trailed off, unsure what to ask. Unsure what he even wanted to know. This was what he'd been most afraid of for the past nine days.

"The Maker," his mother said for him. "Yes, I did. Would you like to hear about her?"

Her, Horace thought. He poured all his warm, worried

hope into the box, trying to calm himself. He could only nod.

"She passed through just once, on her way west, and came to the Warren. She had a small collection of Tan'layn to leave with Mr. Meister and Mrs. Hapsteade. Deliveries of Tan'layn happened from time to time, in the hopes that Mr. Meister and Mrs. Hapsteade could try to find a match. Usually, the instruments were nothing major. But when Falo showed up, she—"

"Falo," Horace interrupted.

"Sil'falo Teneves. The maker of the Fel'Daera. That was her name."

The maker of the Fel'Daera. Sil'falo Teneves. "What did she . . . ?"

"You want to know what she looked like," Horace's mother said. "You've seen the Riven, and you're wondering if Falo looked like that."

Horace could only nod.

"Have you ever encountered a Mordin?"

An image of Dr. Jericho rose up in Horace's mind, impossibly thin and monstrously tall, with his cruel face and savage hands. Much taller than ordinary Riven, the Mordin were fearsome and relentless hunters of Tanu, and Dr. Jericho was perhaps the most fearsome and relentless of all. Worse, he had a particular skill for being able to sense and track the Fel'Daera. Horace's skin went cold, remembering his last encounter with Dr. Jericho. "Yes. Very much so."

His mother pressed her eyes closed for a moment and

then looked out the window. "Well," she said. "Let's just say that Sil'falo didn't . . . *feel* like a Mordin does, or the way the rest of the Riven do, even though she looked similar. Falo was beautiful, in a way, if you can imagine such a thing. The Altari are tall, and long limbed, but full of light and life in a way the Riven aren't." She went on gazing across the lawn for several more seconds and then took a deep breath. "But anyway. Falo brought these Tanu to the Warren. Some of the Tan'layn were quite unusual, powerful. A few of them were her own creations that she'd somehow managed to track down. There were three in particular, really serious instruments. The Laithe, the Box of Promises, and—"

"Wait," Horace said. "The Laithe." He remembered the tiny, miraculous globe from the House of Answers, the warehouse where he'd found the Fel'Daera. The same globe he'd later seen on Mr. Meister's desk. "The Laithe of Teneves, right? She made that?"

"Yes. You know it?"

Horace nodded. "I think so. I think it was one of the other Tan'layn there when I found the Fel'Daera."

His mother considered this thoughtfully. "It makes sense that Mr. Meister might present them both to you. The box and the Laithe had the same Maker. And I suppose they are similar, in a way."

"In what way?" asked Horace.

But his mother shook her head. "I can't tell you that. Tuners aren't supposed to reveal the inner workings of the instruments they cleanse. But let me finish. All these Tan'layn that Falo brought were in serious need of tuning—especially the Fel'Daera and the Laithe. Messy, scarred up, badly imprinted, the Medium knotted and torn inside."

Horace shifted in his seat uncomfortably, rubbing his thumb across the lid of the box, but his mother seemed not to notice, caught up in her memories. Chloe shot him a sympathetic glance. "Mr. Meister brought me to the Warren to tune the box and the globe, but . . . it was hopeless. Not only were they wrecks, but they were the most complex instruments I'd ever seen. I worked on the Fel'Daera like a dozen times, with several different harps, but I couldn't do a thing. Same thing with the Laithe. Falo felt sorry for me, I think." She cocked her head, her voice suddenly dreamy. "She was nice to me, which meant a lot. I was probably fourteen at the time. Every kindness loomed large."

"So if you didn't tune the Fel'Daera, who did?" asked Horace.

His mother absently plucked a string of her harp. "There was another Tuner working for the Wardens, a girl four or five years younger than me. At first, she didn't have any more luck with the Fel'Daera than I did, even though she was more talented. But Falo had brought an unfamiliar harp with her. Very old. *Very* powerful. They let this girl try it, and . . ." She shook her head in rueful admiration, looking down at the Fel'Daera. "I watched her tune the box. What she did with that harp was so complicated I couldn't even follow. Afterward, I tried to use it to tune the Laithe, but the harp was beyond me. Too many threads—far too many, more of a cloud, really. And the threads had to be worked with the mind instead of the hands. I was totally lost. But the other girl took over for me, and she tuned the Laithe easily. I was so embarrassed. I felt like an amateur." To Horace's surprise, a little bit of blush rose in her cheeks.

Chloe sat up. "Well, I don't know about this other girl, Mrs. Andrews, but I just want to say that however badass I thought you were before, you're like twice as badass now."

Horace's mother laughed merrily. "Thank you, Chloe. I don't know if that's true, but I do want you both to be impressed. Not by me, necessarily, but by Tuners in general."

"Why?" said Horace.

"Just for example?" His mother leaned forward, her face suddenly serious. She placed all ten fingers on the threads in some complex symmetry he couldn't quite discern, adjusting their positions meticulously. Then she glanced up at him and pushed inward all at once.

The Fel'Daera, a constant presence in Horace's mind, instantly vanished from his thoughts. He heard himself let out a choking gasp. He could still see the box, there his hands, but he couldn't feel it. He started to drift into a familiar sick gray—this was just like passing through the Nevren. The Nevren was a kind of energy field that the Wardens used to protect the entrances to their strongholds. Within it, Keepers were completely cut off from their Tan'ji, unable to use its power or even sense its presence. Horace was feeling that now. He heard Chloe speak, a sludgy drawl of concern that he couldn't comprehend. But before he sank too deep into the void, the box was back again. The connection coursed through him once more.

His mother pulled her hands away from the harp and looked at him ruefully. "Sorry," she said. "I know that doesn't feel good."

"You severed him?" Chloe asked sharply, sounding shocked.

"Yes. We Tuners can manipulate the Medium, remember? We can even cut it off completely. For a while, anyway—it takes effort to keep it up."

Horace looked at the harp with renewed respect. "Mrs. Hapsteade told us that if a Keeper stays severed for too long, they can become dispossessed. Permanently cut off from their Tan'ji. Can a Tuner do that too?"

Chloe's face was rigid, her gaze distant.

"Not me," Horace's mother said. She gestured to the bouquet of daisies on the table, glowing in the afternoon sun. "Think of it this way. Imagine that the connection between you and your instrument is one of these daisies. The Medium is the sun, bringing power and life. Cutting off the flow of the Medium is like blocking out the sun. This is severing." She cupped her hands around a single flower, encasing it in darkness. "The flower starts to wilt, but usually no real damage is done. If it stays in the darkness long enough, however, the flower—the bond—will die completely. That's dispossession, and it is permanent." She dropped her hands. "I'm not strong enough to sever a Keeper for so long that they become dispossessed. Especially not with anything as complicated as the box, or the dragonfly. But the best Tuners could certainly do it, if it was required."

"Like the girl you worked with," Horace suggested.

"Yes. Also, you should know that dispossession isn't the worst thing a Tuner can do to you."

"It's not?" Horace said. He couldn't imagine anything worse than losing the bond permanently. And the way he understood it, Keepers didn't generally survive being dispossessed.

"No." His mother grabbed a daisy by the stem. "The very strongest Tuners could grab hold of the bond directly and tear it apart by force." With a savage flick of her thumb, she popped the head of the daisy completely loose. It tumbled onto the table. "Cleaving, they call it. Supposedly the agony is unimaginable."

Horace realized his face was frozen in horror. He smoothed it and resisted the urge to clasp the box to his chest. Why had no one told them about this before? He expected Chloe to be just as outraged, but she hardly seemed to be listening, still lost in some dark thought.

"Cleaving," Horace said, looking at the decapitated flower head. "So basically, Tuners are potentially very bad news."

"Potentially, yes."

"What about the Riven? Are any of them Tuners?" he asked.

"Not technically, no. You need the Wardens to become a Tuner. You need Mr. Meister."

Chloe stirred. "Why?"

Horace's mom hesitated. A shadow seemed to flit across her face, and then she said, "It doesn't matter. The point is that without Mr. Meister, none of the Riven, as far as I know, can become Tuners. But remember . . . that doesn't mean they don't have any Tuners on their side."

Horace understood. He remembered Ingrid, the flute-playing former Warden who had last been seen in the nest, right by Dr. Jericho's side. A traitor. "How many Tuners are there?" he asked.

"Not very many, I think. I've only met three others."

"But they were friendly, right?" Chloe asked.

"Friendly, yes, but . . . there were issues with the girl who tuned the Fel'Daera."

"What kind of issues?" asked Horace.

"Well, she kept using that same crazy harp, off and on, for a couple of years afterward. But it was too strong, even for her. She couldn't totally control it. She was pretty temperamental to begin with, and when she got angry or frustrated, those emotions would come out through the harp. She would sever people—just for a second, but with no warning, for no reason. She'd be tuning, and all of a sudden it'd be like the power went out, for every Tan'ji in the area. Heck, I couldn't do that, no matter how hard I tried." She rocked her harp absently on the tabletop. "Thank god no one ever taught her how to cleave."

"So what happened to her?" asked Horace.

"She ran away. Or she was banished, depending on how you look at it."

"Banished," said Chloe. "By Mr. Meister, you mean."

"Yes." Horace's mother frowned, remembering. "Being a Tuner isn't easy. Since we're not Tan'ji, our instruments aren't really ours to keep. The only reason I still have mine is because Mr. Meister let me take it when I left. And I think he did that only because he felt guilty about what happened with the other girl."

"Why did he banish her?" asked Horace.

"She wasn't happy being a Tuner. She wanted to be a Keeper. After she got a taste of this new harp that only she could use, she started to act like she was Tan'ji. She actually seemed to think she could *become* Tan'ji, if only Mr. Meister would let her keep the harp. But Mr. Meister would never let us take the harps home with us. He was always reminding us that the harps weren't ours, and he would only let us use them in the Warren. She blamed him for the problems she had controlling the harp—she was sure there was a way to fix it." Her voice grew stronger, more agitated. "She was so young. It wasn't fair what happened to her. Mr. Meister makes her a Tuner, and then he gives her this crazy powerful harp, and then he—" She stopped and shook her head, her eyes faraway.

"Is that why he banished her?" Chloe asked. "Because she wanted to keep the harp for herself?"

"Oh, it went way beyond wanting. One day, a couple of years after she tuned the Fel'Daera, she snuck into the Warren and she stole that harp. The Nevren is no obstacle when you're not Tan'ji, so she just walked right in, took the harp, and walked back out again. She disappeared. The Wardens tried to track her down but couldn't. So instead Mr. Meister banished her. Permanently."

Horace frowned. "But . . . why banish her if she'd already run away?"

"For the Wardens, banishment isn't just a warning not to come back, Horace. They make it so that you're physically unable to ever find the Warren again."

Horace and Chloe glanced at each other. It made sense that the Wardens had such a power, but Horace had never considered it before.

"Anyway," his mother said, "I was deeply disenchanted when I learned that they'd banished her." She tilted her head thoughtfully, as if measuring something inside herself. "She and I weren't exactly friends—we didn't hang out or anything—but we were . . . close, in our own way. And I was sixteen by then. It was easy to get passionate about things. I kind of drifted away from the Wardens not long after. I think Mr. Meister understood—he knew I was done."

Chloe said, "And meanwhile, this girl is still out there somewhere—or woman, I guess."

"I assume so. I never saw her again. I always wondered what she would do, once she realized she wasn't going to magically become Tan'ji just by having that harp all to herself. She wanted so badly to be a Keeper, and she was sure there was a way. She was convinced the Wardens were holding out on her. Holding her down."

"Do you think she still thinks that, wherever she is?" asked Horace.

"I don't know. She was so stubborn, so fierce. I remember she had flaming red hair, and it suited her—like she would set fire to anything just to get what she wanted." She looked out the window, across the lawn toward the sun. "But life passes. Obsessions fade. I genuinely hope, after all this time, that she's found new things to fight for."

CHAPTER FIVE

Traveling Companions

"*WHAT DID YOU DO?*" APRIL ASKED AGAIN, HER VOICE GOING—OR not going—out into the void. Red. Green. She was so cold. It was so cold without the vine. So cold and numb she couldn't even remember what the vine was, or why she cared.

Something moved. Red hair. *Isabel.* That was a name. The name had done something—stolen something and left her alone—but why?

And then abruptly, warmth poured through her. As quickly as it had disappeared, the vine returned. She was April again. Arthur's alert curiosity and the hum of the forest blossomed again in her mind. April took a deep breath and unclenched her fists.

Isabel was watching her, her face half angry and half apologetic. "You're okay," she said flatly.

"What did you do?" April asked for the third time, or

90

maybe the first time. The wicker sphere—Miradel, that was its name—was small and dark again.

Isabel crossed her arms. "I told you to stop."

"You cut me off," said April.

"I warned you."

"Yes, and I tried to stop. But I didn't know you would do that. I didn't know it was *possible* to do that."

"Now you know," Isabel said, wrapping her hand around Miradel.

April collected herself. She had to stay calm. She had to keep still. "I'm wondering what Miradel actually is," she said quietly. "And if I'm an empath, what are you?"

"I'm—" Isabel began, and then started over. "Miradel is my harp. With it, I can protect you. But you have to listen to me."

"And if I don't, will you punish me by cutting me off again?"

"Severing isn't a punishment. I told you—I'm trying to protect you, not hurt you."

Except that it *had* hurt. Even the sound of the word itself was cruel—*severing*. April stood there in silence, letting her sour face speak for her.

Isabel shifted uncomfortably. "Look. I'm not going to apologize for severing you. I'm not even going to tell you it won't happen again. And if that scares you, fine. Now you understand why the Riven fear me too."

Comprehension dawned over April. "The Riven weren't running from Arthur. They were running from you."

Isabel shrugged. "The Riven enjoy being severed even less than you do."

"But if they can be severed, that means they're Keepers like us."

"Not like us. They don't call themselves Keepers. But yes, they are Tan'ji. And because they are Tan'ji, they fear me. Now you've got proof that I can help protect you while we're together."

"And if we're not together?"

"The only way to be truly safe is to retrieve your missing piece. The sooner the better." She turned to leave.

April clambered to her feet. She really did need Isabel's help to find the missing piece, that much was becoming clear. But she also needed answers. "Truly safe, you say. I would like to know how, please. Specifically."

Isabel hesitated, heaving a long sigh. Then she bustled back to April so fast that April almost recoiled. But instead of scolding her again, Isabel began to explain, her voice low and swift.

"The Riven that are hunting you now aren't ordinary Riven. They're Mordin—taller, fiercer, more cunning. They can see in the dark, can disguise themselves. Most importantly, they have instruments that make them especially good at sensing and tracking down Tan'ji. But you're lucky. You're an empath, and empaths aren't easy to detect. Empaths are passive—receivers instead of transmitters—and ordinarily, even a Mordin might not sense one from more than a hundred feet away." Her eyes flitted over the vine almost apologetically. "Ordinarily," she repeated.

April soaked this in as Arthur rummaged through the underbrush. Trying not to sound sullen, she said, "So while I'm broken, I can't use the vine at all, or the Mordin will hear me."

"You can't completely hide a broken Tan'ji from the Mordin," Isabel replied. "Even if you never use the vine, your amputation is going to leave a faint trail. That's not all bad—it means that taking little sips from the vine won't make the situation much worse. But don't get greedy. The harder you push your broken instrument, the louder you get. The more you struggle to bring an animal mind fully into your own, the more danger you're in. And if you go so far that you lose yourself . . ."

"My whiteouts," April murmured.

"Yes. Our instruments are like . . . filters for the Medium. Valves, I guess. The veins of the Medium enter and get put to use. Energy turns into function. But your instrument is missing an important valve, some crucial function—"

"I wish you could tell me what," April said.

"I can't. But when you pull too hard, you're taking more of the unfiltered, uncontrolled Medium into yourself than one person could possibly handle. It's dangerous, and your body rejects it. And when that happens, every Mordin within a dozen miles can feel it. That's how I first heard you."

"But once I find the missing piece—"

"Yes. We have to find the missing piece. We need to go now."

"And until we find it, I can still use the vine. Sparingly."

Isabel nodded, then held up a finger, her eyes flashing. "But when I say stop . . ."

"Stop," April agreed. Off in the distance, in the direction of the city, the missing piece seemed to burn ever more brightly now, promising her everything. To be safe. To be whole. To be back home again—even though she'd only just left!

"One last question," April said. "What would the Mordin do if they caught me?"

"They'll try to get you to join them. If you refuse, they'll take your Tan'ji from you and try to find one of their own who can bond with it, who can use its power."

April gritted her teeth, flushed with rage. "Is that possible?"

"Possible, but unlikely, even among the Riven. They'll try to convince you to join them before they . . ." She trailed off.

"That's not okay with me," April said grimly. "To say the least."

"Nor with me," said Isabel.

April felt a tug on her shoelace. Arthur had untied it in a single yank and was now gazing proudly up at her, snapping his thick beak. April squatted and retied it, double knotting it, noting how carefully Arthur watched her. She sipped cautiously at the vine, wary of Isabel but trying to calm herself by focusing on Arthur's fascinating mind. He was hungry and expectant, perhaps smelling the dog food in her pocket—though from what she could tell, having a sense of smell didn't seem like a major part of being a bird. More likely he was simply remembering all the treats she'd brought him in the past.

Isabel watched with scowling interest, but said nothing about using the vine. Apparently April was doing it right—or maybe Isabel was waiting for April to slip up again. "Tell me about the bird," Isabel said suddenly. "Arthur, you called him. Is he a pet?"

"No, he's . . ." April struggled to find the right word, but couldn't. "A bird," she finished lamely. She felt strangely disappointed that it had been Isabel, not Arthur, who'd scared off the Mordin.

"Birds are a good omen, you know," Isabel said.

"I don't believe in omens."

The woman rolled her eyes. "Then how about this—birds hate the Riven, and vice versa. Ravens especially. He probably did want to protect you." She studied the bird a moment longer, and then said just about the last thing April could have expected. "Bring him with us."

"What? But . . . he's wild." Arthur tugged at her laces stubbornly again, then gave her his cutest coo when he failed to untie them.

"He doesn't look very wild," Isabel said dubiously.

April explained the circumstances briefly and confessed to the dog food in her pockets. "But I can't just *bring* him."

Isabel, listening with obvious interest, frowned. "Why not?"

"*Wyenot?*" Arthur wailed. "*Wyenot?*"

95

Isabel laughed, clearly pleased, but of course Arthur had no idea what he was saying. He was only doing the tricks April liked, anticipating a treat.

"I can't take care of a wild bird," she protested, remembering every lecture Doc had given her on the subject of wild animals. "And anyway, it's bad. He has to learn to take care of himself."

"Suit yourself," Isabel said with a shrug. "All I'm saying is, a bird might be useful. Besides, it's easy between the two of you. Quiet." She wove a wiggling hand through the air from April to Arthur. April realized she must mean the Medium.

"Really?"

"Yes. But whether he comes or not, we need to go. Now." She turned and started down the trail.

April stood there for a moment, unsettled by Isabel's impatience. Why was she in such a hurry? At her feet, Arthur preened himself fussily. April made a quick decision, reaching into her pocket. She pulled out a fistful of kibble and dropped a chunk onto the ground. Arthur snatched it up at once, tossing it back into his gullet, and then opened his beak for more. "You're supposed to be wild now, but you're acting pretty tame," she told him. She began walking slowly backward, following Isabel. She dropped another chunk of dog food on the path, and Arthur waddled after her to grab it. "I guess I'm the opposite—supposed to be tame but acting wild. Maybe we can balance each other out?"

Arthur warbled at her sweetly, then shocked her—and

thrilled her—by flying up and attempting to perch on her shoulder. He was small for a raven, but still a big bird, and as he landed, his wing boxed her in the ear, hard. Then his talons sank painfully into the flesh of her shoulder. She cringed, trying to bear the pain—thankfully her backpack straps took the brunt of it—but in the same moment, Arthur took off again, releasing her.

April could sense that the raven was almost as surprised by what he'd done as she was. He flew away and landed in a nearby tree, croaking uncertainly in a way that seemed to ask for her reply. His mood was curious and wary, but warm. Companionable.

"It's okay," April said, feeling her shoulder. He'd put a couple of small holes through her shirt and torn a gash in the strap of her backpack, but she wasn't bleeding. Arthur continued to croak. "It's okay. You just want to be friends. So do I." She tossed a chunk of dog food in his direction. This time he just eyed it where it landed.

She sighed, unsure what to do. "I'll tell you what," she said at last. Arthur fell silent, listening hard. "I'm going to keep walking. I'm going to occasionally drop some food. If that idea interests you at all, maybe you can follow. If not, I guess . . ." She felt herself choking up a bit, but shook it off. "If not, then I guess it's been nice knowing you. Sound okay?"

Arthur cocked his head and ruffled his wings.

"Okay," April said. She hurried down the trail after Isabel. Arthur didn't move, but she could still feel his attention on her. She knew she'd lose him after fifty feet or so, but just as she was about to pull out of range, she felt him swoop down from the tree and swallow the kibble she'd thrown. Smiling to herself, she waited until she was sure his attention was on her. He watched keenly as she dropped another piece of food. "I'm sorry, Doc," she said into the air. "But I could use a friend right now."

Isabel, far ahead along the path, stopped and turned around, waiting impatiently for April to catch up. Miradel was a round cloud against her chest, full of dark shapes and shadows. April clung thoughtfully to the presence of the vine, to the power it gave her, to Arthur still following behind, to the lost and distant missing piece—remembering how Isabel had used her own power to take that all away from her, and how the woman refused to promise that it wouldn't happen again. Protection, yes, but at what cost? April muttered softly to herself, "I could really, really use a friend."

SHORTLY BEFORE SEVEN, April and Isabel arrived at the abandoned barn. Out here in the meadow, free of the trees, the sun still shone brightly, lifting April's spirits even though she was generally a fan of cloudier days. The barn, which had once been white and tall, sagged into the high grass around it like some great animal squatting low. Derek was always warning April that the barn was unstable, that she shouldn't go inside, but she'd been ignoring him for years. To her, the barn looked like an aching old beast that had at last found a comfortable position that might suit it forever, a final seat from which it was unlikely to ever stir.

Isabel seemed equally unconcerned about the possibility of the barn collapsing. "I'll be right back," she said, and then ducked through the canted opening into the dark interior. A soft flurry of manic, merry thoughts sprouted in April's brain, and a moment later two swallows darted out of the barn. April watched and listened for a moment, marveling, as the birds began to flit acrobatically after unseen bugs in the evening air, all grace and precision. She longed to open up wider, to revel in their flight, but she kept herself quiet and passive. Very still. The swallows scattered when Arthur glided in and landed on the ragged edge of the barn roof. He watched April expectantly.

"Man, you sure do love dog food," April said. But then she realized the bird was full. His anticipation wasn't hunger; he had other ideas on his mind. And he held something in his beak—something shiny and round.

"What's that?" April said, pointing.

Right on cue, Arthur flicked his head, tossing the object onto the ground at April's feet. She bent and picked it up—a bottle cap, rusty and flattened. As she examined it, Arthur squawked at her. His bright black eyes shone as she felt his anticipation grow. He was eager. Hopeful. All at once she understood—this was a present.

April choked up a little. "Thank you," she said, holding up the bottle cap. She touched it to her upper lip and then slipped it into her pocket. "Thank you."

Arthur bobbed his head, gurgling happily. *"Henkyoo,"* he crooned. *"Henkyoo."* And then he strutted up the roof, feeling very pleased with himself.

Fingering the bottlecap in her pocket, April wandered around to the back of the barn. Years earlier she'd discovered a strange semicircle of stones here, half buried in the ground. Each one was about the size of a watermelon, each one a different chunky shape—this one like a face, this one like a tilting house, this one a sleeping bear. She stepped onto the first stone and took a long stride onto the next, following the crescent. Off to the left, inside the arc of the crescent, a flat stone lay exposed in a patch of dirt, different from the others. Broken in half and weatherworn, it was shaped and colored like a blue jay, badly faded. When she was little, April had liked to imagine that this spot was once the site of a bird kingdom, and that these were the remains of some bird king's palace. But now those thoughts seemed simple and far away.

April stepped from stone to stone, pinwheeling her long arms to keep her balance, wondering what was taking Isabel so long. Arthur, now at the peak of the barn, watched her in confusion. When she reached the last stone, she leapt out and landed with both feet on the cracked stone jay. Arthur complained softly, annoyed at her antics for some reason. "Sorry," she said. "Was this guy a friend of yours or something?"

"What are you doing?"

April startled. Isabel stood in the shadow of the barn,

watching. A small figure trailed behind her—a boy, eight or nine years old. He had dark, curly hair, and was dressed in a strangely overformal way, a button-down shirt tucked into long pants. Isabel's son? Or no, maybe not. The boy had deep olive skin, whereas Isabel's skin was fair and freckly.

"Just waiting," April said, stepping off the stone. "I used to play out here when I was little."

Isabel came nearer, the boy cautiously following. A large patchwork bag was hoisted over her shoulder. Isabel saw the stone jay and looked sharply around for a moment, but didn't comment. "Joshua, this is April," she said. "April, meet Joshua. He'll be coming with us."

"Hey," April said, trying not to sound surprised. She gave the boy a little wave that she hoped seemed friendly. She liked kids okay, but didn't have a lot of experience around them. And of course—in this place, in this company—she had to assume Joshua was probably not what you would consider a normal kid.

Joshua walked up to her, eyes cast downward, and held out a hand. It took April a moment to realize he wanted to shake. When she offered her hand, he pumped it once, dropped it, and then said stiffly, "I have shyness issues."

"Oh," April said. "Well, you don't seem very shy. You shook my hand."

"You're supposed to do that. When you meet somebody new. And if you're shy, you should make an effort."

"I guess that's true. Are you . . . ?" She started to ask him if he was Tan'ji, but maybe that was a rude question. "How old are you?" she asked instead.

"Eight and a half."

"Oh. I just turned thirteen."

"I saw your house."

"You did?"

"Yes. I like to know where things are."

"Oh."

Isabel waved a hand through the air as if to clear away the awkward chitchat. "We'll have plenty of time to talk on the road," she said. "April, any change from your missing piece?"

"It's stronger. It's been getting stronger all day—"

"No. You're just getting better at hearing it." April barely had time to absorb that notion before Isabel crossed her arms and demanded, "Point to it."

"There," April said, raising her arm without hesitation, pointing out across the meadow.

Isabel looked intently at Joshua and said, "Tell me where we're going."

"Southeast." Joshua turned so he was facing in the direction April pointed. "Southeast by south, actually."

Confused by the question—and the answer—April didn't comment. She wasn't sure southeast by south was even a thing.

"And what's out there?" Isabel prompted the boy.

Joshua shrugged. "Lots of stuff. If you went in a straight line, you'd be in downtown Chicago in thirty-seven miles."

April dropped her arm. "That's pretty smart," she said. "You're good with maps, huh?"

"Just wait," Isabel told her. "Keep pointing, straight at it. Go ahead, Joshua—tell us what's out there. Be specific. Be precise."

April raised her arm again, and Joshua moved so that he was directly under it. He looked up at her pointing hand, gauging it, then shut his eyes. "Goose Island. The confluence of the Chicago River branches. Downtown Chicago."

April felt her eyebrows lift.

Isabel, meanwhile, clapped her hands together softly. "Where downtown? Remember to be specific." Her voice was eager, her eyes lit with an almost hungry glow.

"Um . . . the Loop. The Art Institute. Grant Park. The Aquarium." He opened his eyes and turned, his face all innocence and hope. "Are we going to the Aquarium?"

But Isabel ignored the question. "This is good. This is very good. We're headed in the right direction for sure."

April was still staring at Joshua. "You're Tan'ji."

"No. I don't have an instrument. But Isabel says I have potential." He pronounced the word carefully, like it was a password to get into a secret chamber.

"But if you're not Tan'ji, how did you do that?" April asked.

It was Isabel who answered her. "You might as well ask the same of yourself. How did you learn to be good with animals? Everyone who becomes a Keeper has some kind of natural talent or interest to begin with. It's a sign, a hint as to the kind of Tan'ji you'll eventually—hopefully—discover."

April considered this. "So you think Joshua will become a Keeper."

"No reason not to think it. I can see more than just the talent on the surface."

"And will his Tan'ji have something to do with . . . maps?"

"Yes, yes, probably," Isabel said, hefting her bag once again and turning away. She sounded as if she didn't want to discuss it.

"I would think, though," April said, "that there are a lot of people who have talents who never manage to find their Tan'ji. Or don't have one to find. Not all people with talents are meant to be Keepers, are they?" As soon as the words were out, she regretted them. Joshua's face grew long and sad, and he looked questioningly up at Isabel.

Isabel said, "Not everybody has me. Joshua's lucky to have me." She looked over her shoulder at April. "And I'm lucky to have you. Now let's get going."

They started off across the meadow, passing through the long shadow of the barn. Insects droned and sprang and soared through the tall grass all around. Arthur kept pace with them, leapfrogging ahead along the tree line and then falling behind again. His continued presence was a comfort to April, especially since everything else was feeling so . . . foreign. So odd. Isabel was keeping secrets, that much was clear.

The missing piece, apparently, lay somewhere in the

heart of Chicago, and it seemed Isabel had been expecting this. And then there was Joshua, walking silently at April's side. He seemed decent and harmless, and she worried for him. All this talk of potential, and becoming Tan'ji. April wondered whether Isabel was just humoring the boy. Whatever else April knew or didn't know, she didn't think Keepers and their Tan'ji were a dime a dozen.

She cleared her throat and looked down at Joshua. "I'm sure you'll find it."

"Thank you," he said, and they fell back into silence. But now the boy began to sneak curious looks over at April, and after a minute or two he said, "Do you think about it a lot? Your Tan'ji?"

"Um . . . pretty much. I'm not very good at ignoring it." The question got April thinking about the vine, about how present it was in her mind. She put her hand on it now, comforted by its presence. It had only been two weeks, but she felt like she could not remember a time when the vine hadn't been with her. She listened to Arthur, directly above, gliding along with them. The bird pulled ahead and climbed higher, rising out of the range of the vine, then circled lazily back again, alert to April's presence—a strange sensation that she couldn't quite name but was learning to recognize. Joshua, noticing, looked up with her.

"Isabel said you talk to animals," he said.

"That's not exactly true. I can't *talk* to them."

"Then why is that crow following you?"

"He's not a crow. He's a raven. His name is Arthur. And I don't actually talk to him—I only listen to his thoughts."

"Oh," Joshua said. April couldn't tell if he was disappointed or not. They watched as Arthur landed in a tree off to their right and began to complain noisily. "So what does Arthur think about?"

April laughed. "Food, mostly. Flying. Shiny things. Grooming himself. But mostly food. That's why he's following me—I have food he likes."

"But he likes you too. I bet he thinks about you."

April considered it, thinking about how Arthur had tried to land on her shoulder. "He likes me fine. Mostly he thinks of me as a snack-delivery system." But then she recalled the powerful surge of gratitude and affection she'd felt just after she'd freed the bird.

Joshua whacked at the weeds with his stick. "I think he's nicer than that. I think he's your friend."

"I hope so."

Joshua shot her a nervous look. "Can I . . . see it? I promise I won't touch."

April understood immediately—her Tan'ji. Strangely, she found she wanted to show it to him. "Sure, okay." She pulled back her hair. Joshua leaned in close to examine the vine, his hands behind his back. He let out a long, breathy sound of admiration.

"How did you find it?" he said, clearly awed.

Now Isabel did glance back at them, obviously interested

in the question herself. April was reluctant to tell the story, but she didn't want to leave this strange, sweet boy hanging. "I found it at a flea market, believe it or not," she said. When Joshua looked confused, she explained. "It's like a really big yard sale, where lots of people come and sell their stuff. Mostly junk."

Isabel stopped and turned. "You *bought* your instrument?" she asked dubiously, as if that were bad. And for some reason, her disapproving tone encouraged April to confess the whole story.

"Actually, no. I would have, but I didn't have any money left."

"They gave it to you?" Joshua asked.

"Not . . . exactly," April admitted.

Isabel broke into girlish laughter, leaning back and clapping her hands together. "You stole it!" she cried. "You stole your own Tan'ji!"

April blushed furiously, and her shame only deepened as Joshua's eyes grew wide. "It just sort of happened," she explained. "I was browsing through this tray of old junky jewelry marked a dollar. I don't know why. I don't even like jewelry. But then I saw the vine and I just—" She shrugged.

"You had to have it," said Isabel, an eager light stretched across her face.

But no. That wasn't right. Those words weren't big enough for the sensation—the pure, certain knowledge that had rushed through April when she first set eyes on the vine.

She shook her head. "More than that," she said meaningfully. "It already belonged to me. I saw it, and I just . . . I knew absolutely that it was mine. It was mine *before* I even saw it."

Isabel wasn't laughing anymore. She was staring at April with a furious intensity, nodding. She clutched the wicker ball. "You knew it. I knew it too. It was just like that for me."

"And so I . . . took the vine." April swallowed and gave them both an apologetic look. "In fact, to tell the truth, I *did* have the money. I had like three dollars. But I just couldn't make myself pay for something that already belonged to me."

"Damn right," Isabel said. "And you shouldn't."

Joshua was still looking at April with skeptical wonder, like she was something halfway between a criminal and a unicorn. "Stealing's bad," she told him. She found herself pointing a finger at him like a lecturing adult. "Don't get me wrong. I never stole anything before this, and I never will again." Then she stopped, remembering. "Well . . . that's not totally true. Once when I was four I stole a roll of Scotch tape from the Farm and Fleet. But my mom caught me playing with it in the car, and she turned around and drove me back to the store, and made me go in and confess to the cashier, who was probably only sixteen or something. I remember I was crying, and my mom was crying, and then this poor cashier girl started crying, and it was actually pretty terrible. I was traumatized. I never stole anything again after that." She looked up at them, shocked that the story had popped out of her like that. She hardly ever talked about her mom and dad, even with Derek. "Well, I never stole anything else until now, I mean," she finished awkwardly.

Isabel was still nodding. "We're getting to know each other," she said flatly. "This is good." She turned and began walking again, April and Joshua following close behind.

After a minute or two, Joshua poked April solemnly in the shoulder. "I would steal mine," he said quietly. "If I had to."

"Your Tan'ji?"

"Yes."

"You really think it's out there somewhere?"

"Yes. Someplace secret. Someplace safe. Like in a tower, or deep underground."

April recalled what Isabel had said about a secret place in the city. A fortress filled with people like them. Keepers?

"Deep underground, huh?" April said to Joshua, playing along but feeling uncomfortable about it. "Sounds scary."

"I'm not scared," Joshua said confidently. "I would go wherever I had to go. I would steal it if I had to."

April nodded, the boy's words echoing her own undeniable need, the constant ache of the missing piece.

Suddenly Isabel spoke, her voice solemn and sure. "It'll be underground."

"How do you know?" asked Joshua.

The woman shrugged and kept walking. "Because," she said. "That's where these things are."

"Mine wasn't," April pointed out.

"His will be," Isabel said flatly, then turned away.

CHAPTER SIX

Detour

HORACE WATCHED THE CITY INCH BY SLOWLY AS THE CAB CREPT through rush-hour traffic, headed for the Mazzoleni Academy and the Warren beneath it. Chloe slouched beside him, fiddling with the Alvalaithen. She hooked the cord around her bottom lip, letting the dragonfly hang there like it had landed on her chin.

They'd been discussing Horace's mother, of course, not caring that their driver might be listening. Beck was a person you could trust. Plus, it wasn't clear whether Beck could even talk. But Chloe wasn't doing much talking either.

"My mom said something about Falo heading west," Horace said. "What do you think that means?"

"Don't know," Chloe said with a shrug.

"Do you think that's where the Altari are?"

"Don't know," she said again, and looked at the driver.

"What about you, Beck? You seem like you've been around for a while. What do you know about all this?"

The driver—bundled from head to toe as always, with nothing but eyes and fingertips showing—shrugged. Beck looked up at the mirror, bright eyes catching Horace's, eyebrows lifting in what seemed like a gesture of apology. Horace had no idea what to make of that.

Chloe let out a long, considering hum. "I respect your mysterious nature, Beck."

Beck nodded solemnly and flashed a thumbs-up.

They lapsed into silence. The cab moved on. The downtown Chicago skyline slowly grew higher, the Sears Tower looming in the foreground. Such a big city, and so many strange dangers hidden below the surface—or walking around in plain sight, if you knew what to look for. Ever since Horace had gotten off that bus back in May, following the sign that led him to the House of Answers and, eventually, the Fel'Daera itself, the city had become a very different place for him.

They passed into the tunnel under Ogilvie Center. Chloe spoke in the sudden darkness. "When she severed you, was it just like the Nevren?"

Horace, who had been thinking about the mysterious Sil'falo Teneves, was confused for a moment. "My mom? Yeah, pretty much. But more sudden."

"You didn't feel it coming."

"No," said Horace.

"Why wouldn't the Wardens warn us about something like that?"

"Well, it sounds like there aren't very many Tuners. There are bigger things worth worrying about, I guess—although the cleaving she was talking about sounds pretty horrible." He shivered a little, remembering the decapitated daisy.

Inexplicably, Chloe waved this off as if it were no concern of hers. "But the severing. There's no way to stop it?"

"I don't think so."

"Do you think one Tuner could stop another?"

"I don't know, Chloe."

Chloe slipped a mint into her mouth and leaned her head against the window. In the glass, the reflected white of her eyes shone, and the gleam of the dragonfly, and the occasional flash of teeth. Something was bugging her, but Horace didn't understand what. Chloe was rarely afraid of anything. The cab crossed the river and made a left. There were nearly there.

"So what do you think is going on at the Warren?" Horace asked.

"Beats me," Chloe said, as if it hardly mattered.

"What did Mr. Meister say again?"

"'Something long asleep has awakened,'" she recited dully.

"You don't think that sounds like a big deal?"

"I don't know, Horace. How about we just wait and see?"

He frowned at her, annoyed. "Two hours ago, I was the

one in a funk. I guess it's your turn now, for some reason."

"Yup. Times change. You of all people ought to know that."

Horace turned away, annoyed. But then at last he spotted the towering green doors of the Mazzoleni Academy half a block up. Beck began maneuvering the cab into an open spot at the curb.

"Sorry, Horace," Chloe said. "I just—"

Unexpectedly, the cab's engine roared, and they dove back into traffic. Horace toppled over almost into Chloe's lap. Horns blared. He grabbed for the strap overhead, struggling for balance. On the cab's meter in the front seat, the red readout under *Extras* switched from *0.00* to *DET.*

"What's happening?" Horace cried. "Beck, what are you doing?"

"Detour," said Chloe. She slithered out of her seat belt and got to her knees, peering out the back window. Horace twisted in his seat, following her gaze. At first he saw nothing, but then he spotted a towering figure on the sidewalk behind, just passing the steps of the academy.

"Mordin," Chloe said. She pointed suddenly. "And look, there's another. And another. Three of them—a whole hunting pack."

Horace saw them all now, towering scarecrows that stood four feet taller than the pedestrians around them. Besides the one in front of the academy, there were two more across the street. Because the Mordin used mysterious Tan'ji to disguise their true appearance, no one on the sidewalk was paying any attention to them. But Horace and Chloe, being Tan'ji themselves, were much harder to fool. Apparently, so was Beck.

Horace scrutinized the three Mordin as they drove away. To his relief, none of them were Dr. Jericho.

Chloe turned to Beck. "Do they know we're here?"

In the front seat, the great bundled head shook back and forth. Beck's hand went up and covered the rearview mirror momentarily.

"They can't see us," said Chloe, interpreting.

Beck gave another thumbs-up and swung the cab into a squealing left turn. The Mordin, and the academy, disappeared around the bend.

"Why would they be there?" Horace asked. "Why would they happen to be there right when we arrived?"

Chloe didn't answer.

Beck took two more right turns and then, to Horace's great surprise, pulled up to the curb again and came to a halt. Horace reckoned that they were no more than two blocks from the academy and the roaming pack of Mordin.

"Shouldn't we keep moving?" he asked. "Get farther away?"

Beck leaned into the passenger seat and pointed out the window, into the sky. Horace and Chloe both bent over and craned their necks to see. Outside, peeking over the top of a rounded stone wall, were the spindly, jumbled limbs of a ginkgo tree.

"A cloister," Horace said. One of the Wardens' tiny safe havens. After Horace and Chloe's escape from the golem at the House of Answers, Gabriel had escorted them through a series of tunnels, emerging at last into a cloister like this one. Tiny walled gardens, completely enclosed, cloisters were protected from the prying eyes of the Riven.

"You want us to go there?" Chloe asked Beck.

Beck nodded and held up a hand, flashing all five fingers.

"Five? Five what?"

Beck laid the index finger of one hand against the wrist of the other, then pointed at the cloister again.

"Five minutes," Chloe said. "Someone will come for us inside? Five minutes?"

Two big nods, two big thumbs up.

"Thanks, Beck," Chloe said breathlessly, and before Horace could even absorb what was happening, she was out of the cab and onto the sidewalk.

Horace slid out cautiously after Chloe, who was already weaving through pedestrians, passing beneath the outstretched branches of the ginkgo. They approached the cloister and began searching for the way in. A cloister had no outside doors, just a passkey—a hidden Tan'kindi that would allow the user to step straight through the wall to the safe courtyard inside. But they would need to find the passkey first, somewhere along the curving stone wall.

They followed the snaking wall, searching, and came around to the backside. A large steelwork wall rose high behind them, too, so that they were in a kind of canyon, completely sheltered from view.

"It'll be here somewhere," Chloe said, and a moment later she pointed. Just over her head, a paler kite-shaped rock was embedded in the dark stonework of the cloister wall. It was not the sort of thing a person would usually notice, but it was obvious to a Keeper's trained eye.

Chloe moved two steps down the wall from the rock. With the dragonfly, of course, she had no need of passkeys. In fact, she had been warned to steer clear of them. The reasons for this were unclear, but Horace imagined that the dragonfly, with its similar powers, might create some kind of interference with the passkeys. Chloe seemed endlessly irritated that passkeys even existed. "Go on ahead," she growled. "I'll come in behind you."

Taking another quick look around to make sure no one had followed them, Horace stepped up to the stone. He put his fingers against it and felt them slide inside it like it was liquid. Within, he found the passkey itself—a small, chunky object not much bigger than a marble. He gripped it between his fingertips and stepped into the wall, closing his eyes. He felt a cold tingle as his body passed into the stone. The passkey rotated with him, and then he was through. He made sure he was free of the wall before removing his fingers last.

Off to one side, Chloe emerged through the wall herself, the wings of the dragonfly an almost invisible blur. She threw a surly glance at the kite-shaped stone that hid the passkey, and then the Alvalaithen went still.

Inside the cloister, almost all the sounds of traffic and construction and humanity dropped miraculously away. The afternoon sun somehow found its way between buildings and cast dappled shadows through the ginkgo tree. Horace took a deep breath, one hand and half his thoughts resting lightly on the Fel'Daera. This cloister was as peaceful a place as one could find in the city. Peaceful, and safe.

Like the last cloister they'd been in, this one had an odd assortment of chunky stones embedded in the brick floor in the shape of a circle. In the center was a flat black stone in the shape of a large bird. It was a leestone, a Tan'kindi that ensured that the cloister could not be detected by unwanted visitors—especially the Riven. The Wardens used leestones to protect all their sanctuaries. Horace even had one in his house, a statue of a turtle with a raven in its back. This one here in the cloister looked like a raven too, but it had white on its belly and wings.

"What kind of bird is that supposed to be?" Horace asked.

Chloe considered it. "Penguin," she said.

"Very funny."

"What? I'm not a bird expert."

Horace looked at the stone again, wondering how it worked. "Why birds, anyway?"

"I don't know. Birds are old. They're the dinosaurs that survived, which seems respectable. They have complicated cultures, actually. And they're smart, too—especially the cor-vids."

Horace stared at her blankly.

"You know," she said. "Crows and ravens and jays, stuff like that."

"I thought you said you weren't a bird expert."

"I'm not, but . . . you're the science guy. You've heard that crows are smart."

"I have, but I never heard the word 'corvids' before."

"Well," Chloe said, shrugging, "I read a lot. You know that." She scratched at one of her new scars. "What time is it? Has it been five minutes yet?"

"Not quite." Horace wasn't wearing a watch, but of course he didn't need to. He knew without thinking that it was six thirty-three, and that four minutes and thirty-seven seconds had passed since they exited the cab. Keeping track of time had always been his talent, a very useful skill for the Keeper of the Fel'Daera. And ever since the Find, he'd been getting better and better.

At four minutes and forty-six seconds, a loud metallic screech made them both jump. A set of heavy cellar doors embedded in the ground were being pushed open from below. A moment later, a dark figure strode up out of the opening, a long staff at his side. The new arrival cocked his head, lis-tening.

"Gabriel!" Horace called.

The teenager turned toward them, his milky white eyes

gleaming brightly against his dark skin. He was breathing deeply and smoothly, as if he'd been running but was too polite to show it. "Keepers," he said formally, and then his voice grew slightly warmer. He smiled. "Horace. And Chloe. Good to see you."

Chloe was not particularly talented at hellos—or good-byes, for that matter—and Horace half expected her to make an awkward joke about a blind person saying "Good to see you." But instead she only frowned critically at Gabriel and said, "You look taller."

"I think I'd have noticed," Gabriel said, hefting his Tan'ji, the Staff of Obro. He prodded its silver-clawed tip against the ground.

The last time the three of them had been together, they had pulled off the daring rescue of Chloe's father from the nest. Without Gabriel's bravery and endurance—and the incomparable power of his Tan'ji—Horace and Chloe would never have escaped. Two or three times that night, they had eluded capture in the humour, the featureless gray fog Gabriel could release from the Staff of Obro. Everyone trapped in the humour was rendered utterly blind, and half deaf. Everyone but Gabriel, that is. The humour gave Gabriel an incredible awareness of his immediate surroundings, an awareness that went far beyond sight. The humour was so sensitive that Gabriel had once used it to read the dates on coins in Horace's pocket. Meanwhile Horace hadn't been able to see his own nose. The humour was ideal for hiding and fleeing from the

Riven, with Gabriel as guide.

"Beck took a detour," Gabriel said now. "What happened?"

"There were Mordin outside the academy," Horace replied, wondering exactly how word of the detour had gotten to Gabriel.

"I thought so. Lucky for us, Beck always knows where to go." Gabriel stepped aside and gestured down the steps he'd just climbed. "After you."

They clambered down a set of steep metal steps into the darkness below. Horace's claustrophobia squeezed him like a great black hand, but he kept his breathing steady. He tried not to think of the boiler. Strangely, the faint stink of sewage here seemed to help.

"Tunnels with Gabriel," Chloe said lightly as she climbed down. "That takes me back. Will we have to walk in the dark again? I would have brought my jithandra, but, it was confiscated in a crisis of faith."

"I've got it covered," Gabriel said. He reached into his collar and pulled out a finger-sized crystal on a chain that immediately blazed to life. A jithandra, the calling card of the Wardens. Horace had often wondered if Gabriel even had a jithandra—the light it cast would be of no use to him, and he got around amazingly well in his constant darkness with the help of the Staff of Obro. But Gabriel's jithandra was startlingly bright and colorless, gleaming with a sharp silver light. The crystal, as with all jithandras, was set in a cluster of curling silver flower petals.

Horace's own jithandra had been destroyed by Dr. Jericho in the nest. And he had a pretty good guess what Chloe meant when she said hers had been confiscated. The night of the rescue, Chloe had intentionally allowed herself to be captured by Dr. Jericho and taken back to the nest. The Wardens must have taken her jithandra from her beforehand. Chloe's capture was a future Horace himself had seen through the Fel'Daera, and it had been the right path—the willed path—but apparently the Wardens hadn't trusted Chloe enough to let her keep her jithandra. Not with the Alvalaithen lost to her in that moment, traveling through time.

Gabriel stretched up and pulled the overhead doors closed, sealing them in. Horace let his eyes adjust and saw to his relief that they were in a large drainage tunnel, as wide as a car. Gabriel turned and began to lead them deeper into the passage. "Sorry about the detour," he said, his voice echoing, "but it happens sometimes. The Mordin patrol this part of the city pretty regularly. It was pure chance they were nearby just as you arrived."

"I thought the Warren was supposed to be hidden," Chloe said.

"We can't totally disguise its existence. Any time large numbers of Tanu are gathered together, the Mordin will be drawn to the area."

Horace said, "But you—we—have leestones that keep the Warren safe. I've seen them."

"Yes. Leestones, and more. Even the very structure of the Warren diffuses the signal of all those Tanu—and ourselves—over several city blocks. It's highly unlikely that the Riven will ever find us. The academy is extremely well protected, and the Warren even more so."

"Very unlikely, you said," Horace pointed out. "But not impossible."

"We've found it's best not to speak in terms of the impossible," Gabriel replied, and this struck Horace as such a good policy that he said no more.

They walked on for a quarter mile or so, Gabriel moving surely through the dark tunnels. Horace wondered briefly if Gabriel had used the humour on his way out to meet them. Surely he had, with no one around to be troubled by it.

They used another passkey—or rather, Horace and Gabriel did. At one intersection, Horace glanced down a side passage and thought he saw a narrow set of train tracks, far too small to belong to a normal-size train. He was about to ask about them when Chloe spoke.

"Here's what I'm wondering," she said. "Why are we here?"

Gabriel cocked his head back at her. "You mean, why do we exist?"

"Ha ha. That's hugely hilarious. No, I'm wondering what's up, why Mr. Meister called us in."

Gabriel slowed to a stop and turned to an innocent-looking patch of wall. He felt around until his fingers sank into the stone. Another passkey. "I'm not sure why he called you in today," he said. "He didn't tell me." And then he disappeared through the wall, leaving them in the utter dark.

Horace followed behind, groping for the passkey clumsily and emerging into a much smaller tunnel that sloped steeply downward. Chloe came through last again, beginning to talk even before she had fully emerged, her voice erupting bizarrely as her throat cleared the stone. "—ntell you? I thought the old man told you everything."

Gabriel rubbed a thumb over the dragonlike head of his cane. "Why would you think that? All I know is that Brian has made a discovery."

"'Something long asleep has awakened,'" Chloe recited.

"Yes."

Horace remembered the pale, ponytailed boy he'd glimpsed twice before in the Great Burrow. Brian was twelve or thirteen—about the same age as Horace. "Brian is a Warden, right?" he asked.

"Yes. And a friend."

"Well, if he's a friend," Chloe said, "he probably told you what he discovered."

Gabriel didn't respond.

Chloe pounced on Gabriel's silence. "He *did* tell you. You're not a total Boy Scout after all."

"Or maybe I am," Gabriel said smoothly. "Maybe I like to be prepared."

"So what did he tell you?"

"He told me company is coming."

"What kind of company?" Chloe insisted.

But before Gabriel could answer—or more likely, refuse to answer—they came through an arched opening into a large space Horace recognized at once. They were at the opening of Vithra's Eye, the underground lake that served as the entrance to the Warren. Horace could smell the water, see its smooth dark surface glistening ahead. On the far shore, he knew, lay the tunnel that led to the Great Burrow. A brick walkway led straight across the lake, but that path was unusable for Keepers.

Along the near shore, meanwhile, there were three more archways to their right, one of which led up to the Mazzoleni Academy—the way they would have come were it not for the detour. Horace couldn't help wondering how many ways into the Warren there were, and how safe and hidden those entrances could be. But of course, they hadn't quite reached the Warren yet. There was one more obstacle in front of them.

The Nevren was here in Vithra's Eye, powerful and wide, emanating from a source somewhere along the brick path that bisected the lake. The Nevren here was so strong that no one wielding a Tan'ji could hope to pass close to its source and survive, which was why that path was unusable. To cross the lake, one had to walk atop the water itself, along the weak outer edge of the Nevren, and the only way to walk atop the water was with a jithandra. Jithandras were specially made to work in the presence of the Nevren, but only here in Vithra's

Eye. They were like keys to the Warren, and no one but a Warden could be enstrusted with them. Horace couldn't really blame Mr. Meister for taking Chloe's away from her before she went out on her risky mission that night.

Gabriel moved to the lake's edge, far from the brick walkway and the source of the Nevren. He undid the chain around his neck, dangling it to its full length, so that the jithandra slid to the bottom. He held it out, letting the crystal hover an inch above its own reflection in the water. Gripping the Staff of Obro firmly in his other hand, he said, "Let's go."

Horace and Chloe knew the drill, of course. They lined up tight behind him. One of the chamber's owls swooped in low over their heads, black and silent. Gabriel dipped his jithandra into the dark water, making barely a ripple. With a great crackling sound that echoed through the chamber, the water around the crystal seemed to gather itself. It pooled toward the jithandra, growing lighter and lifting slightly—becoming solid.

Gabriel stepped onto the charcoal-colored patch, still holding the jithandra out in front, where more water continued to crackle and gather and become firm. Horace followed cautiously behind, with Chloe in the rear. The newly formed walkway was smooth like ice, but neither cold nor slick. They eased out onto the water, keeping close to the outer edge of the lake, where the Nevren would be the weakest. The sheer stone wall of the chamber rose high on their left.

Once they'd gone twenty feet or so, the gray trail behind

them began to dissolve, returning to liquid again with a soft hiss. They would have to keep moving along this temporary path or sink into the murky depths, an experience they'd been assured they did not want to have.

It began to get cold. The already cool air became bitter and still. Horace prepared himself, but still he gasped as the bone-cold grip of the Nevren swept over him. The box vanished from his mind. Even though he was braced for it, the loss was crippling. The world faded around him, freezing and numb. He felt his limbs begin to sag. He shuffled forward, knowing there was a far side, trying to believe it. An endless stretch of time passed, seconds he could not count, an eternity without the box, and then, suddenly—

Dawn broke explosively inside his head. He was through the Nevren. The box was with him. It had never left him, of course, but now he could feel it again. He was Horace, Keeper of the Fel'Daera. Behind him, he heard Chloe growl appreciatively as the Alvalaithen returned to her.

Horace could see the far side now. Two small figures stood there, one in a dark, prim dress and the other in a bright red vest beneath a tangle of white hair. Horace stumbled a bit at the sight of Mr. Meister, reminded of the startling secret the old man had been keeping from him all this time. His own mother—here in the Warren, years before. In a strange way, the thought comforted him. He belonged here. He had a history here. But he could not understand why that history had been kept from him.

As they stepped onto dry land, Mrs. Hapsteade swept forward to greet them, small and shadowy. Dark hair, dark dress, dark face—even the jithandra that shone around her neck was dark, casting an eerie bluish-black light. "Keepers," she said. Before anyone could reply, she held up a finger and dug into her front pocket with her other hand. "First things first. These are unmistakably yours." She pulled out two dark crystal pendants, one red and one blue, each set in the mouth of a curling silver flower.

Horace took his jithandra gratefully. Immediately it began to glow a deep electric blue. Chloe brought her gleaming scarlet crystal so close to her face that her eyes crossed.

"I would've given yours back to you sooner, Chloe," Mrs. Hapsteade told her. "But a new one had to be made for Horace, and we thought it best to wait."

So apparently it had been Mrs. Hapsteade who had confiscated the jithandra. Chloe eyed her warily. "Is that an apology?"

Mrs. Hapsteade smiled thinly. "Are you saying you deserve one? That it was wrong for me to take it, under the circumstances?"

Chloe opened her mouth, then shut it again. "Just checking," she said. "I wanted to make sure you're not getting soft."

"Only in the flesh," Mrs. Hapsteade sighed.

Mr. Meister ambled forward. His bloodred, many-pocketed vest gleamed in the dim light. His watery eyes loomed hugely behind his glasses—especially the left eye.

The left lens of his glasses was actually a Tan'ji called an oraculum, which allowed him to see Tanu in a way others could not—in fact, Horace now realized, it must allow him to see the Medium.

Mr. Meister gave one of his little bows. "Thank you for coming, Horace," he said warmly. "It is good to see you again."

For a moment, Horace thought the words might barrel out of his mouth right now—*You knew my mother?* But instead he mumbled, "Yeah. Good to see you."

"You are well, I trust?" Mr. Meister asked. "The Fel'Daera is well?"

"Yes, I . . . haven't been using it much."

"As you should not, if you have no need," Mr. Meister said. "But soon we may have need indeed." He straightened and turned, jerking his head for them to follow. "Come."

They followed him down the trail and into the Great Burrow, the topmost level of the Warren. If seeing Mr. Meister again hadn't exactly stirred Horace's sense of adventure, the Great Burrow did. Here, huge rough columns, twenty feet wide and twice as high, rose haphazardly throughout the massive chamber, like an underground forest of stone. Most of the barrel-shaped columns had doors and windows, with crude living spaces inside. Dobas, they were called, and though nearly all of them were deserted now, Horace could easily imagine that the cavernous hall had once been filled with Keepers.

Halfway through the Great Burrow, Gabriel and Mrs. Hapsteade peeled off, waving good-byes and going their own way. Mr. Meister trekked on, leading Horace and Chloe on past his own massive doba to the very back of the chamber. Here, a tall, dark gap opened up between the final two dobas. The trio stepped out onto a ledge overlooking a deep chasm that sank out of sight. At their feet, a steep staircase wound down the sheer face of the cliff, on into darkness.

"As you may have heard by now," said Mr. Meister, "one of our fellow Wardens has made a discovery I want you to see. I don't believe you've been formally introduced to Brian, but we'll find him below. We must descend into the Maw." He started down the precarious steps, then turned and said, "I am sure I do not need to tell you to watch your step." He pointed to the rock wall, where crooked words were engraved deeply in the stone:

THE PERILOUS STAIRS
Swallow up your fear,
or be swallowed up yourself.

Perilous. Abruptly Horace remembered the last words Dr. Jericho had said to him during their first encounter: *"Curiosity is a walk fraught with peril."* Since then, Horace had been surprised to learn how much of the peril he faced seemed to come from the Wardens themselves.

He peeked over the edge into the black abyss—the Maw. A cold, dry draft rose out of the depths, ruffling his shaggy hair. He tried not to imagine a bottom covered with jagged rocks—not that it would matter, at this height.

Chloe started down the Perilous Stairs after Mr. Meister gracefully, surefooted as always. Horace brought up the rear, descending more cautiously. He wasn't afraid of heights, but the steps were steep and narrow, and his big frame wasn't exactly designed for nimble work like this.

"So . . . what does Brian do, exactly?" Horace asked as he eased his way down. The last time he'd seen Brian, the boy had been descending these very stairs. What was he doing down below? What was his power?

"You will see. I have given him permission to share everything with you." Mr. Meister faltered on the next step and cocked his head as though reconsidering. "'Permission' is a strong word. He does not need my permission. Let us say I have given him my blessing."

"If he's a Warden," Chloe asked, "how come he didn't help us when we raided the nest?"

"That is not his function."

Chloe glanced back at Horace. *Function?*" she mouthed.

Mr. Meister almost seemed aware of the gesture, tipping his head thoughtfully again as they cornered a sharp bend on the stairs. "I am not explaining this well. I sometimes get flustered when it comes to Brian."

Horace and Chloe exchanged another surprised look. Hearing Mr. Meister say he sometimes got flustered was kind of like hearing a rainbow say it sometimes got depressed.

As they rounded another switchback, Mr. Meister paused.

"Brian is an exceptional Keeper, in more ways than one. I hope he will not . . . how can I put it?" He looked pointedly at Chloe. "Rub you the wrong way."

Chloe glared back at Mr. Meister. "I'm not a cat, you know," she said, looking for all the world exactly like one.

"Nonetheless," Mr. Meister said simply.

At last they reached the bottom of the Perilous Stairs. The Maw still yawned into darkness below, but a great bridge stretched across the chasm to what looked like a wide-open balcony on the far side. Mr. Meister, however, ignored the bridge, turning instead toward the cliff face. There, a large, square-cornered tunnel cut back beneath the Great Burrow far above. Bizarrely, just ten feet in, this passage narrowed to the size of an ordinary doorway, and within that space the path disappeared instantly into complete darkness—a slab of black so utterly deep and blank that no natural phenomenon could explain it. Horace knew at once that some Tanu had to be at work.

"Brian's workshop is just through here," Mr. Meister said. "But there is a trick to getting there, as you can see."

"You say that like sometimes there *isn't* a trick," Chloe said.

Mr. Meister raised an eyebrow at her. "We do our best to make ourselves comfortable, but do not forget that above all, the Warren is a stronghold. We have many secrets that must remain protected." He gestured at the unforgiving darkness. "This is an oublimort, perhaps the last of its kind. It is a confounding but harmless device. Let me demonstrate for you the worst that can happen." Mr. Meister stepped into the doorway made of shadow. He vanished immediately, as if swallowed, but no sooner had he gone than he reappeared, headed back toward them—so instantaneously that he seemed to be finishing the same step he had taken going in.

"Whoa," Horace said.

"Wicked," Chloe agreed. "So how do we get through?"

"It's quite simple, once you know the secret," Mr. Meister said, and then checked himself. "Well . . . simple to describe, not so simple to do. All you must do is close your eyes."

"Close our eyes," Chloe said skeptically. "That's it."

"Yes, and do not reach out for the walls."

"And why is that not simple?"

"When you step into the oublimort, you will feel no ground beneath your feet. You will feel that you are falling. You will want to open your eyes, to reach out to catch yourself. But you must do neither. You must simply keep walking. Otherwise, you will end up back where you started."

"And there is no actual falling," Chloe said.

"No indeed. But you will not be able to escape the sensation, and you must not hope to save yourself. Instead, you must believe you do not need saving."

"So this time it's 'swallow your fear or be spat back out,'" Horace said.

"Just so."

Chloe eyed the doorway with her typical fierce lack of

respect. She stepped right up to the edge of the darkness and stuck her leg into it. Her foot vanished completely from sight, as if it had been amputated. "Oublimort," she said. "That sounds like French words mashed together. It's like 'forget death' or something."

"Quite right," Mr. Meister said. "Very good."

"Well, that's the story of my life," Chloe said, and she stepped into the black.

PART TWO

The Sundered Bloom

CHAPTER SEVEN

———∽∾∽———

Brian's Brain

WHEN CHLOE STEPPED INTO THE SHADOW OF THE OUBLIMORT, Horace had no doubt she would pass through on her first try. She was as stubborn as she was brave, and if all she had to do was stay calm, surely she would have no difficulties. To his great surprise, however, Chloe disappeared into the dark doorway and reappeared instantly, heading back the way she'd come. Her eyes and mouth were open, her hand clutching the front of her shirt.

When she saw Horace and Mr. Meister, Chloe's shocked face collapsed into a knot of irritation. "Dammit," she said.

"Remember, resist the urge to open your eyes," said Mr. Meister.

"Yeah, I heard you the first time." Chloe whirled around and marched into the shadow again—but again she went in and came right back out. This time, to Horace's great surprise,

Mr. Meister actually snickered softly.

"Dammit!" Chloe cried, blazing with fury. Horace bit his lip to keep from smiling. Now the Alvalaithen's wings flickered into motion, and Chloe turned to the oublimort for a third time. Horace half expected Mr. Meister to stop her from attempting the doorway with the dragonfly activated, but the old man said nothing. And it didn't matter—once again Chloe disappeared and returned in the blink of an eye, the dragonfly still whirring. This time she said nothing, just balled her hands into fists and bobbed up and down angrily as only she could, her feet sinking into the stone floor beneath her and popping back up again, over and over.

"I guess there's something you can't go through after all," Horace teased. He wasn't used to seeing Chloe fail.

"It's harder than it sounds," she snapped at him. "Let's see you do it."

Horace shrugged. "Why not?" he said.

Chloe stepped aside, still fuming, as Horace approached the wall of blackness. He stopped and studied the oublimort, considering. There was nothing to see, but of course he'd been wondering how it might work, and he already had a hypothesis. If the oublimort made you feel like you were falling, but actually you weren't, that meant it had to be messing with your senses. And earlier that very day, Horace had gained some experience in having his senses messed with, courtesy of his mother. Horace had a hunch that the oublimort worked in a similar way.

Horace closed his eyes. He stepped into the doorway, into utter darkness. As his foot came down, instead of feeling firm stone, he felt . . . nothing. He started to fall forward. He flashed back to the last time he'd had this unpleasant sensation, at his cousins' cabin two summers before, when he'd walked off the edge of the porch in the dead of night, thinking the stairs were there. He'd shrieked—yes, shrieked—and fallen six feet onto a gravel slope below.

But he wasn't actually falling now. His brain merely thought he was. Horace squeezed his eyes shut, refusing to panic, and let his step continue, a step that according to all his senses was into thin air—the longest step he'd ever taken.

He felt himself pivot until he was plunging headfirst, falling from a great height at a great speed, and it was all he could do not to look. He was about to throw up his hands, bracing for an unseen crash, when his foot landed, ever so lightly, on solid ground. He felt bizarrely as though he'd rotated a hundred and eighty degrees, and was now walking upside down on the underside of the path he'd started on, heading back in the opposite direction. But he took another step, and the sensation faded, and he opened his eyes.

He was through. Ahead, the square stone tunnel widened and continued. He could see bright light thirty yards ahead. Behind him, the dark void of the oublimort loomed. Through it, he heard Chloe's voice, shrill and angry: *"Dammit!"* Clearly she'd realized he'd made it—and on his first try, too.

"It's easy," he called back, and then grimaced as he

139

realized how that must sound. He pictured the face Chloe would be making. "It's only two seconds, and the landing is soft. It's just an illusion."

There was a long pause, and then another angry roar from Chloe. Apparently she'd tried and failed again. "That's more than two seconds!" she shouted.

She was clearly frustrated. She knew better than to question Horace on matters of time. "It only feels like that," Horace assured her. He did a quick and dirty calculation in his head, using an equation he'd memorized for falling objects. Take the number of seconds, multiply it by itself, and then multiply that by sixteen. In this case, two times two was four, and four times sixteen was sixty-four. Sixty-four feet, or about six stories—that's how far something would fall in just two seconds. Horace was sure that if he fell out of a sixth-floor window, it would feel like a lot more than two seconds had passed before he hit the ground. But two seconds it would be.

Chloe's voice rang out again. "I'm going around," she said, and then apparently spoke to Mr. Meister. "Can I go around? How big is this thing?"

"I do not know how far it extends, exactly," Mr. Meister replied, his voice thoughtful. "But one would think that encountering the oublimort while embedded in solid stone would be a distinctly unpleasant experience. Perhaps even a dangerous one."

"I'm having a distinctly unpleasant experience right now," Chloe said.

"Nonetheless, I suggest you keep trying."

But it was another three minutes before Chloe finally made it. When she came through at last, Horace almost burst out laughing—she'd pulled the collar of her shirt up over the top of her head, covering her face so that only a small round crown of black hair poked out the neck hole. Her pale belly showed, the tip of the scar the golem had given her just peeking out, pink and coarse. "Don't tell me I'm back again," she said, her voice muffled inside her shirt. "I swear I didn't open them."

"You made it," Horace said. "You're here."

Chloe yanked her shirt down, her head popping into sight again. She looked around, clearly relieved. "Oh, thank god," she said. A moment later, Mr. Meister stepped out of the oublimort, opening his eyes calmly at the precise moment his face emerged from the gloom. "And here we are," he said, as if there had been no delay whatsoever. "Come. Brian's workshop is just ahead." He swept past them, leading the way.

As they followed, Chloe shot a nasty look back at the oublimort and then thrust a finger in Horace's face, glaring. "This is not a thing we discuss, okay?" she whispered insistently.

"Hey, everybody has issues," Horace replied. "Better you had yours here instead of someplace where something bad could've happened, right?"

"Something bad did just happen," she said. "Repeatedly."

The tunnel opened up into a brightly lit space, a sprawling

natural chamber in the rock that twisted and rambled in every direction. Strangely, a half dozen ordinary fluorescent lights hung from the ceiling, like the kind you'd see in a garage. And beneath them—at least to Horace's science-loving mind—lay a veritable hall of wonders.

The chamber was a jumble of tables and shelves and workbenches, all piled high with tools and equipment both familiar and exotic. A microscope, a sledgehammer, a rock tumbler, a balance scale, an assortment of saws and knives. He spotted what looked like a kiln in one corner, and in another—unmistakably—an anvil. One long table seemed to be covered entirely in jagged sheets of stained glass. Another held a row of bins, a couple of which had clearly come from the House of Answers. Unfamiliar objects and devices, some of them obviously Tanu, were scattered here and there around the room, many in various states of disassembly.

Against one wall was a kind of living area, with a kitchen table, a ratty green couch—Horace shuddered to imagine carrying that through the oublimort—and a couple of bean bag chairs. An ancient-looking TV sat on an equally ancient-looking end table, and there was a framed picture on the wall of Thomas Edison standing next to an elephant. Horace frowned at that one.

Brian himself stood bent over one of the workbenches, focusing intently through a pair of magnifying goggles he wore on top of his regular glasses. His ponytail had fallen forward over his shoulder. He held some sort of tweezerlike tool in one hand and a minuscule chunk of something golden in the other. He wore a black T-shirt that made him look even paler than Horace remembered.

Mr. Meister cleared his throat. "My apologies. I hope we're not interrupting anything delicate."

Brian didn't move an inch. "So delicate," he said, "that the entire fate of the world may hang in the balance." With the tool, he pinched cautiously at the small gold nugget, as if he were unwrapping a tiny present, and stared closely at it for several more seconds. He then abruptly straightened and unceremoniously threw both the tool and the golden thing into a drawer. "But I'm bored with it now." He stood, stripping off his goggles, and came toward them, studying them with thoughtful blue eyes. He bowed awkwardly, his ponytail and his long thin arms dangling. When he straightened, Horace saw that his shirt read VITAMIN D. "The newbies made it through the oublimort, I see. Didn't you love it?" His eyes seemed to linger on Chloe for just a moment longer.

"A delight, as always," Mr. Meister replied. "And how is our . . . other project? Any changes?"

"A little roaming around, maybe. But that could change at any moment."

What on earth did that mean? Horace thought he noticed a slight frown of worry on Mr. Meister's face, but then the old man nodded and moved smoothly into introductions. "Horace Andrews and Chloe Oliver. Brian Souter. I believe you've all encountered one another in passing, yes? But never been formally introduced?"

Brian pointed at Horace. "Once in passing." He then pointed to Chloe and said, "Once in passing, once in Princess Charming mode."

"What are you talking about?" Chloe demanded.

"After Horace sent the dragonfly through the box," said Brian. "You spent the day here before you went back to the nest, remember? You were *so* pleasant." He gave Chloe a wide, sarcastic smile.

Chloe crossed her arms, her face thunderous. "That day is kind of fuzzy for me, thanks," she spat. "But just so we're clear, I only have one mode—and it's not princess anything."

Brian gazed back at her for a long moment. "Fascinating," he said.

"And so we begin," Mr. Meister murmured with a tired sigh. "As we discussed, Brian, you have much to tell our new friends."

"You still think this is the time?"

"I do," Mr. Meister said stiffly. "There are certain secrets that must be revealed before we can proceed."

"Fine." Brian turned to Horace and Chloe. "Here's the big secret . . . you two ready?" He spread his palms wide, like a magician. "It's turtles all the way down."

"I'm reasonably sure it isn't," Mr. Meister said drily. "I will give you a half an hour to introduce yourself more fully, and then we will attend to the pressing matter at hand. Alert me if anything changes." He turned to leave, laying a friendly hand on Horace's shoulder as he passed. They watched him vanish into the shadows, and eventually his soft footsteps receded into silence.

Nobody said anything. Horace examined a particularly powerful-looking heat gun, wondering what was going on. Chloe backed against a workbench and hopped up to sit on it, her feet dangling. She picked up a hunk of metal shaped like a seahorse, studying it closely, and cursed a question softly to herself before setting it down again. Brian regarded them both skeptically for several seconds, and Horace realized he was taking a long, hard look at the Fel'Daera and the Alvalaithen.

"So, newbies," Brian said at last. "Make yourselves useful. Tell me what it's like outside."

The question threw Horace, but Chloe didn't bat an eye. "Today, or just in general?" she asked, her voice full of thorns. Clearly Brian, as Mr. Meister had predicted, had rubbed her the wrong way.

Brian turned toward her, apparently unruffled. "Just in general, of course."

"Oh, yes, of course," Chloe said sarcastically. "What do you want to know?"

"Let's see . . . pretend I haven't been outside in three years."

"Three years. Wow, you've missed a lot. We have flying cars now. Also it rains every day from two to two thirty, but it smells like hand sanitizer. And squirrels are the size

145

of dogs." She stood there staring laser beams, but Brian just looked back at her placidly, his mouth crooked with amusement. "Oh," Chloe said, looking anything but amused, "and popcorn is legal again."

Horace started to laugh but choked it back. He had no idea what to say, not with Brian being so unexpectedly weird and Chloe feeling feisty. Probably better to sit this one out and just enjoy it.

Brian nodded at Chloe with mock seriousness. "Your stories of the overworld fascinate me," he said. "Tell me, is the squirrel situation related to the rain thing?"

Chloe's scowl only deepened. "What's your deal, anyway?"

Brian sighed. "Oh, man, where do I start? I tell you what. Let's start here: I haven't been outside in three years."

Now Horace leaned forward. "Wait, you were serious about that?"

"Yup."

"Like you haven't been out of the Warren?" Horace exclaimed. "In *three years*?"

"Roughly, yeah. I'm a valuable asset. Too precious to go outside, I'm told. But I'm also told that being stuck down here makes me 'difficult.' The stress makes me 'challenging' to deal with—or so the rumor goes. It's also why I have this lovely complexion." He struck a dramatic pose, gesturing grandly down his face and one bony, pale arm.

"So you're a *prisoner*?" Chloe said. Horace could hear her disdain.

"I'm a reluctant—but voluntary—resident. Look, it's not all bad. Sounds like your squirrels are out of control at the surface. That's one bullet dodged."

Suddenly, the wondrous workshop seemed a little less enticing. Brian had been here for three years? Three years ago, Horace had just finished third grade. It seemed a lifetime ago. Why on earth had Mr. Meister kept Brian down here for all that time?

Brian's blue eyes darted back and forth between the two of them. Horace realized he and Chloe were both staring at him like the new animal in the zoo. Brian said, "You guys get that I'm kidding about the squirrels, right? I know there's no giant squirrels. Or flying cars."

"Yeah, I think we got that," said Horace.

"Not everybody does. Some folks down here take things way too seriously. I think Mrs. Hapsteade thinks I'm insane."

Chloe scoffed. "Maybe she has a point. You've lived underground for three years. Voluntarily."

"Maybe. But maybe you'll feel different when I explain why I can't ever leave—why the Riven can't know I exist. It's because of what I do."

"And what do you do?" Horace asked.

"I make things." He gestured to the jumble of the room all around. "Clearly."

"Like what?" Chloe asked, still suspicious. "Muffins?"

Horace laughed, but Brian remained serious. "No," he said. "More like . . . Tanu."

147

The very idea staggered Horace for a moment. "What . . . *what*?" he said lamely.

Chloe pointed at Brian. "You," she said, her voice dripping with disbelief.

"Me, yes. Hi."

"You make Tanu," Chloe pressed.

"That's right. Hello." Brian flashed a curt wave.

"Wait a minute," said Horace. "You're a Maker?"

"That's not a word I like to use," Brian replied. "I'm not Altari, obviously. I'm a Tinker just like you. I mostly make relatively simple things—mainly Tan'kindi. Let's see . . . you've both been to the warehouse on Wexler Street. You saw the little round sign on the front door. 'State your name your state your name,' et cetera?"

Horace remembered the sign on the door to the House of Answers. The door opened only when visitors honestly stated both their names and their mental state. And of course, Horace realized now—it had to be Tanu. "Are you saying you made that?"

"Yup," said Brian. "Meister wanted something that would only grant entry to people who weren't hiding anything. Basically, the sign was just a lie detector—tell the truth, and the door opens."

Horace, deeply impressed, had to keep his mouth from hanging open. "Wow," he said, his brain scrambling to imagine how such a device might work.

Chloe, however, rolled her eyes. "Yeah, wow, great idea,"

she snarked. "Too bad it didn't work."

Horace understood at once. "Chloe," he chided, embarrassed for Brian.

"It's okay," Brian said softly. He seemed to understand too. His eyes dropped thoughtfully to the Alvalaithen, gleaming at Chloe's throat. Clearly he'd heard about the day the Riven invaded the House of Answers. They'd brought with them a huge and powerful Tanu called a golem—more creature than device, like a living river of stone. Horace and Chloe and Mrs. Hapsteade had barely escaped, but not before Chloe, using the Alvalaithen, had actually gone into the belly of the golem to rescue Mrs. Hapsteade's Tan'ji.

"The sign at the warehouse wasn't really meant to keep out the Riven," Brian explained. "The Riven should never have been able to find the door in the first place."

"But they did," Chloe said. "And they got past your little sign."

"Because of you," Brian shot back. "I heard a rumor that the Mordin had been stalking you for weeks before you came to the warehouse. You were the one that led them there."

Chloe hopped down off the bench. She lifted her arms up toward the cavern walls all around them. "Well, at least I'm out there *doing* something. At least I'm not letting someone lock me up my whole life so I can futz around making stuff that doesn't even work."

"Chloe—" Horace began again, but again Brian interrupted him.

"Oh, I see," he said. "Not only am I weak, but I suck at what I do. Meanwhile, you're the hero."

Chloe shrugged. "Your words, not mine."

"You have no idea what I do or how I do it. Look, you guys probably think very highly of your Tan'ji. The Fel'Daera, the Alvalaithen—Meister struts around here bragging about the new recruits and their instruments of legend." Brian held up his hands. "And I'm not saying that's wrong. No disrespect. You guys are packing some serious heat. But you have to understand." He bent his head. His voice got heavy as he began to speak—no, not speak, recite.

"From the starlit belly of the Loom, the Firstfound,
the nine Loomdaughters were drawn.
And from these few, the One and the Nine,
everything after came."

Horace and Chloe stared at him. Chloe looked as though someone had just asked her for directions to the moon.

"What the hell was *that*?" she said.

"Old words. A translation. The original version rhymes, if that makes you feel better."

"I don't understand," she said.

"How do you think Tanu get made?" Brian asked. "Including yours?"

"I never thought about the actual process," said Horace, a little embarrassed that he hadn't.

Slowly, as if he were talking to small children, Brian said, "You have to wield an instrument to create an instrument."

"Duh," Chloe said, as if all of this had occurred to her before. But her face was lit with interest, her keen eyes locked on Brian.

Brian continued as if he hadn't heard her. "Generally speaking, Tanu can only be made by the Keepers of very specialized Tan'ji. And only ten such Tan'ji have ever existed: the Starlit Loom itself—the very first Tanu—and then the Nine. The Nine are the Loomdaughters, rough copies of the Loom. Every Tanu worth mentioning that has ever existed was made either with the Loom, or with one of the Nine."

"So are you the Keeper of the Starlit Loom?" Horace asked.

"Big no. If I were the Keeper of the Starlit Loom . . . well, that's major superstar territory. But I am the Keeper of one of the Nine." He pushed his glasses up on his nose. "Behold the secret of Brian," he intoned, briefly striking a pose and making jazz hands. "Meister didn't want you to know about me, not at first. But you've been spilling your hero juice all over the place. He trusts you now. Why it had to be today, of all days, I don't know. But he wants me to show you."

"So show us," said Chloe.

Without another word, Brian turned and led them deeper into the workshop. He led them around a bend and through a low opening that led into a separate cramped round chamber beyond. Horace's claustrophobia clutched at him again as he entered, but quickly loosened. The room felt vaguely churchy, somehow sacred.

There was a faint electric smell, like the scent of an old vacuum running. Illumination filtered down from the amber light that fumed dimly above, falling onto a stout wooden table that seemed to float in the gloom. Atop the table sat an oval block of stone, dusty black, about eight inches thick and eighteen inches across. The stone was massively and unmistakably Tan'ji, like nothing Horace had ever seen before. It burned with power, and Horace thought of the flows of energy his mother had described to him. He felt almost as if he could sense that energy himself now, coursing deep through the heart of this stone.

They approached the table, Brian going around to the far side. He looked different as he leaned over the stone—older, taller, more severe. The top surface of the mysterious Tan'ji was rough, unmarked except for a narrow ridge around the edge and, near each end, the deep outlines of two crude circles.

"This is a Loomdaughter," Brian said. "One of nine. Her name is Tunraden." He held up his hands. And now Horace saw that a thin, dark band tightly encircled each of Brian's wrists, glinting in the dim light. Brian let one hand dangle over each of the two crude circles in the stone. Horace stepped nearer still, but even as he did, he was aware of Chloe taking a step back.

"What's the matter?" he asked her.

"This is serious stuff," she said.

Brian looked at her quizzically. "There's nothing to be afraid of."

"I'm not afraid, caveman. I just . . . don't want to be any closer."

"Some don't," Brian said. "Being this close to the raw Medium makes some people feel sick."

Horace just had time to register the word—*the Medium!*—when Brian said, "You may want to close your eyes."

And then he plunged his hands into the stone.

His hands vanished to the wrist inside the crude circles, and the surface of the Loomdaughter exploded into golden light. Horace cried out and leaned away, throwing up his arms. The air all around him began to quiver and thrum, making his hair stand on end. He clutched at the Fel'Daera, feeling from it a sensation he'd never encountered before—not alarm, but a kind of knife's edge of exhilaration, like a strong tree bending deeply in a raging wind.

Chloe, meanwhile, had taken another step back. She held one arm in front of her face, shielding her eyes, while with the other she clutched at the Alvalaithen. Its wings beat furiously. Her lips were parted wide in shock.

Brian leaned back, his lit face straining slightly with effort, and from the glowing pit the Loomdaughter had become he pulled a great pile of—there was no other word for it—light. Thick, drooping coils of light, golden and smooth and pulsing and heaped in his hands like the tentacles of some ocean beast, running through his fingers like honey. He spread his hands, and the light moved with them, looping and curling.

"The Medium," Brian said quietly, and at first Horace couldn't understand why he didn't have to shout—but of course the storm that rampaged now wasn't real, or if it was real it was happening only between the boy's hands; the room was utterly silent. The circlets around Brian's wrists glowed brightly.

Brian reached into the Loomdaughter again and pulled out more of the golden substance. He pinched some between his fingertips and pulled it into a webwork of lace that thinned into nothingness. "This is what we weave into the Tanu," he said. "The presence of the Medium gives the Tanu their power, and the pattern of the weaving gives them their function."

He carved off a piece of the Medium with the edge of his hand. The chunk coalesced briefly into a sphere and hovered over his palm. Grooves began to appear across the surface of the sphere, rows of furrows that interlaced and spread, like a tapestry, or a circuit board. Eventually so many lines scored the sphere that it was sliced into pieces, and the pieces poured back into and over Brian's hand like salt, rejoining the rest of the Medium. Horace watched the display in wonder, transfixed. He had never seen anything so beautiful before, so . . . *elemental.*

"Stop it," Chloe said. "Put it back. Let it go."

Brian looked up, his hands still full, his pale skin glowing.

"It's not alive or anything. Don't be upset."

"I'm not upset. It's just those colors . . . they hurt my eyes."

"Colors?" Horace said, squinting into the yellow fire of the Medium. Brian bent forward, dropping the thick cables of light into the Loomdaughter and spreading his arms toward the ends of the oval surface. He pulled his now-empty hands up from the stone, the rings around his wrists reemerging, black once more. Abruptly, the stone swallowed the light whole, and the room plunged into darkness. The electric smell was thick in the air.

Horace stilled his own heavy breathing. Across the way, he could hear Chloe's breath hissing sharply in and out through her nose.

"You saw colors?" Brian asked, still unseen.

"Yes," Chloe replied. "At least, I think so. There were these . . . these thin jagged lines. Like bolts of electricity."

Horace had no idea what she was talking about. He'd seen nothing like that.

"That's right," Brian said wonderingly. "But normally only Tuners can see the colors. Tuners and Meister and, well, me."

The room was coming back into focus now as Horace's eyes adjusted to the dark. Horace spotted Chloe's small, solid form, far back against the wall. "Whatever," she said. "It doesn't matter." She pushed off the wall and walked up to the table. Leaning over the Loomdaughter, she held a palm above the surface, as if feeling for heat. "Do you know how old it is?"

"Let's see . . . what's today? Tuesday?" Brian ticked off some numbers on his fingers. "Five thousand years, give or take."

"Holy freaking cow," Horace said. That was older than the pyramids.

The room went quiet. All their gazes lay heavily on the Loomdaughter. Tunraden, Brian had called it. Had its Maker given it that name? And who had that Maker been? Chloe gnawed intently at the corner of her mouth, her face troubled. At last Brian said brusquely, "Let's go. This room isn't really for talking." He stepped around the table and slipped through the door, leaving Horace and Chloe to follow.

CHAPTER EIGHT

The Daktan

BACK IN THE WORKSHOP, BRIAN TOOK HIS SEAT AT THE WORK-bench again. He glanced at something unseen across the room and then glanced at his watch. He picked up a tiny vial of some glittering red substance and examined it closely. He seemed suddenly reluctant to talk.

But Horace, riled up by what he'd just witnessed, wanted to hear more. "How does Tunraden work, exactly? I mean, what do you do with the Medium?"

"Man, I don't know. How does an egg become a chicken? I guess the simplest way to say it is that the Medium can be structured, kind of like a very complicated circuit board in three dimensions." He glanced at the Fel'Daera. "Or four. The structure determines the power. Once I have the structure I want, I connect it to a physical object, let the energy flow, and presto: Tanu. I was messing around in there just now, but the real thing is very time-consuming. Exhausting."

"So only Tuners and the Keepers of the looms can manipulate the Medium," Chloe interjected, listening intently.

"Basically, but Tuners can only manipulate the Medium in structures that already exist," Brian said. "They can't make anything new because they can't permanently attach the Medium to an object. Even if they did manage to create a new structure, it would be simple and temporary—a flimsy knot instead of a heavy anchor. But Tuners are actually way better than me at tweaking the flows between an instrument and its Keeper."

"So you can't sever like a Tuner can?" Chloe asked.

"I don't unmake. I make." Brian slipped the red vial into a small rack full of similar vials, each with a tiny amount of powder in them, each a different color. "Why are you so interested in Tuners?" he asked.

Horace hastily changed the subject. "So basically in order to do what you do, you have to be the Keeper of the Starlit Loom, or of a Loomdaughter."

"Yes."

"And there are only ten of those."

"Not even. I am an extremely rare commodity. Many of the Loomdaughters have been destroyed, and apparently most of the ones that remain don't have a Keeper. The Riven would give anything to have me on their side—or, failing that, to take Tunraden away from me, in the hope that one of their own might have the talent to use it."

"The Riven don't have anyone like you?" Horace asked.

"Not quite. Let me explain. The first Keeper of the Starlit Loom used it to make—what else?—copies of the Loom. And that's all she made. Not that you can really blame her, because the Loom was the only thing there was to imitate. There were no other Tanu. And even though she didn't know how to make anything else, she did get better and better at copying the Loom. Each Loomdaughter she made was more powerful and more refined than the last. Eventually the Loomdaughters found Keepers, too, and each instrument was named after its first Keeper." He paused and then began to recite softly: "Sephet, the first. Dalrani, the second. Aored, Nev'fel, Domari, Filfora, Lan'ovro, Tunraden. Viskesh, the ninth."

Chloe fussed intently with the tail of the Alvalaithen. Horace followed her gaze back into the dark room behind them, where the curving bulk of Brian's Tan'ji could no longer be seen. Now that he knew it was there, though, Horace was sure he could still feel its massive presence.

"Tunraden is the eighth?" Horace asked. "That means it's powerful."

"Yes. The *most* powerful, because Viskesh, the ninth, was destroyed a long time ago. But none of the Loomdaughters are anywhere near as powerful as the Starlit Loom itself. Keepers of the Loom have been few and far between, and instruments made with it are extremely rare." He pointed casually at the Alvalaithen, and at the Fel'Daera at Horace's side. "That's why everyone's talking about you. Your instruments were made with the Starlit Loom."

The news hit Horace like a slap of cold water, invigorating but shocking. He found himself feeling monstrously small, once again overwhelmed by the hugeness of this story into which he had wandered.

"But we're not the only ones," said Chloe, who never seemed to have much difficulty taking her rightful place in things. She nodded back into the dark toward Tunraden. "Your instrument came from the Starlit Loom too."

Brian gave her a thin smile. "True. I guess that makes us like . . . littermates or something, doesn't it?"

"I'm going to try *not* to think of it like that," Chloe replied.

Horace was only half listening, his thoughts churning forward. If Brian was right, that meant Sil'falo Teneves, maker of the Box of Promises, had once been the Keeper of the Starlit Loom. "So where is the Starlit Loom now?" Horace asked. "And what about its Keeper?"

"I don't know," Brian replied. "The location of the Loom is a major secret, obviously. Sometimes Meister tries to imply that the Loom is gone forever, but . . ."

Gone forever. Would that mean Falo was gone too? "But you think he's wrong," Horace prodded hopefully.

Brian shrugged. "The Loom still exists. I can't tell you how I know, but I know."

Horace was very familiar with that sensation—knowing things without knowing *how* he knew. Talking to Brian

160

was stirring something big and powerful inside Horace. It was partly the thrill of peeking beneath the surface into how Tanu were made and how they worked, a process that pushed every nerdy button in Horace's brain. But it was also the sensation of sinking deeper into this long story, and getting glimpses of the bottom. The very first Tanu. The names of Keepers long dead. A boy whose Tan'ji was so old and valuable he couldn't even be allowed to leave the safety of the Warren.

Perhaps sensing the floodwater of questions Horace was barely holding back, Brian poked around on the workbench some more. He glanced across the room at something again, as if checking a timer, and let loose a frustrated sigh. "Meister should be back any minute now," he said. "Not sure why it's taking him so long."

Horace followed his gaze, but the chamber was so cluttered it was hard to tell what Brian was looking at. Casually Horace started strolling in that direction.

"So what's the fanciest thing you've ever made?" asked Chloe, seemingly unaware.

"Mr. Meister's vest," said Brian immediately. "My first Tan'ji."

That stopped Horace in his tracks. "The red vest?" he said. "What do you mean?"

"It's Tan'ji," Brian said with a grin. "One hundred percent homemade. You might not have noticed right away because it's a little rough, and not the genuine Altari article."

"Mr. Meister already has a Tan'ji," Chloe pointed out. "The oraculum."

Brian shrugged. "Yeah, well, Mr. Meister has his ways of breaking rules the rest of us can't—or won't. That's why he's the boss."

Another surprise. "But the vest is definitely Tan'ji?" Horace said.

"Oh, yeah. It doesn't always work like it's supposed to, but only Mr. Meister can use it. I got the idea when I saw his office. He likes red. I designed the vest, Mrs. Hapsteade actually sewed it, and then I strung the function into it with the Medium."

"What do you mean, the function?" Horace asked. "What does it do?"

"Almost every one of those pockets—there are a hundred and sixty-seven of them, if you ever wondered—connects to a compartment in Meister's office upstairs in the Great Burrow. He can reach into different pockets and pull out items from his office, even when he's away. Didn't you ever notice?"

Horace thought the surprises would never end. "I knew something weird was going on. I guess I never thought it through. But how do you do something like that?"

"It's not that complicated, really. A little triangulation, a little entanglement. Even then, the vine only has a range of about fifteen miles. The hardest part was making it Tan'ji instead of just Tan'kindi. Meister insisted that it could work only for him. It took me weeks, and I gave him a lot of headaches—literally—but I finally did it."

Horace clung to every word, fascinated. *Not that complicated. Triangulation and entanglement.* He barely even knew what those two words meant. "So basically you're a genius," he blurted out.

"Oh, lord," Chloe muttered.

"That's what I've been trying to say," Brian told Horace. "Without actually saying it."

"No wonder they don't let you leave," said Horace.

Chloe sighed dramatically. "I was just starting to enjoy myself, and now there's all this bromance in the air. Or no— not even bromance. Nerdmance."

"Don't poop on my parade, Chloe," said Brian. "Maybe it might occur to you that I get a little lonely down here."

Chloe slipped another mint into her mouth.

"Anyway," Brian said. "I see you got my presents."

"Presents?" Horace said.

Brian pointed to Horace's neck and down to his chest, where the jithandra lay beneath his shirt.

"Our jithandras," said Horace. "Of course . . . you make these."

"That I do. I had to make a second one for you, Horace. Luckily, I still had enough of your dust left."

"Wait . . . dust?" Horace said.

"Ink dust. From the Vora."

"Mrs. Hapsteade's quill?" The Vora was the first Tan'ji Horace had even laid eyes on, before he became a Keeper.

With the quill, he'd written in the guest book back at the House of Answers, the blue of the ink he produced supposedly a sign as to his talents and potential.

"Yes," said Brian. "You write in the guest book, Mrs. H brings the book to me, and I harvest the dried ink. I turn it into a powder. It doesn't make much, a couple hundred milligrams, but it's totally useful stuff. It's like the essence of you—or your affinities, anyway." He reached into the rack in front of him and plucked out the vial with the red powder again. He held it up and shook it gently. "Powdered Chloe."

Chloe let out an indignant huff. Brian said, "I know. It's sort of gruesome. But necessary." Brian pulled out three more vials—purple, blue, silver. "This purple one is Neptune. And Horace is blue, of course. The silver is Gabriel."

"This is why they made us write in the book," said Horace.

"They're sampling us," Chloe offered.

Brian shrugged. "Basically, yeah."

Horace stepped forward and held his glowing jithandra against the glittering blue vial. It was the same deep, lustrous shade. "And you use the dust to, like . . . personalize the jithandras."

"Yes. The jithandras are your personal keys into the Great Burrow, after all. But I use the dust for lots of other devastatingly clever things too."

Chloe rolled her eyes. "You could stand to be less cocky."

"Said the kettle," Brian added.

Horace laughed, but Brian didn't join him, instead

glancing across the room yet again. This time, the nervous tension in his shoulders was unmistakable.

"What do you keep looking at?" Horace said, unable to take it anymore.

"Oh, nothing much. Just a time bomb. No biggie." Brian glanced back at the entryway, as if hoping to see Mr. Meister there.

"It's the reason we're here tonight, isn't it?" Horace said. "It's the thing that woke up."

Brian's face twisted with a sour uncertainty. "Woke up. Waking up. Wide awake now. We have to do something soon." He stood slowly and started across the room, leaving them to follow. "I noticed it last week. But this morning something changed. Something big. And now, well . . ."

He stopped in front of a table, upon which sat a large felt-lined tray. Across the red felt, a few dozen strange, tiny objects were neatly arranged. Not Tanu, as far as Horace could tell, though they were certainly odd—a precisely coiled strand of gold like a narwhal's tusk, a kidney-shaped slab of the whitest stone imaginable, a dodecahedron that looked like it was made of maple syrup, an inch-long silver replica of a human forearm and hand.

"Here," Brian said, pointing one bony finger at a tiny black object in the center, smaller than a pea. It looked like a minuscule bell—or no, a metal flower blossom, with tightly seamed petals that flared into gentle points at the opening. It reminded Horace of a lily of the valley blossom. Back at home, a patch of the miniature white flowers grew behind the toolshed, blooming in the late spring. Except this flower was gleaming black instead of shining white.

A deep unease settled over Horace as he examined the little flower. His first instinct told him that it was in fact Tan'ji, but there was something sickly about it, something cruel and sad—as if it were a half-crushed insect, barely alive, still trying to crawl. And as he stared at the tiny metal blossom, he could almost swear that it *did* move, trembling ever so slightly. But maybe that was just his imagination.

"What is it?" he asked. "And what's wrong with it? It feels like Tan'ji, but it seems . . . bad."

"It *is* Tan'ji." They all jumped as Mr. Meister's voice rolled across the room. He strode toward them, his gray eyes as wide as ever, and bent over the table. "But it is not bad—not in the way you might suspect. This little flower is daktan."

When Horace frowned, Brian explained. "Daktan means sundered." Horace shook his head, still clueless. Brian gestured toward the Fel'Daera at Horace's side, toward the dragonfly around Chloe's neck. "This flower is a . . . missing piece."

Horace clutched at the box. "A missing piece . . . of a Tan'ji, you mean?"

"Yes."

Suddenly the flower looked even more horrible, like a chunk of dissected flesh. Horace glanced at Chloe. Her face too was wrinkled with disgust and alarm. "But who would break a piece off a Tan'ji?" he asked.

"Someone who could not bring himself to utterly destroy the instrument in question," said Mr. Meister.

"I don't understand."

"Remember that basically there are two kinds of Tanu: those that require a Keeper, and those that do not. Those that do not, we call Tan'kindi. Those that do, of course, we call Tan'ji—but only when they are bonded to their Keepers. When such a Tanu is dormant—when it is without a Keeper—we call it Tan'layn. The unspoken."

Horace had heard that word earlier, from his mother, but she'd defined it as *"unclaimed."* Somehow, *"unspoken"* sounded even worse.

"As you know," Mr. Meister continued, "we have been actively seeking new Keepers for the Tan'layn we've collected. But as you also know, that search can be dangerous. Every time we seek a new Keeper, we risk alerting the Riven. And there was a time, not so very long ago, when the Wardens were unwilling to take that risk. Instead of allowing the Tan'layn to find new Keepers, the Wardens kept the instruments hidden deep, where no one could hope to find them, friend or foe." He sighed remorsefully. "But in time, even hiding wasn't enough to ease their fears. The Wardens began to deliberately sabotage some of the more powerful Tan'layn, amputating crucial pieces. They moved the Tan'layn—now greatly reduced in power—to other strongholds, leaving the daktan here. Essentially, they hoped to keep the instruments safe by crippling them, making them less valuable to the Riven."

"Less valuable to *everyone*," Horace said, appalled.

"Precisely. But the Wardens reasoned that if a human Keeper was somehow found for one of these Tan'layn, the instrument in question could—with a little luck, in the right hands—be reassembled. Repaired." He glanced at Brian meaningfully.

Brian shifted slightly, looking down at the floor. Of course—Tunraden. But Brian's expression seemed to suggest that reassembling a sabotaged instrument would be no small feat.

"So let me get this straight," Chloe said. "It's like if I didn't want someone to steal my car, I'd break the steering wheel off and hide it."

"A fair analogy, yes."

"Well, that seems like a terrible plan."

"Just so. Terrible and cowardly. And now we are left with some of the remnants of those hopeless days." Mr. Meister swept an arm across the cluttered display case in front of them. "An inventory of steering wheels, if you like."

Chloe shivered. "Wait—these are all missing pieces? They're all . . . what did you call them?"

"Daktan," Mr. Meister said.

"Right," said Chloe. "But the rest of these don't look like this little flower does. This flower makes me want to vomit. The rest don't even feel like Tan'ji."

"That's because the instruments to which these other daktan belong have not yet met their Keepers. They are still Tan'layn." Mr. Meister bent low over the tray, practically pressing his nose against the tiny black flower, cocking his head to the right to stare at the blossom through the great left lens of the oraculum. "But the instrument from which this floret was taken has very recently been *Found*." The heavy way he said the word left no doubt as to his meaning. Again Horace saw, or imagined that he saw, the little blossom tremble.

"So this piece is missing from some new Keeper's Tan'ji," Horace said, trying not to think too hard about how that might feel. "But is that Tan'ji even working?"

Brian glanced at Mr. Meister, who was staring silently at the daktan. "Yes," Brian said. "But we can't say how well, or even what it does."

Mr. Meister said, "Very likely even its Keeper cannot say how well the instrument is working, though he or she is certainly aware that something is amiss."

Chloe raised an eyebrow. "And you know this because . . . ?"

Brian shrugged. "I've been keeping an eye on this little flower since I first noticed it coming to life. I can sense changes in the Medium, remember?"

Mr. Meister pointed to the oraculum over his own left eye. "As can I, in my own small way."

Brian continued. "And then this morning, something major happened. The Keeper became conscious of the daktan for the first time. He or she heard the call of the missing piece. It's been growing stronger hour by hour all day, and now . . . it's big-time."

Fascinated, Horace gazed at the little flower. "Can you two hear the call?" he asked.

"In a manner of speaking, but only in the presence of the daktan," Mr. Meister said. "You might say that when we observe the daktan, we are aware that someone else is aware."

"It's like hearing one end of a phone conversation," Brian said. "This isn't a signal you could actually intercept."

"Right," Chloe said. "But do you wonder twins have any idea where this Keeper actually is?"

Somewhat creepily, both Brian and Mr. Meister raised a silent arm, pointing back over their shoulders in the same direction. Chloe's eyes grew wide. Horace was a little disoriented, deep underground, but the two Wardens seemed to be pointing vaguely to the north. "It is hard to tell how far away, precisely," Mr. Meister said. "Brian is better at such things than I am. He believes the Keeper is outside the city."

"Within fifty miles, I think," Brian added, but he sounded distracted. He looked up into the air as if hearing a sound no one else could detect. "Maybe forty. Neither of us can tell the exact location—only the direction and a rough idea of distance."

"But who is this Keeper?" Horace asked.

"We do not know," Mr. Meister replied. "All we know is that the Keeper is feeling the irresistible pull of this small piece, even from far off. They have sensed the wound in their instrument, and will soon be on the move. Even as we speak, they are being drawn to this place, to this very chamber. And despite all our efforts to keep the Warren hidden, they will find us." His tone sounded ominous, though Horace wasn't sure why.

"You say that like we should be worried," Chloe said.

"Perhaps we should," said Mr. Meister grimly, looking down at the metal blossom again. "I said we do not know who the Keeper is, but let me be clear—we do not even know *what* the Keeper is."

"Wait a minute," said Horace. "Are you saying that it might not be a human out there . . . that it might be a Riven?"

Mr. Meister blinked at him with those great gray eyes of his. "That is correct. A visitor is coming to the Warren, and we cannot assume it is a friend."

CHAPTER NINE

—⟨∞⟩—

Prairie Lake Station

APRIL EMERGED FROM A CORNFIELD ON THE EDGE OF TOWN with Isabel and Joshua, feeling—for the first time—very much like a runaway. She was only a couple of miles from home, after all, and if they were headed into town it was possible someone who knew her might spot her. That simply wouldn't do. She tried her best to look innocent and anonymous. She told herself she had every right to be here—the call of the missing piece could not be ignored. It was as simple as that.

But maybe they weren't headed into town. Up ahead, the amber lights of the local Metra station glowed. The station sat between two vast commuter parking lots, each one as wide as a football field. Since it was nearly seven thirty, with the trains only running every hour or so, the lots were all but empty.

At some point on their hike, a subtle shift had occurred in their little group. Joshua had begun to lead the way, no doubt using his keen sense of direction to take them wherever they were going. But so far, instead of leading them toward the magnetic call of the missing piece, he'd been taking them away from it. For April, this was beyond frustrating, and frankly a little worrisome. When she'd politely asked where they were headed—how they were planning to get into the city—Isabel had said only, "Arrangements have been made." But now, as Arthur drifted overhead and dropped into the parking lot, April looked at the train station in the distance and felt her heart slump in her chest.

"We're taking a train?" she said.

"What?" Isabel said blankly. "No . . . no train."

April breathed a sigh of relief. The thought of getting a raven on a train was problematic, to say the least. But it still didn't answer the question of how they were getting to the city.

They started across the parking lot, weaving between the dozen or so cars that still remained. Arthur meandered alongside, exploring, warbling low to himself. He hopped briefly onto the hood of an SUV, clearly in a good mood. He stopped to examine something small and shiny—a coin or a pop top, maybe—and then began tossing it into the air. He was playing. Isabel watched him with a smile. Meanwhile, keen little sparks of mischief fired in April's head.

There were nearly to the station when a northbound train came and went. A lone woman got off and headed toward them. April hid her face as the woman passed them, but the woman barely glanced their way. As they crossed the tracks, Arthur swooped in silently and took up a perch on the near end of the long station building. April continued to sip at his happiness, his contentment, his still-blooming wonder at being free and able to fly again. His carefree mood was the perfect remedy for her own stewing worries.

Isabel glanced over at her. "Keep it low," she murmured.

"I am," said April.

They cut across the empty platform, headed for the far end of the darkened station building. But just as they moved under the shadowed eaves, Arthur's mood abruptly shifted. April stopped dead.

A sudden alertness. A jolt of alarm.

She spun and looked back over the abandoned parking lot, toward the dark sea of corn beyond. The woman who had gotten off the train looked to be headed for a car at the end of the lot. "Someone's out there," she said.

Isabel turned, pressing Joshua against the wall. "I don't see anyone. I don't feel anything."

"But Arthur does." April closed her eyes, wary of opening herself too much to the vine. If only she could *know* what Arthur was seeing. If only the vine weren't broken. His keen eyes had spotted something moving out in the distance beyond the woman, something—

"Easy," Isabel warned.

April couldn't see, but Arthur's perceptive mind began to fill in some of the blanks. Shapes approaching from the field beyond the lot, following their trail, headed this way. Unnatural shapes. Hated shapes.

She opened her eyes. "Riven," she said. "Mordin. They're coming."

Isabel didn't hesitate, didn't question. She grabbed Joshua's hand and broke into a sprint. April followed, her backpack bouncing as she ran. She quickly moved out of range of Arthur, but they all heard his hoarse, challenging cry as it echoed across the entire station: *"Rrrawk! rawwk! rrawwk!"*

April dared to look back as she rounded the corner of the building. A hundred yards off, she spotted the Mordin in the fading light. Two tall and angular forms like living trees, like praying mantises stretched into grotesque, humanlike form. Her heart fluttered as they passed by the woman from the train, but the woman merely nodded at them. April ducked quickly out of sight after Isabel.

A tall hedge lined the tracks behind the station. The threesome slipped behind it and kept running, Isabel in the lead. They turned and hurried up a long gravel drive that ran behind an auto repair shop closed for the day.

Isabel stopped behind the garage and took a knee. She began digging through her pockets, breathing hard. "They're on your trail," she muttered.

"I've been careful," April said. "Barely sipping."

"You've been fine. It's your wound they're following, but even then, they've been lucky to be doing so well."

"I thought maybe they wouldn't follow us into town,"

April said. "That they'd be afraid of being seen. But that woman in the parking lot saw them and—"

Joshua shook his head gravely. "Only people with the talent see the Mordin how they really are."

April wondered if that included him. "So they'll follow us wherever we go," she said. "But they'll keep their distance because of you, right, Isabel?"

"Yes, but we have a bigger problem now. I promised our ride there was no danger. She won't be happy if we show up with Mordin in pursuit."

Our ride. Apparently they were meeting someone who would drive them into the city. "So what do we do?" April asked.

"I can't do anything about your wound, but maybe I can use it." Isabel pulled something small and silver from her pocket—a paper clip. She began to unfold it. "I need your help, April. Drink from the vine. Deeper than you have been."

"But won't the Mordin feel it?"

"That's what I want—I need you to bleed."

Bewildered, April probed at the vine. Arthur was nowhere nearby, but down in the gravel driveway, a bug was crawling. She spotted it at once—a beetle, clambering over tiny stones as big as boulders. She invited the beetle's dull, robotic mind into her own. Plodding and purposeful, some deep instinct was driving the bug, some instinct April didn't recognize, something as crucial as hunger but less . . . selfish.

"More," Isabel said. At her chest, Miradel began to swell. "Quickly."

April closed her eyes and opened herself wider. Not too wide—she couldn't risk a whiteout—but still she felt a buzzing in her temples. The vine's amputated stem throbbed. Surely the Mordin could sense her now. She tried not to think about it, concentrating on the beetle instead, and all at once she understood what the bug was doing. It was a female, bloated with eggs. Heavy and urgent. Vital. It was looking for a place to lay them. The need was primal and powerful and—for April—a touch embarrassing. She let it pour through her.

Suddenly she felt a tug. Not a physical tug, but a kind of mental pull through the vine, as if her thoughts were made of fabric and a burr had become snagged in the threads. A moment later, the snag pulled free, taking something with it. Her eyes flew open. "That's enough," Isabel said, staring down at the paper clip, which was now a flat figure eight. "Shut the vine down now." When April didn't react right away, still drawn by the beetle's lovely, life-filled need, Isabel said harshly, "Shut it down, or I'll do it for you."

April did as she was told, yanking her thoughts away from the insect. She silenced the vine as best she could. She glanced back toward the train station. No sign of the Mordin. She thought maybe she saw a flicker of black in the sky—Arthur?

Isabel unhooked Miradel from around her neck and held it in her palm. In a wink, the already swollen sphere

177

expanded to the size of a grapefruit, crackling audibly, its woven surface breaking open. Green light flickered within, every shade of emerald. "One second," Isabel said, and she slipped the bent paper clip into the sphere. It dropped to the center and hovered there. Isabel held Miradel between her hands—one above and one below—her face rigid with concentration. The paper clip twisted in place at the core, glittering and weightless.

April could tell by Joshua's face that he was as bedazzled as she was. His little mouth hung open. "What are you doing?" April whispered at the woman.

"I'm buying us time," Isabel replied, staring intently into the wicker ball. A moment later, she lifted the wicker sphere with her top hand. The paper clip fell through a hole in the bottom of the ball. She caught it deftly and stood up. "This," she said, holding out the paper clip, her eyes gleaming.

"What is it?"

"A decoy. A thread of your injury, spun into a loop. It's louder than you. It'll wind down eventually, but for now—" She tossed the paper clip high into the air, onto the roof of the garage. April heard it skitter to a landing. "We can get away while they investigate. Now let's move."

Isabel took Joshua's hand once more and ran. April peeked back around the corner again, hoping to catch a glimpse of Arthur, but what she saw instead nearly froze her. The two huge Mordin were crossing the train tracks now, still distant but coming ever closer, their strides long and purposeful. As she watched, one of them stepped calmly over a bench as if it were no more than a fallen log.

April turned to run. But just then, from directly overhead, she heard a familiar crooning call. She looked up and saw Arthur perched on the roof of the garage, peering down at her. She'd been so furiously trying not to use the vine that she hadn't even noticed him coming closer. The raven held something tight in his beak. A stick? A wire? Arthur turned his head and the fading sunlight caught the object just right—a flat and zigzagging figure eight.

"Hey!" April whispered, waving her arms at him. "Put that down!"

Arthur ruffled his feathers and crooned at her again, using only his throat so that he would not drop the paper clip. The vine practically screamed at April, tempting her to tune in to the bird, to figure out what—if anything—he intended to do. She fought off the urge as best she could.

"Listen," April pleaded. "You can't follow me. Not with that thing. I'm going this way. You go that way, okay?" She began to back up as quickly as she dared. "No following."

She'd gotten thirty or forty feet away when Arthur lifted his wings and launched himself into the air, straight toward her, still carrying the paper clip. Panicked, she crouched and scooped up a handful of gravel, then hurled the stones underhand at Arthur. She didn't want to hurt him, of course, but she needed him to go away, to go anywhere but here. And for his own safety, she needed him to drop the paper clip. The bird dodged the stones acrobatically, coming to a near stop in the air. The vine brought her an unmistakable—and so unwanted—stab of astonishment and confusion, of rejection and betrayal. She understood in a flash that the paper clip was a present. A gift for her. Unwilling to drop it, Arthur veered away and flew back toward the train tracks and out over the parking lot beyond, taking the paper clip with him.

April thought her heart would break, but she told herself there was no time to feel bad. She pushed the vine's talk down again and turned and ran. Isabel and Joshua were nowhere in sight. Surely they hadn't abandoned her? She ran blindly up the drive and came out into a neighborhood of cozy little homes. A voice called to her.

"April! Here!"

April turned. Isabel was crouched down between two houses with Joshua, waving frantically. April hurried over.

"What took you so long?" Isabel demanded.

"Arthur took the decoy. He flew off with it. I—" She could not bring herself to admit that she'd had to chase him off.

"Will he be okay?" Joshua asked, his eyes wide with fear.

"He'll be fine," Isabel said. "This is good luck. The bird will draw the Mordin away and he'll—" She stopped and looked up at April sharply. "How many Mordin were there?"

"Two."

"You're sure."

"Yes. Why?"

Isabel stood. "Mordin hunt in packs of three. We need to move. Joshua?"

Joshua led the way. They walked swiftly, not quite running. He cut through the backyard and then through the playground of the neighboring Catholic school. He led them through the park, and across the nearly dry bed of Boone Creek. All the while April kept the vine silent, trying not to listen for Arthur. But every time she saw a bird bigger than a robin, she couldn't help but look twice.

"Where are we going?" April asked. Small as the town was, she didn't spend a lot of time here, and she was half lost now.

"The post office," Isabel replied curtly.

"Is that where our ride is?" April asked, tired of the half answers. "Or are we going to mail ourselves into the city?"

Isabel didn't laugh. "Our ride is waiting at the post office. She's a Keeper like us, and she'll take us where we need to go. We'll be gone before the Riven even know it."

Gone. But what about Arthur?

They walked on, Joshua in front. He never said a word, never once hesitated. He seemed totally confident in where he was going.

"I suppose you memorized the location of every post office in the country or something, huh?" April asked him after a while.

"No," Joshua replied lightly. "Just Illinois."

They passed almost directly beneath the town's water tower, then headed uphill to a manmade pond. On the far side, they crested the high, grassy bank and found themselves atop a long slope covered in sickly looking ash trees. At the bottom of the hill, April recognized Route 120, the two-lane highway that cut through town. There was the funeral home, just across the road, and a few blocks beyond that, she could see the faded flag of the post office. Joshua had gotten them there much more quickly than April would have believed.

"Isabel," Joshua said quietly, pointing, his voice a worried whisper. "Look."

April looked, and goose bumps poured down her arms. On the far side of the highway, a monstrous figure stood in the shadows of the funeral home. A Mordin—apparently Joshua *could* see the creatures truly. April was pretty sure this Mordin was the same one that had spoken to her in the woods. Not only did he seem bigger than the others, he also had an arrogant bearing that gave him a distinctive air of command.

Isabel growled low. "He thinks he can't be fooled," she muttered, as if she knew the Mordin personally. But then she gasped as another figure walked up and joined him. It was clearly one of the Riven—same pale skin, same long arms— but it was much smaller, no taller than a tallish human. This one had a distinctly feminine look, perhaps because of its long hair pulled back into a thick braid. The braid was so blond it was almost white.

Isabel grabbed April and Joshua by the arms and pulled them down onto the grass, behind the lip of the embankment. "Quiet!" she said. April was shocked to see real concern in the woman's eyes.

"What is that?" April whispered. "It's not a Mordin."

"No. Another kind of Riven—an Auditor." Isabel grimaced as if she hated to say the word. "We're in great danger."

Isabel's apprehension began to seep into April's own bones, chilling her. "Why?" she asked, as calmly as she could. "What's an Auditor?"

"The Auditor won't be afraid of me like the others are. Now be quiet. Be quiet and don't move. Don't even think of the vine—I can't risk severing you now."

Joshua burrowed up against April, interrupting her thoughts. "Did they see us?" he asked.

"No," April said firmly. "They won't find us." But inside, she felt no such confidence. Isabel had promised to protect her, and April had gone along with it—even risking the terrible misery of severing. And now, as it turned out, Isabel seemed to be saying there were things she couldn't protect them from.

"If they do find us," Isabel said grimly, "run. I will fight them. I can't promise how it'll turn out, but I'll try. Be quiet now. Let me think."

They waited. They could see nothing but the square pond just below and the bare, slender branches of ash trees stretching over the water. Tiny frogs croaked among the reeds around the pond, but April kept them shut out, refusing to add even the tiniest trickle to the vine's presence. Distantly she became aware that she could catch snippets of the Riven talking, their voices rising occasionally over the murmur of traffic. Their speech was crackling and hissing, like wet logs burning. It made April's skin crawl. And then, suddenly, she couldn't hear them anymore.

"They're gone," Joshua said, as if he too had been listening. He made as if to rise, but April grabbed his arm.

"No," she whispered, staring into the sky.

A small black shape was gliding toward them, dropping out of the twilight. Wings spread wide, it banked gracefully and then alighted on a branch out over the water. As it bobbed its head at them, April struggled not to reach for the vine.

Arthur.

He was all right. He'd found her. But he was strangely silent, and with a creep of horror April realized why—he still held the decoy in his beak. The paper clip glinted keenly against his black feathers, presumably still broadcasting a loud, false echo of the vine's wound.

Isabel saw it too, or perhaps sensed it. "Send him away!" she hissed urgently at April. "Tell him to go!"

But of course that wasn't how being an empath worked, and Isabel had to know it. The vine was a one-way street. Much as she hated to do it, April would have to scare Arthur off, just as she had before. She groped desperately through the grass for something to throw. All she found was a twig, which she flung at the bird, but Arthur only watched as her sad throw fell way short. April dug into her pocket. Dog food—no good. But there was something else there, something round and smashed flat.

The bottle cap. A gift from Arthur. She wouldn't throw

it, no, but . . . maybe she didn't have to. She looked up at the raven, at his crystal-black eyes. She looked at the shimmering water below. She looked up at the precious, shining figure eight in Arthur's beak.

It was a gift. Another gift for her.

April nodded at him. "Yes, thank you," she called out softly. "Thank you."

Arthur cocked his head. He shuffled from side to side, clearly unsure what to make of the situation.

"Thank you," April said again, making her voice as sweet as she could. This had to work. It would work. The Riven were coming.

Arthur fluffed his feathers. Through the vine, a tiny stab of happy hope. *"Henkyoo,"* he crooned at last, and as he spoke, the paper clip tumbled from his open beak, falling toward the water below.

CHAPTER TEN

The Hedge Witch

ISABEL'S DECOY FELL, GLINTING IN THE LAST RAYS OF THE SINK-ing sun. They all—even Arthur—watched the paper clip drop into the dark water of the pond with an almost inaudible *plorp!*

"Go, go!" Isabel said, shooing them forward. "They'll be here to investigate in no time."

They ran, back around the pond the way they'd come. Isabel led them over the embankment and cut left into a sub-division, parallel to the highway. Soon they were lost among the wooded backyards. Even without tapping into the vine consciously, April was aware of Arthur following them, his presence seeping up through the vine like the heat of the sun from a summer sidewalk.

After a few blocks, they crossed the highway, headed for the post office. As they crossed, April glanced back toward the pond on the hilltop and saw the massive silhouette of the tall Mordin lurking beneath the ash trees. The Auditor was at his side.

"It worked," she said aloud.

"Of course it worked," Isabel said without looking back. "He's never seen that trick before. Even better, the decoy will be dying out any moment now, but the trail your bird made with it is still there. With any luck, the Riven will follow it all the way back to the train station." She sounded so satisfied, so sure. April hoped she was right.

They walked in silence for another few minutes, Arthur keeping pace. At last the post office came into view across the street. A garishly painted van was parked out front, the only vehicle in the lot.

Isabel turned to April. She pulled April's hair forward over the tip of the vine. "Keep it hidden," she murmured. "She can't know about the wound."

April nodded, and the three of them started across the street toward the van. The driver-side window rolled down and a woman's head poked out, her hair long and grizzled. She waved, and Isabel waved back. Faintly, April could feel Arthur watching from somewhere behind, alert to her whereabouts but distracted by a plastic wrapper tumbling in the wind. That was good—no Riven in the area.

As April drew closer to the van, however, she became aware of a new presence trickling through the vine, dour and slow and distinctly unpleasant. She stopped in the middle of the road, startled. This presence was like nothing she'd ever felt before, and she sipped at it cautiously. Definitely unpleasant, and definitely . . . old. To her great surprise, it seemed to be coming from the van. But what was it?

A passing pickup truck honked, startling her, and she hurried the rest of the way across the street. When she arrived at the van, the driver leaned out and looked April and Joshua up and down. She was wrinkled, with heavily lidded eyes, and gave off a spicy, incensey smell.

"You're the ones, then, eh?" the woman said in a heavy British accent, her voice as leathery as her skin. "Not much to look at."

Joshua stepped forward and held out his hand. "I'm Joshua," he said.

The woman raised a bushy eyebrow. She nodded but didn't take the offered hand. "Ethel," she said.

"Ethel is going to take us into the city," said Isabel. "She's one of us."

Ethel started to laugh raspily. "Oh yup," she said. "One of us."

"You're Tan'ji?" Joshua asked.

"In the flesh," Ethel said, and laughed so hard she began to cough. She sounded like she was about to lose a lung. Her nose was pierced with a braided silver hoop. Was that her instrument? "Mind you," the woman continued, when she'd found her voice again, "I'm not one of your fancier types. I'm just a simple hedge witch."

Joshua stepped back and grabbed April's hand at the word

witch. She gave him a squeeze back that she hoped was comforting. "I don't believe in witches," April said.

Ethel lifted her eyes, almost sleepily. "And who are you?" she asked.

"I'm April."

"Well, April, I don't believe in love, but it's happened to me once or twice nonetheless."

April peered into the darkened van, trying to identify the source of the mysterious presence she felt through the vine. She was surprised to see a large bird skull hanging from the mirror. She was pretty sure it was from a raven. Meanwhile, the creature she felt was definitely not a bird. It was so cold, so dreary—so *slow.* "You've got an animal in there," April said. "I feel it."

Ethel's face went sharp. Her drooping eyes flew open wide as she stared accusingly at Isabel. "An empath? You didn't tell me you were bringing an empath."

"Does it matter?" Isabel said.

Ethel measured April up and down once again. "Not as long as she keeps herself to herself. She might not like what she finds, after all."

The words filled April with dread. But instead of fretting, she focused on the tug of the missing piece. Unpleasant as she was, this woman could take April where she needed to go. "I'll mind my manners," April said stiffly, unsure what that would even entail. "I just . . . we need to get to the city."

Ethel frowned suspiciously. "Tell me then, love—what's

in the city that's so important?"

"It's the boy," Isabel interjected with a sidelong glance at April. "He has . . . potential."

"I see," Ethel said, peering down at Joshua. "Looking for something, are we?"

"Yes ma'am, I think so," Joshua replied, and the answer was so immediate and earnest that it seemed to satisfy Ethel.

"Come on around, then," she said, beckoning them with a tilt of the head. "Climb in."

As they circled around the back of the van, April murmured to Isabel, "This is a person you trust?"

"I trust her when I need her," Isabel said in a whisper. "She can get us where we want to go."

April, still listening to that far-off beacon, couldn't deny the thrill those words gave her. But there was a problem. "And what about Arthur?"

"Bring him along," Isabel said, as if that were the easiest thing in the world.

April frowned inwardly. She took Isabel by the elbow and stopped her gently, trying to be patient. "You do know I can't actually *control* animals, right? I can't make them sit and stay, can't make them follow, can't make them be friends. That's not how the vine works."

"I'm aware of that," Isabel said. "But you seem to be doing fine so far."

"It might take me a minute to coax him into the van. What about the Riven?"

Isabel scowled. "I told you not to mention that," she whispered. "Ethel's jumpy about the Riven. That's why we had to come to her instead of the other way around. But don't worry—that bird skull hanging from Ethel's mirror? That's a leestone. Protection against the Riven. Not terribly strong, but you're less detectable standing beside this van right now than you have been since the start."

That was reassuring, but April still roiled with doubt. What if she couldn't get Arthur to follow? And what about the strange animal she could sense inside the vehicle?

"Everything okay?" Ethel called out.

"Fine," said Isabel, turning away.

They rounded the van, and Isabel threw open the battered sliding door. A cloud of spicy scent billowed out, cloying and unpleasant. Joshua held his nose. The van had two bench seats in the back, the cargo space beyond crammed with junk. Up front, Ethel watched them intently from the driver's seat. The passenger-side seat, meanwhile, had been completely removed. In its place was a large ornate rug that must have been colorful once but was dingy and slick now. Standing on that rug was a large tortoise, well over a foot long, its sinewy neck extended toward them.

When he spotted the staring tortoise, Joshua jumped and burrowed against April. She could hardly blame him. This was the creature she'd been feeling, of course, and it looked every bit as unpleasant as it felt. The tortoise's face was frozen in a permanent scowl of disapproval, its eyes as heavily lidded as its owner's. Something yellow and vile was oozing out of one corner of its mouth. The vine continued to bring April the same steady flow of dreariness and cold indifference, as if the creature was beyond caring about anything at all. There was some intelligence there, but otherwise the tortoise seemed as flat and as soulless as a slug. And there was something else about the tortoise, too—a quality April couldn't quite identify, much less name. Something unnatural. Something twisted and wrong.

"This is Morla," said Ethel. "She's beautiful, I know, but you'll have to resist the urge to get friendly. You're likely to get bitten." She grinned a long-toothed smile, making April wonder who exactly would be doing the biting.

"We'll try to control ourselves," April said.

"It's only you I'm warning, love," Ethel said coldly, her eyes locked on April.

April didn't reply. She nudged Joshua forward into the van. He scrambled into the backseat, as far away from Ethel and Morla as he could get. Isabel climbed in behind him.

"One minute," April said.

When Ethel frowned, Isabel explained. "We're waiting on one more passenger."

Ethel's frown deepened. "Not another child, I hope."

"Not quite." Isabel gave April a nod.

April turned, pulling her attention away from the wretched tortoise and out toward Arthur. He was scavenging happily in the parking lot. She crouched down, holding out her hand to him. To her surprise, he skipped over eagerly.

Ethel, craning her neck to watch, let out a laugh that could only be described as a cackle. "A raven," she said. "You say you don't believe in witches, but you've got yourself a familiar? And a raven at that? That's witch business, through and through."

"Is that what Morla is?" April asked, trying to keep her tone polite. "Your familiar?"

"Oh, she's more than that, love," Ethel said with disquieting glee. "She's the dearest friend I have."

Arthur, listening to their conversation, was perturbed. He didn't like the sound of Ethel's voice. Didn't trust it. Doubt and evasion. April was sure that if she got into the van and drove away with Ethel, Arthur would attempt to follow, but getting him into the van would be another matter entirely. "Quiet, please," she said. "He's still wild."

Ethel chuckled. "I can—"

"Quiet, please," April repeated calmly.

She pulled a chunk of dog food from her pocket. Arthur hopped forward alertly, hungry again. Backing into the van, April laid the food on the doorstep. Arthur looked into the open van dubiously, then chirruped at her. Asking if it was safe. Locked doors. Imprisonment. April thought back to the crate at Doc's house and understood.

"It's fine," she told him. "It's safe. Just for an hour or so, then you'll be free again."

Arthur couldn't understand the words, of course, but her

tone got through to him. Trust. Friendship. To her relief, he croaked warmly and hopped up into the van with a beat of his wings. For the first time, April felt a ripple of change in Morla's brooding consciousness as the tortoise saw the raven—a slow bubble of irritated surprise. Morla yanked her head back, still staring. Arthur, choking down his food, seemed not to even notice the tortoise.

April stepped in quietly behind him and slid the door closed, trying to be gentle. But the mechanism was awkward and unfamiliar, and the door ended up slamming shut with a painful bang. Arthur squawked and rose into the air in a panic, flapping his great wings and calling out in alarm. One of his wings smacked Joshua in the face, knocking the boy off the bench.

"Arthur!" April said, holding out a palmful of dog food. "Arthur, here. It's okay!" But the bird was too frightened and angry to listen. He was trapped again, after only a few hours of freedom. Rage. Betrayal. He careened about ever more wildly, looking for a way out, still shrieking. He thumped his still-healing wing hard against the roof and April knew that it hurt. The bird blustered over the back of the seat and got his feet tangled in Isabel's red hair. The woman cowered and cursed.

Ethel, meanwhile, was watching calmly from the front seat. "Control your bird," the woman said coolly over the din, "or I'll do it for you."

What does that mean? April wondered, but she said only,

"He'll be fine! I just startled him." But Arthur grew more and more hysterical, beating his wings madly about Isabel's head. At last he pulled loose, yanking out a tuft of red hair and bashing his way toward the back of the van. Isabel howled in pain and in the next moment—

April felt it before she saw it. Morla's presence was a dull, smooth rock in April's mind, a cool forgotten stillness all but asleep below Arthur's red-hot panic. But now, abruptly, that presence was . . . taken. It was taken the way a cloud takes the sun, a towering shadow of interference. It was an alien presence, something not-Morla, taking Morla over and . . . pressing. Crushing. Subduing. There was no pain, just a terrible pressure, and April understood—Ethel was doing this. Ethel was in the tortoise's mind, in her bones, her thoughts making a fist inside Morla's being.

Morla was Ethel's Tan'ji.

Scarcely had the horrid thought formed when something utterly new occurred. Arthur's panic still bubbled ferociously in April's brain, but now, inside that panic, a new presence began to sprout—a mind within a mind within a mind. It was Ethel, reaching out through her Tan'ji. April exhaled in shock, all her breath leaving her. This new presence was so cold. Icy calm. Numb surrender, dreamless sleep.

Arthur's panic froze into stillness like a waterfall in winter. He stopped struggling and dropped onto the backseat beside Joshua. He blinked his black eyes—oh so slowly, impossibly slow—and folded his wings to his sides. His thoughts were muddled and sluggish, moving like molasses, so slow they couldn't be anything but calm. The sensation was so powerful that April had to shake off her own drowsiness, pushing the bird's mind out of her own to avoid falling under the same spell.

She kept herself open to Morla, unable to turn away. Her heart hammered. Ever so slowly, that cruel, clenching grip inside the tortoise subsided. The looming shadow retreated, and Morla was free.

"There now," Ethel said with a smile. "All better, are we?"

April struggled to find her breath. "You're disgusting," she said. "You should be ashamed."

Isabel, who was fussing with her tangled hair, whipped around, her face a knot of anger and shock. "April!" she spat.

But Ethel only laughed her bony, rasping laugh. "So some say. But it served you well, didn't it? Got your familiar settled. Without me—without Morla—you'd have had to leave him behind."

"What did you do to him?"

"I brought him oblivion. I slowed him, made him forget. I brought him peace. That's what Morla brings—peace."

April felt terrible. Arthur was calm now, yes, and she was sickened by her own relief—because meanwhile Morla was flat and spent, like a blade of grass that has been trodden on too many times. No wonder Morla had seemed so sour, so corrosive. April's distaste for the tortoise was swept away, replaced by pity. "You don't know what you're doing to her," April said.

Ethel rose out of her seat, looming. "You think you know my Tan'ji better than I do? If you've got a mind to step between a Keeper and her instrument, love, your second step can be right out that door and back onto the streets."

April bent her head, fuming, not feeling particularly chastised but aware that continuing to argue would only jeopardize the entire trip. She burned inside, burning for Morla, but she knew she couldn't say more.

Isabel said, "April's just a neophyte. She doesn't know any better. She's still learning."

Ethel's eyes flared. "I can teach her, if I have to."

"No," April said. "I'm sorry, Keeper."

But Ethel wouldn't stop. "You and the Do-Rights, you think you know what's best. You forbid what you don't like and then embrace it when it suits you."

"To be fair," April shot back, "I don't even know who the Do-Rights are."

"You'll find out, I'm sure. The Wardens. The All-Stars. They'll be happy to snap you up. They'll be happy to teach you their rules. Isabel knows all about it. They did her wrong, didn't they? Set her plenty of rules, then used her up and tossed her out. Left her broken."

Isabel sat up straight. Her face was cloudy and livid. Green light flickered inside the wicker sphere. Holding Ethel in her icy stare, she said, "You think you know all about it, do you, Ethel?"

Ethel watched the red-haired woman silently, concern creeping over her face. No, not concern—something closer to fear. "I've heard your stories," Ethel said at last, cautiously.

"Then you'll know it was a long time ago," she said. "You'll know that things didn't work out the way the Wardens intended."

"I do know it, sister."

"Remember it. And take us where we need to go."

Ethel gave a deep nod and turned away.

With the mood in the van suddenly heavy with tension, April kept her mouth closed. She wasn't sure she liked the sound of the word *Wardens*—it made her think of prison guards. Prison, or worse. She'd left home for one reason, and one reason only—to find the missing piece. But she hadn't imagined any of the obstacles she would face. She hadn't considered the depth and scope of the world she was stepping into. She'd have to learn fast, or risk losing her way.

She took a deep breath and told herself firmly that she could do that. She could find her place among these strange people, at least for a while. The missing piece was all that mattered. She sat back in her seat, calming her anger, listening to the still sleepy tranquility of Arthur's mind. How long he would stay like this, she didn't know, but the bird seemed at ease, resting easily beside her, barely startling when the van's engine roared to life and they pulled away from the curb.

Joshua pulled a book out of Isabel's bag and began to read. Or no—not a book. A road atlas. No surprise there, April supposed. April considered getting out one of her magazines, but instead she watched Morla. The tortoise gazed back at her with lifeless eyes, her head bobbing slightly with the motion of the van. On an impulse, April pulled a piece of dog food from the bag and rolled it quietly across the floor toward her. It tumbled to a stop right between Morla's front feet. Slowly the tortoise looked down at it, blinked, and then turned away. Not a flicker of hunger or interest came through the vine. Nothing. April shuddered.

"What did I say about trying to get friendly?" Ethel said suddenly.

"Sorry," said April. She looked away and tried to push the wretched creature from her mind.

No one spoke for several minutes. April jumped when Joshua finally broke the silence. "Isabel's not broken," he announced petulantly, not even looking up from his atlas.

Isabel looked back and gave him a smile. "Thank you, Joshua. That's very kind of you to say."

Up front, Ethel scoffed and reached for the radio dial, as if intending to drown out any further attempts at conversation. "Where you're going, loves," she said as she fiddled to find a station, "you'll need much more than kindness."

CHAPTER ELEVEN

Hints and Promises

HORACE STARED AT THE LITTLE BLACK FLOWER IN MR. MEIS-
ter's hand. According to the old man, the Keeper of the Tan'ji
from which this flower had been taken was coming here.
Soon. And they had no idea whether it was friend or foe.

Chloe said, "So basically, the Tan'ji this came from might
belong to one of the Riven. One of the freaks could be out
there right now, homing in on the Warren. And leading all the
rest of them here."

"That is the worst case scenario, but quite possible," said
Mr. Meister. "On the other hand, it could be a harmless young
soul out there, just as lost and uncertain as you once were,
thick in the Find. Completely alone, perhaps. And with a crippled Tan'ji."

"But there's no way to know which it is?" asked Horace.
"Friendly human or unfriendly Riven?" He looked at Brian

for an answer, but Brian seemed lost in his own thoughts, staring at the daktan and glancing over his shoulder now and again.

Mr. Meister shook his head. "There is no way to know."

"And even if it's a human," Chloe pointed out, "that doesn't necessarily equal *friendly*."

"Just so," Mr. Meister said sadly. "We must act. Soon. The unknown Keeper is still far off, but—"

Brian held up a hand and said, "Actually . . ."

Mr. Meister looked at him sharply, then turned to the north again. The two of them stood there, Mr. Meister staring hard, Brian squeezing his eyes closed but clearly locked in concentration.

"What's happening?" Chloe demanded.

"The Keeper of the daktan is on the move now," Mr. Meister said. "Moving fast."

"How fast?"

"Vehicle fast," said Brian, opening his eyes. "Car or bus or train. Coming closer."

Horace tried not to look shocked. "But if they were only forty miles away, that means they could be here in less than hour."

"Forty miles as the crow flies," Brian clarified. "By road, it might take an hour and a half to get here, all things considered." He said this as though the extra half hour made it that much better, but Horace could see the concern in his eyes.

"So what will we do?" Horace asked.

Mr. Meister turned and leaned toward him. "That's precisely what I was hoping you would tell us, Keeper."

Horace hesitated. He looked at the old man, his soft steady gaze. Brian had the same expectant expression, and even Chloe—though she was tugging grumpily at a lock of her black hair—seemed to be waiting for him to respond.

"The lost Keeper is coming, Horace," Mr. Meister prompted softly. *"What will we do?"*

"You're asking me," Horace said, stressing the word *asking*.

Mr. Meister nodded. "I am."

Horace glanced again at Chloe. She yanked at her hair and gave him a single brusque nod. "Fine, then," Horace said. He pulled the Fel'Daera from the pouch at his side. He sensed a sudden rise in alertness from Brian, felt the boy's keen and curious eyes on him. Horace tried to brush the attention aside. Instead he let his mind settle across the box's presence, so much a part of him, so reassuring and constant. His inner clock, always accurate, told him it was 8:02.

The box could show him the future twenty-four hours in advance—one possible future, anyway, here in this place, here in this room—but only if he concentrated hard on the path he already walked. In order for the box to see tomorrow truly, Horace had to think hard about the past, present, and future— where he was, how he'd gotten there, who else was with him at the moment. The path they all walked. The miserable daktan before them, calling out like a beacon. A new Keeper, a crippled Tan'ji—friend, or foe? What path forward could embrace both of those possibilities? The box would tell him.

In chess terms, Horace knew he was more of a positional player than a tactician, more suited to considering long-term advantages instead of short-term attacks. So he thought long. And when he thought long, he kept coming back to one idea: whoever this new Keeper was, it seemed likely he or she would never stop hearing—and heeding—the daktan's call.

Cradling this thought, Horace pressed his thumb against the box's silver seam and twisted it open. The lid split and spread wide like wings. And inside, through the box's blue glass he saw—*tomorrow's workshop, sharp and clear, apparently empty; the fluorescent tube lights overhead burning like laser beams.* He bent over the table where today the tiny black flower still sat.

Gone.

Horace felt a flutter of alarm, but quickly calmed it. Someone was going to take the flower away, but it was no good leaping to conclusions. He had to keep his mind open. He turned, seeing nothing else out of place in tomorrow's workshop, and then, directly behind him—*Brian, pale and stark, looking in Horace's direction, a faint smile on his face; one finger pointed at his own black T-shirt, at the sharp white letters there:*

GO TEAM!

Horace frowned, but then, as he watched, the Brian of tomorrow turned, revealing more words on his back:

NO, SERIOUSLY, GO.
DON'T WORRY ABOUT ME.
I'LL BE FINE HERE.

Horace laughed and lowered the box thoughtfully, sliding the lid closed. He mulled over what he'd seen.

"Well?" Chloe intoned after a moment. "Care to share? You were laughing, so I'm assuming you caught Brian with his shirt off."

"That's not so much funny as it is scary," Brian said, looking down at his own ghostly arms.

"Shirt, right," Horace said. "Brian, do you have a T-shirt that says *GO TEAM!* on it?"

Mr. Meister let out a sigh. Brian said with a wry smile, "I do, but I'm told it's bad for morale."

"Okay," Horace said, "so you're alone and wearing the shirt tomorrow. That tells me everything is fine here. And the little flower—the daktan—is gone. That, and the shirt, seems to suggest that we leave, and that we take the daktan with us."

"But where do we take it?" asked Chloe.

"Out of the Warren. We need to make sure that this new Keeper, whoever it is, comes to us in a safe place. We can't put the location of the Warren in jeopardy. It has to be someplace where we can be waiting for them." Horace furrowed his brow, concentrating. "It seems obvious now that I say it." He glanced at Mr. Meister, but the old man's face was as blank as ever.

"So we set up an ambush," Brian said.

Horace shrugged. "Or a welcoming party."

Mr. Meister nodded. "Horace is right. We cannot risk revealing the location of the Warren to the Riven, but neither can we abandon a new Keeper who might be friendly to our cause. We will take the daktan to a location where we can control the manner in which the inevitable encounter will unfold."

Brian circled a pointed finger in Mr. Meister's direction. "You're doing that thing where you say what somebody else said, but way smarter. Are you trying to impress us?"

"I am merely thinking out loud. I certainly won't apologize for having an organized mind." He clapped once and rubbed his hands together. "Let us go. The sooner we get in front of this, the better. Horace, since we do not know what to expect from our visitor, I'm guessing the Fel'Daera will be of great use to us today. Chloe, I'll ask you to carry the daktan, please." He reached back without looking and plucked the tiny daktan—the little black flower—from the table. He held it out to Chloe, who took it in her hand like it was a mouse turd. Mr. Meister seemed not to notice. "Brian, if rumors move as swiftly between you and Gabriel as they usually do, I'm assuming he and Neptune already know about our potential visitor."

"Uh . . . ," Brian began nervously.

"As I thought. I will let them know what we have decided to do. Horace and Chloe, meet me in the Great Burrow in ten minutes." He spun on his heels and marched down the passageway, leaving the three young Wardens alone.

Brian watched him go with a sigh. "So I guess I'll just be here. Ready for my big wardrobe change tomorrow." He looked down at the daktan in Chloe's hand. "But the mystery guest is still coming—coming fast—and you guys are the hero types. I'll just be glad to get this thing out of here."

Grimacing, Chloe slipped the daktan cautiously into her pocket. She wiped her hand against the edge of the table as if to rid it of filth, and considered Brian for a moment. "I can't tell if you feel sorry for yourself or not."

"Constantly. And never."

"I don't feel sorry for you," she said.

"That's a lie. But thank you for it."

Chloe flinched slightly, yet had no answer. She turned to Horace and cocked her head. "Ready to go, then?"

Brian shifted uncomfortably. "Actually, if I could . . . have a second. With Horace."

Chloe's eyebrows knifed up as high as they could go. "Just Horace?"

"Just Horace," Brian said, not a hint of apology in his voice. "Man talk."

"Okay, well . . . if you're sure you guys qualify for that, I'll leave you to it." She slipped a tiny nod to Horace and turned away, slinking silently down the passage.

Brian watched her go. "Watch out for the oublimort," he called after her. "That first step's a doozy." She didn't react, and once she was out of sight Brian sighed and said casually, "I'm going to marry her."

Horace almost choked. "What?" he gasped.

"Or maybe not. I kind of just wanted to say that out loud, see how it sounded."

"It sounded creepy."

"Maybe *you're* going to marry her."

"No one is marrying anyone," Horace said firmly, feeling his cheeks burn.

Brian's eyes dropped to the box at Horace's side. "Not today, no. Or tomorrow. Did the Fel'Daera tell you that?"

Horace sighed. So that was what this was about. Brian was going to ask him about what he'd seen—about whether Brian would actually have to go through with wearing the *GO TEAM!* shirt tomorrow or not, as Horace had foreseen. "I suppose you've got questions," he said.

"Not exactly. That was the first time I've seen you use the Fel'Daera."

"And?"

"Well, first of all—totally wow. I've never seen a Tan'ji so majorly complicated, never seen the Medium used that way. It's wickedly cool. But look—we didn't need the Fel'Daera to know that taking the daktan out of here was the best plan. It was the *only* plan. And I think Mr. Meister knew it."

Reluctantly, Horace had to agree that this made sense. All the box had revealed was that the flower was gone. The rest was only logical. "Okay, but then why did he want me to use the box?"

"Meister never does anything without a reason," said Brian. "And there was really only one reason to get you to use the box just now." He shrugged and then gestured down the length of his own body with both hands.

Horace stared, still flummoxed. "You?"

"Me."

"You're saying he wanted you to see the box in action? But why?"

"Because he knows that I'll tell you things I shouldn't."

Now Horace was completely lost. He glanced back down the passageway. Chloe was nowhere to be seen.

"Look," said Brian. "Tan'ji don't come with instruction manuals, right? Instead, we go through the Find. We're supposed to figure it all out on our own."

"Right."

"Well, now that I've seen you use the Fel'Daera first-hand, I can tell you"—he paused and looked around conspiratorially—*"you haven't figured it out yet."*

Horace leaned back. A hot blossom of indignation exploded in his chest. He laid a hand on the box. "I know I'm not perfect, but I—"

"No, I mean . . ." Brian gestured at the box, flapping his hand. "Take it out, take it out."

Horace reluctantly slid the box from its pouch and held it forward. Immediately Brian thrust a finger at it, pointing at the silver spoked star on the side of the box. "Never wondered about that?"

Horace, of course, could have drawn a picture of the star in his sleep. Not just *a* star, but *the* star. The sun. Twenty-four wavy spokes—twelve long and twelve short—radiating out from a smooth, rounded circle in the center. "One ray for each hour of the day," Horace said. "The box sees one day into the future. This is like a symbol. A decoration."

Brian shook his head. "Nope, not just a decoration. It does something. It *wants* to do something, actually—that's what I saw when you had the box open. But I also saw that'd you'd never done it. As far as I can tell, no one's done it in years."

Horace's heartbeat began to rumble forward, gathering speed. He rubbed his thumb across the silver sun. Nothing happened. "But what? What does it do?"

"I don't know. Meister probably knows—he's the historian. But he's too old-fashioned to tell you."

A cold stab of something like loneliness swept through Horace, desperate and fuming. Brian had seen something about the Fel'Daera that Horace knew nothing about. Perhaps his mother had seen it too and said nothing, a deeply shameful thought. He pressed the smooth black mound in the center of the silver sun. Nothing. He tried to twist it. Still nothing.

"Not like that," Brian said. "It's telemetric."

"Telemetric?"

"You control it with your thoughts. Your mind."

Horace concentrated but felt nothing. He'd never sensed

the silver sun in any special way before, and couldn't do so now. "Tell me," he said, feeling sick and desperate.

Brian shook his head. "I can't. Besides, Meister's right that we don't want all the answers given to us. The more our hands are held while we bond with our instruments, the less our instruments belong to us. You have to do this on your own, man. I just didn't feel right saying nothing."

Which was probably exactly what Mr. Meister had counted on. Horace tried the box again, staring hard at the star. But he was too angry and full of rage to concentrate.

"Nope, nope nope," Brian said, waving his hands impatiently. "Stop it. Put it away. Take the hint home and figure it out."

"I can't!" Horace cried. "Daktan? Lost Keeper? Remember?"

"Right," Brian said, looking chagrined. "Sorry, I forgot."

"You *forgot*?"

"I'm sorry, okay? I've been down here for so long that sometimes I—" He stuck his fingers under his glasses and rubbed his eyes, then started over. "Look, nothing ever *happens* down here. Ever. All that stuff you guys do up above—it's all stories to me. And when all you get is stories for three years, it's not always easy to remember that it's real." He threw up his bony arms. "Heck, I've never even seen a Riven!"

That was a surprise. Horace took a breath and tried to calm his sizzling nerves. "You're not missing much, believe me," he mumbled.

"Oh, yeah?" Brian said angrily. "Want to trade?"

They stood there staring at each other, until at last Brian looked away. He plucked at his *VITAMIN D* shirt and scuffed one foot thoughtfully against the stone floor. Horace calmed himself, forcing himself to put the box back in its pouch. Maddening as this new mystery was, Brian was only trying to help, he knew that. And he also knew that he could not begin to fathom a life like Brian's.

"Hey," Horace said, trying to sound kind. "Can Tunraden actually be moved?"

"Yes. I can draw on the Medium to lift her. But if you're going to suggest maybe I can take her outside, get above ground for a minute—forget it. Way too risky, even for me."

Going outside was precisely what Horace was going to suggest, but he understood the reluctance. "Okay, so maybe you could just leave her here for a little while. I know it hurts a bit when we move far away from our Tan'ji, but—"

"I can't do that," Brian said.

"Maybe just for a—"

"You're not getting me. I mean I physically can't leave Tunraden behind." Brian held out his arms, exposing his wrists and the thin black bands. "These bands bind me to Tunraden. I can only get maybe two or three hundred yards away. Enough to get me up the Perilous Stairs. Enough— barely—to get me to Vithra's Eye."

"And what happens if you go farther than that?"

"Let's just say my license would be permanently revoked.

211

Tunraden generates a new pair of rings, and waits for a new Keeper."

"But would you be okay?"

Brian just looked at him, flat and unblinking. "Being the Keeper of a Loomdaughter is serious business, Horace. *Seriously* serious."

Horace eyed the bands with a new understanding. They looked painfully tight, almost melded into Brian's skin. He said quietly, "I thought you said you weren't a prisoner."

Brian rubbed the ring around one wrist with the opposite hand. He glanced down at the Fel'Daera. "We're all prisoners, man. Some of us just have the luxury of pretending we're not."

CHAPTER TWELVE

Sent

WHEN HORACE GOT BACK TO THE OUBLIMORT, HE WAS RELIEVED to see Chloe had already made it across. He found her on the far side, standing at the bottom of the stairs with her chin held high, her dark hair ruffling slightly in the wind that rose up from the Maw. "First try, in case you two were wondering," she said, her voice lifting on the breeze.

"We weren't, but good. I'm glad."

"So what was that all about?"

Horace wasn't sure what to say, part of him still thinking about Brian and his long confinement underground, part of him still probing discontently at the Fel'Daera's mysterious silver sun. "We were just . . . talking."

"You guys besties now?"

"I like him. You do too."

Chloe frowned. Side by side they started back up the

Perilous Stairs, Horace still holding the Fel'Daera in his hands.

"He's kind of annoying," Chloe said.

"He's smart," Horace pointed out. "You like smart."

"I do like smart, but I'm not sure he qualifies. He's not smart enough to stop Mr. Meister from imprisoning him down here."

Now it was Horace's turn to frown. "You should probably cut him some slack on that."

"Why?"

"Just trust me."

"You say that a lot."

"Yes, and you keep doing it."

Chloe sighed. After a few moments she elbowed him gently. "See, Horace, *you're* smart."

They climbed on. Horace ran his thumb in circles around the silver sun. A single thought kept burning at him like a nest of angry bees in his stomach, getting buzzier—Brian knew something about the Fel'Daera that he didn't. And Mr. Meister too. It made him want to retch. He flicked the box open and closed, open and closed, watching his own feet disappear on tomorrow's stairs. Gradually he became aware that Chloe's eyes were on him. He started to put the box back into its pouch but couldn't quite bring himself to let it go.

"I'm feeling . . . antsy," he said before she could ask. He gripped the box hard and shook it. "Actually, you know what? I feel like I'm going to explode."

Chloe came to a dead stop on the stairs. "What's going on?"

Horace closed his eyes and probed at the box, trying to think of it as a machine—an assemblage of parts. For a moment, he imagined he could feel the silver sun, but then it slipped away. He clenched his teeth and looked over at Chloe. "Brian told me something."

"Right, I know. Man talk."

"No, I mean he told me something about the Fel'Daera." Feeling weirdly ashamed—almost as if the box had betrayed him, he realized—he told her what Brian had revealed, and what he had not.

Chloe listened carefully and considered it. She kicked a cluster of loose pebbles over the edge and watched them disappear into the gloom below. "So there's something new to learn. Don't freak out. That's *good* news. We learn new stuff about our Tan'ji all the time. Look at me—I've been Tan'ji for seven years and I only recently learned how to go underground."

"But that's because you were *afraid* to do it," Horace pointed out, making Chloe scowl. "This is something totally new—something I never even imagined."

"Okay, so, you'll just have to figure it out."

"When? I don't have time."

"That's ironic."

"Very funny," Horace said. He kicked his own shower of grit out into the Maw. "What I mean is, I'm not going to be able to stop thinking about it until I figure it out. And I can't figure it out here—not with all this going on, with that thing in your pocket. Not with us heading off to set our trap. Or our rescue, or whatever it is."

Chloe turned and started climbing again. "So don't go. Stay here and figure it out."

"How can I not go?" Horace said, following after her. "You heard Mr. Meister—*the Fel'Daera will be of great use to us today.*"

"You're not Brian. You don't have to do what Mr. Meister tells you."

"Easy for you to say. You do whatever you want."

"Well, maybe you should too." When Horace grunted skeptically, she threw up her hands. "Look, I don't know what to tell you. Just be Horace. Be the Keeper of the Fel'Daera. That's who you are, and nobody can change that."

Horace lapsed into silence. How could he be the Keeper of the Fel'Daera when others knew something about it that he didn't? They climbed the rest of the way without speaking. When they got to the top, Chloe kept moving, heading for Mr. Meister's doba.

They found the old man inside, sitting at his desk. As they entered, he was peering at a large roll of parchment. A chart or a map of some kind, it looked like. Around it lay the usual assortment of Tanu, both familiar and strange—the massive book with pages a half inch thick, the golden dial with a red needle centered on Mr. Meister; a delicate silver filigree crown; a life-sized, paper-thin oak leaf that appeared

216

to be made of wood. Neptune was here, too, floating easily ten feet off the ground with her cloak wrapped around herself as if she were cold. She waved down at them. With her Tan'ji, a small stone called a tourminda, she could escape the force of gravity—not to fly, as she liked to point out, but to float.

Higher still, the pocketed red wall of the place curved into a high dome. Every inch of the wall was covered with shelves and nooks and cubbies, containing all manner of wonders. Horace spotted the little cyclops owl with the gleaming yellow eye, and the heavy chest that held the burned-out crucible. There were bird-related things everywhere, including some actual living birds. And then he caught his breath. The Laithe of Teneves sat high on a shelf behind the desk. The little globe spun slowly, blue and white and brown and unmistakably alive. Horace gazed at it, feeling woozy. The same hands that made this had made the Fel'Daera.

"Are we all right?" Mr. Meister said.

"Super," said Chloe. She nudged Horace.

Horace pulled his eyes away from the Laithe. Now that Horace knew Brian had made Mr. Meister's red vest, he recognized it as Tan'ji, but it was a strange kind of recognition, like a faint reflection on the surface of rippling water. Once again he wondered how it was possible to have two Tan'ji at once. He watched Mr. Meister roll up the parchment and noticed his Möbius-strip ring. Was that yet another Tan'ji? Somehow the very question—maybe being reminded of everything that had been kept from him, and all the things he still didn't know—made Horace's outrage flare up again. The silver sun. Sil'falo Teneves. His mother.

"I was just talking to Neptune," Mr. Meister said, "and she thinks she knows of a place where we can—"

"I can't do that right now," Horace said.

Mr. Meister blinked. A little black bird flitted by overhead, from one compartment to another. "Is that so?"

"Yes. I need you to tell me about the silver sun."

Mr. Meister's thoughtful gaze lit across the box, then back up to Horace's face. He took a deep breath. "No."

Neptune drifted slowly to the floor, her wide, innocent eyes stretching even wider. "You'll want some privacy, of course," she said, nodding her way out of the room. She and Chloe murmured terse, polite good-byes to each other. Chloe apparently had no intention of leaving.

"I need to know," Horace demanded. "Brian already told me the silver sun does something."

"Did he?"

"Yes. You knew he would. You wanted me to open the box in front of him."

"I made no mention of the box."

Horace couldn't remember if that was true or not, but the old man's flat, reasonable tone aggravated him even further. "I wish you wouldn't pretend. You wanted Brian to see me use the box."

Mr. Meister spread his hands, conceding the point. "I admit I thought it would be informative, yes."

"So that he would tell me I've been using the box wrong."

Mr. Meister leaned forward abruptly, bushy eyebrows working hard. "You are a brilliant Keeper, a prodigy. You have astonished us all. Never once have I said or thought you were using the box in the wrong way." He held Horace's gaze steadily.

"But?"

Mr. Meister sat back in his seat, tugging at his red vest. He fiddled with the Möbius-strip ring on his finger. "But," he said at last, "if you are asking me if untapped potential still remains within the Fel'Daera, the answer is yes." He spread his hands wide. "A month ago we sat in this very room and I practically told you as much."

"And what is that untapped potential?"

"I cannot tell you that."

"Cannot?"

"Will not."

Horace began pacing, fuming inside. He felt like he was in the Find all over again, sick and lost and desperate for answers. The Fel'Daera buzzed in his hand, as if sensing his frustration. He glanced up at the Laithe of Teneves, and for a moment almost spilled everything he knew about his mother. But no. Not now. He kept his anger in focus. "You have all these rules about not teaching us how our instruments work. About letting us figure it out on our own. But you break those rules all the time, whenever it suits you."

"For example?"

219

"For example, you told me how the very act of opening the box changes the future I see. You told me all that stuff about free will. Why did you tell me that? Why didn't you let me find that out for myself?"

"I confess I have walked a thin line. But those were refinements of ideas you had already begun to explore yourself. It was you who figured out that the box could send objects into the future. It was you who realized the box allowed you to actually witness the future firsthand."

"But you gave me help even before that. The very first day I found the Fel'Daera—remember? You told me I can't keep anything inside the box. You told me not to open the box without reason."

"Mere hints whose true meanings you had to come to on your own. They were distant beacons, not explicit instructions."

"What's the difference?"

"You think I am toying with you. I assure you I am not."

"I think you don't even know what your own rules are."

Mr. Meister clenched his jaw. "I freely admit that sometimes I do not. But once again, Keeper, you have fallen victim to your own tendency to underestimate both me *and* the dangers we face. Yes, every Keeper should navigate his own path through the Find. Yes, I took risks with the hints I gave you the day you claimed the Fel'Daera—hazy though those hints were. Yes, every time I talk to you about the function of the box, I risk tainting the bond." His voice grew stern, and one of his bony hands balled into a trembling fist. "But the times are desperate, and as you say, the caution is mine to exercise or ignore as I see fit."

"Why? Because you're the Chief Taxonomer?"

Mr. Meister looked startled. For a moment Horace could almost have sworn that a flicker of sadness swept across the old man's face. "If you like, yes," Mr. Meister said. "What I say and do weighs heavy on you all."

Chloe spoke for the first time. Horace had almost forgotten she was even there. "A month ago—in this very room—you told us you weren't the chief of anything."

"Titles are irrelevant. Only our abilities matter. But because of my abilities, my word carries weight—with you, Chloe, and with Gabriel, with Neptune. With all the Tan'ji gathered in this place. And particularly with you, Horace. I cannot allow my word to fall too heavily, to influence you too much. You must trust me on this."

"Why particularly with me?"

"Because as others influence you, so in turn do you influence the Fel'Daera. And this can lead to disaster, because what the Fel'Daera reveals affects us all. Have you forgotten the message you left in your toolshed, the night of the fire? How Chloe's determination to leave compelled you to see a future in which you felt safe allowing her to do so?"

Just being reminded of that mistake, a mistake that had almost cost Chloe her life, made Horace's anger flare higher. "So you won't tell me about the silver sun."

"I will not."

"Then I need time to figure it out—on my own, apparently."

"We do not have time. The Keeper of the crippled Tan'ji approaches even as we speak, drawn by the daktan. We do not know what to expect. We need the Fel'Daera's help. Your help."

"I can't help you right now. I can't even think straight. Maybe you should have thought of that before you got Brian to tell me how little I actually know about my own Tan'ji."

"Apparently I should have. And had I known you would pout like a child when you discovered you still had more to learn, I never would have opened that door. Your pride does you no credit, Keeper."

That was more than Horace could take. Horace whirled to face Chloe. He thrust out his hand. "The daktan. Give it to me."

Chloe's eyes narrowed curiously, but she dug out the little flower without a word, dropping it into Horace's hand. It felt clammy, slightly electric—revolting and dismal. He spun back to Mr. Meister's desk and laid down the Fel'Daera, twisting the lid open with his free hand.

"What are you doing?" the old man said, his great left eye shining behind the oraculum.

Horace dropped the daktan into the open box. It clattered tinnily against the blue bottom. "You say the Keeper of the daktan is on his way here. You say he's following the call of

222

this missing piece. Well, I can fix that."

"Horace—" Chloe began, but he cut her off.

"Everyone wants me to be the Keeper of the Fel'Daera. Fine. That's what I'm being."

He looked Mr. Meister straight in the eye, and then he flicked the box closed. He felt a shivery tingle roll through his hands, and it was done. The daktan was gone. It would be nowhere on this earth until it reappeared in this exact location in twenty-four hours. Let the lost Keeper try to track it down now.

The old man took off his glasses and squinted at Horace, as if barely recognizing him. He opened his mouth, but no words came out.

Horace shrugged. He picked up the now-empty Fel'Daera and slid it into its pouch. "I told you," he said. "I need more time."

PART THREE

Little Bo Peep

CHAPTER THIRTEEN

Adrift

APRIL BOLTED UPRIGHT IN THE SPEEDING VAN, HER BREATH seizing in her chest. She swayed, disoriented—as if the only star in a moonless sky had winked out, leaving her dark and directionless.

The missing piece was gone.

For a moment, she couldn't even remember what that meant. A numb spot burned in her mind, and the snipped memory struggled to re-form. April tried to remain calm, reaching out through the vine, her thoughts spilling out of the broken stem, but she still couldn't sense anything, finding only cold silence where before there had been a warm summons.

The missing piece. Gone.

"Stop," she said weakly.

Ethel, bent over the steering wheel, gave no sign that

she'd heard. Arthur stirred, but seemed untroubled. But Isabel turned around to look. "What's wrong?" she said. She studied the air all around April's head, and her curious face wrinkled into consternation. "Why are you doing that?"

April pushed out harder through the vine, desperate to find the signal again. She unbuckled her seat belt and stood up. "Stop," April muttered again, and then again, louder: "I said *stop*!"

Morla lifted her bony head, a small blip of interest crossing through her sluggish misery. Ethel, meanwhile, glanced back in the rearview mirror but didn't slow.

Isabel lifted a hand to Ethel and said softly, "The girl told you to stop."

Though they were on the expressway, Ethel hit the brakes at once and swung smoothly onto the shoulder. April grasped the seat to keep from toppling over. Joshua, who had been snoozing fitfully, woke with a sleepy, "Are we there?"

They rolled to a halt along the guardrail. Cars continued to whiz by on the left, rocking the van where it stood. Ethel turned and glared at the three of them suspiciously. April ignored her, pulling her hair back, not caring that she was exposing the vine's wound.

Ethel caught sight of it and inhaled sharply. "This is no shopping trip for the boy, is it?" she said.

April pressed her fingers hard against the vine. The missing piece—what had happened to it? Had it been destroyed? "It's gone," she told Isabel. "I can't feel it."

"You just lost it for a moment," Isabel said, but her face was wrinkled with worry.

"No. It's just . . . gone."

"They know," Ethel said abruptly. Her squinty eyes were locked on to the vine's broken stem. "They've got your dak-tan and they know you're coming."

April skipped right over the unfamiliar word, understanding Ethel at once. "The Wardens, you mean," she said, not bothering to pretend anymore.

"The Do-Rights, yes."

Isabel rounded on Ethel. "Hush!" she said sharply.

But Ethel paid her no mind. "They don't want to be found. They've destroyed what you need. It's too late for you now."

"Quiet!" Isabel bellowed, rising to her feet. "You don't know *anything*." Morla cowered into her shell, her wretched presence shriveling into an icy tremble.

And then, abruptly, Morla was gone. Arthur was gone. The vine itself vanished from April's mind. A single look at Ethel's stunned face confirmed that she too had lost contact with her Tan'ji.

Isabel had severed them all.

Isabel yanked the van door open, letting in the sounds of roaring traffic and the smells of exhaust. "Out," she commanded, staring down at April. Arthur was out the door before April could even react, his wings blurring past April's face. *Gone.* She tried to make herself stand, to make herself leave.

But it was as if she'd forgotten even how to stand. *Gone.* And then she felt a small hand in hers, pulling her forward. "Come on," said a voice, simple and sweet.

She stumbled out into open air. She lost her balance, lost the small hand she was holding. Sharp pain flashed through her knees. And then suddenly, miraculously, she was warm again. The vine opened once more in her thoughts. She could breathe. She reached out through it, felt Arthur down over the edge of the highway, on a grassy slope whose low murmur she could also sense—but still she could not feel the missing piece.

"You can go now," someone said imperiously, and she looked up to see Isabel looming overhead. But the woman wasn't talking to April—she was talking to Ethel. April locked eyes with the driver and knew that the mixture of dismay and confusion and relief she saw on Ethel's face must be echoed on her own.

Morla, meanwhile, had entirely disappeared into her shell, and from her April felt a painful waking from a deathlike sleep, a torturous unlimbering from the void. Ethel was in the tortoise's mind again, rousing her and testing the bond after the brief severing, as if Morla were a great rusted machine whose parts could be hammered senselessly into motion. And April realized that that's what Morla was—a machine. A machine with an animal's soul beaten thin and trapped alive inside. She wondered how old Morla really was, and whether she would ever—*could* ever—die. Maybe death would be a relief.

April threw up, still on her knees there on the shoulder. Her stomach emptied itself in two convulsive heaves. It was all too much, all of it, everything that was happening—too sad, too sick, too hopeless. Joshua backed squeamishly away. Isabel seemed not to notice, still facing the van.

"Go," Isabel said again.

"Ask her to tell you the truth, love!" Ethel called out. "Ask old Isabel what she really is. She's no Keeper."

April wiped her mouth and looked back at Ethel. "What?"

"Go *now*," Isabel said, taking a step toward the van.

"She says she's Tan'ji, but she's not one of us!" cried Ethel. "And she never will be!"

Isabel took another step forward. And now, on the fringes of Morla's mind, April felt a new presence, thunderous, coming down hard along the line of thought that burned between Ethel and the tortoise. This new presence began to push—so heavy, so sharp—and Morla made a sound that April heard through the vine, a sound of bone-deep anguish, the sound a person might make while being torn in two.

Suddenly the van roared to life and sprinted away, the door still open. Bits of gravel kicked up, spraying them. Horns blared. Tires screeched. Within seconds the van's taillights were distant swerving dots in traffic. Ethel and Morla had escaped whatever Isabel had been doing to them.

Isabel bent over April, fists on her hips. The wicker sphere dangled above April's head. "Don't listen to Ethel. She lies."

"I felt you inside Morla," April said. "You were tearing

231

them apart. Not just severing—more than that."

"Severing's too good for her," Isabel said, but explained no more. "Come on. Let's get off the road."

April got to her feet, avoiding the pool of sick there on the shoulder. As she bent to wipe bits of grit from her bloodied knees, she saw Joshua was holding her backpack. She took it from him gratefully.

"You okay?" he said.

"Not really. But I'm not going to barf again, if that's what you mean."

Joshua made a face but reached out and placed his hand on April's arm in a comradely sort of way. "I barfed once," he said earnestly, and the gesture broke April's weary heart just a little.

They climbed over the guardrail and down the grassy slope. The sun was fully below the horizon now, but barely—a peachy glow still crouched low across the sky. April veered away from Isabel, heading instead for Arthur, who sat all but invisible in the darkening grass. She opened herself to the bird, wanting to cleanse herself of Morla's wretched presence.

Arthur was still calm after what Ethel had done to him—tamer than April had ever felt him—but his playful curiosity was beginning to surface again. She walked up to him and sat in the grass a few feet away. He hopped right over and plucked at the hem of her dress. When she held out a piece of dog food for him, he snatched it out of her hand.

Joshua came and joined them, sitting a respectful distance

away. Isabel followed behind but didn't sit. Behind her, back up the slope, the interstate traffic continued to thunder by.

April had no idea what to say to the woman, no idea what to even think. The missing piece was gone. Everything they'd done was all for nothing. There was no hope in the world anymore. The trip had been nothing but uncertainty and fear and danger, and now . . . what was she supposed to do? Go back home? She could barely even muster up the idea of a future.

Joshua scooted closer, his eyes wide and hopeful. "Can I feed Arthur?" he said.

April managed to smile. "Go ahead. He likes you."

Joshua took some food tentatively. Arthur saw the exchange and hopped toward the boy expectantly. When Joshua just sat there, Arthur let out a low, rattling warble that April thought of as his purr. Joshua startled and hurriedly tossed the food. Arthur caught it out of the air nimbly and squawked in gratitude, rustling his wings. Joshua's face lit up with wonder.

Isabel, however, did not seem impressed. "Where are we, Joshua?" she said impatiently.

"Northbrook," the boy said at once, still watching Arthur.

"How far to downtown?"

"Eighteen miles, in a straight line."

"As the crow flies," April told him. "That means in a straight line—it's a saying."

"Eighteen miles as the crow flies," he said. "Or maybe the raven."

Isabel sighed. "But we won't be able to walk in a straight line. It'd take us all night to walk that far, and it's already quarter til nine."

April stood up. "I'm not walking anywhere except home."

"Home?" Isabel said incredulously. "No, no, you can't go home."

"Yes. I never should have come in the first place. But I did, and whoever had my missing piece knew it, and they destroyed it. It's gone." She keep her voice even, but her insides were burning wreckage, a world on fire.

"It's not destroyed—if it was destroyed, you'd have felt it." Isabel clutched at April's shoulder, almost pleading. "*I'd* have felt it."

"Ethel said it was destroyed."

"I told you—don't listen to her."

"She also said you're not Tan'ji. I don't understand why she would say that, unless it's true. And if you're not, you can't help me. Or Joshua. Can you?"

"She lies. People lie."

April thought quietly for a moment, struggling to keep her head above the smoke. She was not much of a liar herself—not because she was so opposed to lying, necessarily, but because she was terrible at it. And because she was terrible at it, she often had trouble telling when other people were lying. But the more time she spent with Isabel—the more the woman kept hidden, the more she let slip, the more severing she did with that wicker sphere of hers—the harder it was to trust her.

"I think *you* lie," April said firmly.

April half expected Isabel to sever her then and there, given what she'd seen of the woman's temper so far. Instead, though, Isabel seemed to sag. Her face filled with sorrow. "This is no place to talk. Let's find someplace quiet, someplace private. Let me explain."

"I'm trying to imagine what you could possibly explain that would keep me out here—miles from home, without permission—when the missing piece is . . ."

"It's not destroyed, April. I'm almost sure of it."

"But it's nowhere. If it's not destroyed, what is it?"

"Severed."

April hesitated. She found herself wanting to cling to the idea. She probed at that numb corner of her mind—not so much a corner as a kind of blind spot, shifting and swallowing her thoughts whenever she reached out for the missing piece. "Is that even possible? To sever just the missing piece?"

"There are ways it could be done, yes."

"Could you do it?"

"Yes."

"Then could you undo it?"

Isabel shook her head. "Not from here. From the other end . . . maybe. It depends what's happening there. But the severing won't last. If we just keep moving, the call will return, I promise—"

"You lied about being Tan'ji, didn't you?" April interrupted.

Isabel glanced at Joshua. He was pulling up tufts of grass and tossing them into the air while Arthur watched, but it was clear the boy was listening to every word.

April said, "You're asking for so much trust from us. You've already lied to us. We need to know the truth now, or we're leaving. I'll take Joshua with me."

A pack of loud, rumbling motorcycles passed by on the highway above, filling the air with jackhammers and rattling April's chest. Isabel let them pass, sputtering into the distance, before answering.

"I told you I'm a Tuner. What I didn't tell you is that being a Tuner is . . . not a very respected profession. Tuners use Tanu called harps to clean and tune other people's instruments. They get treated like maids, like garbage men. They are expendable. Even their harps are borrowed instead of owned." She held up the wicker sphere, gritting her teeth. "But my harp is different. Miradel is more powerful than other harps, and I'm more powerful than other Tuners. With Miradel, I am . . . I am *like* Tan'ji. I have the bond. Just like you." She let Miradel dangle again and twisted her wooden ring restlessly, clearly waiting for April to respond.

"I don't understand how you can be *like* Tan'ji," said April.

"Miradel only works for me," Isabel insisted. "I'm the only one who can use her—the only one who can control her."

April nodded, choosing her words carefully. "But do you have the same bond with Miradel that I do with the vine? Like, for example . . . can you be severed?"

236

Isabel turned away, which was all the answer April needed. "No one else can do what I can," Isabel said stubbornly.

"But you're not Tan'ji."

"Not . . . completely. No." She briefly made fists, then unclenched them. "I never had the chance."

Joshua stood up. He walked stiffly over to April and put his arms around her, hugging her tight. Surprised, April patted his back awkwardly. Still holding her tight, Joshua looked over at Isabel and said, "You lied to me."

"It's not that simple, Joshua."

"Yes it is," he said.

"I can still help you," said Isabel. "I can still take you to your Tan'ji."

Joshua shook his head. "Maybe there is no Tan'ji."

A cop car sped by on the highway above. As it passed, April thought she saw the brake lights flare. "We should go," she said.

Isabel nodded. "Yes. Someplace quiet to spend the night. Someplace we can all rest and talk. Somewhere I can *explain*."

April glanced down at Joshua and frowned. Would they be safe on their own? Could she keep *him* safe? April shook her head then looked up at Isabel.

"Okay, but what about the Riven?"

"We've left them far behind," said Isabel. "Plus, the lee-stone's effects will linger with us for a while. As long as you don't push the vine too hard, it'll be hours before they even have a hope of tracking us down—maybe a full day."

That was a relief. "So where should we go?" April looked down the road, where a hotel sign rose high into the sky. But she was pretty sure Isabel didn't do hotels.

"I know a place," Joshua said, peering up at April. "It's not far."

Holding April's hand, Joshua led them a half mile down the frontage road to a highway that crossed back under the interstate. On the far side of the expressway, a large patch of darkness lay before them, stretching for what looked like a mile in either direction, with just the one road cutting through.

"What is this place?" April asked, startled to see such wilderness this close to the city.

"Lagoons," Joshua said. "The Skokie Lagoons. Lots of trees. Islands. Places we can spend the night."

He led them on into the darkness, searching, then seemed to get his bearings when he found a paved bike path that led along the edge of the woods. But instead of following the path, he cut straight through the trees. Before long, April could hear the sound of falling water. They emerged onto the shoreline of a murky-looking lake. Water rushed over a low dam, really more of a spillway—only about a couple of feet high. As they stood looking at it, Arthur alighted in a tree just overhead. April could feel how happy the woods made him, how at home he felt.

Joshua pointed at the tiny dam. "If we cross here, we can get to that island on the other side before it gets totally dark. No one will find us there."

The dam was less than a foot wide and probably a hundred feet long. Water ran smoothly over the top of it.

To April's surprise, Isabel was already slipping off her shoes. "Perfect," the woman said. "Thank you, Joshua." And then she stepped out onto the spillway.

April watched in astonishment as Isabel easily navigated the slippery stone path, the water parting around her feet with each step. She never once lost her balance. When she reached the far side, dim in the wooded twilight, she waved her hands and shouted, "Come on across! If an old lady can do it, so can you."

April and Joshua went next, Joshua in front. The water was shockingly cool. Joshua moved slowly, as if he were on a tightrope across Niagara Falls. He stopped several times, hesitating, but each time April said calmly, "All you'll get is wet," and then he started up again. April herself almost stumbled once, when she caught a whiff of a turtle drifting in the water nearby and thought of Morla. But this turtle was wild and alive and undeniably himself. April regained her balance and eventually—after what seemed like an eternity—she and Joshua made it to the far side. Seconds later, despite his confusion, Arthur joined them.

The island itself was overgrown and as wild as anything around April's house. There were footpaths, unmarked and clearly little used. They found a clearing and set up camp there. Unsurprisingly, the mosquitoes were terrible, and everyone wanted to use April's bug spray. April was slightly conflicted about the bug spray, since she could feel it every time the hungry drone of a mosquito turned to poisonous revulsion. But not only was it better than getting eaten, the bug spray also kept Isabel from swatting the mosquitoes to death against against her flesh. Bugs might be small, their minds meager, but for April, feeling even a tiny life snuff out inside her brain was like a miniature implosion of pain and blindness.

April broke out the beef jerky, which Joshua and Arthur both loved. As for April, she ate one apple and twenty-two potato chips, determined to ration things in a sensible way. Isabel, meanwhile, ate nothing.

They spoke little, until at last they settled into their blankets, staring up at the darkening sky overhead. Arthur, who had been daringly social all evening—even with Isabel— retreated into the shadows just above. April tuned herself to him until she felt him drift toward his version of sleep, a strange sensation she'd picked up before—half his brain faded into oblivion, while the other remained semi-alert. She envied it, and wished she could embrace it fully. But she couldn't even try, not with the vine the way it was. Isabel had said she was *not completely* Tan'ji, a notion that seemed ridiculous. But as she lay there rubbing her thumb across the broken stem of the vine, April had to wonder if she herself wasn't completely Tan'ji either.

Joshua stirred sleepily. "April?"

"Yeah?"

"How does Arthur sleep? In a tree, right?"

"Yes. He's right above us."

"Did he make a nest?"

"No. Nests are just for eggs, really. Arthur roosts on a branch."

"Really? But how—" Joshua paused and yawned prodigiously. "How does he stay on? How come he doesn't fall off when he goes to sleep?"

April laughed, glad for the distraction. She'd asked Doc Durbin this same question the first night Arthur was in the pen. "Ravens are what's called *passerine*. Most birds are passerines—especially songbirds, or really any bird you'd see at a birdfeeder. Passerines have special feet. They have three toes pointing forward, and one toe pointing back." She looked down at her own feet, almost feeling the illusion of Arthur's feet inside them even now—his feet, when relaxed, naturally curled shut. He had to consciously flex them to open them.

"Passerine feet are very good for gripping branches. So good, in fact, that their feet stay gripped to the branch even while they're asleep."

"Ohhh," Joshua said, but April could tell he was already mostly asleep himself. A moment later he began to gently snore.

"Passerine, eh?" Isabel remarked, watching April keenly. "You know a lot about animals."

April shrugged. "I like animals, that's all."

"Like I said, all Keepers have a natural talent to begin

241

with. And now here you are, an empath."

April watched Joshua sleep. "And what about Joshua? Do you really think he's going to become Tan'ji?"

"I said so, didn't I?"

"You say a lot of things. But what would his Tan'ji be?"

"I wouldn't want to guess," Isabel said quickly. "That's why he's been traveling with me. I thought maybe he'd be drawn to what he's looking for if he got close enough. We were headed into the city to see how we fared, but then I sensed you bleeding. We were lucky to find you. Very lucky."

That seemed like a curious thing to say. April sat up and studied the woman. "We're looking for the Wardens, right?" she asked. "The ones Ethel was talking about? I'd like to know who they are."

Isabel sighed. "They're Keepers, like us," she said, and then winced. She clutched at Miradel. "The Wardens collect Tanu of all shapes and sizes—everything they can get their hands on. They have huge hoards of Tan'ji."

"That's why you think they had my missing piece."

"*Have*," Isabel corrected. "I think they *have* your missing piece, yes."

April couldn't even respond to that. "And you think they have Joshua's Tan'ji, too?"

"I think there's no better place to look. That's all I'll say."

"You were one of them once, weren't you? Ethel said they kicked you out."

Isabel scowled. "Ethel lies. She doesn't know. She wasn't there."

April couldn't help but feel that even though Isabel might be telling the truth now, she was leaving plenty of space for lies. April sat very still, trying to piece together everything Isabel had said that morning, everything Ethel had hinted at in the van. Abruptly, comprehension dawned over her. "Oh my god," she said, and then said it again. "Oh my god—you're just using us."

"What are you talking about?"

"No, please don't do that," April said, still thinking it through. "Don't pretend. You're trying to find the Wardens, but because you don't know where they are, you need us. First Joshua, hoping you'd get him close enough to his Tan'ji that he'd feel it, leading you to the Wardens. Sort of a desperate plan, I think. But then you came across me. With the missing piece I'm like . . . your guided missile. A homing device."

Isabel squirmed, and April knew she wasn't wrong. "I'm not using you," Isabel protested. "We're helping each other. All of us."

"But why do you even need our help finding the Wardens? If you were one of them—"

"I worked with them," Isabel interjected. "I was never one of them."

"Either way, why don't you know where they are now?"

April could hear Isabel grinding her teeth. "When the Wardens don't want to be found, they can't be found," she said.

April leaned forward. "And why are you so desperate to find them?"

Isabel was silent for a long time. As April watched, the wicker ball swelled slightly and then shrank again. Over and over it grew and shrank slowly, like a beating heart. Isabel didn't even seem to be aware it was happening. Watching her face, April became sure that the woman was going to evade April's question now—or at least, that she was going to twist the truth. April promised herself that her decision about whether to stay with Isabel or not would hinge on whatever the woman said next.

At last the wicker ball stopped pulsing.

"I need to get back," Isabel said slowly. "Something happened that I . . . that I'm not proud of. I want things to be set right." Her eyes were faraway and cloudy, and April was sure that those words—whatever they meant—were the truth. But then Isabel shook herself and glared at April. "It doesn't matter. I'm helping you get where you want to go. I've saved you twice already."

"You've severed me twice, too."

Isabel stared back, unflinching. "It could be worse."

"I'm sure it could. And I could walk away. Good luck finding the Wardens then."

"Good luck becoming whole. Good luck with the Riven."

They stared at each other for a long moment. April kept her fear shoved down deep. If Isabel wouldn't flinch, neither would she. She would be brave. But the truth was, Isabel was the best chance she had at finding the missing piece, if it still existed. And as for the Riven . . .

244

"I'm going to sleep now," April announced. "In the morning, I'll decide whether to go back home or not."

"You can't go home, and you know it." Before April could protest, Isabel pointed to the vine against April's skin. "You don't have a choice. Tan'ji don't have a choice. You'll keep searching for the missing piece forever." She lay back on her blanket and rolled onto her side, her back to April.

April sat there, watching the woman breathe, trying to convince herself that Isabel was wrong. But of course, she wasn't wrong. Somewhere far off, an owl's call sounded, first loud and then soft. The change in volume was an illusion to fool prey, April knew. The owl was only pretending to move away. The thought made her remember Isabel's words: *"When the Wardens don't want to be found, they can't be found."*

April had asked her why she wanted to find the Wardens so badly. But maybe she should have asked a different question.

Why didn't the Wardens want Isabel to find *them?*

April couldn't quite make herself ask it out loud. Instead she said quietly, "What did the Wardens do to you?"

Isabel shrugged. She wrapped her arms around herself. The owl called again, softer still. "They made me who I am," Isabel said simply. "That's what they do."

CHAPTER FOURTEEN

Closer

"I'm telling you," Chloe said, for like the seventh time, "that was brilliant."

Horace forced a smile. They stood in his driveway, where Beck had dropped them off after leaving the Warren. It was 9:30, long past dinnertime, but food could not have been further from Horace's mind. A part of him swelled proudly with the notion that sending the daktan through the box had been clever. Inspired, even. The Keeper of the Tan'ji from which the little black flower had been taken could not possibly track the daktan down now. Not while it was traveling. The Keeper would be utterly lost, and—for the time being, at least—the Wardens were safe. And it was all thanks to Horace.

Or was it?

"Brilliant," Horace repeated. "Right." Without Mr. Meister's trickery and Brian's gossip, would he even have stumbled across the mystery of the silver sun? Would he have thought to send the daktan? For all he knew, sending the daktan was precisely what Mr. Meister had hoped he would do. "My Tan'ji has a power I know nothing about. That's how brilliant I am."

"Doesn't matter," Chloe said. "You're the Keeper of, like, the most wicked Tan'ji ever. And I'd bet anything it's about to get . . . wickeder. You'll figure it out before we have to deal with whoever's coming for that flower thing."

Horace nodded. The problem of the unknown Keeper could be set aside, but not for long. He had twenty-four hours to learn what the silver sun could do. He couldn't afford to be distracted or uncertain about the Fel'Daera once the daktan had returned and the lost Keeper was once again on the move.

Chloe studied his face. "I think you want me to stay."

"For dinner?"

"Sure, yeah, but I meant for the thing. The figuring out whatever you have to figure out."

"Why the heck would I want you to stay for that?"

"What are you going to do, just ball up in your room and think real hard?"

Horace shrugged, not bothering to admit that that was pretty much his plan.

"Look," Chloe said. "We've got until, what . . . eight o'clock tomorrow night before the daktan reappears?"

"Eight thirty-one," Horace said automatically.

"So by eight thirty-one tomorrow, you'll figure it out. I'm

staying to make sure that happens. Now take me inside and get me invited to dinner, like best friends are supposed to."

Horace closed his eyes and laughed. "You are my best friend, you know," he said.

"Duh," said Chloe.

They went inside. Horace's mother was in the living room, working on a crossword puzzle.

"Hey," said Horace, not quite meeting his mother's eyes.

"Hey, Mrs. Andrews," Chloe said.

Horace's mother looked startled. "That's the first time you've called me that."

"I think it might be the first time I've called you anything," Chloe said.

"Well, if you're going to call me anything, I prefer Jessica." She pushed her reading glasses up onto her head. "Dad already went to bed, but there's plenty of leftover pizza if you're hungry. That goes for you too, Chloe."

"You don't have to feed me, but I'm planning to stay. If that's all right."

"If you stay, you eat. But I gather there's a situation."

"There is, in fact," Chloe said. "It's a box thing."

Horace looked at Chloe incredulously.

"What?" Chloe said with a shrug. "You weren't going to tell her?"

"Ah," Horace's mother said knowingly. "Tan'ji troubles."

Horace wanted to die. He wanted to get out of her sight—could she see what was wrong with the box even now?

Chloe seemed to catch his mood. "Uh, Horace has some things to figure out. I'm here for moral support, and tomorrow night some stuff is going to go down."

"Things and stuff, I see," said Horace's mother. She hesitated and then said, "Is the stuff dangerous?"

Though her tone stayed light, Horace thought he could hear a little strain in her voice. He glanced at Chloe and said, "Mr. Meister seems to think it's fifty-fifty on the danger issue. With the stuff."

His mother laughed ruefully. "If he thinks it's fifty-fifty, it's probably more like eighty-twenty. On the dangerous side." She smiled faintly, then waved her hand toward the kitchen. "Get yourselves some food. Then you can get to work on the things."

They carried plates of warmed-over pizza and bottles of root beer up to Horace's bedroom, where Chloe closed the door and immediately started into a monologue about how awesome Horace's mother was. "You don't even know how lucky you are, Horace. My mom is—was—a zero. Literally. That's the score you get when you abandon your family. But your mom was already a ten, and now that it turns out she knows all this stuff, she's like an eleven. Plus she wants me to call her Jessica." She frowned suspiciously, as if trying out a new, dubious-looking food. "Jessica. Jessica."

"That's not so weird," Horace said. "Besides, your dad knows stuff too."

"Not like this. And I love my dad, but your mom is . . ."

She trailed off, looking suddenly conflicted.

"I think it's safe to say my mom has had an easier time than your dad," Horace pointed out gently.

Chloe sank onto Horace's bed and huffed out a sigh. "Fair," she said, and took a huge bite of pizza.

Horace wasn't hungry. He took the Fel'Daera out of its pouch, trying to clear his head. He examined the silver sun. It seemed so obvious now that it wasn't a mere decoration. But what was it?

"Anyway," Chloe said, mouth full, "about tomorrow night. You realize that if this mystery Keeper is human, and we go out with the daktan to lure them in, we're basically going to be recruiting for the Wardens." She pointed her pizza slice at him. "We'll be doing exactly what the old man wants us to do."

"Why do you say that?"

"You heard what he said before: 'We can't abandon a new Keeper who might be friendly to our cause.'"

"So?"

"So Mr. Meister doesn't care about the person. He's just hoping to find another soldier for his *cause*." She took another bite.

"Meanwhile, you care deeply about the person—if it is a person," Horace said skeptically.

"You're missing the point. We don't even know what the old man's cause *is*."

This was a conversation they'd had before, and it always

made Horace uncomfortable. He remembered the claims of Dr. Jericho, on that long, terrible night in the nest: the Wardens kept secrets; the Wardens were simply using the young Keepers to achieve their own hidden goals; the Wardens marched toward ruin.

"We're Wardens ourselves now, remember?" Horace pointed out, trying to push the memories away. "We joined them because they want to keep the Tanu safe from the Riven. Including our own Tan'ji. That's the cause. Whatever else we don't know about Mr. Meister, we know that."

"I'm just saying, sometimes he seems more like a collector than a protector. I mean, look at Brian—he's like a bug in a jar."

"Come on. That's not fair."

"It's not even about Brian. It's about what Mr. Meister is willing to do to us. Look, I'm on this team, okay? I'm on *your* team, and Gabriel's and Mrs. Hapsteade's. The Riven hurt my family and you guys helped me save my dad—but that doesn't mean I just blindly accept everything Mr. Meister tells us. He wants us to go out there tomorrow with the daktan—the bait—in the hopes that we'll catch him a new recruit and a new Tan'ji. But we don't even know if the lost Keeper is human. We could be walking into danger."

"Since when are you so worried about danger?" he said. He pointed to the scars on her arms, her shins, her throat.

Chloe uncapped her root beer, took a long swig, then belched profoundly. Beside her, Loki's eyes opened wide and his ears went flat. "Good point," she said, wiping her lips with the back of her hand.

Horace pushed his still-untouched pizza away. All of that stuff could wait. He needed to figure out the silver sun. Maybe then the Fel'Daera would give them the answers they needed. He bent over the box again, trying to concentrate.

A minute later, Chloe peeled a pepperoni from a slice of pizza and held it up. "If you sent this through the box right now, it'd come out tomorrow still warm, right?"

Horace nodded, knowing from his experiments that it would. Items came out of the box exactly as they went in, as if no time had passed for them while they were traveling.

"That's fabulous." Chloe held the pepperoni out to Loki, who sniffed it politely and then looked away. She bent down and asked the cat softly, "You don't even like people-food, do you?" The cat touched his nose to hers. "What about time-travel food?" she cooed. "Would you like that?"

"I thought you came here to help," Horace said.

"I am helping. I'm trying to keep your brain moving."

"My brain *is* moving." He threw up his hands. "We get here and all you can talk about is awesome mom blah blah and Mr. Meister secret agenda blah blah, and when you finally do want to talk about the Fel'Daera, it's about future pizza. How is that helping?"

She blinked at him. "I like to be distracted when I'm trying to figure something out. Usually it just comes to me."

"Have we even met? That is not how things work for me."

Chloe slid to the floor beside him, wiping her hands on her thighs. "Sorry," she said. "Show me."

"Okay, thank you," Horace said. He laid the Fel'Daera on the floor between them. "So like I said, whatever it is I'm missing has something to do with this." He touched the silver sun, its rays gleaming around a glossy dark center.

Chloe bent to look close. "Maybe it's like a switch. Or a dial."

"Maybe, but not a physical one. Brian said I'd control it with my mind. Telemetric, he called it."

"Like with me and the dragonfly," Chloe said. On cue, the dragonfly's wings whirred to life again for just a moment.

"Right," Horace said. "So how do you do that?"

"Beats me." She swung her eyes toward the ceiling, thinking. "It's like I . . . let myself flow into it? But it seems like you should know."

"Why? The box is mechanical. I open the lid, I look."

"Yeah, but it's all mental once the lid is open, isn't it? Your thoughts affect the future you see."

"That's true. But I don't really feel like I'm controlling anything, making it happen. I'm not pushing a button."

Chloe leaned back against the side of the bed. "The problem with you, Horace, is that you're too logical. I'm telling you, you've got to think less and feel more."

Horace rolled his eyes. This was one of the fundamental differences between them. Chloe had mastered the Alvalaithen largely through intuition, through gut and instinct.

Horace, however, was methodical and clinical. The more he understood about the box's function, the better.

"You're rolling your eyes," Chloe said.

"I'm not like you," Horace said. "I'm a scientist. I need to be logical."

"Okay, so let's logic it out. How could the box do more than it already does?"

Horace sighed. "It could be more accurate."

"It's super accurate now. That night in the nest? You saw pretty much everything true."

"I could do better. But yeah, I don't think the box has a focus knob or anything like that. The accuracy thing, that's on me."

"Maybe you could see farther away—to other places," Chloe suggested.

Horace made a face. "No, that doesn't make sense. The box is a window. I look through it and I see what's on the other side of the glass. The location doesn't change, only the—" He stopped, an idea suddenly blooming in his head. He scooped the box up off the floor.

Chloe sat up straight. "What?"

"Maybe I *can* see farther away. But not to different places. To different times."

"What do you mean?"

Horace clutched the box to his chest. "Maybe I can see farther into the future."

"Try," Chloe said, her face alight with excitement. "I

won't say anything. Pretend I'm not here."

Horace tried. He pushed his thoughts toward the Fel'Daera and the silver sun, trying to let himself flow into it.

Suddenly Chloe gripped his arm. "Wait. What if you see too far?"

"What does *too far* mean?"

"I don't know. What if you see like . . . twenty years into the future, and you find out we're married, with three kids?"

Horace just stared at her, waiting for her to realize what she'd just said, or to say she was only joking, but she just shrugged at him angrily. "Well?" she insisted.

"Well, I can only see the future right where I'm at, so . . . if I see both of us *still here in this room* in twenty years, I think we have bigger problems than having three kids."

She released his arm and chuckled.

"Besides," Horace continued, "Brian says *he's* going to marry you."

Chloe sat up straight so fast Loki flinched. "What?!"

"Quiet, please," Horace said, bending over the box. "I'm concentrating."

Horace pushed his thoughts toward the Fel'Daera and the silver sun, trying to let himself flow into it—whatever that meant. He didn't expect to feel anything—half his brain was thinking about Chloe—but after a full minute of gentle questing, his thoughts settled into a kind of hollow. A fingerhold. A ripple in the box's function. "Wait," he said, breathless. "Wait."

It was there—not a structure, but an idea. A passage deep in the black center of the silver sun, pulsing with power. He pressed against it, ever so gingerly. He sensed the sun's gleaming rays, so bright, so unknowably full, a balloon about to burst. He pushed harder, hoping to push that power further into the future. But almost at once his focus slipped, and he lost hold.

"I almost had something," he said.

Chloe clapped softly. "Try again. You can do it."

He tried. He found the fingerhold more easily this time, but again when he pushed it, it slipped away. He closed his eyes for a moment. He could feel the silver sun there, waiting, swollen with energy but still somehow resisting him. "It's there," he told Chloe. "I can feel it. It wants to move. I just can't quite get it."

"You will, though."

But he wasn't sure he would. And Chloe's unwavering belief in him—while well intentioned—was not actually helping. "I wish you wouldn't say that," he said. "You make it sound like it should be easy. It's not easy."

Chloe frowned. "Nobody said anything about easy," she growled. She watched in sullen silence as Horace kept trying. She finished her pizza, then ate most of Horace's without asking. Eventually she clambered onto his bed, reaching up to pull a small selection of books off Horace's neatly crowded bookcase. She curled up and began to read.

Horace spent the next hour trying in vain to push the

Fel'Daera's sight farther into the future. He tried pushing with the box open, and then with the box closed. He tried it with a marble inside, and then tried again as he sent the marble traveling. He tried pulling, even though that seemed wrong. Nothing happened. Chloe spoke only once the whole time, muttering directly to the book in her hands, slowly and scornfully, "Nice pants, Lurvy." But still she kept reading, leaving Horace to his work.

Hopeless work, it seemed. At last, at quarter past eleven, he stopped trying. According to Brian, whatever the silver sun did was something the box *wanted* to do. And it clearly did not want to be pushed like this. He examined the silver sun again and laughed ruefully. Twenty-four spokes. Twenty-four hours.

"I'm so stupid," he said glumly, his voice croaking hoarsely. He looked up and saw Loki on the bed, watching him through thin-slitted eyes. He was surprised to see that Chloe had fallen asleep, a book beneath her head like a pillow.

"I can't see any farther into the future," he told the cat. "It's twenty-four hours. It's always been twenty-four hours." Loki let his eyes float closed, purring gently.

"I should just give up, is what you're saying," Horace said. He laid back on the floor, frustrated and exhausted, and set the box on his chest.

Suddenly Chloe murmured sleepily. "Never give up," she slurred.

"You're asleep," Horace said, and then he waited for her

to tell him that she wasn't. To tell him again to keep trying.

But the words never came.

HORACE WAS STILL lying there a half hour later when his mother knocked and leaned in. She smiled at Horace and the box, then caught sight of Chloe's tiny sleeping form.

"She really asleep?"

Horace sat up. "She was mumbling a while ago, but I think she's out."

"Should we move her?"

"No, it's okay. I'll just . . . sleep on the floor or something."

"You say that like you might not sleep at all," she said, nodding at the box in his hand.

Horace weighed his next words, looking down into his lap and wondering if he was brave enough—or weak enough—to ask his mother what she knew about the silver sun. But before he could even make the decision, she asked a question of her own.

"Horace, how long were you in the Find? A few weeks?"

Horace swallowed, thinking. "A week. Not even."

"Not even a week! Are you aware how fast that is? Especially for something like the Fel'Daera?"

He shrugged, embarrassed and irritated at the same time. "I had help," he said, thinking of Mr. Meister's hints and advice.

His mother laughed. "What, from Mr. Meister? Not much, I bet. If the Find was an avalanche, he'd bring you a teaspoon and politely suggest you dig yourself out."

"That's . . . pretty accurate, actually. But so what? So the Find was fast for me—so I'm a prodigy or something. Is that supposed to make me feel better? Because it doesn't. It mostly just feels like a lot more pressure."

His mother plucked at the carpet with her bare toes. "I get that," she said earnestly. "Success yesterday is no guarantee of success today."

"Exactly!"

"But it *is* evidence, objectively speaking, so treat it that way. The Find was fast for you. Maybe you should ask yourself why." She reached out and rapped him softly on the head. "Keeper," she said, and then left the room without another word.

Evidence, Horace thought. Right. The Find had been fast—a simple fact. It didn't prove anything, or promise anything. The truth was, he'd gotten through the Find partly through hints and partly through dumb luck, but also partly—maybe even mostly—through his own inquisitive nature. He had asked questions and looked for answers. That's what he'd always done. That's what he had to keep doing now.

And there was another fact, as simple and as true as anything else he knew. Even his mother had said the word. No matter how it had happened—fast or slow, easy or hard, help or no help—he *was* the Keeper of the Box of Promises. And the silver sun, whatever it did, was a part of the box.

Horace decided to go back to basics. He pulled his

thoughts away from the silver sun and instead prepared his mind for opening the box again. He thought about his long day—his mother, the harp, Gabriel, Brian, the daktan, Chloe sleeping. He thought about how tomorrow night, he and the other Wardens would be headed out to track down the mysterious Keeper. He reminded himself, though, that there were no guarantees. The Box of Promises made no promises.

When he was ready, he pointed the Fel'Daera at Chloe lying curled on the covers, and then he opened the lid. He peered through the blue glass at tomorrow's room, blue and crisply rippling—*his own barely touched bottle of root beer sitting on the desk; a pillow slumped over the back of his chair; the three empty spots on his bookshelf full again; the clock with its sharply knifed numbers reading 11:55; an empty, rumpled bed.*

Tomorrow's bedroom was empty, he assumed, because he would be out with Chloe and the other Wardens by this time, dealing with the unknown Keeper. They'd be out dealing with it whether Horace solved the mystery of the silver sun or not. He glanced over the top of the box to where Chloe lay snoozing peacefully in the here and now. Sleeping was about the only time when she didn't look ready for a fight. He shifted his gaze back and forth between today and tomorrow. Chloe here, *Chloe gone*, Chloe here, *Chloe gone.*

As he looked, Horace asked himself questions about the Fel'Daera. *Why blue?* No idea, but presumably unavoidable. *Why oval?* It was a good shape for looking through, clearly. *Why so small?* Maybe this was as big a window into the future as was possible to make. *Why one day exactly?*

He paused and thought about that one. He couldn't think of a reason why the gap would be a single day. And it was strange, really, how everything that happened between now and then was unknown to the box. For example, even though the box told him that Chloe would get up sometime in the next twenty-four hours, Horace had no sure way of knowing exactly *when* she would get up—or how, or even why. A lot could happen in twenty-four hours that the Fel'Daera couldn't see. It was like having a map where everything between where you were and where you wanted to go was blacked out.

But maybe that wasn't quite fair. Maybe a better analogy would be human eyes. After all, his own mother saw things fine when they were far away, but she struggled with close-up things. She was always having Horace read labels for her when she couldn't find a pair of reading glasses. With the reading glasses on, though, she could focus on things much—

"Closer," Horace said aloud.

The realization came to him fully formed, with so much utter surety that his heart did not even skip a beat. "Closer," he said again. He shut the lid of the box. He shut his eyes. He took hold of the silver sun with his mind. Concentrating hard, he slowly became aware again how the sun's rays seemed rich, dense with potential and change. The silver rays—brimming with all the coming day's unseen possibilities—were so full. But maybe they didn't need to be so full. It was as simple as that.

The box seemed to hum in his hands, welcoming his understanding, tuning itself to him as he learned. Closer, not farther. He didn't have to push. He didn't even have to pull. He felt his thoughts catch on that tiny dimple he'd been poking at all evening. Not a fingerhold, but a gateway. He gripped it with all the confidence he could muster, and he began to close it.

Almost immediately, something gave. It was as if a great rusty wheel, long stuck, surrendered at last beneath an unexpected weight. The subtle gateway began to shrink, and the flow of power moving through it started to slacken. Horace breathed, deep and slow, eyes still closed. He was doing it. This was what the box wanted. He kept going, narrowing the gap fraction by fraction, cutting off the flow. It became harder as he went, and he knew he wouldn't be able to cut the flow off entirely, but there was so much sheer pleasure in the act, exercising a muscle that hadn't been used in . . . well, as Brian said, *years*.

He shrank the opening until it would shrink no more. Only a trickle of power flowed through it now. Instinctively he pinned the opening in place—he couldn't even have said how, but he locked the gap where it was. Eyes still closed, he probed at the box. It felt . . . different. It felt empty. Not bad empty, just . . . simpler.

He opened his eyes. He stared. The silver sun wasn't silver anymore. Every ray had gone as dark as the center.

Every ray but one.

The topmost ray still gleamed brightly.

Horace's heart swelled. He thought he understood. He opened the box again, knowing precisely what to look for next. Experience—and logic—told him that every clock looked the same through the Fel'Daera as it did in real life, because he was looking exactly twenty-four hours ahead.

But not now.

He turned toward his clock, its glowing numbers reading 12:02 in the present. He lifted the box and looked—into the future, yes, but not into tomorrow.

Through the box, the clock and the table it sat on were almost painfully sharp. And his clock read simply—incredibly—*12:42*.

Straining to keep calm, Horace snapped the box closed. This was it. This was what Brian had seen—what Mr. Meister had probably known all along. Yes, the Fel'Daera could look one day into the future. But it could look nearer to the present, too! He'd adjusted the Fel'Daera so that it was seeing only forty minutes into the future, a dizzying thought.

He brought the box close to his face, looking again at the single silver ray that still shone brightly. He realized now that it wasn't completely silver—a small portion of the ray had also gone dark like the rest of the sun, leaving only two-thirds of it shining and silver.

Horace clutched the box to his chest, grinning. The silver sun *was* a kind of dial after all, complete with its own system of measurement. If each ray represented an hour, he could tell how far into the future he was looking by counting the number of silver rays. Right now, only a single ray was shining—actually, only *two-thirds* of a single ray.

Two-thirds of an hour. Also known as forty minutes.

Horace blazed with a satisfaction so deep and affirming that he was sure there was no word for it. The box was so logical, so ordered. Never had he felt more strongly that the Fel'Daera was his, and his alone, no matter how many Keepers had come before him. He stood there, marveling, thinking he would explode with the knowledge. He had to tell Chloe.

Chloe.

Horace looked over at her. Still asleep. He opened the box again, and through the glass—*Chloe here; Chloe sleeping; Chloe as she was now*. But not exactly now. Forty minutes from now. He compared the two sights of her, inside the box and out. Inside the box—*her head tilted slightly skyward from where it was now, her mouth a half inch farther open.*

Horace closed the box gently, hardly able to believe he could have missed this for so long. "All this time," he whispered to himself, and then looked down at the box and laughed. "All this time."

He looked over at Chloe again, aching to wake her. But he wasn't about to contradict this new future he'd seen, a future that was so close!

He would wait. If she was still asleep in forty-one minutes, he'd wake her then. He sat down on the floor, suddenly ravenously hungry, and started in on what remained of the pizza. It was cold, of course. He couldn't help but think that two hours ago—if he'd known what he knew now—he could have taken Chloe's suggestion and sent some warm pizza through to this exact moment in time.

He froze, clutching a stiff remnant of a slice in his hand. If he could *see* forty minutes in the future, surely he could *send* something, too. Right?

And he knew just what to send. Chloe wanted time-travel food? Well, she could have some. He peeled the last remaining pepperoni from the half slice in his hand, then crept up onto the bed beside Chloe as gently as he could.

Horace settled his mind, thinking about the path he was on and where he wanted it to lead. Then he opened the box and looked, forty minutes into the future. Through the blue glass he saw the future beginning to unfold, the future he was already planning—*Horace's own hand, shaking Chloe awake; her eyes opening, confused and angry; Horace's hand again, putting an empty plate into her lap.* Horace had to stifle a laugh.

He knelt carefully over the still-sleeping Chloe of now, over where her waking self would be forty minutes from now. Through the Fel'Daera—*Chloe's mouth opening in a cranky snarl, unheard words forming on her lips*—this was the moment. Horace rose up on his knees and put the pepperoni into the box, aiming carefully, holding it directly above the plate in future Chloe's lap. It was 12:08.

He closed the box. He felt the tingle that meant the pepperoni was gone. Chloe stirred a little in her sleep, her

265

lips falling slightly open. Horace eased himself off the bed, watching her carefully. If the box worked like it should—and he knew that it would—the pepperoni would arrive at 12:48. He'd wake Chloe up, just as he'd witnessed, and then she'd see. Time-travel food, extra rush delivery.

He sat back in his desk chair to wait, feeling exhausted and invigorated all at once. He'd done it. He'd figured out the silver sun. He lay back for several minutes, looking up at the ceiling's glow-in-the-dark stars, and just reveled in the idea. But soon enough, as always, he found that having the answer just led to more questions. In particular, *how* had he changed the time, exactly? And could he change it again?

He spun around and set the box on his desk. Once more he let his thoughts settle across the sun's snaking rays and into that tiny passageway, knowing better what to feel for now. When the box was set at twenty-four hours, all of the silver rays were shining. The passage was wide open and the power—the Medium, of course!—was at full force. But when he turned that power down, the box saw less far into the future. That only stood to reason. Fewer things could happen in forty minutes as opposed to a day or even a few hours. Fewer branching paths, fewer possible outcomes. So now if he wanted to see farther into the future again, he had to widen the channel, increasing the flow of power. He hoped it would be as simple as that.

It was now 12:13. "Let's try *four* thirteen," he murmured to himself. "Four hours. Four rays." With his thoughts, he found the same subtle hole he'd latched on to before. Instead of closing it, he began to pry it open. He assumed it would be hard, but it began to widen almost at once. He watched the silver rays begin to fill, like mercury rising. He could almost feel the power flowing—all the change and chance and probability and possibility coursing outward into the sun. A kind of inertia took over, a heavy movement like a slow, wide river. Horace waded in it, let himself be taken away by it, sure he knew where it was going, sure that he—

The flow came to an abrupt halt, so sudden and jarring that he could have sworn it made a sound. He realized his eyes were still open, but that he wasn't seeing anything. He squeezed them shut hard, making himself see stars.

He checked the silver sun. All twenty-four spokes were full and shining. He tried to hit four hours and had overshot it by a mile. He felt disoriented, strangely displaced. But why? And then he checked his clock and got a surprise.

It was 12:16.

"Whoa, what?" he said aloud. He'd started pushing at 12:13, and his inner time sense told him that only a dozen seconds had passed. But apparently two or three minutes had gone by. For a moment, he was sure there was something wrong with his clock. That it had malfunctioned. But of course that wasn't very logical. It wasn't the clock; it was himself. Something about pushing the box forward in time had messed with Horace's own inner clock, normally accurate down to the minute.

The clock blipped to 12:17, snapping him out of it. He looked down at the Fel'Daera. "What did we do?" he asked it, but he got nothing in return. No reassurance, but also no alarm, either. Maybe this was just a side effect. Maybe he could learn to adjust to it.

"We'll figure it out, right?" he said to the box. "We are figuring it out." He let his mind drift through the Fel'Daera, and he felt the passageway—a kind of conduit or valve, really—that caused the silver sun to brighten and dim.

He felt ready now to face the coming day, and the reappearance of the daktan—in fact, he felt more ready than ever. Think of it! With any luck, he'd be able to reveal not just what was going to happen in twenty-four hours' time, but within just a few minutes. He couldn't wait to show Chloe what he'd learned.

But he would have to wait. He checked the clock again, relieved to find that his sense of time was returning. It was 12:20. He set the Fel'Daera aside and waited for another twenty-five minutes, until at last it was 12:47. He grabbed an empty plate and climbed onto the bed, shaking Chloe awake, just as he'd seen himself do through the Fel'Daera. Finally she sat up, her face cross.

"You're a terrible person," she snarled.

"Here," Horace said, putting the plate into her hands.

Chloe looked down at the plate, puzzled. "What?" she slurred sleepily.

"Watch the plate. Trust me."

She yawned grumpily. "This better . . . be better."

"Than what?"

"Dream," she breathed with a smile, but she kept her sleepy eyes on the plate. A second later she startled as the pepperoni materialized with a soft *pop!* right in front of her face. She watched it flop down onto the plate.

"Hey . . . ," she said agreeably. "Future food." Then she frowned. "Wait," she said, blinking and staring. She sat up straight. "Wait." Almost giddy with anticipation, Horace waited for her to figure it out. She checked the clock, then checked the window with the dark night sky outside. She looked up at Horace, her face full of dawning wonder. "Wait, is this . . . did you . . . ?"

"Yes," Horace told her simply. He held the box out toward her with one hand, shaking it gently. "Not farther," he said, still trying to catch his breath. "Closer."

CHAPTER FIFTEEN

Falling

APRIL WOKE INTO COLD. COLD AND DARK. SHE TRIED TO STAND but couldn't find her feet. She couldn't find . . . anything. She shot her hand up to the vine curled around her ear. It was there, but she couldn't sense it.

She was severed.

Where was she? Shivering, she looked around desperately. Trees. Night. It was so dark and she was so lost and confused and slipping, falling, sinking into a place far from everything she'd ever known. But what did she know? She knew the vine. Except the vine was gone now, taken. She was alone.

No. Not alone. There—two sleeping figures. A jolt of red hair. *Isabel.* Isabel was doing this, cutting her off. Isabel was curled into a fitful ball on her blanket, murmuring and muttering with eyes closed, apparently dreaming. Had the woman severed April in her sleep? Was that even possible?

April tried to call out, to wake Isabel, but couldn't remember how to speak. She tried to crawl forward. And then she collapsed. She fell on something soft and hard. It squirmed beneath her, pushing, and then a voice.

"April?" the voice said. "April, what's wrong?"

Joshua. She knew that voice. Some part of her did. She tried to answer it but couldn't speak. She couldn't breathe. She was so cold, so gone. Everything was going cold, going frozen gone.

"Isabel!" the voice cried. "Isabel, wake up!" But there couldn't be voices here. It was too cold, too cold and lonely and—

Then the woman shot awake and April felt sudden warmth flooding her. She took a great gasping breath, filling her lungs so full her ribs ached, and there on the crest of that breath was the vine, golden and shimmering, present again. She was April. Arthur was overhead, alert and watching. Murmuring bugs wove through the air between the hum of the trees. Tiny kinetic fish darted along the shoreline a dozen yards away. A handful of toads were awake and doing their nightly deeds. Life all around swept through April, loud and comforting.

Isabel was sitting up, a few twigs and leaves caught in her curly hair, Joshua kneeling beside her. "Did she make it?" the woman asked groggily. "Is she okay?"

"You're having a nightmare," Joshua said somberly, as if that explained everything. He shook her shoulder gently.

"But is she—" Isabel blinked and caught sight of April, still drinking deeply from the vine, and hurried closer. She reached out for April's shoulder, but April drew away. "You," Isabel said. "I'm sorry."

"You severed me . . . in your sleep," said April, hardly believing it.

Isabel worried her wooden ring. "I'm so sorry. It won't happen again."

"In your *sleep*," April repeated. She sat in silence, gathering her thoughts as best she could. "You said you were the only one who could control Miradel. But you can't control her at all, can you? This is the third time you've severed me, and I think only one of those times was really on purpose."

Isabel sank back onto her haunches. "It happens sometimes when I get angry. Or scared." And she did look scared, her knees huddled against her chest like a little girl's. But somehow April had the impression that for Isabel, angry and scared often went hand in hand.

Keep calm, April told herself. *Keep still*. "What were you having a nightmare about?" she asked.

"Old times. A bad day." She dragged a hand down her face. "And then Wardens were there, and an Auditor."

"You're afraid of the Auditors."

"Yes. But they're exactly as afraid of me as I am of them. That's how they work."

Still awash in the aftermath of being severed, April found it hard to summon up much worry about the Auditors just now. She was far more worried about the woman sitting right in front of her, and her own terrible powers. But of course April couldn't just come out and say that. She came at it gently, sideways. "No offense, but you don't really know how horrible it feels," she said.

Isabel scowled silently at the reminder that she wasn't Tan'ji.

April said, "I would like to be told if it's dangerous."

"It's not. Not in and of itself."

That sounded more like a yes than a no. "Okay, but maybe there are . . . related dangers. Dangers I ought to know about."

Isabel sighed. "If you're severed for too long at one stretch—"

"How long is too long?" April interrupted, steeling herself to hear the rest.

"It's different for everyone. Seconds for some, minutes for others. But at some point, the bond between Keeper and instrument dissolves. Permanently."

"I see," April said serenely. "I feel like I ought to tell you that that terrifies the hell out of me."

"And it should, but—"

"What if Joshua hadn't been here just now? What if he hadn't woken you up when he did?"

"Very strong Keepers—stubborn Keepers—can survive being severed for a long time. An hour, maybe."

"So you're saying I'm strong."

"I'm saying you're *something*," Isabel said with a cautious smile. "And I've never severed anyone for more than a few moments—not accidentally, anyway."

Now that she had Isabel talking, there were other things April wanted to know. "Back on the highway, by Ethel's van, I felt something in Morla's mind—it had to have been you. You did something to them, or at least you started to. It was ugly."

Isabel's smile vanished so quickly it made April shudder. "I thought Ethel was my friend," she said sulkily.

"Maybe she's thinking the same thing about you right now. What were you doing to them? You weren't severing. It was . . . worse than that."

Joshua looked up at Isabel, clearly troubled. "What were you doing?"

"Just a warning, that's all," Isabel said defensively. "I'd never actually have done it."

"Done what?" April pressed.

Isabel seemed to consider her words. When she spoke, her voice was low and clear and serious. "The bond can dissolve slowly, but it can also be ripped apart by force. It's called cleaving. I would never actually have done that to Ethel, though. I wouldn't do that to a human, even by accident. It takes a lot of effort, and it's cruel."

April swallowed. "You would do it to the Riven, though?"

"Would and have," Isabel said coldly. She got to her feet and shook out her hair. "But with the Riven, cleaving isn't usually necessary. The Riven's bonds are bone-deep. They can't survive even a few moments of being severed. Take the

Mordin, for example—when they promise themselves to their Tan'ji, and bind themselves the way they do, they can't afford to lose that bond, even for a moment." She tore a piece of bark from a tree and snapped it in two. "That's why they're afraid of me. It's also why you're safer with me than without me."

April took a deep breath and let it out slowly, watching Isabel carefully and trying to decide what to do. She did her best to keep all her confusion and uncertainty confined to a single small fire in her belly. It occurred to her now, watching Isabel with her arms still wrapped around her legs like a child, that maybe Isabel was not the monster she sometimes seemed to be. She was searching for something, just like April was. And despite all her experience, in some ways she seemed in over her head just as deeply as April. Both of them broken, neither one of them completely Tan'ji.

Joshua crawled toward April. He surprised her once again by lying down and putting his head in her lap. "I think we should stay together," he said, as if he'd been reading April's thoughts. "All of us."

April put an awkward hand on his shoulder and squeezed. "You do, huh?"

"Yes. I think everyone can help everyone."

"That's right," said Isabel, her voice hopeful. "I can help you. I can help you both."

April knew that much was true. At the very least, Isabel could protect them from the Riven. Joshua looked up at April. "What do you think?"

"Oh, Joshua, I don't know." She squeezed his shoulder again. "I left home, you know. I left my family behind."

"Do your mommy and daddy worry about you?"

For some reason, the innocence of the question and the way he put his words—*mommy, daddy*—stabbed April deep, in a way that she hadn't felt in years. For a second all that old pain was raw and new again, and she blinked back a sudden push of tears. She caught sight of Isabel in the dark, and was surprised to see Isabel's face thick with compassion, her eyes soft and warm and almost maternal.

April nodded, her body rocking gently. "They would if they could," she said.

THE NEXT TIME April woke, it was to mid-morning sunshine, and to a noisy crowd of busy thoughts that weren't her own. A gaggle of geese was drifting by just offshore, several adults and a multitude of adolescents. The adults were crabby and spoiling for a fight—even grumpier than usual because they were molting and couldn't fly very well at the moment—but April lay there and listened to the youngsters, to the cacophony of optimism and confidence bubbling from them. Their first flight was still ahead of them. They were, she supposed, not so different from April herself, and the idea made her strangely happy. But then as the geese pulled out of range of the vine, a new thought came to her, this one all her own: she still could not sense the missing piece.

She felt gingerly around the edges of the blind spot where

the absence of the missing piece still hung. When she imagined her life spread out before her, that hole always there, year after year . . . she wouldn't give up on it, not yet. She wasn't about to go back home, but she didn't know how to go forward, not without the missing piece.

Arthur's signal suddenly came through loudly, the way it did when he was thinking about her. He knew she was awake. He was proud, hungry, frustrated—working on something he wanted her to see. She rolled over and discovered that he'd gotten her backpack open—zipper and all—and had pulled out a wide strip of beef jerky. He was standing on it with both feet and tearing at it with his great beak.

The raven saw her looking and bobbed his head.

"You love that jerky, don't you?" she asked him.

"Dontchoo," Arthur replied agreeably. *"Dontchooo."* The jerky was tough, even for him, and he wanted assistance.

"Let me get this straight—you steal food from me, and now you want my help eating it? I don't think so."

Arthur cocked his head back and forth, not understanding her tone. *"Dontchoo?"* he asked hopefully.

"I knew it," said a voice suddenly. Joshua was propped up on one elbow, watching with wonder, his curly hair an adorable wreck. "You *can* talk to him."

April laughed. "I can say words at him, yes. So can you. That doesn't mean he really understands us."

"But he answered you."

"He's just imitating me, like a parrot. He knows I like it

277

when he talks. He thinks if I'm impressed enough, I'll help him with his food."

"I don't know," Joshua said slowly, his brow creased with importance. "I don't think you're giving him enough credit."

"Maybe you're right," said April, playing along even though she knew better. She was certainly the most qualified person in the world when it came to knowing what was and was not going on in Arthur's brain. He was smart, yes—smarter than she'd realized animals could be. She knew from researching it that ravens had a kind of language of their own, both verbal and nonverbal, and through the vine she'd learned it was far more complicated than any other animal talk she'd yet encountered.

But compared to the mighty forest of human language, raven language was as simple as a blade of grass. This was not Doctor Dolittle. She and Arthur were not going to be having any long conversations about feather grooming, or people food, or the shininess of various objects.

But she could still understand him. And he was still completely amazing.

Plus, when she found the missing piece—*if* she found it—she knew she would understand him even more. It was probably silly, but sometimes she imagined that if only the vine were whole again, she could actually *become* Arthur. That she could see and hear and feel and think everything that flowed through his fascinating mind. She watched the bird eat for a while, imagining the strength in his beak, the powerful muscles in his neck as he tore at the jerky. For a moment she almost—almost—thought she could taste the surprising saltiness of the meat on the bird's tongue.

"Are you staying with us?" Joshua asked. "I want you to stay."

"I'm staying."

Joshua clasped his hands together and bounced on his knees. "Yes," he hissed, making a celebratory little fist. "Will Arthur come, too?"

"I think he'd better, don't you?"

"*Dontchoo?*" Arthur crowed, throwing his head back. "*Dontchooo?*"

"I *do*," Joshua said, nodding emphatically at the bird.

Isabel was still asleep, so April and Joshua talked quietly for a while. They shared a breakfast of beef jerky, apples, and some gaudy but travel-worn Pop-Tarts. Arthur stayed close, and was rewarded when Joshua broke the crusts off his Pop-Tarts and tossed them to the bird. Joshua watched him eat, talking to him, trying to get him to say "Pop-Tart." April couldn't bring herself to explain to Joshua that Arthur didn't like Pop-Tarts too much.

"He doesn't chew much, does he?" said Joshua, frowning as Arthur ate.

"He doesn't have any teeth," April reminded him.

"Who needs teeth when you have claws?" a thick sleepy voice said. Isabel was awake. Her face looked drawn and even paler than usual.

"Didn't sleep well?" asked April.

"Tried not to sleep at all. I was up until dawn. What time is it?"

"Elevenish, I think," April said. She assumed Isabel had tried to stay awake to avoid more accidents, and she appreciated the gesture. A thank-you didn't seem quite appropriate, but because April had made up her mind about sticking with Isabel—for now, anyway—she wanted to keep things as civil as she could. And because she was not a good liar, she cast about for something honest to say. Not just honest, though—*earnest*. "I have nightmares sometimes, too, you know."

"Oh?" Isabel said. "What about?"

"Different stuff. Usually something to do with being alone. Like really uncorrectably alone, forever. Huge empty spaces, like abandoned malls. Falling through space." She sighed. "Losing important things I'll never find again."

Isabel looked at her hard. "You've made up your mind."

April nodded. "I'm coming."

"We'll have to walk. It'll take hours to get where we're going."

"If that's what it takes. Maybe by the time we get there, I'll feel the missing piece again."

"Yes," Isabel said, avoiding the word *maybe*. "Yes."

They packed up their little camp. Before they left, April took her backpack and slipped off to a private spot to change her clothes—a new set of clothes for a new day. She didn't smell too great, but the way she figured it, none of them did.

And she had bigger concerns right now.

They crossed the secluded island and came back to the dam. On the opposite shore, the park was now filled with activity—joggers and cyclists, boats on the water. The three of them started across the slippery dam, April in front and Isabel bringing up the rear.

Just as April had nearly reached the far side, she heard a shout and a splash. She turned and saw Joshua flailing in the shallow water. "Ow! Ow! Ow!" he cried.

Isabel rushed across the narrow dam like a cat along a fence. When she got to Joshua, she lifted her skirt and stepped into the water, sinking in up to her knees. "Did you hurt yourself?"

Joshua grimaced. "My ankle."

Isabel helped him clamber back onto the dam, and he crawled the rest of the way across, flopping onto the shore. He was soaked through, his ankle beginning to swell like a balloon.

"It's broken," he said flatly.

Isabel reached out and pressed along his leg above his ankle. "Does it hurt here?"

"No," said Joshua tentatively.

"Can you put any weight on it?" said Isabel. "Try to take a step."

Squeezing April's arm so hard she thought it would pop off, Joshua stood and managed a single, limping step. Then another. "It's definitely broken," he said.

But Isabel shook her head. "No, just sprained. Here. Let's sit." She and April helped Joshua hobble over to a nearby bench. As they sat down, Arthur swooped in and started strutting around in the grass along the shoreline, immediately starting a shouting match with a crow farther down the bank.

Isabel dug into her bag and pulled out a long, thin scarf. She proceeded to wrap Joshua's ankle in it. "Walking's out of the question now," she said. "Any ideas?"

"Um . . . we could call Ethel again. I'm sure she'd love to see us."

Isabel knit her brows, unamused. "Let's call that Plan B."

Joshua held up his hand as if he was in school. "I have an idea," he said, and pointed out into the lagoon. A hundred yards off, two people were paddling a silver canoe across the glassy water.

"Wait, is that even possible?" April said. "How close could we get to the city in a canoe?"

"All the way," Joshua said. "Right into the city. And it's all downstream." He started to carve shapes in the air with his hands, seemingly drawing the map from memory. "These lagoons go into the Skokie River, which meets up with the North Branch of the Chicago River. Then the North Shore Channel. Goose Island. Chicago River." He said this last one with an air of finality, making a lopsided Y with his hands. "That's downtown. Right in the direction you said you felt your missing piece."

Isabel leaned over and wrapped the boy in a hug. "It's

perfect," she said. "You're perfect."

"I don't know how to drive a canoe, though," Joshua said through her curly red hair.

"That's okay," Isabel said, releasing him. "I do."

"Okay, so . . . we boat it," said April. "But where do we get a canoe?"

Isabel gestured off to the left, where another silver canoe was rounding the corner. "There must be someplace that rents them nearby. I'll find out." And then with an abruptness that startled April, she stood and stalked off determinedly, without another word. If nothing else, April thought, at least she was decisive.

While Isabel was gone, April helped Joshua get to a nearby restroom so he could change. They laid his clothes out in the bright sun to dry. Arthur left them for a while. Joshua seemed more worried about his absence than Isabel's. April wasn't worried, however, and not surprised in the least when the bird returned twenty minutes later. He was full. Satisfied. She tried not to think too hard about what he might have eaten, or whether it was dead or alive when he found it. Ravens, she knew, would eat just about anything.

They waited for Isabel. Joshua kept apologizing to April for spraining his ankle, saying he'd messed everything up. April tried to reassure him, and eventually found him a walking stick. Once he'd practiced hopping around with it a bit, he seemed to feel better. Occasionally a passing adult would stop and ask if they needed help, not just because of the hopping, but also because of Joshua's wet clothes conspicuously laid out on the grass. Each time Joshua said simply, "No, thanks, my ride will be here soon," as if he'd said it a thousand times before.

At last, after an hour, Isabel returned. She looked furious, her face as red as her hair. "I found a place, but they're no good. They wouldn't give me a canoe without an ID or a credit card."

April stared. "And . . . you don't you have those things?"

"No. Do you?"

"I just turned thirteen. I don't even have a wallet yet." April had never heard of an adult who didn't have a credit card, much less some form of ID. Even Derek had a credit card. She started to wonder how it was Isabel managed to survive, how she made her way in the world. "So what do we do?"

"We wait. We wait until tonight, when the boat rental place closes. Then we help ourselves."

It took April a moment to understand. "We're going to steal a canoe?"

"You're not opposed to a little stealing, I hear," said Isabel. "When it matters."

"When I have to," April clarified.

"I suppose we could take a train instead, but . . ." Isabel glanced meaningfully at Arthur, who was busying himself moving pebbles around on the shore, concentrating hard on some birdly task.

"No," April said at once. She wasn't leaving Arthur, especially not when she couldn't even feel the missing piece anymore. But then she looked at Joshua's worried face. If she stubbornly refused to take the train now, was she putting them in danger from the Riven? "The canoe is fine," she told Isabel, "as long as you think it's safe to stay here today."

"It's never going to be safe with a wound like yours," Isabel said. "But I'd be surprised if the Riven find us before nightfall. And by then, we'll be sailing downstream."

In a stolen canoe. April could hardly even believe she cared about that, but she did. "Fine. We'll wait here and take a canoe. But I have seventeen dollars, and I'm leaving it when we go. We're not stealing. Deal?"

Isabel nodded. "Deal."

"Deal," said Joshua.

"The boat place doesn't close until eight," Isabel said. She squinted into the sky, where the early afternoon sun was still heating up overhead. "And it's going to be a hot day. That can only mean one thing."

"What's that?" April asked, sure that the answer was going to be some new trial, some fresh danger Isabel had neglected to mention.

But instead the woman only grinned at them both. "Ice cream," she said.

——∿∾——

CHAPTER SIXTEEN

The Chaperone

HORACE WATCHED AS THE DAKTAN MATERIALIZED OUT OF THIN air at exactly 8:31 on Wednesday evening, arriving with a *pop* and tumbling onto Mr. Meister's desk. The little flower bounced slightly and rolled to a stop.

All the Wardens were crowded into Mr. Meister's office for the daktan's return. For Horace, it was a strange gathering—it was the first time all seven of them had been together at once. Brian wore his *GO TEAM!* shirt, leaning against the desk, eyes bright and fascinated. Neptune was sitting—if that was even the word—cross-legged in the air above the others, trying to get a better view. Gabriel cocked his head alertly at the sound of the daktan's arrival.

"And so we return to where we were a day ago," Mr. Meister said, plucking the daktan from the desk with two knobby fingers. "Let us hope we have lost less than we gained in the last twenty-four hours." He glanced at Horace with an unreadable glint in his great left eye.

Horace nodded, understanding full well what the old man meant by *gained*. He had already told Mr. Meister about figuring out the silver sun on his own, careful not to sound like he was bragging but also not wanting to sound bitter. Mr. Meister had said very little, remarking only, "Ever is our faith in you justified," which, Chloe quietly pointed out to Horace, was just a fancy way of saying *I told you so*. But Horace didn't mind. He could tell the old man was pleased. And he wasn't bitter about yesterday, not really. Even if he didn't understand Mr. Meister's rules about what could be explained and what could not, still Horace was gratified to have solved the riddle of the silver sun himself. Or at least, *mostly* solved. It hadn't even been a full day since his breakthrough, and naturally there were still some . . . uncertainties. Uncertainties he hadn't gotten around to sharing with Mr. Meister yet.

He and Chloe had spent the entire day experimenting. He was getting better with the silver sun, but he still couldn't quite get control of the gap. When he tried adjusting the time window to ten hours, for example, he might end up with something like twelve hours and fourteen minutes. Not great.

Also, for reasons he couldn't begin to fathom, it was still very easy to overshoot when trying to push the time window *forward*. More often than not, the box ended up back at the maximum twenty-four hours. Horace knew this was partly because the box had been at full power for years. He sensed that it had become a kind of default setting, a kind of rut the box was in, which also helped explain why he hadn't discovered the new power on his own.

But the slipperiness when pushing the window forward also had something to do with himself. His own sense of time seemed to dissolve whenever he tried to make the box see farther. While opening the passageway and letting power flood into the silver star, Horace always felt that mere seconds were passing. When he finished, though, it would always turn out that minutes had gone by. Chloe had watched him do it, and afterward had reported that for those few minutes—minutes that felt like seconds to Horace—his eyes had "glazed over like dead doughnuts."

It was frustrating for sure. But his frustration was tempered by the wonders that the Fel'Daera's new power had revealed. He'd discovered that when the box was looking just a few hours into the future—as opposed to a whole day—his viewings were much clearer. This clarity only made sense, of course. Less time meant less change. Less change meant less uncertainty, less blurriness.

Even better—or at least more entertaining—there was a new thrill in being able to see a future that was so tantalizingly close. At around noon, after squeezing so hard he thought his head would burst, he'd managed to get the time window down to just three minutes. Only a tiny fraction of the topmost ray still gleamed on the silver sun. He and Chloe had spent an hour messing with the possibilities. They hung a plastic orc from a string taped to the ceiling and set it swinging, then made bets to see if it would still be swinging in three minutes. The box revealed that it would be, barely.

Next Chloe had bragged that if she took a deep breath, while at the same moment Horace looked three minutes ahead at her future face, she'd still be holding that same breath. The box revealed that she wouldn't be—barely. And the queasy discomforts that came with the Fel'Daera—the strange things its viewings could do to moment-to-moment life—were very much intact.

For example, while the box was still set on that three-minute gap, Horace and Chloe had decided to have a contest to see who would be able to balance an egg on its end first. They got two eggs from the kitchen and marked them—Horace's with a capital H, Chloe's with a doodle of a rather insane-looking chicken standing on one leg. Before actually starting the contest, they checked the Fel'Daera to see whether either one of them would manage to get their eggs balanced within the next three minutes. The Fel'Daera revealed that *both* eggs would be standing on end. They then spent a strangely tense and unpleasant three minutes attempting to balance their eggs, trying to create the future the Fel'Daera had promised. But in the end, Chloe had given up in disgust and Horace had balanced *both* eggs himself, getting Chloe's upright with just five seconds to spare. What they had seen had come true, but not how they had expected. It was a reminder for Horace that even when the Fel'Daera saw clearly, and even when the time window was so short, still there was no way of being sure what exactly would happen in that unseen gap between one side of the blue glass and the other.

And now, of course—now that the daktan's twenty-four-hour absence from the world was at an end—they were about to find out what had become of the little flower's mysterious Keeper during the daylong gap. Without the daktan, Brian and Mr. Meister had been blind. They had no way of knowing if the Keeper had come closer or wandered off course.

But now the daktan was back, and Mr. Meister and Brian both bent over it. Brian had his chin in the air, as if trying to detect the source of a faint smell. All at once he turned and looked distantly over the heads of the other Wardens, up and out through the walls of the doba. A moment later Mr. Meister turned in the exact same direction, slightly west of north by Horace's reckoning. "There," the old man said, pointing.

"How close?" Gabriel said.

"Maybe twenty miles, but not moving now," Brian replied thoughtfully, and then he startled, as if a bug had flown in his face. "But she feels the daktan again." He looked at the daktan and flinched once more. "She feels it hard."

"She," Horace said.

"Bo Peep," said Brian. "That's what I've been calling the Keeper in my head." He looked around the room. "You know—Little Bo Peep."

"Lost her sheep," Neptune offered from overhead.

Brian nodded, indicating the daktan.

Mr. Meister closed his eyes patiently.

"You don't even know if it's a girl," Chloe said.

"Correction," Gabriel said. "You don't even know if it's *human*. What if the Keeper is one of the Riven? What if it's a Mordin?"

Brian shrugged again. "*Little Bo Peep* kind of takes the edge off, right?"

"I like it," Mrs. Hapsteade said, the first words she'd spoken. Surprise popped up on every face in the room, but no one responded.

Mr. Meister shook himself as if trying to forget a foul taste. "Regardless. It is time to go." He turned to Chloe and held out the little black flower. "Once more, I'll ask you this favor. Because we do not know the intentions of our lost Keeper, the daktan will be safest with you."

Chloe looked knowingly at Horace and mouthed a single word that he recognized at once: *Bait*.

Mr. Meister caught it, too. "You are not bait," he said. "You are a chaperone. We cannot prevent the lost Keeper from sensing the daktan, and therefore we must give the daktan to the only one among us who truly cannot be caught. We need your abilities, Keeper."

"You say that like flattery will get you somewhere," Chloe said.

"It is not flattery. It is fact."

Chloe eyed the little flower warily. "I don't like the feel of that thing."

"Nor do I," Mr. Meister said lightly, pushing his hand forward another inch.

Chloe rolled her eyes, then reached out and took the daktan without further comment. Just as before, a ripple of disgust crossed her face as the flower touched her skin.

"Thank you," said Mr. Meister. "I'm sure I do not need to tell you to be on guard. You are now the beacon our mysterious visitor pursues. But even if the lost Keeper is human, we must all prepare ourselves for the likelihood that the Riven will be present tonight. Mordin, certainly."

That was startling news. "Why certainly?" Horace asked.

Mr. Meister looked pointedly at the daktan in Chloe's hand. "A wounded Keeper draws extra attention," he said simply.

Wounded. The word cast a pall of silence over the room. Chloe tucked the flower protectively into her front pocket. Horace, meanwhile, felt a deep stab of guilt over his snap decision to send the daktan through the Fel'Daera. If this Little Bo Peep was a human, lost and wounded and pursued by the Riven, how much more danger had the delay caused? How much pain and confusion? He knew what that was like. He was still mulling this over darkly when Mrs. Hapsteade gestured for everyone to head outside.

As they filed into the Great Burrow, Horace held Brian back. Somewhat guiltily, he asked, "If Little Bo Peep turns out to be friendly, will you be able to fix her Tan'ji?"

Brian hesitated, though he'd clearly already been considering it. "I can stitch the parts together, and I can pump power back into it. But I'm pretty sure that's the same thing Dr. Frankenstein said in his lab."

Mrs. Hapsteade, listening in the doorway, laughed fondly. "He can fix it. Brian is an artist, not a madman."

With Brian blushingly furiously, they stepped out into the Great Burrow. For reasons he did not explain, Mr. Meister stayed behind with Brian while Horace and the rest of the Wardens headed for Vithra's Eye. Mr. Meister was planning to go with them on their expedition, of course—other than Brian, he was the only one who could sense the direction of Little Bo Peep—but apparently they would meet the old man at a nearby cloister.

Mr. Meister gave the other Wardens a stern nod as they left. Brian, meanwhile, called after them solemnly, "Fear is the stone we push. May yours be light." When both Horace and Chloe turned back to look at him, surprised by the serious farewell and his somber tone, he grinned and gave them a gangly wave. "Bring me back something nice!"

Horace waved back and Chloe frowned, and then they hustled after Mrs. Hapsteade, marching up the slope toward the lake. Gabriel and Neptune glided easily beside them, Gabriel with his long, steady stride and Neptune with the customary effortless glide her gravity-defying Tan'ji gave her.

"Mr. Meister never crosses the lake," Chloe said suddenly. "What's up with that?"

Horace realized with a start that it was true—he'd never

seen the old man cross the black water.

Neptune looked at them with her wide, innocent eyes. "There's a back door to the Warren, of course," she said. "He goes that way."

A back door. Horace pictured the stone bridge that spanned the Maw at the bottom of the Perilous Stairs. That must be the other way out. But what was the back door like? And what protected it?

"That's kind of a nonanswer," Chloe told Neptune. "You know what I think? I think he *can't* go this way. I think he *can't* cross the lake." And now Horace remembered something Mrs. Hapsteade had said on their first visit, when he'd asked if there were any Keepers strong enough to cross through the heart of the Nevren in Vithra's Eye: *"Mr. Meister least of all."*

"It's true that Mr. Meister does not cross the lake," Gabriel said. "Just as you, Chloe, do not use passkeys. Just as Horace does not disregard the revelations of the Fel'Daera. Our powers come with limitations. Sacrifices. Ill effects. Let us leave it at that." Neptune threw him an approving glance, her wide eyes shining with admiration. Horace was mystified, but also relieved in a strange way to discover this weakness—if it was a weakness—in the old man.

They caught up to Mrs. Hapsteade at the water's edge. If she'd overheard their conversation, she gave no sign. He followed Neptune, and Chloe went behind Gabriel, walking their narrow paths across Vithra's Eye and through the soul-sapping void of the Nevren. On the far side, the group then made the long trek back up to the Mazzoleni Academy. Five people in the tiny, ancient elevator that led into the school was about five people too many for Horace, but he made it.

They passed the omnipresent chubby lady in the front office, who waved at them through the round window, and outside they found Beck's cab waiting for them at the curb. Gabriel and Mrs. Hapsteade squeezed into the front seat and Horace piled into the back with the girls. As Beck pulled away, the readout on the meter for extras flickered to *HAP*.

"So," Chloe said. "We're going to pick up Mr. Meister now. From yoga class or something."

Gabriel shook his head slightly. Neptune sighed musically and said, "I'm not sure why you need to poke at it."

"I'm not sure why I need to *not* poke," Chloe replied.

Mrs. Hapsteade glanced back and said, "Henrik is a complicated man. Leave it at that."

After a short drive, Beck pulled over on Randolph Street. Mr. Meister was already waiting for them, standing alertly beneath a flowerpot that hung from an old-fashioned streetlamp. Behind him, the shadow of a ginkgo tree rose high into the night sky over a tall brick wall, a cloister Horace had never been to before. Mr. Meister looked somehow both out of place and utterly in command, as if he had owned this particular corner, and the cloister that stood there, since long before the city around it even existed. Horace found himself wondering just how far the network of cloisters extended, and how old they were.

Mr. Meister slid in beside Horace. The already-crowded cab became very tight indeed. As soon as the door was closed, the cab's meter switched from *HAP* to *MEI*, and the old man was immediately all business. If Chloe really did intend to ask him about Vithra's Eye, she had no chance.

"Our Keeper is on the move again," Mr. Meister announced briskly. "I can't gauge the distance like Brian can, but he now estimates fifteen miles and shrinking, as the crow flies. Please head northwest, Beck—along the Kennedy. Stay off the actual highway, though. I don't want to get too close just yet." As the cab swung into traffic, he turned to Horace. "So. We are on our way to meet the lost Keeper at last, with the daktan in hand. Our day of delay has caused no harm, it seems."

Horace could only nod.

"And you have mastered the silver sun," Mr. Meister said.

"Well, I wouldn't exactly say—"

"No one masters the Fel'Daera," said Mrs. Hapsteade abruptly.

To Horace's great surprise, Mr. Meister shot an unmistakably irritated glance at the back of her head. "Yes, thank you for your opinion, Dorothy," he said, sounding anything but grateful.

Chloe elbowed Horace hard in the ribs—whether at learning Mrs. Hapsteade's first name or hearing the snark in Mr. Meister's voice, Horace wasn't sure. He refused to look at her, focusing on his feet instead. "I'm not claiming I'm the master of anything," he said, for the benefit of everyone in the crowded car. "And with the silver sun, I can only move the . . . whatever you call it . . . the amount the box looks forward in time—"

"The breach," Mr. Meister said.

Horace snapped his head up. "That's the name for it?" Mr. Meister nodded solemnly. The breach. The word felt so right that Horace could not stop himself from asking the next question. "Did Sil'falo Teneves tell you that?"

Mr. Meister inhaled sharply at the name, and Mrs. Hapsteade whirled around in her seat. She and Mr. Meister exchanged a concerned look, a look that—strangely—seemed to soften quickly into warmth, the terse exchange of a moment ago apparently already forgotten.

Horace's heart was galloping. With one casual question, he'd just let slip that he knew his mother's secrets.

"She did," Mr. Meister answered Horace, his tone fond and genial. "And the fact that you know that name tells me that certain buried seeds have at last come into the sun. I am glad this is so. When the urgency of the daktan has passed, I hope we will discuss it more."

"Sounds good," Horace said, trying to sound serious and mature, but feeling more sheepish than anything.

Beside him, Chloe whispered hissily into Horace's ear. "Seeds? Dude, I think he just called your mom a plant."

"Tell me, Horace," said Mr. Meister. "When you adjust the breach, can you set it accurately?"

"Not very," Horace admitted. "Sometimes I'm way off."

"Let me tell you what I have in mind. I hope to find an ideal location for the coming encounter, somewhere we can establish our presence and wait for the lost Keeper to arrive. While we wait, you can adjust the breach accordingly and then witness the arrival through the box. Then we will know what lies in store for us."

"You make it sound easy," Horace said.

"I make it sound possible. Please tell me if that is too optimistic."

Horace felt for the breach, testing it gently. "I can do it. Or at least, I can try."

"Excellent."

"So what kind of a location are we looking for?" Chloe asked.

Neptune answered her, as if reciting a conversation she and Mr. Meister had already had. "Someplace not too far off Bo Peep's current course. We don't want to alarm her. Someplace where we can see her coming, but can stay hidden ourselves. Someplace outdoors, but secluded. Darkness would be nice—we have advantages in the dark."

Horace nodded. The humour of Obro made darkness irrelevant for Gabriel. And then there was Neptune's ability to sense objects—including people—via their gravity, without the need for sight.

"Also," Neptune continued, squirming, "the cab is maxed out already. If we're adding one more to the mix, it would be a bonus if there were a cloister nearby."

"A *working* cloister, yes," Mr. Meister agreed, whatever that meant.

They drove on. The bag that hung from Beck's mirror swayed to its own strange rhythms as the cab slid in and out of traffic. Once or twice Mr. Meister gave soft instructions to Beck, guiding the driver on toward the Keeper that only the old man could feel. Soon downtown was far behind them. The sky outside was almost completely black now—technically, Horace knew, reaching the end of what was called nautical twilight, when even at sea the horizon would be lost in darkness.

Horace wasn't paying too much attention to where they were, only that they were still headed northwest. But after about half an hour he spotted the tall shadow of the Central Wet Wash chimney, and he realized he knew precisely where they were. They were just a few miles from Horace's own neighborhood.

"Our lost Keeper is a human," Mr. Meister said, looking out and up into the night air. His breath fogged the glass as he spoke. Gabriel turned sharply toward the old man, his pale eyes seeming to shine in the darkness, but he said nothing.

"How do you know?" Horace asked.

"I do not," Mr. Meister replied. "But I feel . . . a simplicity in the urgent search to find the lost daktan." Then he frowned and squinted. "Beck, pull over, please."

Beck obeyed, swinging the cab neatly into a darkened parking lot. Mr. Meister got out at once, beckoning for Chloe to follow him. She clambered over Horace, and the old man took the daktan from her. He held it in his palm, wandering across the asphalt, gazing down at the daktan and then off to the northwest, his chin high. He stood there for a full minute, then began to spin in a slow circle, peering all around through the thick lens of the oraculum. After another minute, Mrs. Hapsteade slipped out and joined them, and the three of them had a murmured conversation that Horace could not hear.

"I wonder what's happening," Neptune said breezily, phrasing it as a fact instead of a question.

"Me too," Horace said. "He seems . . . confused."

"They are discussing the signal," Gabriel said, his ears apparently picking up what theirs could not. "Mr. Meister *is* confused. Now he is lamenting the fact that Brian could not be with us—Brian's senses are keener about such things than Mr. Meister's are."

Outside, Mr. Meister continued to try and get a bearing on the mysterious Keeper. At last he handed the daktan back to Chloe and returned to the cab, the others in tow. He leaned against the open door but did not get in. He looked grim. "I worry that our lost Keeper has encountered difficulties," he said.

CHAPTER SEVENTEEN

What Belongs

WHEN THE MISSING PIECE RESURFACED IN APRIL'S MIND, HER
knees almost buckled beneath her. For a moment she thought
she was actually fainting—a queer and distressing notion—
but she locked her knees and clenched her hands at her sides,
and managed to stay upright.

The missing piece. *Her* missing piece. Against all hope, it
was back. It still *was*. She had felt so broken, and here was her
cure. Closer than ever. The entire ocean of her consciousness
seemed to pour into the vine at once, spilling out the broken
end before she could stop it, reaching urgently out for that
distant, beautiful beacon. Every cell in her body seemed to
scream at her to go find it, claim it. They should have taken
the train. She should have left Arthur behind. She stood there
quivering impotently for . . . she didn't know how long, letting
this new desperation—so foreign and yet so familiar—pour

out of the broken stem of the vine like water from a pitcher.

Abruptly April was pulled out of herself. Someone was shaking her. Hard. "What are you doing?" Isabel spat. "Every Mordin for miles can feel that. Stop it!"

April found she hardly cared. "It's back. The missing piece. I feel it again."

Isabel's face seemed to shudder, wavering between rage and fear and sudden hope. "I told you," she said, clearly struggling to control her emotions. "I told you so. But you're bleeding now. You've got to stop."

April nodded and tried to get her own instinctive yearning under control. She pulled back from the missing piece—so hard to do so soon after it had returned!—and was at last able to draw all her longing and hope and need back into herself. The effort made her feel hollow and overstuffed at the same time.

"Good," Isabel said, satisfied. She looked around cautiously, as if expecting to see Mordin closing in. But there was no one. "I'm sorry I shook you. You weren't hearing me."

"It's okay." So April had been too far gone to even hear Isabel talking—that was distressing news. She struggled to regain her bearings. They were still at the lagoons, hunkered down in some trees near the water. The sun had just set. Joshua was beside her, looking worried. Arthur was overhead—and had April really just wished she'd left him behind?

"Can you follow it?" Isabel asked. "Can you find it—quietly, without disturbing the wound?"

"Absolutely," April said. The missing piece burned like the sun now. "If it lasts, that is."

"Good." Isabel turned and looked over at the boat rental place, a hundred yards away alongside a pull-off near the water. The place had officially closed half an hour before, but a couple of workers were still there, dragging canoes and kayaks into a storage building. It wasn't completely clear how Isabel was planning to get in, but she'd said she planned to do it "the old-fashioned way." April took this to mean she was simply going to break in but didn't want to say so in front of Joshua.

Now that the missing piece had reappeared, April could hardly wait to get started. She watched the men working impatiently. It seemed like an eternity passed before at last they got in their cars and drove off, leaving the storage shed abandoned. Isabel commanded April and Joshua to wait where they were, here along the dark edge of the trees, well back from the road, waiting for her signal.

They waited. April unwrapped Joshua's swollen ankle so he could flex it a bit, then tried her best to rewrap it.

"Are you okay now?" Joshua asked.

"Yes. Don't worry. Was I really that out of it?"

Joshua made three big, slow nods. "You were like a zombie. But your eyes were all . . ." He made a catatonic face—sagging mouth and crossed eyes—and wiggled his fingers through the air.

"You lie," April said, embarrassed.

"No. But it's okay. You looked happy."

April went back to work on the wrap, doing her best not to think about the missing piece, whose glowing presence she could still feel in her gut. Happy was not the word for what she was. There was no word for what she was. Tragistupid? Crippletastic?

"I don't see Arthur," Joshua said.

April finished the wrap, tucking it into itself and hoping it would hold. "Don't worry. He's here," she said, pointing. The raven was perched thirty feet up in an oak tree with white-bottomed leaves.

"Animal check?" Joshua asked hopefully.

April gave him a patient smile. He'd been saying that all afternoon, wanting to know how many animals were around them at any given moment, and what those animals were thinking about. It was a way to pass the time, like a game for him. "I feel like I better not use the vine too much right now," April said. "But I can tell you that there's definitely a whole bunch of little mammals in a burrow right underneath us. A mother and babies, hiding underground—chipmunks, I think."

Joshua's eyes grew wide as he looked at the ground between his feet. "What are they doing? What are they thinking about?"

April sipped at the vine—just a cautious little peek. "Sleep. Milk. Warm. Safe."

"Sounds nice," Joshua said, his voice dreamy.

"It sure does," April agreed.

April stood and looked over at the boat place. No Isabel, but it had only been a couple of minutes. And then, unexpectedly, alarm knifed through her. A split second later Arthur cawed sharply, twice. Warning calls. Fierce. Hateful. April turned and saw a woman crossing the road, coming straight for them, watching them closely. No, not a woman. Not a human woman, anyway—pale skin, long arms, white-blond hair pulled back into a braid. Arthur's distress was drowned in a flood of April's own full-blown fear.

An Auditor.

Arthur squawked wildly again, furious. He was even angrier now than he had been when he'd chased off the Mordin back home, so angry that April had to struggle to keep from being overwhelmed by his rage. The Auditor glanced up at the bird and seemed to scowl. Over at the boat rental place, meanwhile, still no sign of Isabel. As the Auditor came closer, April surprised herself by moving in front of Joshua instinctively, her heart pounding.

"There you are, girl," the Auditor said as she approached. Her voice was both velvety and crackling at the same time, like skates on ice, or a match being struck. Her face was surreally smooth, angular and stunning, one horrid step sideways from being unspeakably beautiful. Her green eyes should have been cold, but instead they were dark and warm, almost moss-colored. On her forehead, close to her hairline, a single red gemstone gleamed, bright as blood against her ghostly skin. Triangular, about the size of a marble, the gem seemed to actually be embedded in her flesh.

The strange creature circled them and stopped just a few feet from April. "I've been looking for you," she said.

"I guess you found me, then," April said, trying not to stare at the red gem. She would stay calm, stay still, even for this. "But I don't know why you bothered."

The woman spread her arms gracefully, so unnaturally slender and long, her fingers like wands. "We just want to talk. That's all we ever wanted."

We. But in her head, April knew that all of Arthur's attention was on the Auditor. If there were any other Riven in the immediate vicinity, the bird was unaware of it—and Arthur was never unaware. The Auditor was alone. "I'm not very interested in talking to you," April said, determined to stay bold.

"But you've been talking to your companion. The Forsworn." The Auditor glanced around, nonchalantly scanning the area. The Forsworn—apparently that meant Isabel. April couldn't imagine what the word might mean, but it didn't sound good.

Despite the Auditor's casual manner, April could see the wariness in her tiny black eyes as she searched for Isabel. What had Isabel said? Auditors were just as afraid of Isabel as Isabel was of Auditors. So they were evenly matched, then? "I don't see her now," the Auditor continued. "Did she tire of you? The Forsworn are notoriously temperamental."

"She's coming back any minute."

Joshua piped up suddenly. "She always comes back."

The Auditor seemed to notice Joshua for the first time. "You trust her, then?"

"Yes," Joshua said firmly. The Auditor's eyes slid over to April's face.

April hesitated, and then said, "More than I trust you."

"You trust her more than you trust a complete stranger." The Auditor laughed. "How touching."

"You're not a stranger," April said. "You're one of the Riven. And I want nothing to do with you."

The woman grinned and tipped her head, the red gem glinting in the twilight. She pulled her long white braid over her shoulder, stroking it. Her smile was wide and toothy, ravishing and horrible. "You know all about us, then?" she crooned. "How we'll tell you truths you'll never hear from your fellow Tinkers? We can teach you things, you know. Things about your Tan'ji." She raised her lovely eyebrows. "Why, we can even make you whole again."

Whole again. For a moment the words tugged at April hard, and her need began to trickle out of the broken stem. The Auditor was so beautiful. Her voice was soothing and reasonable. She seemed to understand April.

But then Arthur screeched in anger. The sound startled her as much as the jolt of rage that came with it. April let the Auditor's words roll off her, refusing to believe. And suddenly it occurred to her that the Auditor wanted the same thing

Isabel wanted. She wanted April to lead her to wherever the missing piece was now. No one cared if April really became whole again or not. Not even Isabel. She was on her own.

"Fine," said April, feeling as stubborn as Derek always accused her of being. "Bring me my missing piece, then."

Surprise lit the Auditor's face, and April knew she'd said the right thing. But then the Auditor stepped in close. "You don't understand," she said. "We would *like* to be friends. We would *like* to help you, if you help us. But your cooperation does not need to be voluntary."

And then something terrible began to happen.

The Auditor took hold of the vine. Not with her hands, but with her mind, slipping right into the vine alongside April as though she belonged there. Her presence was foul and shocking and wrong. April could scarcely move as the Auditor's thoughts reached out along the channels of awareness that were supposed to be April's alone.

The Auditor was not just inside the vine, but was *using* it—feeling the vegetation all around, feeling the mindless whisper of a passing moth, feeling the sleeping bundle of chipmunks beneath them. April could still feel these things too, but they were no longer private. For the moment, the vine was not purely hers. The Auditor was inside it. This was beyond theft, beyond violation. April wanted to vomit.

"Now you understand," the Auditor said softly, and then continued on in a harsh, slashing language April couldn't understand: "*Nothra kali naktu kali ji*—what belongs to you

308

belongs to me, if I so choose."

The Auditor turned and looked up at Arthur, still squawking high overhead. April was powerless to stop her taking the raven's thoughts, basking in them. The very idea that she would—that she *could*—be eavesdropping on Arthur this way was humiliating and infuriating.

"Filthy animals," the Auditor said, examining Arthur inside and out as though he were something stuck to the bottom of her shoe. "Carrion eaters. Opportunists. But he worries about you. I feel that, just like you do." She turned back to April and gave that wicked smile again. "You don't look well. You thought your instrument was yours alone, no doubt. You thought you were truly Tan'ji. Every Tinker does. But you are merely an aberration, like all the others, and you cannot stop me from stealing what you wrongly call your own."

April fought off her doubts, and the strange knife of jealousy the Auditor's grip on the vine was plunging into her gut. "You're not stealing," she said. "You're only imitating. You're just a shadow of what I am." The iron in her own voice surprised her.

The Auditor laughed. "You could learn to be strong, you know. Perhaps you could even learn to resist me. We could teach you, if you only—"

The Auditor whirled around. Mercifully, her presence in the vine winked out like a candle, tugging a gasp of relief from April. The vine was pure again, hers again, but she hardly had time to register it before the Auditor crumpled to the ground, clasping her head and keening. She rocked in place, wailing as if she were in great pain.

"Run!" someone shouted.

Isabel. She stood down the street, halfway to the boat place, beckoning them frantically. "Hurry! That won't last forever."

April slipped her bag onto Joshua's shoulders, hoisted the boy onto her back, and began to run as best she could. The Auditor, still on her knees, swiped at April with the long fingers of one hand—too long, too many knuckles, sickening.

April dodged her. Joshua was heavier than she had imagined, but she ran. By the time she reached Isabel, gasping, she thought her ankles would snap off. No sooner had she lowered Joshua to the ground than Isabel scooped him up and began to run. "No vine now," the woman commanded. "Leave no trace."

April did as she was told, shutting down the vine as best she could. She glanced back and saw Arthur following after them. They ran around the far side of the storage building, out of sight of the Auditor, and began trotting down the grassy slope toward the water. A canoe lay at the water's edge, two plastic oars and two blue life jackets inside.

"You in front, April. Take a paddle."

April stepped into the wobbly canoe, making her way unsurely to the front. She'd never been in one before and had only a rough idea how to work one. She took the front seat, paddle in hand. Joshua crawled aboard, sitting on the floor in the middle as Isabel instructed, and then they shoved off, Isabel in the rear.

"Paddle," Isabel said. "Hard as you can."

April was flustered, and still reeling from the Auditor—eager to get away from the horrible creature. Twice she almost dropped her paddle, but she kept at it, her arms burning. Arthur flew by, curious, but kept his distance from all her flailing and splashing.

They paddled for several minutes, Joshua directing them across the open water and into a narrow channel. Soon they were deep in the shadows of bending trees overhead, hidden from sight in nearly every direction. "Okay," Isabel said. "Rest for a while if you like."

Relieved, April stopped, clinging to her oar. Isabel kept paddling, pushing the canoe forward with such strong surges that April now realized she hadn't done much to contribute, despite her efforts.

"What did the Auditor say?" Isabel asked.

April tried to remember the Auditor's words, but everything she'd said had been erased by what she'd *done.* "She took over the vine. She used it."

"I know," Isabel said. "Are you all right?"

"What do you mean, she took it over?" Joshua asked.

"That's what Auditors do," Isabel explained. "They draw upon the powers of whatever instruments are around them. Even multiple instruments at once, if they're good enough. It's the only power they have, imitating the powers of others.

They're parasites, but they're dangerous."

April squeezed her eyes shut, trying to forget the sensation, trying to fight off the urge to reach for the vine and make sure it was still clean and right and hers again. "You should have cleaved her," she said. She was surprised to hear the words come out of herself, and even more surprised when she realized she didn't want them back, wanted the Auditor dead.

"Auditors can't be cleaved," said Isabel. "They're not Tan'ji, so there's no true bond to tear apart. But don't worry—I clipped her threads. Tied them in knots. It'll be a bit before they untangle and flow again."

"But if she's not Tan'ji, then—"

"You saw the crystal on her forehead? That's where their power comes from, but it's not Tan'ji. We call them ghost stones, although the Riven don't give them names at all. Even the Auditors themselves aren't given individual names—they call themselves Quaasa, and don't distinguish themselves from one another. They're chosen early, and train hard to become what they are. Years of training. Their ghost stones are physically bound to them, to replace the bond of being Tan'ji. Rumor has it the red you see in the crystal is the Auditor's own blood, flowing through the stone."

"I'm not sure I believe that part," April said reflexively, even though everything else Isabel was saying had her transfixed. "They can really hijack any instrument that's around?"

"The instrument's owner must be present, but yes—almost any instrument."

"Even harps. Even Miradel. That's why you're so afraid of them. She could do to you what you just did to her."

"Yes. That's why they're just as afraid of me as I am of them. When I battle an Auditor, it comes down to who's faster."

April thought about that, and the speed with which the Auditor had spun and then collapsed. Isabel was fast, she had to give her that. But if an Auditor was only as dangerous as the most dangerous instrument around, an Auditor around Miradel was dangerous indeed.

"The Auditor called you something strange," said April. "Forsworn, I think. What does that mean?"

Isabel pulled her oar quietly through the water. The canoe continued its slow slide across the lagoon. Far ahead, some white waterbird skimmed low and ghostly over the surface of the water. "It means they pity me," Isabel said at last. "But I don't need pity, least of all from the Riven. No more questions now. Keep paddling. Let's get to where we need to go."

CHAPTER EIGHTEEN

Hope for No Regret

"WHAT KIND OF DIFFICULTIES?" GABRIEL ASKED.

Mr. Meister stood in the parking lot, daktan in hand, watching it closely. "The Keeper is several miles away yet, still headed in our general direction. But the movement is slow. Far too slow for a vehicle—and even somewhat slow for walking. Worse, though, it seems the Keeper is wandering wildly, as if lost." He raised a hand and wove it through the air. "It's almost as if the daktan's call were hard to hear."

Horace stayed silent, beginning to wonder if he'd somehow damaged the daktan by sending it through the box. Had he scrambled the signal? But just then Chloe climbed into the cab again, the Alvalaithen swinging in Horace's face, and he remembered—the Alvalaithen had once gone traveling too, and afterward it had worked just fine.

He set his doubts aside and tried to be logical. He

considered the evidence: the Keeper's meandering approach; moving forward at the pace of a slow walk; the current location somewhere vaguely to the northwest of where they were now. He summoned up what he knew about the area, and as soon as he did that, it all came together for him. "The river," he said at once. "Bo Peep's on a boat in the river."

"River?" said Chloe. "What river?"

"The North Branch. It winds all around like crazy, especially up here. That explains the wandering. And the speed."

She looked at him blankly.

"The Chicago River," he clarified. "I swear, half the people in this city think the Chicago River ends after downtown. But the river comes in from the north, from way outside the city. Me and my dad go canoeing on the North Branch all the time. Lots of people do."

"That old red canoe in your yard?" Chloe said, her voice thick with disbelief. "You actually put that thing in water? And then you get *in it*?"

Horace shrugged. "It floats."

"Yeah, so does a marshmallow. But you're not going to see me—"

"If you two are quite finished?" Mrs. Hapsteade said briskly, cutting Chloe off. She turned to Mr. Meister. "The river—that could explain it."

"I believe it does," Mr. Meister said thoughtfully. "And if that's where our Keeper truly is, perhaps we can find a secluded spot along the bank for our encounter."

315

"We definitely can," Horace said. "All we have to do is stay on this road for another ten minutes or so, and we'll practically hit the river. There's a big stretch of parks and trails right there—woods and stuff on both banks."

Mr. Meister's left eye shone like an owl's eye, keen and almost predatory. "Show me," he said thickly, and he and Mrs. Hapsteade scrambled back into the crowded cab.

As Beck pulled out of the parking lot, growling slightly in an echo of the engine's roar, Chloe nudged Horace. "So, canoeing. Wow."

"What, you've never been in a canoe?"

"When I was little, yeah. But I didn't know you were so outdoorsy."

"We own a canoe. We go camping all the time."

"Uh-huh."

"I look at stars for a hobby."

"True, but you also play marbles."

"Marbles is really supposed to be an outdoor sport, you know."

She snorted. "Sure. When I think of outdoor sports, I think of marbles right up there next to snowboarding and polo."

"I'm sorry, is there a reason you're so feisty tonight?"

Gabriel spoke without turning around. "She carries the daktan. I imagine it is not an easy task to stomach."

Chloe opened her mouth to fire back—about to say something juicy and cutting, judging by the look on her face—but then she closed it again. She crossed her arms and exhaled bullishly through her nose. Several seconds later, Horace was shocked to feel a dazzling and indescribable swell of energy creep slowly into his left foot, a universe of stupefying sensation. He caught his breath and held it.

He knew at once what was happening, didn't need to look over at Chloe to see that the dragonfly's wings were whirring. She'd gone thin, and placed her own foot entirely inside his. He could feel her pulse, the electric signals in her muscles, even the curl of her toes. Past it all he could hear the faint, sweet music of the Alvalaithen, a humming, soaring chorus. But there was something else too, something fainter still. Something far more simple, and utterly sad, like a fish out of water gasping for breath, or the eyes of an abandoned child.

The daktan.

Horace tilted his head toward Chloe and felt her tilt back in return. "Just so you know how it feels," she whispered, so low that only he could hear, and then she pulled her foot from his, leaving him empty with his thoughts. Mr. Meister gave them a pensive glance but didn't comment.

A few minutes later Mrs. Hapsteade spoke, startling Horace. "Tell us when, Keeper."

Horace looked around, trying to clear his head and find his bearings. "We're getting close," he said, and then he pointed to a road he recognized, running along a large uninterrupted patch of forest. "This is the way we usually go when we're canoeing—there's a landing somewhere over there in those trees. But I'm not really sure where the best spot for us would be. I've only really seen the whole woods from the water."

"Perhaps we can get a better lay of the land," Mr. Meister said, leaning forward and looking meaningfully across at Neptune.

"I'm on it," she said, and began rolling down her window. A rush of cool night air poured in. And then, before Horace knew what was happening, Neptune started to hoist herself out the window. In a flash, she was outside, clinging to the side of the moving car, her free hand gripping her tourminda tight. Her cloak fluttered madly behind her.

Horace tried not to stare. No doubt Neptune had done this before, and no doubt it was perfectly safe—probably— but this was like a movie stunt.

"Why did no one tell me this is a thing that happens?" said Chloe. "Is this, like, what you guys do for fun on Wednesdays?"

Neptune ducked her head and peeked in. "Go on into the park," she said. The rushing wind tore at her voice. "I'll be back down in a jiffy." And with that she pushed off with her powerful legs, launching herself into the sky and cruising quickly out of sight.

Horace and Chloe both leaned over, craning their necks to watch. "That is . . . kind of awesome," Horace said, wondering how far the momentum of the car would carry her.

"Hmm," Chloe said skeptically. "I bet she gets bugs in her teeth."

Everyone looked at her, even Beck. "What?" she said innocently. "Professional hazards, right? We all have them." She pointed at herself, Gabriel, and Horace in turn, reciting: "Scars and broken bones . . . pissing off all your friends . . . possibly shredding the very fabric of space-time." She shrugged and sank back into the seat. "All I'm saying is, maybe swallowing a few mosquitoes isn't so bad."

The cab rolled on into the park. They passed an aquatic center, complete with a pool and twisting water slides, closed for the night. Beyond, an unlit parking lot was surrounded on all sides by dense woods. Somewhere in those trees, Horace knew, the North Branch of the Chicago River snaked by. If he was right, Little Bo Peep was somewhere upstream, following the call of the daktan that Chloe carried.

If he was right.

Beck slid into a spot at the far end of the darkened lot and shut down the car. Mr. Meister and Mrs. Hapsteade got out at once, and everyone but Beck followed—in fact, as Horace closed the door he could have sworn that the driver leaned back and drifted immediately to sleep, snoring softly.

Once outside, Horace stretched his legs, his foot still tingling with the memory of Chloe's flesh inside his own. Meanwhile, Mr. Meister led Chloe aside and had her take out the daktan again, quickly focusing all his attention due north. Horace tried to remember what he could from river maps that he and his father had printed out. It was practically impossible to memorize the meandering river's exact path, but he did

319

recall that it took a big swing out to the west and then back east again, snaking all around as it went. If Little Bo Peep really was following the river, and if she was due north right now, he figured she must be about four or five miles upstream.

Horace tipped his head back and gazed into the clear sky above. The moon hadn't risen yet into the night full of stars, and he could easily see Polaris almost directly over Mr. Meister's head. He'd first learned to identify the North Star by tracing a line from the last two stars in the bowl of the Big Dipper, but now he could recognize it on sight. Meanwhile, off to the east, the Summer Triangle shone plainly—the bright stars Vega, Deneb, and Altair.

Abruptly he became aware of Gabriel beside him. "Can you see Neptune?" the older Warden asked, as if he somehow knew Horace was looking at the stars.

Horace laughed slightly. "The planet, or the person?" The planet Neptune couldn't be seen with the naked eye, but most people didn't know that.

"Either," Gabriel replied good-naturedly.

Horace sighed and scanned the sky. "Neither," he said, but no sooner had he spoken than there was a soft rustle overhead, and Neptune—the person, of course—dropped out of the darkness, slowing her fall with her cloak and alighting like a leaf right in front of them.

"I found a spot," Neptune said as the other Wardens quickly gathered around. She led them north out of the parking lot and onto a well-worn path. They followed it for a hundred yards or so and then broke off into the dark woods. Neptune and Mrs. Hapsteade took out their jithandras. The combined violet-black light cast a sinister, magical glow onto the dark trees and made long shadows bob and sway all around. Sticks and leaves snapped and rustled unnervingly underfoot.

Horace glanced at Chloe and saw that her face was crumpled with worry and distaste. Part of this was the daktan, no doubt, but Horace suspected that some of it was the forest itself. Not everyone liked the wilderness, even a tiny slice of it like this one. He thought back to that first night he'd followed Chloe, before he even knew her name, and how she'd hidden from Dr. Jericho inside a tree. He hoped there'd be no need for that here tonight.

At last, perhaps a quarter mile from the parking lot, they came to the river. The North Branch was a smallish river, only thirty or forty feet wide, trees crowding both its banks. Horace hadn't been exaggerating when he'd said the river wound around like crazy. Just here it bent severely, like the end of a paper clip. It flowed up from the south on their left and turned sharply to head back southward on their right, leaving them on a kind of peninsula. There was a good-sized clearing here, too, rocky dirt and patchy grass sloping gently down to a muddy bank. It was a good location for the coming encounter. Anyone—or anything—hoping to sneak up on them would need to come through the woods behind, or over the water ahead.

"Just so," Mr. Meister said, nodding approvingly. He

turned to Neptune. "And now it is time we laid eyes on our approaching guest. You will find our Keeper somewhere directly to the north of us. Follow the river and see what you discover."

"Actually," Horace said. "Don't follow the river. Not only does the river wind, it bends way off course. Little Bo Peep might be several miles away by water, but if she really is due north, she's probably only . . . I don't know . . . two miles away, in a straight line?"

"Understood," Neptune said. "I'll go as the crow flies, then."

"Excellent," Mr. Meister said. "Come back as quickly as you can. Hitch a ride. And remember, Neptune—be cautious when approaching the Keeper. Despite my hunches, we still do not know what to expect."

Neptune nodded, then looked over at Gabriel.

"Fear is the stone," Gabriel said, as if he could see her. "May yours be light."

Neptune smiled. "It always is." She pushed off easily from the ground and drifted into the branches of the tree overhead. High above she caught a limb, planted her feet against the trunk, and launched herself over the river and out of sight.

Mr. Meister turned to Horace. "You know the river. What is the earliest the lost Keeper could possibly arrive?"

"If she really is where we think she is, and if she stays on the river . . . definitely over an hour. Probably closer to two hours."

"My hope, of course, is that you will be able to witness the lost Keeper's arrival through the Fel'Daera. Can you adjust the breach to ensure you do not miss it?"

"I can try," said Horace. "A bit over an hour should do it."

"Excellent. Please proceed, Keeper."

Everyone watched as Horace pulled the Fel'Daera from its pouch. Feeling a bit of stage fright suddenly, Horace focused on the task at hand. It was now 10:20, and he was reasonably sure Bo Peep couldn't arrive any sooner than 11:40, an hour and twenty minutes from now. He would try to set the breach at a bit over an hour, just to be safe, even though he suspected Bo Peep wouldn't show up until closer to midnight.

Ignoring his audience—particularly Mr. Meister and his great left eye—Horace took hold of the silver sun with his thoughts. He found the valve and squeezed it closed slowly, turning down the flow. The gleaming silver rays began to go dark one by one as the breach shrank. Cautiously he kept clamping down. Once the breach sank below the hour and a half mark, he tried to pin the valve in place, stabilizing the flow. Nothing happened. The breach threatened to reopen again. He remained calm and tried again, pressing much harder. At last the breach settled.

Horace examined the single silver ray that still glowed. "An hour," he said. "Almost exactly." That would work fine. He'd just have to keep checking the box during the next forty minutes or so, especially as it got closer to eleven. He squinted at the ray again, another new kind of time sense suddenly shimmering to life inside him. He could tell exactly how full the silver sun was, the same way he always knew the time. "Actually, to be exact, fifty-nine minutes," he said.

"Excellent," said Mr. Meister. "Very well done. And now?"

Right. The job was only half finished. Quickly Horace oriented himself mentally to the moment, to this uncertain game of tracking and baiting and waiting, to everyone's roles so far, and also—as best he could—to the Keeper who was out there somewhere following the call of the daktan. It was 10:21. He was positive Little Bo Peep could not possibly arrive within the next fifty-nine minutes . . . but being absolutely positive was a bad idea when using the Fel'Daera.

He twisted the lid open easily. He blinked at what he saw. Through the Fel'Daera's blue glass, the river itself looked astonishing—*a ribbon of shivering static, both grainy and textureless at once, a fine and crackling misty road.* Horace just watched it for a while. He'd never seen anything like this before—but then, he'd never looked at flowing water through the box before. He reasoned that the static was due to the chaotic turbulence of the water's surface. On the one hand, you had millions of tiny ripples, all connected, whose precise futures were probably impossible to predict. But on the other hand you had the river itself, the whole body of it steady and reliable and constant. Add to that the knife-sharp clarity of the narrow breach, and Horace could hardly—

"See anything?" said Mr. Meister patiently.

"Oh. Sorry." Horace tore his attention away from the spectacle and scanned the bank. There, he saw—*Chloe and himself, sitting side by side; Gabriel standing a ways off with Mr. Meister and Mrs. Hapsteade.* They were clearly waiting. Horace spun in a full circle and didn't see Neptune, but that was to be expected. She was probably high above, keeping watch.

Horace briefly considered trying to widen the breach a little, to push the dial of the silver sun forward in time, but he wasn't confident he could maintain control. Opening the breach was still difficult for him, and the last thing he wanted was to slip forward to a full day. No, he'd leave it at fifty-nine minutes and keep checking.

"We're here. We're waiting. Everything looks fine." He closed the box. "My guess is she'll be here around midnight, give or take ten minutes. Once it gets closer to eleven, that's when I'll really have to keep watch."

"Just so," said Mr. Meister. "We wait."

"So the plan is to wait?" Chloe asked skeptically.

"When one has the Fel'Daera, one does not make plans," Mr. Meister said.

"Okay, but . . . does one at least decide what one will do if this whole thing turns out to be a trap?"

Mr. Meister sighed. "If it is a trap, Horace will see it long before the trap is sprung. Have faith in your friends, Chloe. Time is on our side." He turned and wandered off with Mrs. Hapsteade, the two of them talking quietly and disappearing among the trees.

Gabriel stood where he was, as if he might stay there forever. Chloe took a seat on a large rock, and Horace joined her.

"Sorry," Chloe mumbled, glancing down at the Fel'Daera. "You know I'm not doubting you, it's just that this daktan sucks. It's like a fistful of miserable. I want this to be over with."

"It's okay," Horace said, and left it at that. He was getting used to plans being dependent on his powers, but he preferred not to dwell on it. In the silence, night noises rose around them—pulsing frogs and crickets, the whisper of leaves, the murmur of the river. Only the distant hum of traffic reminded them they were still in the city.

"Anybody got marshmallows?" Chloe said after a while. "We need to start bringing food to our stakeouts."

"So now it's a stakeout?" Horace asked.

"Stakeout . . . trap . . . welcome home party. Helpless human . . . hordes of Riven . . . who knows? I'm just worried that Bo Peep will turn out to be a human who's playing for the wrong team. Remember Ingrid?"

Gabriel shifted uncomfortably but said nothing.

"Ingrid helped us escape from the nest," Horace reminded her.

"Ingrid helped *Gabriel* escape from the nest," Chloe said.

"Same difference."

Gabriel stirred again, and now he did speak. "No. Chloe is right. It's true that Ingrid freed me from the golem that night in the nest, but her actions were . . . personal. After she released me, she begged me never to go back to the Wardens." He drew a line in the dirt with the tip of his staff, then scribbled it out. "She has chosen her side, and it isn't ours."

This was the most Gabriel had said about what had happened after he'd been captured in the nest. "But . . . *why?*" Horace asked. "Why would she choose that side? Why would *anybody*, for that matter?"

Gabriel looked straight at him with those ghostly eyes. "Why does a blade of grass bend one way and not the other?"

"Whoa," Chloe said, waving her hands and frowning. "Let's keep our floaties on, Dr. Deep End. The point is, being human does not guarantee that Bo Peep is on our side. But what will we do if she's not? Do we destroy the daktan?"

"I don't know," Horace said, instinctively recoiling against the idea. "I guess that's why Mr. Meister gave you the daktan in the first place. Only you can keep it safe without destroying it."

"You could do even better. You could send it traveling again. It'd *really* be safe then."

Horace hadn't thought of that. "For a while, yeah—"

"No," said Gabriel. "Mr. Meister gave the daktan to Chloe not just because she can keep it safe, but because she can truly destroy it if need be." Horace and Chloe stared at him for so long he seemed to feel it. He shrugged. "I know how Mr. Meister's mind works. He's prepared to find a permanent solution if he has to. The Fel'Daera is not a permanent solution."

"He's right," Horace said. "Remember the malkund?"

He watched Chloe realize it was true. In order to get the malkund—a cruel, traitorous gift of the Riven—away from Chloe's father, they'd first sent it through the Fel'Daera. But sending it through the box had only delayed their problem, not solved it. And when the malkund returned, Chloe had utterly destroyed it by embedding it in solid steel, a trick she'd learned with the dragonfly. Melding, she called it. Afterward, she'd admitted that she should've melded the malkund in the first place. Chloe opened her hand now, revealing the little flower, black and fragile and hideously sad.

"I'm not positive I could bring myself to do it," she said. "I don't think I could destroy part of a Tan'ji."

Gabriel seemed as surprised by this as Horace was. "You destroyed the crucible," he pointed out.

Chloe hugged herself, hiding the long dark scars on her forearm. "That was different. That was in self-defense. To save my dad."

"But if Little Bo Peep is allied with the Riven, why would you hesitate?" Gabriel asked.

She swung on him, scowling. "Have you ever destroyed a Tan'ji?"

Gabriel was silent for several long seconds. "Yes," he said. "But I have learned to accept certain truths that you—"

He cut himself off, turning to look back through the trees. A second later, Horace heard cautious footsteps approaching. He saw the glint of Mr. Meister's oraculum in the gloom. Mrs. Hapsteade walked beside him like a shadow of a shadow, her jithandra tucked away.

"Pardon our interruption," the old man said. "I'm assuming we have no news?"

It had barely been five minutes since the last check, but Horace oriented himself and looked anyway. Nothing but the gleaming river, himself and Chloe side by side, and Gabriel standing watch. "Still waiting," he said, snapping the box closed. "But that's what I expected. It's too early for Bo Peep. We've got at least another fifteen minutes before I'll see anything."

"I trust your judgment," Mr. Meister replied. The old man walked over to a nearby tree and slowly sank to the ground at its foot, folding his legs neatly beneath him. He let loose a deep sigh of satisfaction. Mrs. Hapsteade stood rigidly nearby, not even bothering to find a tree to lean on.

"I grew up in the woods, you know," Mr. Meister said, peering up into the leaves overhead.

Horace had no words to respond to that. The idea of Mr. Meister being a child was all but unfathomable.

Chloe, however, clearly felt no such reluctance. "To be fair, it was *all* woods back then, wasn't it?" she said.

Mr. Meister chuckled warmly. "You are funny. And you are at your funniest when you are under duress, it seems." He gave her a kind look. "Would you like me to hold the daktan? I could take some of this burden for a few moments."

"No, let me take it," Gabriel said.

"I could hold it for a while too," Horace chimed in.

Chloe glanced around at them. "So chivalry isn't dead after all. It's just really slow." Then she shook her head. "No, I'm fine. But it might help me if I knew some things."

"Such as?" Mr. Meister asked.

Chloe looked him in the eye. "All those daktan you have back in the Warren—have any of them ever come to life like this before?"

The question seemed to make Mr. Meister uncomfortable. He picked at his slacks and flicked an invisible mote of something away. At last he said, "Once."

"And what did you do?"

Another pause, and then: "We destroyed the daktan in question, before its Keeper could find it."

Horace hid his surprise—so a daktan *had* been destroyed before. And as far as he knew, there was only one reason to commit such a troubling act. "Was the Keeper a Riven?" he asked. "Or with the Riven?"

The old man shrugged sadly. "I do not know."

"But . . . if you didn't even know who the Keeper was, why did you destroy the daktan?"

Mr. Meister leaned his head back against the tree and sighed. "This was long ago. At the time, it was not my decision to make. But I was told—and briefly believed—that it was an act of mercy." He looked at them and lowered his voice. "You've seen Tunraden, Brian's Tan'ji. You've seen what Brian can do."

"Yes," Horace and Chloe said together.

"Should the opportunity arise, I have hope that Brian

330

can reattach the daktan Chloe carries tonight. But when the first daktan came to life—this was long before Brian was even born, you understand—no such hope existed. Tunraden had no Keeper, and most of us doubted she would ever find another. And as long as Tunraden remained without a Keeper . . ."

"You had no way to reconnect the daktan," Horace finished.

"Just so. We could not have repaired the broken instrument, even if its Keeper had been an ally. He or she would have remained incomplete forever, always feeling the burn of that missing piece, always crippled by that wound." He shrugged sadly. "And so the decision was made to destroy the daktan."

Horace felt Chloe recoil slightly beside him. He leaned back, looking up and spotting an open patch between the trees where a few unidentifiable stars shone. How must that Keeper of long ago have felt, searching for their lost daktan, only to have it destroyed before it could be found? What pain must that have caused?

Again he thought guiltily of Bo Peep, and his own rash decision to send the flower daktan traveling. Surely she must have assumed the missing piece was destroyed. Surely it must have hurt. Horace tried to imagine the sensation: a piece of the Fel'Daera—the silver sun, perhaps—stripped from the box and shattered, crushed, melted, obliterated. He shuddered and blushed with private shame. He tried to imagine whether Mr. Meister had felt that same shame so many years ago.

"I have another question," Chloe said.

"As you wish," Mr. Meister said, sounding melancholy.

"How many daktan are there altogether, back at the Warren?"

"Nearly two hundred."

"Two hundred! But in a very long period of time—" She interrupted herself and glanced at Mr. Meister. "No offense. You're super old, right?"

"Outrageously old," Mrs. Hapsteade said. Mr. Meister smiled and nodded in agreement.

"Right," said Chloe. "So in a very, *very* long period of time, only two out of two hundred daktan have come to life. Only two of the instruments those daktan came from ever found a Keeper. Why?"

"Partly because broken instruments are less likely to draw potential Keepers near. But even then, the Find is more difficult with a broken instrument—often impossible." He sighed and stroked his chin. "Many Keepers remain trapped in the early days of the Find. They never discover their abilities. They never become Tan'ji."

Silence fell over the clearing. Horace knew they were all remembering the early days of their own Finds, the frustrations and agonies of not yet knowing what *had* to be known. He could scarcely imagine being trapped in that state forever.

Suddenly, startlingly, Mrs. Hapsteade began to sing. Her low voice was surprisingly sweet. The words were "Little Bo Peep," but with extra verses Horace had never heard before, and set to a tune both lilting and sad at once, eerie and light, a tune that trickled out into the woods and sent goose bumps thrilling up and down Horace's arms:

"Little Bo Peep has lost her sheep,
And doesn't know where to find them.
Leave them alone, and they'll come home,
Wagging their tails behind them.

Little Bo Peep fell fast asleep,
And dreamed she heard them bleating.
But when she awoke, she found it a joke
For they were still all fleeting.

Then up she took her little crook,
Determined for to find them.
She found them indeed, but it made her heart bleed,
For they'd left all their tails behind them.

It happened one day, as Bo Peep did stray
Unto a meadow hard by—
There she espied their tails side by side,
All hung on a tree to dry.

She heaved a sigh and wiped her eye,
And over the hillocks went rambling;
And tried what she could, as a shepherdess should,
To tack again each to its lambkin."

Mrs. Hapsteade fell silent. No one else spoke. Not even Chloe had anything to say. At last, after a full minute, Mrs. Hapsteade sighed and said, "There are miseries in what we do."

Mr. Meister hummed thoughtfully in agreement. "Yes, but there are triumphs, too. I have hope that tonight will bring us no new regrets."

Horace knew these words were meant to be inspiring, but once they were out an even deeper silence seemed to settle over the little group. They sat and watched the river slide by, each Warden lost in private thoughts. Horace checked the Fel'Daera every few minutes, but very little changed. It was now getting closer to eleven, and his best guess placed Little Bo Peep's arrival sometime around midnight. With the breach at fifty-nine minutes, he ought to be seeing something soon. But what would he see?

At ten minutes to eleven, Mr. Meister stirred and lifted his head to the sky. A moment later Neptune swept heavily into their midst, sailing in from over the river and coming to a running halt. Her eyes were like moons as she gazed around at the group.

"Not to be a drag," she said, "but we have a problem."

CHAPTER NINETEEN

Witness

EVERYONE SCRAMBLED TO THEIR FEET, THE OLD MAN JUST AS quick as the rest of them. "What happened? Did you find our lost Keeper?"

"Almost definitely. There's a canoe on the river with three people in it. Humans. I didn't get a good look at them—I only sensed them. One is a young kid, but the other two were bigger."

"What, then, is our problem?" Mr. Meister asked.

"For starters, two hunting packs of Mordin are following the canoe. They're creeping along the bank, hanging well back. I don't think the people in the canoe know they're there."

"Two packs?" Chloe said. "What's so special about Bo Peep that they send six Mordin after her?"

Mr. Meister waved his hand dismissively, as if this was a

335

stupid question. "The Riven know she is seeking her daktan, and they rightly assume the daktan is in our possession. No doubt they hope she will lead them to the Warren. That is why we are here, and not back home."

That seemed reasonable to Horace, but he had another question. "Is Dr. Jericho one of the Mordin?"

"Yes," Neptune said.

Horace tightened his grip on the Fel'Daera. With Dr. Jericho around, of course, using the box was risky. For reasons not even Mr. Meister seemed able to explain, Dr. Jericho was especially attuned to the Fel'Daera, able to sense the box being used—not only in the present, but also through time, from the other side of the glass! And Horace had been using the box steadily since they arrived. Had he already given them away?

"Like I said, though," Neptune continued, "that's just for starters."

"Explain," Mr. Meister demanded.

But before Neptune could speak, Chloe said bluntly, "You're all wet."

It was true. Her cloak was heavy and clinging, her wet hair dangling limply. She was soaked through.

"Am I?" Neptune said innocently. She grabbed her cloak and wrung out the end, spilling water onto the ground. "I was following behind the canoe, trying to get closer, and then I—" She made two fists, as if she could not endure what she was about to say, then threw her hands out, fingers spread. "I was cut off."

Mr. Meister took an alarmed step forward. "You were severed?"

"Yes. One second I was drifting over the river, and the next it was like I was in the Nevren. I couldn't feel my tourminda. I got heavy and I fell. I was only about twenty feet up when it happened, but I'm lucky I was over the water." Her eyes grew wider, her gaze sliding into the distance. "Do you know how long it's been since I've fallen? Even slipping on the ice, or tripping on the stairs? I never fall. I almost forgot what falling even *is*."

"But how could you be severed like that, out in the middle of nowhere?" Horace asked, afraid he knew the answer.

Neptune shuddered. "Whoever our Little Bo Peep is, she's got a Tuner with her."

Though he was half expecting to hear it, the word hit Horace like a blow. Gabriel stroked his chin and thumped his cane against the ground. Mr. Meister gazed into his own hand, opening and closing it slowly. His gray eyes were huge with shock. When he spoke, though, his voice was icily calm. "If I may ask, for how long were you severed?"

"I'm not sure," said Neptune. "Who can be sure? A long time, I think—minutes, altogether. But coming out of it wasn't sudden, like the Nevren. It was slow, like I was . . . tangled up—fighting my way up out of a giant bowl of spaghetti."

Mrs. Hapsteade and Mr. Meister exchanged a look, then moved together into the shadows, where Mrs. Hapsteade whispered urgently as the old man dug through the pockets of his vest.

Chloe turned to Horace, clearly unsettled. "A Tuner," she said. "Like your mom."

Neptune's mouth dropped open. "Goodness," she said to Horace. "Someone's been keeping secrets." Gabriel, on the other hand, looked unsurprised.

"It's not my mom out there," said Horace.

"No kidding," Chloe said. "But whoever it is can do the same stuff. Maybe it's the Tuner your mom told us about."

Horace had already considered that possibility. How many Tuners were there in the world?

"There is no reason to think *any* Tuner means us harm," Gabriel said.

"Yes, *I* certainly can't imagine a reason to think that," Neptune said airily, wringing another dribble of water out of her cloak.

"Preach it," said Chloe.

Off in the trees, Mr. Meister and Mrs. Hapsteade seemed to be arguing quietly. The sight made Horace wonder if Chloe was right—maybe this Tuner *was* the same one the Wardens had banished years before.

"Tuners are our allies," Gabriel said with conviction. "Perhaps the Tuner on the river didn't even know Neptune was human."

"Perhaps," Chloe said, crossing her arms. "But these Tuners could be seriously bad news if they wanted to be." Chloe tipped her head apologetically toward Horace. "No offense to your mom."

"None taken," Horace said, only half listening to her. Mr. Meister seemed to be winning whatever argument he and Mrs. Hapsteade were having.

"I mean, a Tuner who wanted to could pretty much wreck us, right?" said Chloe. "And if anybody should be worried, it's Neptune and me. Not you two."

"Wait, what?" said Horace.

She looked at him flatly. "Neptune. Me. Not you. What happens to us if we're using our instruments and we get severed with no notice? Have you seriously not thought about this yet?" She sounded insulted. "You already heard what happened to Neptune. She got lucky landing in the water. And then there's me."

Comprehension dawned over Horace, but Chloe wasn't through with him. She leaned against a nearby tree, and the Alvalaithen's wings started vibrating. Slowly she began to back into the tree, disappearing bit by bit beneath the bark, her eyes locked on Horace. "I do remember the malkund," she said, sinking into the tree until only her head and throat remained. "I remember how I destroyed it."

Goose bumps raced down Horace's arms. "Stop that," he said, his stomach twisting.

"Imagine I get severed right now, Horace," said Chloe, her face seeming to float in the darkness. "I'll be melded. Imagine how it turns out for me." A single hand emerged and drew a finger slowly across her scarred throat. Horace wanted to shut his eyes but could not stop staring. Why hadn't he thought of this before?

Suddenly Mr. Meister was in their midst. "Enough," he said to Chloe. "We do not need this drama. We are well aware of the dangers." Chloe stepped casually out of the tree, throwing a sullen glance Horace's way, which—he knew—was about as close as she got to showing fear.

"Henrik, maybe we should go," said Mrs. Hapsteade. "We weren't prepared for this."

Mr. Meister looked at Horace. Horace wanted to agree with Mrs. Hapsteade. A Tuner, an unknown Keeper with an unknown power, two packs of Mordin, Dr. Jericho. He wanted to agree it would be crazy to stay, except for one thing—the box had repeatedly shown all of them, waiting by the riverbank. According to the box, they would stay. And Horace had learned not to willfully abandon the future the box revealed. There were always consequences.

But then again, now he had new information. Knowledge of the future could change the future. "Hold on," he said. "Hold on." He got his bearings as swiftly as he could, trying to gather all the threads neatly into a single woven braid— so many threads, more than he'd ever considered at once, a dozen individuals, Keepers and Tuners and Riven alike. So much danger just around the bend.

For a moment the image of Chloe's disembodied face surfaced, scattering his thoughts like leaves on an wintry breeze. But he collected himself and concentrated, struggling not to worry about what he might see. "No promises," he murmured, half to himself and half to the others.

"None expected," Mr. Meister said. Mrs. Hapsteade frowned.

It was 10:56. Horace opened the box.

The scene had changed.

Half in and half out of the chattering water, the dark slice of a canoe, hauled onto the bank, Horace himself beside it; a small boy still sitting in the canoe, his face pinched with worry; off to one side, Chloe, standing next to another new arrival—a slender girl almost as tall as Horace, with long straight hair; Chloe rubbing a hand against her own leg.

"They're here," he said hoarsely, barely able to find his voice. The girl was messing with her hair, like she was trying to put in an earring. What was she doing? "There's a girl . . . about my age. I think it's Little Bo Peep. There's a boy with her."

"And the Tuner?" Mr. Meister said grimly. "Where is she?"

Horace spun slowly, noting that the old man apparently assumed the Tuner was a she. There were only two logical assumptions to make of that: either all Tuners were female, or this was the Tuner his mother had told him about. Powerful, she'd said. A thief. Banished. That was all Horace knew, but if it really was her out there . . .

"I don't see her," Horace said, trying to shake his doubts. Through the box he saw—*Gabriel, poised alertly with staff in hand; Mrs. Hapsteade beside him.* But as Horace watched,

341

Gabriel blurred, seeming to split into two. Mrs. Hapsteade briefly became an unrecognizable cloud. "No, no, no," Horace murmured to himself. He turned farther, still looking. *Now Mr. Meister, moving closer, ghosting smudgily through the trees as he approached the girl; something in his hand, a bird's face with a glinting eye—or was it?*

Horace blinked and looked again. *The glinting eye gone now, the empty hand obscured and hazy.* What could that possibly mean? Horace turned in a complete circle and saw no one else, but as he came back to future Chloe and Little Bo Peep, they rippled slowly in and out of sight like stones beneath shallow waves. Another misty form stood by the water—Mrs. Hapsteade? Yes, but fading badly. Gabriel was a smudge of motion. And Mr. Meister, it seemed, had disappeared completely.

Horace snapped the box closed. "It's no good," he said. "It's getting blurry. Nothing is clear. I can't tell if the Tuner is here or not."

"What is the difficulty?" Mr. Meister asked.

"I think it's because I'm . . . incomplete. Not grounded." Horace stopped and gathered his thoughts. It was the Tuner that was unsettling him. His uncertainty about her in the present was rippling forward to make uncertainty in the future. "I'm trapped between knowing and not knowing."

"In what way, Keeper?"

Horace looked Mr. Meister in the eye. "My mom told Chloe and me a story. About a Tuner—someone she worked with, years ago."

Mr. Meister took off his glasses. He pulled a small cloth from a vest pocket and began to polish them. His naked eyes were tiny and troubled.

Horace glanced at Chloe. She nodded, urging him on. "And because of that story," he continued, "there are things I suspect, but don't know. Things you're not telling me. Things that might have a big effect on how tonight turns out."

Mr. Meister put his glasses back on. He looked at Mrs. Hapsteade and she gave him the same nod Horace had just gotten from Chloe. "Very well," he said crisply. "Yes, Mrs. Hapsteade and I believe that the Tuner on the river is the same Tuner that worked for us years ago. She worked with your mother."

"Okay," Horace said. He hadn't quite expected Mr. Meister to admit it. His heart began to race. "But how do you know it's the same person?"

"The way Neptune was cut off from her instrument—the way she had to struggle to become fully connected again. She was not merely severed. Her threads were tied off. I know of only one individual who possesses that particular talent."

"So she's extra powerful," said Neptune.

When Mr. Meister didn't answer right away, Mrs. Hapsteade stepped in. "Her harp is *very* powerful. So powerful that she might not have it completely under control."

That's what Horace's mother had described—people being severed with no warning, for no reason. He glanced at Chloe. She was fiddling nervously with the dragonfly. "My

343

mom said you banished her," he said to Mr. Meister. "Why?"

"She stole from us," Mr. Meister replied. "She fled, and was excommunicated. We proofed the Warren against her return."

"She only stole the harp that belonged to her, though, right?"

Mr. Meister tsked impatiently. "Harps do not *belong*. Tuners are not Tan'ji. Surely your mother told you as much."

Horace tried to ignore a flare of irritation. "So one of your Tuners stole a fancy harp, and you hid the Warren from her. And now—" He laughed wryly as it all fell into place. "Now she's with Little Bo Peep, following the daktan's signal. So she can find you again."

Mr. Meister nodded. "So it seems."

"She wants revenge," Chloe said suddenly.

"We cannot know that. We cannot be sure what kind of danger she poses."

"Why else would she come back?" Chloe scoffed.

"Who can say?" Mr. Meister said, gazing calmly at Chloe. "Perhaps she is seeking forgiveness." At these words, Mrs. Hapsteade promptly turned and walked away. The old man watched her go and then said, "For what it's worth, I do not believe the Tuner will do us any harm when she arrives."

"For what it's worth," Horace said.

Mr. Meister shrugged. "Make of it what you will. Minutes are passing. Let us see what the Fel'Daera reveals."

Horace stepped up very close to Mr. Meister, speaking low so that no one else could hear him. "Or how about this?

You've got some kind of Tanu that keeps the Tuner from finding the Warren again. How about you use it to hide our location from her now?" When Mr. Meister actually recoiled slightly in surprise, Horace explained. "I saw something in your hand, through the box. Just for a second. A bird."

"Remarkable," Mr. Meister muttered. "How strange it is to hear of one's own intentions before they have formed." He reached deep into a large pocket of his vest, groped around for a moment, and pulled a small figurine halfway out, letting Horace peek at it. Horace recognized it from Mr. Meister's office—the owl with a single glittering yellow eye. It occurred to him that the old man was retrieving it from his office right now, using the power of the vest.

"A leestone?" Horace breathed.

"A spitestone," Mr. Meister corrected in a whisper. "It functions like a leestone, but it focuses its energies on a single individual. In this case, the Tuner in question."

For some reason, those last words aggravated Horace even further. "She must have a name. What's her name?"

Mr. Meister's huge gray eyes darted around the clearing at the others. "Isabel," he whispered, tucking the spitestone away. "Her name is Isabel. But the spitestone cannot hide us from her now—the lost Keeper follows the call of the daktan, and Isabel follows alongside."

"Then why did I see it in your hand?"

"I don't know, Keeper. The future is yours to see, not mine."

Horace turned and walked away, mulling over the few

345

new facts Mr. Meister had given him, letting them trickle down through his mind like coins through a sorting machine. He didn't feel confident that he could bulldoze his way logically through this situation, but at least now certain unknown quantities had been named. And the more he knew, the better. But did he know enough?

Chloe followed and planted herself in front of him, hands on her hips. The Alvalaithen seemed to glow in the darkness. His eyes fell on the little scars that surrounded it, made by the Alvalaithen itself getting caught inside her flesh. Another angry stab of worry pierced him as he thought about the mysterious Tuner—Isabel—coming toward them now. How strange that even though Chloe was the most invincible of them all, she always seemed to be in so much danger.

"I was thinking, maybe it's my fault the Fel'Daera is blurry," she murmured. "I put on that little show. I scared you."

"It's not your fault," Horace said.

"You can't be afraid for me. It'll just make things go wrong, like it did that night you left the message in the toolshed."

She was right. Since then, he'd learned not to wish too hard for a safe future, but he hadn't yet learned . . . what? Not to care? Was that the next lesson he had to master?

"I worry about you," he said.

"Well, yeah. Who doesn't?" She reached out and placed a single knuckle against the Fel'Daera, a shocking infraction. Her eyes practically dared him to say something. "You can't

346

control what people do, Horace. You're only a witness." Then she dropped her hand and walked away, leaving Horace there half heartbroken and half fuming, amazed as he always was by her raw courage, and leaving him entirely sure—for just a moment—that there was no more breathtaking thing in the world than being Chloe's friend.

Mr. Meister cleared his throat. "I believe it would be dangerous to assume she means us harm, Keeper."

It took Horace a second to realize he meant Isabel. "Right. But also dangerous to assume she *doesn't* mean us harm."

"Just so," said Mr. Meister, giving him a deep nod of acquiescence.

Horace gripped the box and prepared himself. He felt sure now, more certain about the threads he had to gather. And part of his sureness, strangely, came from his knowledge that Chloe was wrong—he wasn't just a witness. He was the Keeper of the Fel'Daera. He alone had access to what the future held, and whenever he opened the box he alone took the first step toward creating that future. He was a witness, yes—but he was also an architect, a tracker, a seer, a guide. All of those things, and none of them.

He collected his thoughts and felt the path of knowing form, behind and ahead. It was just past 11:01. The breach was still set to fifty-nine minutes. When Horace was ready, he opened the lid and looked ahead into the midnight that awaited.

To his relief, everything was clear and sharp now: *Himself.*

Little Bo Peep. Chloe, standing up straight, her chin high. And someone else—a woman. "I see her," Horace said, not allowing himself to wonder where she'd come from. This was the future as it would be. Isabel was here. "I can't see her face, but it looks like she's talking to us. She's talking to Chloe, I think." *The dragonfly's wings a shining blur; Chloe's brow, wrinkling with irritation; her teeth flashing.* Horace smiled. "Correction. Chloe's talking to her."

"We've seen all we need to see, then," Mrs. Hapsteade said. "Henrik, perhaps we can stop now?"

"Not yet," Horace replied. He kept looking, turning— *Gabriel, off to one side, the boy from the canoe now clinging to his back, piggyback style; a small gauzy cloud surrounding them both.* "I wouldn't exactly say we seem relaxed," Horace said. "Gabriel is over there. He has the boy from the canoe on his back, and the two of them are hiding inside the humour. Just them and no one else. But why?" He continued to turn. "Mr. Meister is standing right there, with Mrs. Hapsteade at his side. She's looking over her shoulder at—"

And then abruptly, the view through the box flickered and became smoky. For the barest of seconds, Horace was sure he'd lost his focus again, that the future was becoming unknowable. But almost right away he knew better.

Gabriel had thrown the humour out wide, enveloping them all.

But Gabriel never used the humour without a good reason. Horace spun back—*Gabriel's eyes, black and bottomless,*

348

his face torn with anger; the humour streaming from the tip of the staff like a flame; the boy on his back with his eyes squeezed shut, shouting words Horace could not hear. And then, farther back in the woods, Horace saw the reason—*several monstrous shapes, spread out in a line among the trees, dark and gaunt and menacing.* Mordin. He couldn't make out their faces, but their shapes were unmistakable. Horace had never seen so many at once.

"Mordin," he said. "Five or six, at least. And now Mr. Meister and Mrs. Hapsteade are—" He stopped, rendered speechless by what he was seeing.

Mr. Meister and Mrs. Hapsteade, running not from the Mordin but toward them; Mr. Meister reaching into his vest and pulling something free; then an approaching Mordin blown back as if struck by a car. Mrs. Hapsteade, wielding a weapon of her own—a wand? Seriously?—flicking it at another running Mordin; that Mordin jerking violently to a halt, as if chained by the neck.

This was a battle in earnest now. A war.

"What are you doing to them?" Horace breathed.

"Nothing yet," Mr. Meister said tersely. "Tell me about the Tuner."

Horace stared for another moment, catching a glimpse of what looked like a large stone, plummeting perilously from the sky and grazing one of the Mordin. That must have been Neptune. He kept turning, looking. *Chloe, arms thrown back and head held high, roaring blindly into the humour; Little Bo Peep, groping slowly with eyes wide open, face lifted toward the sky.*

But where was Isabel? "I lost her," Horace murmured.

But that wasn't all he'd lost. Where was Horace himself?

Horace turned toward the shimmering midnight river and got one of his answers. *His own future self standing beside the grounded canoe, looking across the water, empty hands held aloft—* but no, the empty hands were an illusion. The Fel'Daera was there, invisible because the box never revealed its future self. Obviously Horace would be holding the box an hour from now, using it. He didn't question why, but he dutifully noted the time—a handful of seconds past 11:02. And then he followed his own future gaze across the river. What he saw there turned his skin to stone—*movement in the weeds; a towering figure like a tree come to life, a savage face flickering and melting like a flame.*

Dr. Jericho.

He was forty or fifty feet away but still a giant, several inches taller than every other Mordin Horace had ever seen. He stood alone. Through the box, the Mordin's limbs and head seemed to writhe and divide, becoming many faces, many hands—a side effect of his shifting disguise and the uncertainties of the Fel'Daera. But Horace knew what was coming next—*his many faces collapsing into a single, savage glower; his baleful black eyes seeming to lock on to Horace—this Horace, here and now—through the blue glass of the Fel'Daera.*

"He senses me," Horace said aloud. "He knows I'm watching."

"Dr. Jericho," said Mr. Meister. "He is here?"

"Across the river. He's just standing there, alone. He can feel the open box."

"Shouldn't you close the box, then?" said Neptune.

"No," Horace said. "I want him to know I'm watching. Let him wonder what I've seen. He's the one that should be worried."

"My sentiments exactly," said Mr. Meister. "But where is our Tuner?"

Dr. Jericho held his ground cautiously, apparently frightened of something—the box, or perhaps the Tuner? But there was still no sign of Isabel. Reluctantly, Horace turned his attention away from the scene on the riverbank, wheeling back toward the others and the battle that raged behind. "I still don't see her," he said. "I don't know where she went. Chloe is standing right here. Her hands are wrapped around the Alvalaithen. She's . . . pissed."

He continued to scan the area, pointing and narrating what he saw. "Mr. Meister is out in the trees, there, fighting the Mordin. Gabriel is right where he was. His lips are moving. Oh! Neptune just came down, right there—she's taking Little Bo Peep's hand. Mrs. Hapsteade is backing away from the Mordin, over there, she's got some kind of—"

But as even as he spoke the words, the view changed abruptly—*Mrs. Hapsteade, fading and doubling, a ghost of her future self flickering to life twenty feet from where she'd been, surrounded by a ghostly sphere; now a blurry Neptune, leapfrogging ahead of Little Bo Peep like a film with frames missing.*

"I'm losing it again. What's happening?"

"Maintain your focus," said Mr. Meister. "Find her."

"I trying. I'm looking." But the box was losing clarity, fast.

Was this because of uncertainties about the Tuner again? Or maybe the box had been open for too long—over two minutes now. Unwilling to close the box and reset himself, Horace turned back to the river, hoping to see Dr. Jericho and himself one last time.

And suddenly, there she was. Horace's future self was still holding the box, and Isabel stood right beside him, whispering in his ear. "I found her," Horace said. "She's with me." He couldn't read her lips—between the Fel'Daera's fading clarity and the wispy gauze of the humour, he could barely see Isabel's face at all. She and Horace were both fading, their edges smudging like a chalk drawing.

Meanwhile, across the glittering river, Dr. Jericho stood waiting, his face fixed into a snarl of anger. But he too was beginning to flutter and fade. "Dr. Jericho is still just standing there, across the river. He's outside the humour, so he can't see anything that happening on this side of the river, but . . . would he be able to sense the Tuner? Would he be afraid?"

"Yes and yes," Mr. Meister said.

"I think that's—" Suddenly Isabel fell back, shimmering. She vanished from sight and didn't return. Horace couldn't tell if this was a symptom of the box's fading vision of the future, or something that would actually happen. He needed to know more, needed to see more.

And no sooner had he thought that than Dr. Jericho abruptly stood up tall, as if deeply alarmed. His steady, horrible face began to—there was no other word for it—flip-flop.

From one shape to the other, like a movie flickering back and forth between two frames. And all the while, he continued to fade. What was happening?

A flicker swept across the glass. The view became clearer, and Horace knew why—the humour had been taken down. But even without that cloud of interference, the certainties of the future continued to unravel—*the back of Horace's head flashing, becoming his face; Dr. Jericho flickering between erect and crouching, his body jittering impossibly up and down the bank.* Soon the box wouldn't be able to see anything clearly anymore. "No, no, no," he muttered. "Hang on. Just a few more seconds." Isabel had left his side. The humour was gone. What would the Mordin do now? Horace had to see what came next—just a few seconds more.

And then his thoughts drifted over the silver sun.

Almost before he knew what he was doing, he found himself pushing, trying to widen the breach. Trying to illuminate another tiny slice of the future before it all went haywire. Horace would inch just ten seconds forward, fifteen, ever so slightly, ever so gently, the tiniest nudge. Inside the box, the action sped up, as if he were fast-forwarding through the future. He watched, fascinated. The present dropped away. He kept pushing gently—*the Mordin on the opposite bank, his vicious mouth flashing; Horace himself, holding his ground but winking in and out; Dr. Jericho crouching, his mouth flashing, his long, powerful legs coiling beneath him, and now—*

A sudden leap, the Mordin launching across the water.

Horace panicked. He tried to slam on the brakes but stepped on the gas instead. In his agitated state, his nudge became a shove, and the view inside the box began to flicker nonsensically. Figures darted and vanished, the canoe was ripped away, shapes fell and rose. Meanwhile the shadows around him in the present world were shuddering too, seconds becoming uncountable, and then momentum overtook him as if he were water spilling smoothly over the edge of a cliff, and everything within and without went blue.

Horace blinked. He was kneeling. The box was still open, but he knew without looking that the silver sun was full again, the breach set to twenty-four hours once more.

"Horace."

"No," he murmured. He peeked through the box—*another midnight riverbank, deserted now, no one and nothing.* He closed the box gently.

"Horace." Chloe's voice, close. "Are you back?"

He blinked hard and pulled her into focus. She was bent over him, worried.

"How long was I out?"

"A few minutes. What were you trying to do?"

"It was getting blurry. But I had to see. I tried to push a little forward and I . . . I lost it."

"It doesn't matter. You saw what you had to."

"I can look again. I can readjust the breach. I can start over." He stood and began to push his thoughts into the box, into the power blasting through the center of the silver sun, but he was interrupted by Mr. Meister wandering closer.

"No," the old man said. "Chloe is right. Perhaps there is no need to witness the moment again. Perhaps it would be best to say . . . you saw what you saw."

"Are you telling me not to do it?"

"Certainly not," Mr. Meister said indignantly. "You could narrow the breach and revisit everything you just witnessed for a second time. But I am suggesting you consider how far you could take this particular idea, and whether it seems like a rabbit hole worth falling into."

Horace looked down at the Fel'Daera, frustrated and boiling. Almost at once he realized that if he wanted to, he could use the breach to watch a single moment over and over again, almost endlessly. Witness a moment in the future, narrow the breach, watch the same moment again, narrow the breach, watch again . . .

A rabbit hole indeed. If only he could control the breach down to the second, picking up exactly where he'd left off. Isabel, suddenly appearing at Horace's side and then vanishing, Dr. Jericho leaping across the river toward Horace—those suspended sights were achingly incomplete. Despite his reservations, he itched to look. He was meant to see the future. Seeing was his power, what he could offer to Chloe and the others. Why had everything gotten so blurry, so choppy? Why now?

And then it occurred to him: maybe it didn't matter. Maybe he *would* see the future he had just failed to perceive.

Yes—he would bear witness again, there on the riverbank in an hour's time, just as the Fel'Daera had revealed. Sometime between now and then, he would shorten the breach as far as he could. He would open the box and watch Dr. Jericho on the far side of the river—that's what he'd been doing in the future, standing on the riverbank with the box in hand! Looking mere minutes into the future, spying on Dr. Jericho's actions just before they happened.

The knowledge calmed him, pieces of the puzzle settling gently into place. Gently he slipped the box into its pouch and turned to Mr. Meister. "I know what to do now," he said.

"Good," Mr. Meister said. "And as for our Tuner, it seems you saw nothing to indicate that she means us harm."

"No. In fact, I almost felt like she was trying to protect me from Dr. Jericho."

Mr. Meister smiled with satisfaction. He opened his mouth to say something else, but no words came out. Then he shut his mouth, and after a tiny bow, walked away.

Mrs. Hapsteade cleared her throat, catching Horace's attention. "I've got a question for you, Keeper," she said. "You say Mr. Meister and I were standing over here at first, correct?" She walked over to the spot Horace had indicated.

"Yes, about there."

"And was I on his left, or his right?"

"Um . . . you were on his left."

"Ah, good. Very good." She sidestepped a little, then looked at him as if confused. "How far away?"

356

"I'm sorry?"

"Six inches? Ten? Two feet?"

"I don't really—"

She turned to her right, posing. "And will I be facing him, like this?" Now to her left. "Or will I be like this? And should I hold my chin up or down? Hands raised or at my sides?"

Horace was blushing. He understood the point she was trying to make, but didn't know how to reply. Mr. Meister, meanwhile, was watching silently.

Mrs. Hapsteade pressed on. "Just trying to be accurate. And maybe after you've given me all my instructions, you can do Gabriel. Then Neptune." She clapped her hands together. "Oh, I know! Perhaps we can rehearse it. Let's make sure we all know how to play our roles, right down to the—"

"Okay," Chloe sniped. "He gets it. We all get it."

Horace felt like a fool. He knew very well how hard it was to navigate his own future after he'd seen it with his own eyes. Sharing those details with the others only multiplied the burden, spilling it onto his companions. And now that he considered it, he understood that this was the cause of the blurry, jittery images in the box. By narrating what he'd seen, he'd brought too much of the future back into the present, complicating everyone's course of action. Knowledge of the future changed the future. And by sharing so much of that knowledge, he had overloaded the future with expectations, and his vision had fractured under the strain.

Horace glanced guiltily around. "I'm sorry."

"Don't be sorry," Mrs. Hapsteade said. "Be cautious." She turned and headed over to Mr. Meister.

Gabriel spoke before Horace could say anything else. "No apologies necessary, Keeper. We are all learning."

"Some of us are," said Neptune. "But it's fine. Besides, I already forgot what you said I was supposed to do anyway." Without another word, she launched herself into the air, drifting out over the river to keep watch.

Horace wandered away, feeling grim. Mrs. Hapsteade had never been a fan of the Fel'Daera. She didn't like the way Horace used the box, didn't like the way Mr. Meister encouraged him to witness the future. But that's what the box was meant for, right? He took a seat at the foot of a tree far back from the water's edge. He held the Fel'Daera, wondering if he would ever truly learn to use it properly. Loops of time, lack of knowledge, too *much* knowledge, the stubborn but slippery breach—everything about the box felt like a tightrope act. He understood why the Fel'Daera made Mrs. Hapsteade so uneasy. Still, her unease made him all the more eager to prove that the power of the Fel'Daera was worth the risks.

Chloe sauntered over, the scarlet light of her jithandra making shadows dance on the forest floor. She sank down beside him.

"Don't say you're sorry," she said, just when Horace was about to do exactly that. "I don't need it. Besides, I'm used to you telling me what I'm going to do."

He supposed that was true. She'd done some unimaginably brave things because he'd told her that she would. "I guess it helps that you trust me," Horace said.

"Everyone trusts you, Horace."

"Not Mrs. Hapsteade."

"Maybe not totally, but that's no surprise. I mean, come on—have you seen her hair? Anybody with a bun that tight has *got* to have issues."

Horace knocked his knee softly against hers. "Thank you."

"Yeah, well," she said. "I guess we'll see what happens when it happens."

"Yeah," Horace said. "Actually, that's my plan."

She studied him, glancing down at the Fel'Daera in his hands. "You're up to something."

"I have to be. I saw myself, standing over there by the water, looking through the box an hour from now."

"And?"

Horace rubbed the silver sun, all its rays agleam. "Remember this morning when we tried to balance those eggs? Three minutes?"

Chloe considered him for a moment. "You're going to shorten the breach. You're going to watch the future just a little bit before it happens."

Horace nodded. "I'm going to try. Might as well get ready now." He took hold of the breach again and squeezed. One by one, the silver rays winked out, until only one was left. It always got considerably harder when he got below an hour, but he kept closing it down, straining with the effort. Twenty minutes. Ten. Four. He kept going until a nugget of pain between his eyes grew too sharp to bear, and he pinned the breach in place. He breathed deep, exhausted from the effort.

Chloe's eyes were on the star, where just a dot of silver remained on the topmost ray. "That's better than before," she said.

"Two minutes and two seconds," Horace said, not needing to look. Not as low as he wanted, but maybe better than he could have hoped for.

Chloe shook her head wonderingly. "I don't know if Mrs. Hapsteade is going to love that, but I think it's badass."

Horace thought for a moment, unsure whether to say what he was about to say. "Speaking of badass . . . promise me if you go thin tonight, you'll be careful."

"Because of the Tuner? I thought you said she seemed friendly."

"She didn't seem *un*friendly. But you know how it is. Seeing the future isn't the same as totally understanding it. You have to promise."

"I promise," Chloe said at once, to Horace's surprise. She picked up a twig and twiddled it between her fingers. "Hey, what does she look like?"

"The Tuner? Why?"

"I don't know. Just wondering." She plucked at a weed. "Like, does she look scary? Because your mom doesn't look scary."

"I didn't get a good look at her face," Horace said, remembering. "She was tall. Pale."

"And we're sure this is the Tuner?"

"Who else could it possibly be?"

Chloe shrugged. "I don't know. Homeless person. Santa's elf. Glinda the Good Witch."

"Glinda has red hair," Horace said. "In the books, anyway."

Chloe glanced over at him, clearly amused. "Wow, Horace. Follow the yellow brick road much?"

"I'm just saying. Glinda's hair is definitely red. But the Tuner's hair is blond—way blond. Pulled back in a braid." The Fel'Daera wasn't very good at revealing colors, but the color of the Tuner's hair had been unmistakably blond.

So blond it was almost white.

——✦——

CHAPTER TWENTY

Contact

"Don't turn around," Isabel said, her voice a hush. "But we're being followed."

April nodded in the dark, continuing to paddle steadily forward. She didn't need to turn around anyway. "I know," she said. Behind her in the canoe, a little groan of worry squeaked out of Joshua, but he didn't speak.

They were on the river, and had been in the canoe for nearly two hours now. The river was narrow and winding and had already passed under a number of busy bridges—it felt very much like a secret road into the city, especially in the dark. There had been no sign of the Riven. April had been worried about Arthur, but it turned out he'd been happy to follow the canoe. He even swooped down from time to time and sat on the tip—the prow—emanating a strangely arrogant sense of pride at leading the way.

They'd only gotten out of the canoe twice, each time because of a dam across the river, forcing them to portage around it. April's nautical vocabulary was definitely increasing, but portage, it turned out, was just a fancy word for getting out of the boat and carrying it. It was a word she was happy to learn but not eager to experience too many more times.

Even sitting in the canoe was tiring, despite the fact that Isabel was doing most of the work. April's butt was sore, and her shoulders and back ached, and her knees felt permanently bent. She kept herself distracted by listening to the clouds of fish they passed over, sleepy and sullen, and by chatting amiably with Joshua, who sat on the midthwart, a fancy word for the seat in the middle of the canoe, and most of all by trying not to think too hard about the aching-hot call of the missing piece.

But now they were being followed.

For the last few minutes, Arthur had been agitated by something—or possibly someone?—following behind them. Floating in the air, it seemed. The bird didn't seem particularly alarmed. Mostly confused. Curious. April hadn't mentioned it, choosing instead to concentrate quietly on whatever it was the bird was sensing. April couldn't see it, of course, but it was clearly nothing Arthur had ever encountered before, drifting silently like a balloon. But on at least one occasion, the object—whatever it was—had startled Arthur by alighting briefly in a tree where the raven was perched before launching after the canoe again.

Definitely not a balloon.

"What is it?" Joshua whispered.

"A spy," Isabel said.

"It's not Riven, though," said April. "Is it the Wardens?"

"Doesn't matter. We can't have followers." Isabel quickly pulled her oar into the boat.

"So what do we do?" Joshua asked nervously.

"Not we," Isabel said. "Me."

April turned back. "Are you sure you should—"

"Don't be alarmed, now," Isabel said, her curly red hair gleaming faintly. She grasped her harp. A moment later, there was a startled shout from behind and above—it sounded like a human voice, female—and then a loud *whack* of a splash in the darkness. Arthur, who'd been standing on the riverbank nearby, took wing, wanting nothing to do with the scene. "Paddle," Isabel said. "Now."

They paddled hard, the canoe surging ahead and leaving the sounds of splashing behind. It was minute or two before Isabel spoke again. "Okay," she said. "Rest. I'll steer."

April laid her oar across her lap. Her shoulders were on fire. "You severed someone—whoever that was."

"A tourmindala. They're pesky little Keepers, nothing to really fret about."

April frowned. She wasn't fretting. Worrying, yes, but she kept her worrying on the inside. "These tourmindalas—they have Tan'ji that can let them fly?" she asked.

"Not fly. Float. They sneak and spy. A soft landing's too

good for the Riven, of course, but I don't think that's what we were dealing with, so I made sure there was water below her before I pinched the threads. Either way, they'll leave us alone for now."

Arthur dipped in and out of the darkness and landed on the prow of the boat. He chattered busily at April for a moment, still agitated by the fall and splash. "If that tourmindala was one of the Wardens, though," April said, "I guess now they also know you're a Tuner."

Silence from Isabel. She was silent for so long that now April did feel little trickles of worry creeping across her skin. Isabel hadn't thought it through. She'd given herself away. April turned around and looked at her.

Even in the dark, she could see that Isabel's brow was knitted with concern. But Isabel quickly looked away, pretending to fuss with her bushy red hair and shrugging. "It hardly matters."

"Or maybe they sent someone out here to make sure we're not dangerous, and now you've just convinced them that we are."

"No one got hurt. I made sure of that."

"Maybe they'll make the missing piece disappear again. Maybe they'll even destroy it. I guess you didn't think of that."

Isabel didn't respond, which was fine. The way April saw it, the only good response was regret, and she was pretty sure Isabel had that now. But April had her own regrets. She'd been keeping a secret that might have prevented what had just happened—a secret April could barely even share with herself, for fear of what it might mean.

The missing piece had come closer.

Soon after leaving the lagoons, she'd felt the piece on the move. Moving slowly, yes, in fits and starts, but unmistakably headed straight for them. She'd chosen to say nothing to Isabel, trying to decide whether she was horrified or thrilled. Her stomach sank at the realization that someone else actually had possession of the missing piece—the mysterious Wardens, perhaps?—when meanwhile she herself had yet to even lay eyes on it. But these . . . custodians, as she preferred to think of them—these caretakers—they knew she was coming, and had decided to head out to meet her. They were bringing the missing piece to her, a dizzying thought. The pull became as strong as gravity, if gravity was an electric wire.

Meanwhile the vine's broken stem began to ache like a bad tooth, and she struggled to keep it under control. She sat in the canoe for an hour, measuring the collision course she was now on, trying to grab hold of the idea that this was all *real*.

And then the piece had suddenly stopped moving. It continued to burn hard, closer than ever, but for the past half hour it had simply been lying there all but motionless, somewhere due south of them. Waiting.

Waiting for April.

April was not good at mysteries. Her imagination was

too . . . well . . . stubborn. In her mind's eye, the Wardens had become grim and haughty—stone-faced warriors and long-haired wizards. She pictured them in dark robes and heavy buckles and mighty boots. She imagined the wet and crafty spy Isabel had severed returning to the Wardens with her story. Surely they would confer solemnly and then invoke whatever power they possessed that had made the missing piece vanish before—some kind of cloak, some mystical twisting of the veins—to make it vanish again, maybe for good this time. It felt silly and melodramatic, but hard as she tried to shake the images she conjured up, she could not envision anything else.

"Tell me about the Wardens," April said. "I need to know who they are."

Isabel sighed. "I suppose you're hoping to be one of them now."

"I can't really say," April said, surprised. "I don't even know what that means."

"They'll want you. They always do. You're the right age."

That was hardly enlightening. "Why would they want me? You said they collect Tanu."

"Yes, but they fight the Riven to do it. They recruit new Keepers, to help them."

"Is that how you met them? They recruited you?"

Isabel steered them deftly past a submerged log. "I was too young to know what I was getting into."

Joshua suddenly spoke. "I thought a warden was a prison guard."

"Yes, well that's—" Isabel began, and then started over. "It can mean different things at different times. The Wardens . . . their intentions are good. Someone had to put themselves in charge, and that's what the Wardens did, a long time ago. But people who are in charge don't always . . ." She trailed off again. They floated silently for half a minute. "For us, in our world, difficult choices have to be made. Impossible choices."

"Like leaving home," April said quietly.

"Yes."

"I wonder how the Wardens are going to feel about you returning."

"I don't know. It depends on what I do."

"Last night you said you wanted things to be set right."

"I do. In all the ways. We'll see what happens. We'll see if anyone is willing to listen to me."

"And if no one is?"

Isabel didn't answer. That was fine—April wasn't sure she wanted an answer. They drifted on. April felt strung as tight as a bowstring, waiting for the missing piece to vanish, but it didn't. Her aching muscles were nothing now compared to the shrill pain of the broken stem, calling out to its lost mate. She avoided thinking about it, letting her thoughts run to it and through it, keeping it as secret as she could.

She began paddling once more, to put an end to all this want, all her pointless wondering, to get to the one answer that mattered. Isabel steered them silently through the river's folds, beneath the stone-arched bridges where oblivious cars passed overhead, through dark tunnels of trees that never waned even as the city grew thicker around them. Miraculously—although April didn't believe in miracles, strictly speaking—the missing piece continued to burn.

It must be nearing midnight now. Arthur had nestled himself into a raven-sized hollow just at the tip of the canoe, sleepily watching April's paddle as she switched it from side to side. Joshua curled into a snoozing ball on the floor of the canoe, atop a sodden blanket. Sleep was nothing April could have managed now, despite her exhaustion, not with the missing piece illuminating the sky of her thoughts like a thousand buzzing suns beneath the horizon. They entered into a thickly wooded parkland. The missing piece must now be mere minutes away, she was sure of it.

"Maybe we should stop for the night," Isabel said suddenly. "We have a long ways to go yet."

But that was impossible, of course. That was not going to happen. "No," said April. "Just a little while longer." She plunged her paddle into the water and pulled back hard, willing her tired arms to pick up the pace.

"Wait," said Isabel.

"Just a little more."

"No. Wait. What's going on?"

"Nothing. What do you mean?"

Isabel dug her oar deep into the water and the canoe veered sharply toward shore. April turned to face her, angry to be brought to a halt so close to the finish—but one look at Isabel's face, and April's anger turned to fear. Isabel looked like a wounded and cornered cat, a ball of spite and coiled rage. "You!" Isabel spat at April.

They ran aground against a bundle of tree roots. Isabel scrambled across the canoe, crawling over Joshua to yank April's hair back and glare at the vine. Miradel pulsed faintly, green splinters of light tumbling inside.

"It's close," Isabel said, accusing. "The missing piece. We're close."

Trembling, April didn't know how to be anything but honest. Half of her wanted to shove the woman out of the canoe. "Yes. It's close."

"They brought it out here. They're waiting."

"Yes."

"What's happening?" Joshua said, awake now.

Isabel paid him no mind. "How long have you known?"

"Awhile," said April. "Since the second dam."

"Why didn't you tell me?"

"It wasn't your . . . I wasn't sure what you would do. I didn't want you to—"

"Mess it up," Isabel finished.

"Yes."

"If I'd known they were so close—bringing the piece with them!—I would never have severed that spy. Now who messed up?"

You did, April wanted to say, but she said nothing. She

needed to keep moving. So unbearably close now.

Isabel stood, rocking the canoe queasily. Arthur fluttered into the air, complaining. "I'm getting out," Isabel said. "I need to think."

"I didn't know how to tell you," April said. "I had to keep going."

As Isabel stepped nimbly ashore, Joshua said, "Where are you going? What's happening?"

"Everything's fine," Isabel told him. "Wait here."

Isabel looked back at April. Her small mouth was drawn into a soft frown. "I wasn't ready for this," she said, her voice a boiling brew of scared and sad and mad, and she climbed up the bank and out of sight.

"What isn't she ready for?" Joshua asked April.

"I don't care," April muttered, which was only half true. "Don't worry. She'll be back. She just—"

High overhead, Arthur spotted something. All April's attention collapsed into itself. Something hung in the sky over the river downstream, a distant shape April never could have seen in a million years, but Arthur's sharp eyes had caught it at once. She couldn't see it through his eyes, of course—though the seething vine begged her now to try—but Arthur's reaction to it was crystal clear. He recognized the shape. A new curiosity. Calm vigilance. This was the same figure he'd seen twenty minutes earlier, back upstream.

The spy. The tourmindala.

The Wardens.

371

April picked up her paddle and pushed off from the shore. The current caught the canoe, spinning them, and began to take them downstream.

"What are you doing?" Joshua cried.

"We're going. The missing piece—it's just ahead."

"What? But what about Isabel?"

"She'll find us." April didn't know if that was true—it probably was, because Isabel seemed unstoppable—but right now she didn't care. The missing piece was so close, so *there*. She had to get it. Now. April stuck her paddle in the water and tried to get the canoe pointed in the right direction, but she couldn't control it. She had no idea how to steer this thing. The river spun them until the back became the front. The canoe scraped noisily against overhanging branches on the opposite shore and continued to spin.

April held tight. Once the prow was headed downstream again, she paddled hard. They made some hopeful progress in a straight line but then the river bent and they began to rotate wildly once more, rocking. She told herself it was okay. She couldn't steer, but the river would take them. All she had to do was keep them clear of the banks. The missing piece was so close she could almost feel it in her hand—it was small, so small, but so important. It was everything. It was the tiniest bloom imaginable. A flower. She knew it was. A flower that heard everything.

Wonder filled her, and she turned to say so to Joshua, to tell him what she suddenly knew, but when she opened her

mouth to speak, she realized the boy was sobbing. His crying
hit her ears now and echoed across the black water.

"Hey," she said dropping the paddle into the canoe and
reaching for him. "Hey, it's okay."

"No! You don't do that," Joshua wailed, leaning away.
"You don't leave her." He grabbed her oar and awkwardly
tried to paddle backward. The canoe only spun more.

"She'll find us, Joshua, I promise. But I have to go. My
missing piece—it's so close, and I have to go to it. It feels
like . . . like my heart will explode out of my chest if I don't."
Even as she explained, she hated him for making her explain,
hated herself for hating him. *Always keep calm, always keep
still*—but that was impossible now. She was quivering like a
magnet, drawn by a force she couldn't see or explain or dis-
obey. So close now.

"I know you don't understand," she managed to say. "Just
wait. Please wait. I'm wild right now, okay? Like Arthur. But
I'm not leaving anyone." The beacon she'd been following
was so close, almost in sight now. Joshua stopped paddling
and looked at her hard, no longer crying, his face unreadable
in her blind need, but right this second—more than any other
second she could imagine—she didn't care.

The canoe spun. The river quickened into a sharp hook.
And there on the spit of land it bent around—*there*. The beacon of the missing piece glowed with the heat of an invisible
bonfire. Shapes moved between the trees. Humans. Big and
small. Young and old. Ordinary people—not warriors, not

warlocks. And there was one among them who held what April wanted. The smallest of all, standing boldly on the bank.

The canoe swept around the bend. April paddled for shore with her bare hands, panicked, sure for a moment that they would let her slide by. But then a boy about her age, shaggy haired and husky, waded into the water and clumsily caught the canoe with two hands. He dragged the prow onto dry land.

April stumbled out of the canoe, splashing. She staggered toward the small figure that held the missing piece. A girl. Dark hair. She wore a white pendant around her neck that seemed so . . . *present*, like nothing April had ever seen before—a cross? A bird? The girl stepped toward April, her face so open and fierce that for a moment April thought she was Isabel.

"You have it," April told the girl stupidly. "You have it."

"Yes," said the girl. "I do."

"It belongs to me. It's mine."

"I know." The girl reached into her pocket, into the very heart of the shine that was the missing piece, frowning at April and furrowing her brow. She pulled it from her pocket and held out her hand, uncurling her fingers. "Take it."

There it was. There it was at last. A tiny flower, black as pitch and bright as a star. April tried to make herself reach for it but found she couldn't lift her arms. She was paralyzed, terrified that the girl would close her hand and yank it away.

But instead the girl thrust out her open palm even farther,

her face a knot of displeasure. "Take it," she said again.

The little flower was so beautiful, so perfect. The vine's only bloom. After all the detours and delays, all the searching and losing and finding again, the moment was here, and she couldn't step into it. The moment was here and it was just too—

Suddenly the girl reached out and grasped April's wrist, yanking her arm forward. She unceremoniously dumped the precious flower into April's palm.

"I swear to god," the girl said, practically growling. "Do I have to do everything around here?"

CHAPTER TWENTY-ONE

Then into Now

HORACE COULDN'T HELP BUT SHAKE HIS HEAD AS CHLOE RUBBED her now-empty hand theatrically across her thigh, like she was trying to wipe invisible cooties off her palm. The scene was just as the Fel'Daera had shown, but now he understood the context. The new arrival—Little Bo Peep, here at last—stared down at the daktan with wonder in her eyes, clearly having a moment. Just as clearly, though, Chloe had no interest in letting the moment be.

"I hate to tell you this," Chloe told the girl, with a tone that suggested she didn't hate it at all, "but you've got only a few minutes for your little reunion party. And then some stuff is going to happen that's going to require you to be conscious."

The girl looked up at last, meeting Chloe's gaze with glassy but unflinching eyes. "I wish I could tell you I was ready for that," she said.

Her voice was so earnest and honest that Horace's heart went out to her at once. He still remembered the Find, even if Chloe didn't—the sudden drop, the collapsing of the universe into a single point—and he was guessing the girl was going through something like that right now. Possibly some sadder, crueler version of it. He watched as the girl reached into her hair, as if trying to pin the little black flower to something there. He caught a glimpse of silver beneath the strands of her auburn hair, and knew it was Tan'ji. She was trying to fix her instrument, whatever it was. She fumbled with it stubbornly, but he could see the hopelessness on her face.

Mr. Meister stepped forward. "Not like that," he said kindly. "Not yet."

The girl looked up at him desperately, but then seemed to swallow her need. She nodded and wrapped her fist around the daktan. She glanced about, taking in the group. She even looked up into the sky, as if she could see Neptune overhead. But how could she possibly know Neptune was there? "I'm April," she said. "I guess you were expecting me."

Mr. Meister stuck out his hand, his great left eye riveted to the mysterious Tan'ji buried in the girl's hair. "Indeed we were," he said. "A pleasure to meet you at last. I am Mr. Meister. You are among friends here." He shook the girl's hand and then looked past her. "But it seems you have brought a friend of your own."

The boy in the canoe, who as far as Horace could tell was not Tan'ji, had been watching silently, his fists pressed against his mouth. Now he dropped them and announced robotically, "I'm Joshua. I'm hurt."

"And I'm terrible," April said, wading into the water to help the boy. Mrs. Hapsteade was at her side in an instant, holding her skirt high. "He sprained his ankle," April explained as they lifted the boy from the canoe. His ankle was wrapped in a colorful cloth.

"I fell," the boy added. "I don't always watch where I'm going."

"Neither do I," Mrs. Hapsteade said, which was about as far from the truth as anything Horace had ever heard. "Let's get you over here with Gabriel—you'll be safest with him."

But as they helped the boy limp past Mr. Meister, the old man held out his hand. "Stop," he commanded, the word like a hammer. They stopped, and Mr. Meister bent down to peer at the boy. The quick inspection he'd given April's Tan'ji paled in comparison to the penetrating gaze he leveled at the boy now. It reminded Horace of his own first encounter with the old man, back at the House of Answers on that first fateful day.

"Your name is Joshua," Mr. Meister said after several silent moments.

"Yes, sir."

Another long pause. An interminable pause. Horace counted to ten.

Midnight—and Isabel—was now only three minutes away. What was the old man doing? At last Mr. Meister reached out and clasped the boy's shoulder. "Joshua, I believe I know why you are here," he said.

"You do?"

"Yes. But for now, I want you to stay close to Gabriel. Do whatever he tells you to. Can you do that?"

"Yes."

"Excellent." Mr. Meister straightened as Gabriel stepped forward. "Hold on to him. Keep him safe."

Horace was bewildered, but not even a flicker of curiosity crossed Gabriel's face. He led the boy away, talking to him softly.

Just then Neptune slipped down through the canopy of leaves. She caught a branch and hung in midair overhead, her cloak dangling. "The Riven are almost here," she said, pointing. "There are three packs now, spread out wide through the woods and heading straight for us. They're just a couple of minutes away."

"They hope to pin us against the river," Gabriel said.

Mr. Meister rounded on April. "Not to worry. Nothing we didn't expect. But with the little time we have before they arrive, a question. I believe you had another companion. She carried an instrument—a harp."

"What?" April asked vaguely, watching open-mouthed as Neptune pushed herself back into the sky. She seemed dazed, overwhelmed. "Oh yeah, of course. She got out of the canoe, a little ways upstream."

"Why?"

"Because I . . . I told her you were here."

"She did not wish to meet with us?"

April seemed to scan her memory. "She said she wasn't ready yet."

Horace wasn't sure how to take that—uncertainty, or a threat.

"The Riven have been chasing us," April said. "Those Mordin that are coming—they're after me, I'm sure. I'm sorry."

"Don't be sorry," Mr. Meister said. "That is why we are here. We thought you might need help."

"We escaped from them before. And an Auditor too—"

Mrs. Hapsteade sucked in a sharp breath. Mr. Meister grabbed April by the shoulders. "An Auditor? When? Where?" he insisted, his alarm apparent.

"A few hours ago. Up the river."

"What's an Auditor?" Chloe asked.

Mr. Meister released April and focused on Horace, his eyes slowly widening in realization. "Horace. Please describe to me the woman you saw in the Fel'Daera."

Horace tried not to squirm. Had he screwed up somehow? "I don't know—long blond hair? She was pale. She had a braid."

Gabriel straightened in alarm, gripping the Staff of Obro like a weapon, but Mr. Meister barely reacted. "I see. And she will arrive at midnight?"

"I didn't see the actual moment, but . . . yeah, very close to midnight."

Mr. Meister ran a nervous hand through his white hair. He and Mrs. Hapsteade came together, bending their heads. Horace, standing nearby, could only just hear them. Mr. Meister began to mutter, as if taking inventory: "The Alvalaithen. The tourminda."

"The staff," Mrs. Hapsteade murmured back. "She won't be blind in the humour."

"And what of the Fel'Daera? She could play havoc with the breach, perhaps, but as long as Horace retains possession—"

"Isabel," Mr. Meister whispered, barely audible.

"Is someone going to explain what's going on?" said Chloe.

"A danger approaches," Mr. Meister announced. "Chloe, you must try to get away. Mrs. Hapsteade will take you, and April too."

Chloe crossed her arms. "Thanks, but no."

"This is not a request. Gabriel, stay with me. Keep the boy under curtains as best you can, and may yours be light."

"And yours," Gabriel said with a solemn nod. A second later, he and Joshua vanished as the humour swallowed them—a tiny version of it, anyway. From the inside, the humour was a hopeless gray fog, but from the outside it became a fiendish trick of the light, a slippery spot the eyes refused to focus on. Horace had seen the humour through the Fel'Daera, of course, but the sight gave him no comfort now. Whatever an Auditor was, it clearly had them worried.

"Horace, as for you—" Mr. Meister hesitated, seeming unsure, and then said, "Go with Mrs. Hapsteade."

Horace glanced at Chloe. She shook her head. "But I stay," he protested, pleading with the old man. "I saw myself. So far, everything I saw has come true. I just didn't know—"

"You are leaving. Now."

Suddenly a bird called out furiously from a treetop a little ways upstream, raucous cries that cracked the night open wide. A crow? April spun toward the sound. She cocked her head. "The Auditor is coming," she said.

A split second later, Neptune dropped heavily to the ground and stumbled toward them, breathless. She searched the sky behind and overhead, hands clutched against her chest. "The Mordin have us completely surrounded. There's more of them now—eleven, altogether." Eleven! One short of four full hunting packs. And Horace knew who the twelfth was. "Also?" Neptune said, her voice ragged. "There's an Auditor out there. Very close. She's already—" She swallowed, grimacing as though she'd bitten into something painfully sour.

Mr. Meister eyed her through the thick gleam of the oraculum. "So I see," he said grimly. "Resist her if you can, Keeper. Are you still able to greet our new guests?"

Neptune nodded. She glanced quickly around, then bent and scooped a single hand beneath a half-buried stone the size of a melon. She lifted it as though it weighed nothing—which, of course, it didn't. She tucked it under her arm and sprang into the darkness overhead.

Mr. Meister spun to Mrs. Hapsteade. "Try to get them away. Now."

Chloe threw her arms up in frustration. "Would somebody please—" And then her face went blank with shock. She stumbled back a step. Horace saw with dismay that the wings of the Alvalaithen had begun to flutter madly. What was she doing?

"We are too late," Mr. Meister breathed.

Chloe staggered back another step, holding her hands away from herself as if she were covered in something nasty. "I feel her. Where is she?" She stared around wildly, as if searching for someone. Her eyes were hollow, blazing sockets.

"What's going on?" Horace cried out.

"The Auditor is inside," Mr. Meister intoned gravely.

Horace's skin began to prickle. "Inside—what do you mean?"

And then, like a warrior angel, a tall white figure dropped out of the sky down among them, landing silently in a crouch. It straightened to its full, noble height and looked haughtily around, quickly taking stock of them all.

Horace stared in awe. Here was the woman he had seen. But this was not a woman. This was not even human. It was a Riven, like none he had ever seen. A hair's breadth away from being beautiful beyond measure, the creature had round, brown-black eyes and high white cheeks, a perfect, vicious mouth. Just below her platinum hair, a ruby-red stone seemed embedded in the smooth flesh of her forehead.

This, clearly, was the Auditor.

Chloe stepped forward. She stood as tall as she could and glared up at the creature with burning malice. "Get out," she hissed between gritted teeth.

The Auditor spread her arms wide, and her monstrous hands too—bone white and hypnotically graceful, mesmerizingly foul, an extra knuckle in each of her fingers. "That's no way to treat a guest," she said serenely, her voice like falling sand.

"You are not a guest, Quaasa," Mr. Meister said. "You are a parasite."

"My dear Taxonomer!" the Auditor said with a faint note of surprise, clearly recognizing him. "How funny that you— of all Tinkers—should accuse me of such a thing. Have you brought out your whole collection today? I can't remember when I've encountered such a feast."

"Hey," Chloe said. "Bleachie. I told you to get out. Get out and stay out, or I swear to god, I—"

"You are not allowed to tell me what to do, Tinker," the Auditor said. "*Ruuk'ha fo ji Quaasa*. All doors are open to me."

"Not mine, you sick freak." Chloe bent down and picked up a dead branch as long as a broom and as thick as a baseball bat. She sidestepped into a tree, vanishing, and emerged two seconds later from the other side of the trunk, already swinging the branch with every bit of weight she could muster. Horace had to leap back to avoid being struck, but it hit the Auditor dead on.

And passed right through her.

The unchecked momentum of her swing carried Chloe to the ground. The Auditor laughed, merry and cruel, and then rose slowly into the air. With a grim terror, Horace understood at last. Somehow, some way, the Auditor was inside the dragonfly now, imitating Chloe's power. And apparently she was inside Neptune's tourminda too, using it to defy gravity.

She was hijacking their Tan'ji, using their own powers against them.

Horace hunkered low to the ground and scrambled away, headed for the water, trying to distance himself from the Auditor. His first thought—his only thought—was for the Fel'Daera. Maintain possession, that's what Mr. Meister had said. If the Auditor couldn't actually see into the box, she couldn't use it, right? And Horace, of course, would do whatever it took to never let the box go.

But most of the other Tan'ji here were far more susceptible. The Alvalaithen, of course, and Neptune's tourminda. Horace had to believe Chloe could handle herself, and Neptune too. But what about the Staff of Obro? Would the Auditor be able to see in the humour just like Gabriel could? Would she be able to control it? He was afraid he knew the answer.

And then, from far behind—footsteps, rustling and snapping, approaching the river. A moment later, the biting stench of brimstone.

The Mordin were nearly here.

Horace reined in his panic and stopped, looking back.

The Auditor was floating four feet above the ground, circling the scene. She reached out for a nearby tree and pulled herself clean through it, drifting like a ghost. Chloe was cursing at her. April was backing away, clearly at a loss—what was her power? Was the Auditor tapping into it too?

Beyond them, across the clearing, Horace could barely detect the slick wrinkle in his vision that indicated the unseen cloud of the humour, where Gabriel and Joshua were hiding. Off to the left, Mr. Meister and Mrs. Hapsteade were turning toward the forest, turning to face the looming shadows that now tilted forward down the dark lanes of the trees. Was he imagining it, or had the Mordin actually altered their skin to look more like trees?

But even as Horace looked, the humour was thrown wide, swallowing him with a roar. In his panic, he'd forgotten this was coming. He jumped as the sky and the ground and everything in between vanished into a featureless ocean, the entire clearing and riverbank gone into gray. Every sound became a cavernous murmur—cries of alarm and shouts of command that sounded as if they were deep underwater.

He crouched down again—cowering. He heard the unmistakable high-pitched growl of a Mordin. After that, two muted cracks like distant cannon fire. He'd heard that sound before, he thought, in the tunnels behind the House of Answers after they'd escaped the golem. Horace did his best to ignore the sound now, trusting each Keeper to hold his or her own. He had to trust. The Auditor had erased all their advantages.

Well, almost all. He caught his breath and reasoned it through, trying to calm his nerves, to ignore the senseless sea of chaos around him.

The Auditor was a terrible surprise, and he didn't know who had control of the humour now—Gabriel or the Auditor. But the humour had gone up right on schedule. So far nothing had yet happened that directly contradicted the Fel'Daera's sightings. Not one thing. Perhaps the willed path was still intact.

Horace realized he was counting. He'd been counting off the seconds since the humour had swallowed him—*sixteen, seventeen, eighteen*. It was now one minute past midnight. He'd witnessed this future, of course—fifty-nine minutes ago—and he knew what he had to do. What he was *going* to do. He stumbled as best he could through the horrid nothingness of the humour, assuming he was still headed toward the river. After several steps, he felt spongy ground beneath his feet. He must be near the water. He pulled the Fel'Daera from its pouch and cleared his head, pushing aside his fear and letting his logic come to the surface. If he'd seen truly, Dr. Jericho was due to appear on the opposite riverbank any moment now. The Mordin would hesitate there for a couple of minutes, for a very simple reason.

Fear. Fear of Horace. Dr. Jericho would be feeling the Fel'Daera from fifty-nine minutes ago. He would know that he was living through a future Horace had already witnessed, a stunning disadvantage. Realizing that Horace was a step ahead of him, and worried that whatever move he made might be the wrong one, the Mordin would be hobbled by his uncertainty.

And now, with the breach still set at two minutes and two seconds, Horace planned to add to that uncertainty. Swiftly and surely, he opened the box and pointed it in what he hoped was the direction of the river. He couldn't see through the box in the humour, of course—he couldn't see it at all—but that wasn't the point. When Dr. Jericho arrived, he would be feeling *two* open Fel'Daeras from the past at once! It was a brain-ratttling thought. And when Horace was freed at last from the humour, he would be able to witness the near future unfolding, using his knowledge to do what he could to keep Dr. Jericho at bay, and help his friends.

"Gabriel," Horace muttered quietly into the gray of the humour. He could barely feel the word leaving his mouth. He hoped beyond hope that the Warden could hear him, that the Auditor wouldn't have the power to block his voice.

No response. Horace's inner clock, meanwhile, told him that Dr. Jericho should just be arriving across the river.

"Gabriel," he said again.

Another distant boom. And then, blessedly, Gabriel's powerful voice, quiet but omnipresent. "I'm here," he said, his voice reverberating remorsefully. "I'm sorry for your blindness—I can't stop her. She's blinding you all."

"Can she hear us?" Horace asked. The utter blankness around him was starting to make him lightheaded, and he clenched the box harder, still holding it open.

"I can fend her off for a few moments. She is stretched to her limits, I think. She's inside the staff, the tourminda, the dragonfly. It can't be easy for her to wield them all at once."

Horace's inner clock told him Dr. Jericho had just arrived on the far bank of the river. The Mordin was no doubt standing there, aware that the Horace of an hour ago was watching him through the Fel'Daera, seeing the future unfold. "I have a plan," Horace said. "Well, not so much a plan, but . . ."

"A path."

"Yes. Do you think you can pull the humour away from me? On my mark?"

A pause. "She'll fight me," Gabriel said. "But I'll try."

"You'll do it," Horace said meaningfully. He'd seen it happen.

"Understood," said Gabriel.

Suddenly another voice swept through the humour like fine sandpaper. "What's this?" the Auditor sang. "Secrets? Please share. Whatever is yours is m—"

Her voice was cut off as abruptly as it had appeared—Gabriel's doing, no doubt, wrestling her for control of the humour. Horace thanked him silently.

Horace had every reason to believe that Gabriel would come through. He'd witnessed it.

But there was a problem.

The breach. It wasn't small enough. He'd tried his hardest, but he now understood that two minutes and two seconds was an eternity. The breach was nowhere near narrow enough to be useful. By his reckoning, barely a minute had passed since the Auditor's arrival, and as he listened to the muffled sounds of the battle raging behind him—Gabriel shouting directions, the heavy footsteps of the Mordin, an occasional whale-sized *thpack*—he knew this whole thing might already be over two minutes and two seconds from now.

Horace reached out for the black heart of the silver sun. He caught hold of the breach and bore down on the stream of power that flowed there. At first he couldn't budge it, but slowly the breach began to shrink. It crept below two minutes. Pain crackled between his eyes. He ignored it, thinking of Chloe, and Gabriel, and April, and all his companions—out there doing battle, out there resisting the Riven. He would do his part too. He gritted his teeth, and the breach approached ninety seconds. He wasn't sure what the bottom limit was, but he needed to go farther than this.

No. Not farther.

Closer.

He squeezed harder. The breach plunged below a single minute, Horace's head full of lightning. It was exhausting work, and even as he strained to close the breach, precious seconds ticked by.

And then suddenly—terribly, unforgettably—a presence crept into the Fel'Daera like a cloud of murky ink. An invader, a shadow, a poison. It reached out, fully aware and predatory, groping for control of the breach.

The Auditor. She was inside the box. Horace went numb with shock and then his shock turned to horror as cold lips brushed against his cheek, unseen in the humour. "What have we here, Tinker?" the Auditor whispered coarsely into his ear.

She was right beside him here in the gray. And of course she was—he'd witnessed it, thinking she was Isabel. How could he have been so stupid? Horace couldn't speak, couldn't think. He gripped the box so hard he thought it might shatter in his hands. "Can I play?" the Auditor crooned, and then she pried at the breach, trying to throw it open wide.

On the instant, Horace unfroze. An anger like he'd never felt before exploded in his chest. A roaring wave of will coursed through him, surging into the Fel'Daera. He clamped down on the breach harder than he thought possible, so hard that the creeping presence of the Auditor was blown back from the breach like smoke on the wind. The breach closed even tighter, becoming microscopically small. The flow of power through the silver sun waned to a trickle.

At the uppermost limits of his strength, Horace pinned the breach in place with all the authority he had, hammering it home. A massive thrum of energy tolled through the Fel'Daera, and in its wake, the Auditor's presence evaporated, ejected forcibly from the box. She cried out in astonished rage, her shriek suddenly cut off—whether by Gabriel or by her violent eviction, Horace hardly cared. The Fel'Daera was his again. It would always be his.

Horace nearly fell to his knees, but managed to stay upright, still holding the open box in front of him, out in the gray void of the humour. He couldn't see the silver sun, of course, but he didn't need to. He knew where the breach sat now, though he could scarcely believe it. He'd been trying to get below a minute, and he'd managed that—spectacularly. He felt for it again, just to be sure.

Four seconds.

Too stunned for a moment to remember himself, he spoke with a voice that scarcely seemed like his own. "Now," he said quietly, knowing that Gabriel would hear him, knowing that Gabriel would do as he had promised. The box had shown him as much.

And sure enough, a thin, piercing rumble cut through the air, shaking the earth. The humour vanished. The night returned, but Horace was nearly alone within it. He glanced back, and his eyes slid queasily across the entire clearing and the unseen patch of woods beyond. The battle was still going on, deep within the humour, silent and invisible from outside.

But of course, there was only one thing he wanted to see right now. Across the river, Dr. Jericho stood pale in the darkness, like a dead tree come to life, open astonishment plastered across his face. Horace stepped right up to the water's edge, open box still in hand, knowing the Mordin was now sensing the Fel'Daera not only in the present, but *twice*—once from nearly an hour back, and once from a mere four seconds ago. Horace wondered if the Mordin had ever encountered such a thing before.

Dr. Jericho composed himself. "Ah, my dear Tinker, there you are," he called out, his voice a purr. "And there you *were*," he continued, pointing first at Horace directly and then at a spot farther up the bank, where Horace had been standing fifty-nine minutes ago. "And there you were *again*." He shook his head as if in admiration. "Such a fast learner. In a little over a month, you've mastered the breach. The last Keeper of the Fel'Daera didn't manage that for years. Impressive."

Horace resisted the thin man's taunts about the last Keeper of the Fel'Daera. He kept one eye on the Fel'Daera's blue glass as he replied, channeling Chloe's bravado. "Yes, I'm very talented. Get used to it."

The thin man stroked his chin thoughtfully. "I wonder—what do I do in the next few minutes that is so . . . *vital* . . . that you feel the need to see it twice? You continue to watch me even now. Care to share why?"

The truth was, Horace hadn't seen this future clearly at all. It had been choppy, and then he'd blacked out. But again—there was no reason Dr. Jericho needed to know that. "Not interested in sharing, thanks," Horace said. "You said it yourself: Why would I tell you your own future?"

"Why indeed?" said Dr. Jericho with a menacing smile.

"Tell you what," Horace said, trying to sound more confident than he actually felt. "How about you try something and see how it works out for you."

"Do you know, I would rather not?" Dr. Jericho replied,

but before the sentence was half out, the box revealed the movement Horace had been waiting for, the moment he'd so desperately tried to see beyond, fifty-nine minutes ago—*the Mordin crouching, then leaping across the river straight for him, savage hands outstretched.* Horace nearly flinched, but kept watching—*Dr. Jericho, landing on all fours right where Horace now stood, his teeth flashing.* And then the scene through the Fel'Daera went black, Horace's view momentarily obscured because the Mordin's body—four seconds in the future—was occupying the same space the Fel'Daera was in right now.

Four seconds. Horace would need to dodge at just the right moment. He held his ground, not revealing his hand, letting the future come to him. His automatic counting had begun the instant he saw the future Mordin leap—*one* . . . *two* . . . *three.*

On four, Horace threw himself to the side, tucking the box safely against his belly as he rolled. In the same instant, the Mordin—already airborne—thundered to the ground just as Horace had foreseen, missing him by only a foot or two.

Horace scrambled to his feet, box still in hand. The Mordin laughed with savage glee, measuring him up and preparing for another attack.

But Horace was already ahead of him. Four seconds ahead—*Dr. Jericho, circling to the left; now swiping low with one mighty arm, trying to sweep Horace's feet out from under him.*

Horace crouched. *One. Two. Three.* Horace leapt high on four. The Mordin's arm swept under him, fast as a snake.

Horace barely cleared the blow, stumbling when he landed, but he kept his feet, kept the box open.

"Careful, careful," Dr. Jericho scolded, still circling. "This is a dangerous game you've chosen to play tonight, Tinker."

"I didn't choose it," Horace said, "but I know I win it." That was a bluff, of course, but the thin man didn't know that.

Horace held the box at arm's length, circling with the Mordin and keeping his distance, struggling to watch both now and then at once. It was hard not to be distracted—in the present, the humour was merely an unseeable wrinkle where the forest seemed to buckle and bend. Through the box, though, Horace could see the battle that raged within. He wondered what Chloe was doing. The Auditor would be all but invincible now—flying, formless, and invisible in the humour.

But there was no time to worry. Motion flickered inside the box again—*Dr. Jericho feinting to Horace's left, then lunging to his right.* Horace played into it casually, sliding to his right. *One. Two. Three.* Then he dove to the left, into the thin man's bluff. Now it was the Mordin's turn to stumble as he tried to reverse himself, groping awkwardly. Horace pinwheeled backward, out of his range.

A stab of nausea corkscrewed through Horace's gut. However slightly, he'd just changed the future the Fel'Daera had revealed. He would have to be careful. But the action inside the box wouldn't slow—*the Mordin, reaching high overhead and grabbing hold of a tree branch like some ghoulish, spidery ape;*

lifting himself and swinging forward; now Horace himself, running not away from the attack, but into it, under it.

Horace was already counting, readying himself. *One. Two.* Dr. Jericho stretched upward for the branch. Horace braced himself. *Three.* But just as Horace was about to launch, just as the Mordin's feet left the ground, the Fel'Daera revealed an unthinkable sight. *Dr. Jericho, dropping out of his swing, reaching back with one long arm as Horace sprinted beneath him, catching Horace across the shoulders and slamming him to the ground.*

No. It couldn't happen. Yet Dr. Jericho was already swinging. Horace sprinted toward him just as he'd seen, unsure what else to do. As he ran he cried, "I need help!" He ducked beneath the Mordin's legs, passing him by. He glanced up and saw the Mordin reaching back for him with one great hand, the other still clinging to the thick branch fifteen feet overhead. Dr. Jericho's face was alight with predatory joy. He was going to catch Horace.

And then suddenly—miraculously—a shadow dropped out of the stars. It struck Dr. Jericho heavily in the neck and chest, riding him downward. The Mordin cried out, losing his grip. Even as he fell, he clawed at Horace, his sharp nails raking down Horace's back. The Mordin slammed to the ground, his jaw plowing into the soft dirt.

As Dr. Jericho lay there stunned, Horace scampered away and collapsed against a tree. Another bolt of nausea wrenched him, bigger this time, and a pounding in his head. He'd changed the future yet again—but how?

And then a voice from the canopy. "I see what you're doing, Keeper. Of course you know what's best, but are you very sure this is it?"

Neptune. She'd been floating overhead, obviously, and had heard his cry for help. She'd dropped down onto the Mordin with all her weight and then gone light again, leaping away. Now she stood high in the tree above the Mordin.

"This is the only idea I have," Horace told her.

Dr. Jericho stirred, lifting his head.

"I'm out too," Neptune said. "I'm low on rocks, so I gave him the full Neptune. But that was a twenty-footer I just hit him with, about my limit. And he's still getting up."

Twenty feet! Horace reckoned that with a drop from that height, Neptune had hit the thin man with a force of five hundred pounds or so. But the Mordin staggered slowly to one knee now, shaking his head. He seemed merely dazed.

"It's okay," Horace said. "I can handle this. Help the others."

"They're holding their own. Two Mordin are down, temporarily. Chloe's been calling for you. I came looking."

So Chloe was okay. But of course she was. Horace glanced toward the woods—or rather, tried to. Still the humour rejected being seen. Meanwhile, through the blue glass, Dr. Jericho was nearly on his feet.

"Tell Chloe I'm fine. Tell her not to do anything stupid."

"Considering what you're doing right now, are you sure you're qualified to make a demand like that?"

"Watch out!" Horace cried. Through the blue glass, a genuine scare—*Dr. Jericho groggily regaining his feet one instant; the next, leaping alertly high into the air, swiping viciously at Neptune.* The Mordin snagged Neptune's cloak and yanked her to the ground. But no—this future couldn't come true. Horace wouldn't let it. He cried out, and the box seemed to flicker clumsily. Here in the present, Neptune sprang lightly off the branch, sailing out of sight into the tree. Dr. Jericho got to his feet, glancing up with a scowl, but he didn't even attempt to go after her.

A miasma of queasy pain racked Horace, doubling him over. It was all he could do to keep the box steady as he fought off the effects of this latest—and greatest—refusal to follow the willed path.

"Talented, you say," Dr. Jericho said, watching Horace intently and holding his ground for now—both inside and outside the box. "But not enlightened." The Mordin rolled his neck, as if working out a soreness, and dusted himself off. "Have you not been taught properly?"

"I've been told what I need to know."

"*Need,*" the thin man laughed. "You Tinkers are all alike. You claim not to need what you clearly desire. Don't you wonder about this pain you're feeling now—the pain of disobedience to the box?"

Horace didn't know how to answer. He would refuse to answer. He stood up straight, trying to quell the cramps still roiling in his belly.

"It's called thrall-blight," said Dr. Jericho. "And it's not just you it affects—oh, no. Thrall-blight spreads through the Medium. Even to the Mothergates themselves." Dr. Jericho raised his foul eyebrows in innocent surprise. Inside the box, he had begun to advance on Horace slowly. Horace took a careful step back, his mind reeling with the Mordin's words.

"Has no one ever told you?" Dr. Jericho continued. "Have you never heard the story of Sil'falo Teneves's greatest mistake?"

Despite himself, hearing Dr. Jericho utter the name of the Fel'Daera's maker made Horace's heart skip a beat. "What mistake?"

"The mistake in your hand, of course. The Box of Promises." He spat out the word *promises* as if it were something nasty he'd stepped in.

"Shut up," Horace said. "You don't know anything about it." He kept inching backward. The Mordin kept coming, twenty feet away now, spreading his abhorrent hands.

"I merely repeat what Sil'falo herself has said—allegedly. I am not claiming I agree."

"I know you don't agree," Horace replied. "If you really thought the box was a mistake, you wouldn't want it so badly. You wouldn't want me to join you."

"True enough. And in that regard, am I really so different from your current master? Come with me. Join me. I can teach you things he never will."

His master—Mr. Meister? Horace opened his mouth

to object, but just then the future inside the box went wildly blurry, the ground and the trees and everything in between—including the Mordin—smudging and quaking unrecognizably. He'd never seen anything like this before. What was happening? In the present, Dr. Jericho cocked his head curiously, clearly catching Horace's dismay.

In the next instant, as Horace continued to back away from the advancing Mordin, a sudden tidal wave of sound swept over him—shouts of surprise and roars of anger and a child's plaintive voice calling out.

The humour was gone. But no sooner was it gone than the sounds released by its disappearance also began to fade. In the now-visible patch of woods, Horace saw a scene of chaos grinding to a halt. Mrs. Hapsteade stood exhausted inside the clear protective sphere of a dumin, looking spent, two Mordin lurking outside. Another Mordin, shockingly, had Mr. Meister pinned against a tree eight feet off the ground. The old man wriggled, trying to reach into his vest. Gabriel knelt next to Joshua, staff in hand, his face vacant. April stood behind with glassy eyes. Hardly anyone was moving.

One by one, every figure began to stare, following a peculiar sound—a soft, thin wail of pain. And now Horace saw. A white figure lying on the ground, writhing in pain, hands clutching her head. Her dark green eyes stared into the sky.

The Auditor.

The Mordin began to shout to one another, harsh cries of warning. What was happening? And now another voice, human and familiar: "Horace, look out!"

Chloe. Horace turned toward the sound, but in the same instant backed into something cold and hard—the tip of the canoe, catching him behind the knee. Immediately he was falling, tumbling clear over the canoe. As he fell he caught sight of a new figure, stalking boldly across the clearing. A human. Small, with fiery red hair. At her breast was a small brown sphere, sparkling from within like a night full of green stars.

Horace hit the ground hard, knocking the wind out of himself. The box slipped from his hand and slid away, just beyond his grasp, the lid still open. He strained to reach for it. But what about Dr. Jericho? Looking down along the length of his body, Horace saw that the Mordin had dropped to all fours, his black beady eyes still locked hungrily on Horace— so fixated that he hadn't seen Isabel yet, apparently hadn't noticed or felt what had happened to the Auditor.

But the other Mordin clearly had. They had already begun to scatter, fleeing from Isabel. Mr. Meister's captor let the old man fall heavily to the ground. Another Mordin reached down and helped a fallen comrade to his feet, the two of them sprinting into the woods.

Isabel continued her calm approach. The wicker sphere pulsed and glowed. Without warning—without a sound—one of the fleeing Mordin clutched at its back as if shot. It toppled violently, plunging face-first into the ground. Horace knew without question it was dead.

Breathless, Horace finally grabbed hold of the box. He brought it to his chest and pointed it at Dr. Jericho. He was sure the thin man would run now too, but the box told a different story, promised a different future, horrible and inescapable.

Dr. Jericho, stalking swiftly across the clearing on all fours, stretching for Horace across an impossible distance; his mighty hand wrapping around Horace's lower leg, swallowing it from the knee down. In the present, Horace struggled to scramble backward, counting down even as the events shown in the box began to unfold in the present.

One. Horace slid over a tree root, scraping his hand. He wasn't going to make it. *Two.* The Mordin reached out, his hand opening like the maw of a shark. "No. No!" Horace cried, kicking. *Three.* The Mordin took hold, took hold in the present for real, his hand encasing Horace's leg in a stonelike grip.

In the same moment, another Mordin, galloping away from the scene, crumpled like paper and plowed into a tree with a bone-crunching *thump.* Dr. Jericho, still clinging to Horace's leg, turned swiftly. He saw the fallen Mordin, saw Isabel, saw the Auditor still squirming and keening in the dirt. "No," he said. But he did not relinquish his grip on Horace.

Horace held the box out, staring into it, hoping beyond hope that his fate would be a good one. And then, through the glass, a miraculous sight. An unthinkable sight. Horace's mouth went dry watching.

Dr. Jericho, seizing up as if struck by lightning, his head thrown back in anguish. Horace gripped the box hard, his breath caught in his throat. Time seemed to slow down as he watched—*the*

402

Mordin releasing Horace, then throwing his arms out wide, his fingers as rigid as tent stakes; his many faces collapsing into a single ghoulish skull; and now—now—his long body going slack, collapsing like a rag doll, crumpling lifeless into the mud.

Horace gasped.

One.

Dr. Jericho was about to be cleaved. Tingling with shock, Horace slid his eyes from the box, down along his body to Dr. Jericho. The Mordin looked back at him, furrowing his brow.

Two.

Horace opened his mouth, the words slipping out before he could stop them. "You're next," he said.

Three.

Dr. Jericho's tiny eyes went wide. Twenty feet away, Isabel turned, the wicker harp ablaze. Horace still hadn't taken a breath.

And then, in one fluid movement, Dr. Jericho released Horace's leg, grabbed the prow of the nearby canoe and reared back, heaving hard with a murderous grunt. The canoe left the ground as he hurled it sidearm across his body like an enormous silver spear, straight at Isabel. Horace threw his head to the side and the canoe streaked over his face, missing him by an inch, hissing audibly. Isabel cried out and dropped toward the ground. The canoe clipped her shoulder as it passed, then careened through the trees farther on, tumbling, then crashing to a halt broadside against a thick trunk thirty feet away.

Even as Horace turned to look, his heart pounding like a giant's fist in his chest, the Mordin was airborne, on his feet and leaping back across the river in a single bound. He landed on the far side and scurried up the bank like a nightmare, melting into the shadowy trees. Just like that, he was gone. The woods went quiet again. All the Riven had vanished except for the two dead Mordin and the Auditor, writhing almost silently in the leaves.

Horace fell back, letting the lid of the box slide closed against his belly. He rolled over and vomited, the world spinning around him. So much disobedience, so many willful changes to the futures the box had revealed. And none of them more outrageous than the last one, the worst one. Had he just done what he thought he had?

Had he just saved Dr. Jericho's life?

Chloe squatted down at his side. She didn't touch him—not while he was still throwing up everything he'd ever eaten, plus maybe some things he hadn't yet. But he thought he could feel her concern, warm and feisty. He waited for her to make a joke, but she didn't.

At last his gut stopped heaving. The world began to right itself. He wiped his chin on his sleeve and sat up, slipping the Fel'Daera back into its pouch. He crawled away and propped himself against a nearby tree. He found Chloe's eyes.

"What did I do?" he said.

"You survived. You did it."

"But I—"

"No. No buts. You're safe. Everyone is safe."

Mr. Meister limped over, his eyes on the Fel'Daera. "It is true," Mr. Meister said. "You did well. Everyone did well."

But Horace wasn't so sure. He'd broken just about every rule there was for the Fel'Daera. He'd used it in a way he now felt sure had never been intended. And worst of all, he'd uttered those two simple words—despite the Fel'Daera's predictions—that had saved the life of his worst enemy. He felt miserable. A failure. And judging by the foul expression Mrs. Hapsteade wore at Mr. Meister's side, she seemed to feel much the same.

"Chloe," said a voice. "Chloe, is that you?"

Horace looked up. Isabel. No matter what anyone said, she was the one truly responsible for saving them all. But how did she know Chloe's name?

She'd found her feet and was now approaching, almost drunkenly, clutching her shoulder. The older Wardens backed away silently, faces creased with concern, Mrs. Hapsteade clinging to Mr. Meister's arm. Isabel reached out for Chloe with a trembling, hesitant hand.

Chloe rose to her feet, scowling. "What?" she spat.

The woman's eyes fell on the dragonfly gleaming in the hollow of Chloe's throat. "It is you. I found you. Chloe. Oh my god . . ." She was crying.

Chloe took a step back, studying the woman's face. Her own face became a breaking dam, a wall of furious confusion beginning to crumble. She took another step back, then a half step forward. Her voice, when she spoke, was as fragile as a flower, full of wonder.

"Mom?"

PART FOUR

The Departed

———✿———

CHAPTER TWENTY—TWO

Reunion

CHLOE SLEPT A HORRID SLEEP, AND FOR ONCE, IT WASN'T BECAUSE of the god-awful mattress that smelled and felt like a giant moth-filled sock. Her muscles ached with a deep, all-over ache. Her mind was a nest of surly bees. The bed in her little room at the Mazzoleni Academy rustled and creaked beneath her restless sleep, spilling her from dream to troubled dream— into the tiny prison cell in the Riven's nest, or back to her own bedroom before the fire, or to brightly lit places she scarcely remembered. Her mother roamed them all, red hair ablaze.

Chloe woke slowly, raggedly. She shed her dreams and slipped messily through the wreckage of yesterday's memories. The riverbank, the Mordin, the filthy, miserable Auditor—a creature who deserved to be exterminated if ever there was one. And then, of course, her own mother. Returned against all odds or expectations. Returned not from the dead, but from something like it.

Chloe hadn't seen the woman in seven years. There were a few pictures, of course—or at least, there had been before the fire. That red hair was unmistakable. But now Chloe felt sick at having uttered the word that had risen to her lips in that harrowing moment: "*Mom.*"

Isabel had tried to embrace her, calling Chloe's name over and over, but that wasn't going to happen. No way. Chloe had instinctively gone thin, her mother's arms going right through her. And then Mr. Meister took control, issuing commands in that infernally smooth voice. Immediately Mrs. Hapsteade had whisked Chloe and Horace away, leaving the others behind with the old man.

They'd stumbled along the riverbank, Neptune guiding them from above. They'd crossed a wooden bridge, and then a damp, lumpy meadow. More trees, darker this time, and then a loose and crumbling wall of brick. A cloister. Once inside, Chloe spotted the requisite leestone, flat on the ground and half buried in leaves, this time in the shape of a brownish bird with a splash of blue on the wing. Around the leestone was a motley circle of cabbage-sized stones embedded in the earth. All cloisters had these circles, and Chloe hadn't given them much thought, but now Mrs. Hapsteade and Neptune stalked around the stones intently, clearing away forest debris and examining each curiously shaped rock, Neptune murmuring apparent nonsense: "Wren'laddon . . . Aarnin . . . Navendrel . . . where is it?"

At last Mrs. Hapsteade stopped beside a stone shaped like a half-buried armchair. "Here it is—San'ska." She waved at Horace and Chloe. "Come and see."

Chloe had no idea what she was talking about, and she didn't care. Her mother had returned. Her mother was a *Tuner*. Not only that, but her mother and Horace's mother had actually known each other as children. Impossible. Chloe was so full of rage and confusion—and yes, fear—that she couldn't speak. She thought she might set the air on fire if she opened her mouth.

"Let's go," Mrs. Hapsteade said briskly. "We have to get back to the Warren immediately. Now. The others will meet us there."

The others. Isabel too? Chloe couldn't move her jaw to ask.

Horace asked, "What are these things?"

"This is a falkrete circle," Mrs. Hapsteade replied. "One of only a dozen or so in the city that still work."

Horace, ever curious, stepped forward to examine the chunky stone. "What does it do?"

"It's a transport system. Each of these stones is a gateway to another cloister."

Horace gave Chloe an incredulous look, but she was only half listening. "You mean we're teleporting?" Horace said.

That word got her attention. *Teleporting? What?*

"If you like," Mrs. Hapsteade said. She nudged the stone with one black-booted foot. "This particular falkrete stone

411

leads to San'ska. That's the name of the home cloister—the cloister nearest the academy. But there's a trick to getting there. Neptune, this is your specialty. Would you explain, please?"

Neptune stepped forward, her tourminda in hand. She crouched over the stone, holding her Tan'ji just above the jagged surface. "When you're ready, hold your instrument against the falkrete. You'll immediately split in two, and then—"

Shoving thoughts of her mother aside, Chloe spoke at last. "I'm sorry—*what?*"

"You won't physically be ripped in two, of course," Neptune explained. "Actually what happens is you'll be in two places at once—you'll be here in this cloister, but you'll also be in the destination cloister."

"How does that work?" Chloe said.

"It's a quantum state," Neptune said. "Like Schrödinger's cat."

Horace shook his head. "No way. That's not possible. That only works with, like, atoms and stuff. Really small things."

"You could be right, of course," Neptune said calmly. "We could just be jerking your chain."

Chloe frowned, thinking hard. She'd read about Schrödinger's cat once but hadn't totally understood it. Something about a sealed box with a cat inside that was either alive or dead. And supposedly, according to some crazy law of science, the unobserved cat could be both dead *and* alive at the same time. The moment you opened the box to look at the cat—to observe it—then the cat would turn out to be either definitely dead or definitely alive. But before that, it was *both*. Thinking about it gave Chloe a headache.

"But how do you get through?" Horace asked.

Neptune said, "The trick to moving on through is to decide—to *believe*—that you are in the next cloister. In a way, you have to sort of observe yourself being there, not here. And then you *will* be."

"That's right," said Mrs. Hapsteade. "Once your Tan'ji touches the falkrete and you see both cloisters, be decisive. Move through quickly. We're only doing a single jump tonight, but it will still be disorienting. And the longer you hesitate—the longer you straddle both cloisters—the more disorienting it will be."

"Okay, here's a question," Chloe said to Neptune. "You touch your Tan'ji to the stone, and you'll be in both cloisters at once. But we'll observe you *here*. Isn't that a problem with the whole Schrödinger thing? Won't you be stuck here?" Horace glanced at her and nodded approvingly.

"Actually . . . ," Neptune teased.

They were silent for a moment, and then Horace said, "We can't watch." His voice was dreamy, a sure sign he was geeking out, sucking down this new knowledge like it was candy.

"That's right," said Neptune. "A girl needs her privacy."

Mrs. Hapsteade bustled forward. "Remember which stone it is. We'll go one at a time, while the others wait outside the cloister. I'll go last."

"What about on the other side?" said Horace. "Can we watch people arrive?"

"It can be done, but observing people from the other side yanks them through immediately, and hard. It makes the arrival much more painful. Better to let each traveler come through under their own force of will."

They'd stepped outside the cloister then, giving Neptune a minute or two. Horace had gone next. While they waited, Chloe focused all her mental energy worrying about Horace, even though she was pretty sure he didn't need it. Meanwhile Mrs. Hapsteade eyeballed Chloe steadily. Chloe knew what the woman was thinking, and stupidly took the bait. "Do I have something on my face or something?"

"Chloe, I'm sorry," Mrs. Hapsteade said gently. "We should have warned you."

Chloe shrugged. When she spoke, she tried to keep her voice calm, her tone indifferent. She practically trembled with the effort. "Warnings are overrated. I mean, come on—what's life without a terrible surprise now and then?" She drew on the Alvalaithen's power, letting its song drown out the sound of some of the few words Isabel had managed to say in those few moments on the riverbank: "*I found you. Chloe. Wait, I found you.*"

Chloe stepped into the cloister, feeling the chill of the thick brick wall as she passed through it. Horace was already gone. She slipped the dragonfly from its cord and approached the small, armchair-shaped rock. Part of her hoped that

414

Horace was still in the cloister at the other end, that he would observe her and therefore yank her through without her having to exert a bit of will. She hoped it would hurt.

She tapped the dragonfly's head against the stone. Immediately the world doubled. She was in the city—a sudden canvas of lights overhead, and thin but jarring sounds of traffic—and yet the forest was still here too. The city cloister was cleaner and totally empty; she recognized it as the one where Gabriel had met Horace and her just a few days ago, a couple of blocks from the Mazzoleni Academy.

She looked down at her hand, flexing it. Two versions of her fingers opened and closed, one disorientingly ahead of the other by just a fraction of a second, as if she were watching herself on a video screen. She almost said "Crazy," out loud, but then caught herself—what if Mrs. Hapsteade heard? Wouldn't that count as an observation, of sorts, snapping her back fully into the forest cloister? After her embarrassment with the oublimort, Chloe wasn't going to screw this one up.

She concentrated on the city cloister. In her doubled vision, the leestone there—the black-and-white bird—overlapped the brown leestone in the forest cloister. The other day, she'd joked that the black-and-white bird was a penguin, but now its true name popped into her head. It was a magpie.

She stared at the magpie, willing it to grow clearer even as she let the brown bird fade from her sight. She could only be in one place, and it had to be there, in the city. It had to be. Suddenly a great cramp seized every muscle in her body, and the forest cloister dropped away completely. She fell back onto her rump. Overhead, no longer a forest canopy but skyscrapers soaring high over a single tree. A ginkgo. She'd done it. She'd come fully into the city cloister. But her muscles ached and she felt lightheaded, scattered—as if she'd had a dream in which she stayed in the forest cloister. It felt so real that she had to collect herself for a moment before she felt fully present.

Afterward, once Mrs. Hapsteade had followed, the little group had trekked back to the academy. Without a word to anyone, not even to Horace, Chloe had gone up to her dingy room on the academy's deserted top floor. Her father's room, at the opposite end of the hall, was dark. How long would it be before he found out his wife had returned? What would happen to them now?

An hour later Horace had come to her door to announce that he was leaving, that the others had returned and Beck was taking him home.

"Is *she* with them?" Chloe had asked. "Tell me he didn't actually bring her back here."

"He did—back to the academy. But not down to the Warren. And he took her harp away." He paused and said, "Are you okay?"

"That's a stupid question, Horace," she'd replied, and rolled away from him.

"For what it's worth," Horace said after a while, "I don't think my mom knew that Isabel was . . . you know."

"Of course she didn't, Horace. Your mom would have told me if she knew. Your mother, unlike some, is a good person."

Another long pause. "Isabel saved us tonight."

"Did she?" Chloe had said, and after a painful minute of silence, Horace had left her. Once he was gone, all that was left was a short night filled with long, terrible dreams.

Now Chloe opened her eyes and stared at the water-stained ceiling, lit with sickly morning light. She went thin and stuck her hand outside, her muscles complaining faintly. Even now, the day was already muggy and hot, and promising worse to come. She groaned and rolled over, then opened her eyes wide.

There, sitting silently on the other bed, was her mother. Isabel. The woman made no effort to smile, just gazed at Chloe as if half expecting Chloe to ignore her. Chloe sat up, surprised at the blaze of hurt and rage and doubt that flared up all at once. She corralled it all, finding every bit of braveness she could muster.

"I was beginning to hope I'd imagined you," Chloe said.

"I've had similar thoughts myself," Isabel replied.

"I suppose you're going to tell me you've been sitting there for a long time, just watching me."

Isabel sighed wistfully. "Not nearly long enough," she said sadly. "Or maybe my whole life. I don't know."

The sorrow in her voice was grating, unbearable. Chloe felt herself bristling but couldn't tear her eyes away from that face, so foreign and familiar, the ghost of a ghost. Isabel's hair was even redder than Chloe remembered. Her clothes were travel worn. Isabel worried a brown ring she wore on her right pinky. On her left hand, meanwhile, she still wore her wedding band. Chloe was about to make a nasty remark about that when she noticed the absence of Isabel's harp.

"I heard they took your harp away," Chloe said. "Good for them." She tried to forget what Horace had been trying to tell her—that Isabel's power might well have saved them all last night.

"They didn't take it," said Isabel. "I surrendered it."

"Willingly, I'm sure."

"I knew Mr. Meister would want me to give it up, and I did. Besides, it was the only way."

"The only way to what?"

"To come home."

Chloe made herself laugh, sharp barks that she hoped sounded cruel.

If Isabel flinched, it was hardly noticeable. "I talked to your dad last night," she said.

Chloe stopped laughing, unable to resist imagining it. Isabel had been talking to her dad, just down the hall from here. Had they been reconciling? Crying? Hugging? Possibly all of those things, if she knew her dad. The thought made her boil. "I don't want you talking to him."

"That's not your decision to make. There's a lot for him and me to talk about." Isabel sighed again, and Chloe could hear the exhaustion in her voice. That voice—it registered in some deep pocket of remembrance Chloe hadn't even known she still had. How had that voice sounded to her father?

"If my dad was glad to see you," Chloe said, "it's only because he's been alone this whole time. He's been through more than you can imagine."

"Don't presume to know how much I can imagine," Isabel said low. "But you're right. He's being too kind. He's showing me more forgiveness—more love—than I deserve."

"Spare me," Chloe said, hardly able to stomach the idea. "What about Madeline? Does she know yet?"

Isabel's eyes grew shiny. "Not yet. I so want to see her. How is she? Dad said she's strong, and happy."

"She's the best of us," Chloe said firmly. "No big surprise, though—she knew you the least."

Isabel looked away. She got up and wandered over to Chloe's desk. There wasn't much to see—library books, her stash of wintergreen mints, a chunk of charred brick from the wreckage of the fire. There was also an intricate black key, entrusted to her by Mrs. Hapsteade. It unlocked the elevator that led to the Great Burrow.

If Isabel noticed the key, she didn't comment. Instead she hefted the scorched brick, examining it. "The fire," she said. "Dad told me. I'm so sorry. You lost everything."

"Not everything."

"Not everything, no. Not the most important things. But I'm sorry, Clover."

The all-but-forgotten nickname shocked Chloe, actually

knocking the breath from her. "Do *not* call me that," she spat.

Isabel dipped her head. "Old habits die hard," she said apologetically. "I've missed you plenty."

Angrily, Chloe swallowed the unwanted knot that rose in her throat. This woman had no right to be here, to be saying these things. You shouldn't be able to toss something away and then whine about it being gone. "You'll get over it," Chloe said. "I did."

"Yes," Isabel said lightly. "You really seem over it."

From the desk, she picked up an oversized marble, clear as glass. Like all raven's eyes, this one had started out black, but as it safely absorbed the unwanted attention of the Riven, it had faded from black to purple to transparent until its protective powers were exhausted.

"What a souvenir this is," Isabel said, frowning at it. "A raven's eye, all used up. I wonder how."

"It helped save me during the fire," Chloe said, unsure why she was bothering to explain.

"Can I have it?"

Chloe shrugged. "Why not? It's useless now. And every time you look at it, you can remember how it was there when you weren't."

Isabel tucked the raven's eye into a pocket without comment. Chloe, meanwhile, struggled to keep her bearings. She found herself wishing for Horace, for his steadfast voice and his logical way of looking at the world. If anyone could make sense of this terrible moment, a moment she did not want but had so often imagined, it was Horace.

Isabel sat down on the far end of Chloe's bed. "You seem to have a lot you want to say to me," she said. "But nothing to *ask?*"

Chloe let that one sink like a stone through all the questions she'd wanted to put to her mother over the years, all the things she'd asked her father, all the answers she'd tried to give Madeline. So much, so thick, all so old and dusted and worn down. She went back to the night before, to the moment she'd first recognized that fierce face, so infuriatingly like her own. She went back to the first thought she'd had, and said it out loud now:

"What the hell are you doing here?"

Isabel sighed. "Oh Clover, I came back for you. For you and Madeline and your dad. I've been looking for you all these years."

"All seven?" Chloe snapped, and then winced at how readily the exact number sprang out, as if she'd been counting. As if she'd been keeping track.

"No. Not all seven. I traveled, trying to come to terms with what I did. I worked for a while in various places. Never very far away. But then I came back to find you."

"It doesn't seem like it would be that hard to find someone, if you really wanted to."

"You moved," Isabel said, as if that explained eveything. "Dad left his job."

"He *lost* his job."

"And he changed your name, from Burke to Oliver."

"That was my idea," said Chloe. Isabel frowned sadly. "What, are you really surprised that I didn't want to keep the name of the woman who abandoned me? Abandoned all of us?"

"Maybe it would help if I told you why I left."

Chloe's stomach fluttered. "I can't imagine how, but knock yourself out."

Isabel folded her legs beneath her on the bed and spoke softly, looking Chloe in the eye. "When I was your age, I worked for the Wardens as a Tuner. I was . . . good at it. I was the only one who could use Miradel—the wicker harp."

Chloe was surprised to hear Isabel telling the truth. She was equally surprised to hear that the harp had a name—Horace's mom hadn't mentioned that. And now a watery memory floated to the surface of Chloe's mind. An old photograph of her mother and father lying in a hammock together, looking young and happy. And around her mother's neck, a round wicker pendant. The harp. Aggravatingly, Chloe realized a hunger was gnawing at her quietly now, a hunger for answers she'd never gotten. But she'd be damned if she was going to show it. "I heard a different story," she said. "I heard you couldn't control the harp."

"Sometimes there would be . . . events. Things I didn't intend. Usually it was no big deal."

"Severing people, no big deal."

Isabel winced. "I was getting better," she insisted. "I

needed help. Mr. Meister could have helped me, but it wasn't fair—" Furrowing her brow, she caught herself, rethinking her words. "It was *difficult* for me, because—"

"Because a harp isn't a Tan'ji. *You're* not Tan'ji."

Isabel bared her teeth.

"You're not," Chloe insisted. "You can use it, but the harp isn't even really yours."

"So they always said," Isabel snapped. "They reminded me every day. I could use it when *they* allowed me to. Miradel was on loan to me, like a library book." She gestured at the books on Chloe's desk.

Under the circumstances, Chloe didn't want to admit that these library books weren't exactly *on loan*. "The Wardens didn't let you keep the harp because you couldn't really control it."

"No, because that was the *rule*." She thrust an angry, rigid finger at the floor. "And because of the rule, I couldn't master my instrument properly."

Chloe, of course, was no fan of authority. Much to her dismay, she felt a flicker of anger on her mother's behalf, knowing very well how frustrating the Wardens' rules could be. "So you stole it."

"Yes. Maybe you understand why."

"I don't," Chloe lied. "And I definitely don't understand why Mr. Meister would let you keep it after you stole it."

"Oh, he knew where I was. I was only twelve. He could have come for me."

Chloe had no idea whether that was true or not. "So why didn't he?"

Isabel shrugged. "Probably he was afraid. And he should have been." Her tone was icily casual and tinged with arrogance. "So instead, he banished me. I was excommunicated. I felt it happen." She glanced down at the floor. "It was . . . very bad at first. I'd been to the Warren dozens of times, but after they banished me it was like the sight of it had been erased from my mind. I could picture the neighborhood, but not the academy itself. And even if I'd walked right past it, I never would have seen it."

It occurred to Chloe that Isabel didn't seem to know *how* she'd been banished. She didn't seem to know about the spite-stone. "But now thanks to April, you're back," Chloe pointed out, pressing. "Lucky you."

Isabel twisted her pinky ring. "But I'm not back. Even as I sit here, right above the Great Burrow, I couldn't find my way down."

"Really?" Chloe asked. "Are you saying you could roam the halls of the academy day and night, and still never find the passageway that leads down into the Warren?"

"Is it even a passageway?" asked Isabel. "I have no memories. I can barely even summon up the idea."

Chloe managed not to glance at the black key on her desk. She wondered if Isabel was even able to see it. "Well, shucks, if only you were Tan'ji," she said, making her voice saccharine sweet. "Your harp is down in the Warren, right?

424

The Wardens could never stop you from finding your way to your instrument again—if you really had the bond." She frowned poutily, feigning sadness.

Isabel stopped fussing with her ring and folded her hands into her lap. "True enough," she said flatly.

"I'm still waiting to hear why you left us. Why you left my dad."

Isabel took a long time responding. "I was very young when I met your dad," she said at last. "Very young when I had you. We were happy—genuinely happy. I still had Miradel."

"And you taught yourself how to use it."

Isabel waggled her head ambiguously. "I tried. But there was no real work for me to do, no Tanu to practice on. A harp is pointless without a Tanu there to manipulate. There was no one to teach me how to get better, no one to help fix me. Even so, life was good. Madeline was born. And then, when she was about a year old, and you were five . . ." She trailed off, as if into some sad reminiscence, but Chloe caught something unmistakable in Isabel's expression, a familiar spark Chloe recognized all too well. Anger. And not anger at herself, but anger at some outside thing, some unexpected invader.

And suddenly, like a plane emerging from the clouds, she understood. Chloe rose to her feet, clutching at her own chest. "The dragonfly," she whispered.

Isabel nodded slowly. "Yes. My own daughter—Tan'ji. I knew you had the potential, of course I did, but I never imagined . . . not so young."

"Did you take me to the House of Answers?"

"I have no idea what that means. You were out with Dad. He lost you—you were always wandering off. And when he found you again, you had *that*." She nodded at the Alvalaithen, and Chloe couldn't tell if it was admiration or disgust in her voice. "When you came home," Isabel continued, "I felt you before you even came in the house. I waited for you. You were bursting with power, even though you had no idea what the dragonfly did yet. And the moment I laid eyes on you and your Tan'ji, without thinking or trying or—god, I swear, even *wanting*—I severed you. I severed you clean. You broke into tears."

Chloe had no memory of this, none at all, but a slow realization was beginning to dawn. "You couldn't control yourself," she said.

Isabel took a deep breath. "No. But I didn't see the danger, not at first. I learned soon enough—oh yes I did, as soon as you came through the Find." She interrupted herself with a bitter laugh and then continued in a near whisper: "A daughter with the power to walk through walls. A mother who can sever that power at any moment—even when she doesn't mean to. It . . . it couldn't last."

Chloe felt like she was touching the falkrete again, like the world she knew was splitting itself in two. She clutched the Alvalaithen so tightly it cut into her skin. "The accident," she whispered.

"I hung on for a year," Isabel said grimly. "There were a

lot of accidents in that time. Most of them weren't my fault."

"There was only one that mattered."

Isabel closed her eyes and let her head fall back. After a long, silent minute she spoke, her voice soft and tentative and strangely sweet. "I felt you outside," she explained. "Drinking deeply from the dragonfly. I did my best to ignore it like always. And then suddenly—nothing to do with me—you were screaming. Screaming terribly. I ran outside and there you were, on your knees in the grass. Only you weren't on your knees. The dragonfly's wings were whirring and you were buried. Sinking into the ground. You were clinging to a lawn chair and it was sinking too, like the earth had turned to quicksand right under you. Like it wanted to swallow you up."

Chloe's mouth went dry, remembering. Dark dreams had plagued her ever since that day, a day she'd relived so many times she was no longer sure which of its horrors were real. "And then?"

"I panicked. The veins had you, and it was like they were trying to drown you." Isabel lifted a single shoulder, a seemingly thoughtless half shrug. "And then I . . . took them away."

"You severed me, you mean. With my legs half underground."

Isabel hesitated, then gave a single, quick nod.

"That's how I broke my legs."

"Yes. And worse. Your screams . . . changed. From terror to pain. I let go of the veins right away and the dragonfly came back to life. You crawled out of the earth—I don't know how."

She shook her head wonderingly. "I just watched. I was afraid to touch you. You crawled toward me, and your legs . . ."

"I was six."

Isabel laughed harshly. "You say that like I don't know! Like I didn't have to call an ambulance for my six-year-old daughter. Like I didn't have to invent a story to explain two broken shins—broken ankles, broken feet. Like I didn't have to hold little Maddy while we watched you push bits of dirt and stone out of your torn flesh. Like I didn't have to call your father to explain what I'd done."

Chloe breathed hard, trying to imagine the scene she could barely remember. "And then you left us."

"Yes. To protect you."

"Because you couldn't control your harp, you left us."

"Yes."

"Instead of giving up the harp. Instead of burning it to ashes."

Isabel flinched. "I tried to give it up. I tried. But I could never have destroyed it. Even then."

"You mean you *wouldn't*," Chloe snarled. "Did you try taking Miradel back to the Wardens?"

"The Wardens wouldn't have helped me. They didn't want to fix me."

Chloe shot to her feet. "Fix *you*? You weren't the one that was broken! I was in a wheelchair for four months. You were gone before I could walk again. I thought—" Chloe blinked away sudden tears, furious and fuming with a rage she thought might never die out. "I thought it was my fault you left. Because of what I did."

"I never wanted you to think that, Clover. I just—I couldn't stay."

"No, no. Screw that." She leaned forward savagely, cutting out her words as if made of ice. "You chose the harp over us! Over your *family*. You left us all because you couldn't—you wouldn't—give up the harp."

"I was young. And it wasn't easy. Could you give up the dragonfly?"

"I'm Tan'ji!" Chloe shouted. "You're just a Tuner!"

"I'm more than a Tuner," Isabel insisted grimly. "And Miradel is more than just another harp. She can't be passed around to whichever Tuner drops by—if there even *is* another Tuner who can use her."

Chloe stared in disbelief. "So what do you think you are, exactly? Sorta *kinda* Tan'ji? Like a half Keeper or something?"

"Whatever I am can be fixed. I know it. Miradel belongs to me."

"Obviously not, because she's down in the Warren and you can't even find her. Just like you couldn't find me. The truth is, nothing belongs to you. Nothing belongs to you because you *are* nothing. You left because you could've killed me, and—news flash—you aren't back here now to make it right. You didn't come back for me, or for Dad, or Madeline. You came back because you think the Wardens can *fix you*. Like they can turn you into something you never were, and never will be."

Isabel leapt to her feet. She stepped up to Chloe, her eyes

blazing with a ferocity Chloe had never seen in anyone before, not even herself. "You don't know what I am!" Isabel roared through her teeth. "You don't know what I've been! You think you know Tuners? You think you understand because you're an almighty Tan'ji? I suppose you've been told how Tuners are recruited, then. How a person becomes a Tuner to begin with. Explain it to me, mighty Keeper. Tell me all about myself and how I got to where I am today."

Chloe practically strangled the river of doubt that trickled through her thoughts now. She was so angry and so bewildered that she could barely see. "You got to where you are today," she hissed, "by being the crappiest mother imaginable."

And then, suddenly, strong hands were on her—not grasping, not shoving, but pushing her gently and irresistibly away from Isabel. Her father, tall and sure. His voice, deep and calm, pulling Chloe and Isabel apart. He spoke soothing words Chloe did not understand, held her easily with one great hand wrapped around her arm. She heard him say "Belle," a name she hadn't heard in years, dripping now with sweetness and worry, and she wanted to puke.

Chloe drank hard from the Alvalaithen. Its golden song swelled to life, the chorus filling her. Her father's hand fell away, unable to touch her.

"Did she tell you?" Chloe demanded, peering up at him. "Did she tell you what she did?"

"He knows," Isabel said. "He's always known."

Her father's face wrinkled with an impossible sadness. "Chloe . . ."

The world shrank. Chloe took a step back. Her foot sank momentarily into the floor and she stumbled. "You knew?" she whispered. "All this time you knew, and . . . you still wanted her back?"

Her father put his great arm around Isabel's tiny form and pulled her close. Isabel shut her eyes and leaned her bushy red hair against his shoulder. "She never meant to hurt you," her father said. "She deserves another chance. We all deserve another chance. Don't build new mistakes on top of old ones."

"I saved you," Chloe told him.

"You've saved me every day of your life," he said.

"No, I used my power to save you in the nest. I went underground for you—I faced the fear that *she* created—and even then you couldn't tell me the truth. All these years I thought *I* messed up. I thought *I* made Mom leave."

Her father released Isabel and reached out for Chloe. Still thin, she let him try to hug her, so that he would feel her absence in his arms. She winced as his hands passed through her, winced again as pain slid across his face. "I didn't know that," he said. "I didn't know you blamed yourself. I thought you blamed me."

Chloe shook her head in disbelief. "I never blamed you for anything. Ever."

"Then don't blame me now. Blame can't help us be a family again."

431

Chloe stared at him, hardly recognizing him. "Oh, it can't?" she said. Tears fell from her eyes, fell tingling through her ghostly body to the floor. "Then in that case—*blame*." She thrust her finger at her father. *"Blame,"* she said again, jabbing at Isabel. "Shame on you both. You deserve each other." And then she let herself fall, letting the floor swallow her up, not even bothering to care where she landed.

CHAPTER TWENTY-THREE

The New Recruit

HORACE RETURNED TO THE WARREN EARLY THURSDAY EVENING, exhausted from the night before, still disoriented from the falkrete. He was here to meet with the other Wardens and the mysterious new arrival, April, but he barely felt equipped. His head buzzed with the memories of the nightmare encounter with the Riven—the horrid surprise of the Auditor and the cat-and-mouse game with Dr. Jericho. He still wrestled with the awful feeling that he had saved the Mordin's life, and what that could mean for the future. Above all, he hadn't been able to shake those ominous words: *"Sil'falo Teneves's greatest mistake."* Not to mention thrall-blight, whatever that was. He'd slept with the Fel'Daera beneath his pillow, something he hadn't done since he was in the Find.

And then there was Chloe. Against all odds, her mother had returned—a Tuner like his own mom, but far more

433

menacing. Logically speaking, Horace felt it was too soon to say what Isabel's arrival meant, but last night Chloe had made her own feelings clear: the return of her mother was nothing but bad.

Chloe met him in the front hall of the Mazzoleni Academy, wearing her green hoodie, looking frazzled. She was chewing ferociously on a mint, but her eyes were raw, as if she'd been crying. "I had my little reunion this morning," she announced at once. "Ask me how it was."

"Um . . . how was it?" Horace said.

"Heartwarming."

"Really?"

"Yes, if by 'warming' you mean 'stabbing.'"

The academy was all but abandoned this time of year. As they headed toward the elevator that led down to the Warren, Chloe recounted her conversation with her mother that morning. Filled with horror and sympathy, Horace heard about Chloe's broken legs. She'd mentioned breaking bones before, but he hadn't imagined anything quite so horrible. She told him about Isabel leaving, choosing the harp over her family. "She left us all to protect me—you know, because she's so selfless," Chloe spat sarcastically. "God forbid she give up her damn harp instead."

Horace considered what it would be like to give up the Fel'Daera—to have to choose between family and instrument. But then again, Isabel wasn't Tan'ji. And he knew without question that his own mother would have sacrificed her own harp for him. In a heartbeat.

"That's . . . terrible, Chloe," he said. "I'm so sorry."

"You and me both."

"At least now you know the truth."

"Yup. The whole big truth bomb exploded."

"And now she's back," Horace pointed out cautiously. "She came looking for you."

"Did she, though?"

"What's that supposed to mean?"

"It means I don't trust her. I *can't* trust her. She says she surrendered the harp last night to be with us, but she also says maybe Mr. Meister could fix things for her, or something. She's not willing to give up the harp—not really. I can tell."

They passed by the academy's great leestone, a massive raven launching itself from a branch, wings spread wide. Looking at it, Horace recalled how Isabel's power had mowed down the Auditor and the Mordin on the riverbank. He remembered the shocking sight the Fel'Daera had provided, the moment that—by a whisker, he was sure—hadn't come to pass. Dr. Jericho, cleaved by Isabel, dropping lifeless into the mud. There was no getting around it: a Tuner like Isabel could be perhaps the most powerful weapon they had against the Riven. But of course, Horace couldn't just come out and say it. Not to Chloe, and maybe not at all.

"Well," Horace said instead, "it's still pretty crazy, huh? My mom knew your mom, back when they were kids. Before we were even born. And they don't even know it."

"You didn't tell your mom?" Chloe asked.

"No. It felt like something you should do, if it gets done at all."

"Thank you. I think." Chloe was silent for a several seconds. "It's definitely freaky that our moms knew each other before we even existed. But maybe it's a sign. Maybe that's the reason we get along so well."

Horace bit his lips to keep from smiling. "You mean, that's why I tolerate you so well."

"That's what I said," Chloe replied primly.

When they arrived at the tiny, rickety elevator, Chloe produced her black key and slid back the gate. Horace closed his eyes and stepped inside. He heard her insert her key into the elevator panel and click once to the left, once to the right. The elevator shuddered into motion. As usual, Chloe started up a friendly chatter to keep Horace distracted.

"I heard you were pretty awesome last night," she said. "Neptune said you were like a ninja or something. What was the breach at?"

"Four seconds," Horace said, blushing.

"Four seconds!"

"Yeah. It was stupid."

"Oh, definitely. Totally stupid. But it worked."

Sort of, Horace thought. *Thanks to Isabel.*

The elevator shuddered to a halt at the bottom and they slipped out into the cool tunnels. They took out their jithandras, the red and blue mingling into shadowed purple, and started down the long stairway toward Vithra's Eye. "What about you?" Horace said. "What about that Auditor? She was inside the Fel'Daera for a few seconds, trying to move the breach. It was . . . awful."

"Don't get me started," Chloe growled. "She was in the Alvalaithen almost the whole time. Sometimes she would let go, and if I could have caught her when she was solid I would've tried to meld something inside her—hurt her, you know?" She said this casually, as if embedding solid objects in living creatures was something she did all the time. The startling idea made Horace shudder. "I couldn't catch her, though," Chloe continued. "She'd go up in the air with the tourminda. Plus she was wrestling Gabriel for the humour, and I was mostly blind."

"But was she trying to hurt you?"

"Define 'hurt,'" Chloe said, clearly meaning that having your Tan'ji invaded was injury enough. But then she considered it. "No, she didn't try to hurt us. She tried to wear us down—demoralize us. She kept talking while she used our powers, reminding us how our Tan'ji weren't our own, that our abilities weren't special, that we should stop resisting."

"And was it working?"

Chloe hesitated just a bit before answering. "Not on me."

Horace didn't press the issue. When the Auditor had invaded the Fel'Daera for even those few seconds, it had been like discovering that his own heart was pumping poison into his veins. He could scarcely imagine enduring that violation for several minutes. He let his thoughts settle on the Fel'Daera for a moment, toying with the breach, reassuring himself that it was his now, his and no one else's.

They arrived at the shore of Vithra's Eye. No one was there to greet them. To his surprise, Chloe unhooked her jithandra and let it dangle, stepping up to the water's edge.

"What are you doing?" Horace said.

"What do you think? Crossing."

"But we've never crossed on our own before."

"Well, I've got two things to say about that. Thing one: no one's bothered to teach us. Thing two: how hard can it be?"

But Horace still didn't trust himself in the Nevren. "Nope. I'm not doing that."

"Fine. Then follow me." Chloe dipped her scarlet jithandra into the water. The water rushed to become solid around it, and she stepped out. When Horace didn't follow, she said, "Unless you don't trust me."

Horace sighed. "I trust you."

"Great. That makes two of us. Let's go."

Horace stepped up warily behind her, taking hold of her hood. Unsurprisingly, Chloe moved swiftly and surely, as if she'd done this a thousand times. The walkway that formed just in front of them was faintly red. And whatever worries Horace still clung to didn't last long, obliterated as they entered the hollow terror of the Nevren. Somehow Chloe kept them moving through the cold, even through that stretch when Horace didn't know who either of them was, and before long they were through. They reached the far shore with ease. But when Chloe refastened her jithandra, Horace noticed her hands were shaking.

She caught him looking, her face pale, and she shrugged. "Harder than I thought," she admitted. "But we made it."

They headed into the Great Burrow. They were here to formally meet with April, the girl with the pet raven and the mysterious Tan'ji. When they arrived at Mr. Meister's doba, Mrs. Hapsteade was just leaving with Joshua, April's strange young companion. The boy's ankle was tightly wrapped, and he had only a faint limp now.

"Keepers," Mrs. Hapsteade said with a nod, lingering on Chloe for an extra second. "I see you made it across Vithra's Eye on your own."

Chloe shrugged. "It was Horace's idea," she said inexplicably.

Joshua, meanwhile, seemed starstruck. He bowed so deeply he nearly fell over. "Keepers," he intoned formally. When he straightened, his eyes flitted eagerly back and forth between Horace and Chloe, alighting on the box and the dragonfly.

"What's your story?" Chloe asked the boy, not unkindly. "You a groupie or something?"

"What's a groupie?"

"Like a fan. An inappropriately desperate fan."

"I'm not desperate. I'm going to be a Keeper just like you. Isabel says so."

Chloe grunted at Isabel's name, her eyes narrowing. Mrs. Hapsteade laid a flat hand in front of the boy's face, silencing him. Horace noticed that in her other hand she held a neatly folded piece of paper. He caught a glimpse of shimmering blue ink.

"That's a promise that should never be made," Mrs. Hapsteade said to Joshua, "even if you do have potential."

Potential, yes. And by the looks of that ink—no doubt written with the Vora—it was the same kind of potential Horace himself had. That first day in the House of Answers, Horace had filled out the guest book with Mrs. Hapsteade's Tan'ji and been surprised at the brilliant blue ink that flowed from it—the same ink that had later gone into his jithandra. And Horace remembered Mr. Meister's reaction when he'd first seen the boy on the riverbank the night before. Despite himself, Horace laid a hand on the box.

Mrs. Hapsteade took Joshua's hand firmly. "They're waiting for you inside," she told Horace and Chloe, and with another nod she began leading Joshua away.

"Good-bye," the boy said solemnly.

Horace waved limply, watching him go. He felt Chloe's eyes on him.

"What's up?" Chloe asked. "Seems like that kid is creeping you out."

"His ink. I think it's blue, like mine."

"So what about it? You afraid he's going to take your job or something?"

"Is that a thing that happens?"

"You've got to be kidding me. Come on, forget it." Chloe turned to Mr. Meister's door. She sighed at the ornate red wood and golden doorknob. "I am so surly right now. I'm not sure I'm up for hanging out with Bo Peep."

"She seems nice enough," Horace said, and immediately regretted it.

Chloe made a ferociously sarcastic kissy face at him and then swung the door open wide.

Inside, Mr. Meister sat at his desk, looking at them with the air of someone who had been watching them approach for miles. The spitestone still stood on the shelf behind him, yellow eye gleaming, but Horace was surprised to see that Isabel's wicker harp now lay beside it. Chloe seemed not to notice.

Meanwhile April sat on the couch, wearing another long sundress and chunky, dirty boots. She looked astonishingly lovely, and Horace turned his gaze elsewhere. Her pet raven, perched on a shelf above her head, croaked brazenly, watching Horace with unmistakably intelligent eyes.

Horace hadn't learned much about this girl, or her powers, during those confusing moments on the riverbank; Horace and Chloe had been whisked away almost at once. Nonetheless it was clear that April's Tan'ji—the swirling silver object tangled in her auburn hair—had something to do with the bird. She could control it, or something. Trying to be subtle, Horace studied her, wondering how she'd gotten her crooked nose and whether it actually made her look prettier, until she faintly raised an eyebrow and made him look away again.

Horace had expected that Gabriel and Neptune would be joining them, but the older Wardens weren't present. Instead, to Horace's surprise, Brian was here, waving gaily to get their attention.

"Let's go, heroes," Brian said. "Saved you a seat." He scooted closer to April, opening an unnecessarily large chunk of room on the long, curved couch.

As soon as Horace and Chloe sat, Mr. Meister leapt into action, like a tightly wound toy. "There is much to discuss," he said. "No time for formalities, just simple introductions." He made a karate chop motion at each of them, rattling off their names. "Chloe Oliver, Horace Andrews, Brian Souter. Please meet our new arrival, April Simon."

April ducked her head and muttered a couple of shy but friendly hellos. Horace waved and said, "Hey." Brian shook her hand. Chloe grunted.

"Inspiring," said Mr. Meister.

April looked around at them. "This might be a rude question, but can I ask what you all . . . do?" She nodded at Chloe's dragonfly, making her meaning clear.

"You saw me last night," Chloe said. "I can become incorporeal."

April clearly wasn't thrown by the fancy word. "Totally? You can move through anything?"

"Yes, anything. Wood, stone, metal. Flesh."

"Does it hurt?"

"No," said Chloe, scowling. "Well . . . not normally, no."

"I'm really curious how you actually do that. I've been thinking about it all day. Do you slide between molecules, or do you shift dimensions, or what?"

Horace was impressed. He caught Brian's eye, and Brian mouthed a single word at him, wiggling his eyebrows: *Wow*.

Chloe's scowl grew deeper. "Um, that's not how I roll. I just do it, and it happens."

April hesitated as if she was going to press the issue, but instead she just said, "I wouldn't want to be your enemy."

"No," said Chloe. "You wouldn't."

Clearly perplexed by Chloe's hostility, April tried to smile and then slid her steady gaze to Horace. She raised her eyebrows politely.

"Oh right," said Horace, fumbling for the box. "Well, this is the Fel'Daera. The Box of Promises. It . . . uh . . . opens into the future."

April sat stunned for a moment, and then said, "No, it does not."

"Um, yeah. Yeah, it does. I can see into the future—only as far as a day, though."

April shook her head firmly, her hazel eyes gleaming. "No, you cannot."

"I swear, I totally can. That's how we knew where to find you on the river. I saw you coming."

"I'm trying to believe you."

Chloe scoffed. "Try harder," she muttered under her breath. Horace frowned. What was Chloe's deal?

"I assure you, Keeper, it's quite true," Mr. Meister told April.

"It's not that I don't believe it," she said, watching the box warily. "After everything I've seen this week, I kind of *have* to believe it. But out of every crazy thing I've seen, this seems like the most—"

"Amazing," said Brian.

"I was going to say dangerous."

Horace caught his breath. *Dangerous. Sil'falo Teneves's greatest mistake.* He glanced at Mr. Meister, but the old man didn't reply to April's words—neither agreeing nor disagreeing.

April searched Horace's face. "I'm sorry. I think probably I offended you." She looked genuinely concerned.

"It's okay."

"I'm not sure it is. Just . . . remember that I'm kind of overwhelmed here. Last night was insane, and this is all scary, scary new. I'm just trying not to rock any boats. I'm trying to fit in."

Now Mr. Meister leaned forward. "You want to be one of us?"

"I'm not sure what that even means."

"It means you would join us. You would help us in our fight against the Riven."

"Wow, that's sort of . . ." April began, and then groaned in frustration. "Can I be honest? I'm super glad to meet you all,

444

and I am probably half full of questions for all of you, but right now—really—all I care about is this." She opened her fist, revealing the black flower daktan. Her calm voice cracked as she continued. "I came all this way to find it, and now I have it . . . except I don't. I'm still broken. So when you talk about joining you, and fighting the Riven, I know I should care but I completely don't. I'm sorry, but all I really care about is being fixed. That's all I *can* care about. So I wish you'd tell me—can you can fix me?"

The impassioned plea dove straight into Horace's chest, but Mr. Meister simply sat there serenely. "Let us imagine that we could, hypothetically," he said. "Would you then join us?"

Horace was surprised. Mr. Meister seemed to be bargaining with April, holding out the promise of repairing her Tan'ji in exchange for her loyalty. But then he realized—fixing April's Tan'ji meant revealing the existence of Tunraden, perhaps the Warden's greatest secret. Brian, meanwhile, sat stonily beside April, giving away nothing.

April, to her credit, wasn't deterred. "When I first met you on the riverbank and I tried to reattach my missing piece, you told me, 'Not like that. Not yet.' That didn't sound very hypothetical."

Mr. Meister smiled, apparently pleased. "An excellent point. Let us say for the moment that fixing your Tan'ji is something to be discussed."

"Why?" Chloe asked suddenly.

"I'm sorry?" said Mr. Meister.

"I'm saying fix it or don't fix it. Why are you so eager for her to join us? We don't even know what she can do."

"Chloe," Horace chided her softly, embarrassed on her behalf.

Mr. Meister, however, seemed unperturbed. "April is an empath," he said.

"Oh, thanks, that clears it right up."

"I can listen to animals," April said. "I can hear what they're thinking—*some* of what they're thinking, anyway. Simple things, mostly. Moods, emotions, things like that."

Horace tried to imagine the power she described. How could such a device actually work? And what did animals even think about? He glanced up at her raven, who was preening beneath one of his great black wings.

"But you're right," April continued. "I don't have anything like the kind of power you guys do. I don't know how much I could really help you, even if . . ." She broke off, clenching her fist around the daktan.

"Every Keeper has something to offer," Mr. Meister said. "All the Wardens here have different and important work."

"You can listen to any kind of animal?" Chloe asked April.

"Yes, any kind. Well, any kind but humans."

"What about the Riven?" Chloe pressed.

"Oh, right . . . not the Riven either, now that you mention it."

Chloe laughed. "Well then what's the point? You can tell

me what your bird thinks? We've already got a bird. Her name is Neptune."

"Maybe that's what's wrong with your Tan'ji," Horace offered. "Maybe if it weren't broken, you could listen to hu—"

"No!" Mr. Meister barked, startling everyone—including himself. He straightened his vest fussily. He ran his fingers through his unruly white hair and then continued in a grave tone. "Empaths cannot hear the thoughts of other humans. It is forbidden." He laid a hand on the chest-sized book on his desk. "When the first empathic instruments were made— instruments that allowed the user to understand the thoughts of others—the Makers quickly realized that they had stumbled on a dangerous weapon. One of the most dangerous weapons of all."

Brian looked warily over at April. She flashed an exaggerated monster face at him, holding her fingers up like claws. Brian laughed. Chloe frowned.

But all Horace could think was: *dangerous.* It would have been a mistake to create such an instrument. Was the Fel'Daera a mistake too?

Mr. Meister pointed at his own wrinkled forehead and went on. "Imagine a world where the private mind was no longer private. Where your emotions, your intentions, your hopes, your fears, your histories, your allegiances—all your thoughts—were no longer yours to keep."

Chloe hunkered down in her seat, pressing her knees against her chest, and glowered at the others as if they were trying to read her thoughts right now.

"But wouldn't it be kind of awesome?" Brian said. "We wouldn't have misunderstandings. People couldn't lie. No one could keep secrets."

"Lying is often useful," Mr. Meister said. "And the world cannot function without secrets." He lifted his arms, gesturing to the Great Burrow all around them. "Indeed, without secrets, what would become of us? What would become of our Tan'ji? To create a Tanu that allows us to see into the minds of others is to cross a line. A perilous line."

Chloe eyed him. "And you're sure that line has never been crossed. Not even by the Riven."

"If it had," Mr. Meister said, "we would not be here right now."

"Here's my question, though," said April. "How does the vine even know the difference between humans and animals?"

The question tugged at Horace. "Yeah, we're animals," he said. "So where do you draw that line?" Brian frowned thoughtfully, as if even he wasn't sure how such a thing could be accomplished.

"You underestimate yourselves," Mr. Meister said. "We humans are far more intelligent than other animals."

"But honestly, how are you measuring that?" said April. "By our ability to cut down the forests the animals live in, and poison the oceans they swim through?"

"Preach it, sister," said Brian.

"I wasn't finished," Mr. Meister said coolly. "We are also self-aware—"

"Elephants are self-aware," April said. "If you put a dot of paint on an elephant's forehead and have her stand in front of a mirror, she'll reach up with her trunk and feel her forehead to see what's there. She knows she's looking at herself in the mirror."

"We practice deceit—"

"My *cat* practices deceit," said Horace. April nodded at him approvingly.

"I think I know what the difference is," Chloe said quietly. Now everyone looked at her. "Unlike the other animals, we have the ability to *imagine* that someone might be reading our minds in the first place. We have the ability to imagine what we might then do to such a person. And I can tell you, I am imagining some pretty terrible stuff right now."

Brian stroked his chin, watching Chloe skeptically. "That sort of makes me want to build a mind-reading device," he said.

"It is forbidden," said Mr. Meister.

Chloe ignored Mr. Meister and gave Brian a savage look of warning. "If anyone ever came near me with an instrument that let them read my thoughts, they would be very, *very* sorry."

"What's the matter?" Brian teased. "Afraid we'll discover your secret desires?"

Chloe shot up, fists at her side. "Oh, I've got a desire, all right. Keep talking and you'll find out what it is."

April's raven let out a strange, low warble, shifting nervously. To Horace, he looked and sounded worried. But April was watching Chloe. She said cautiously, "I thought you guys were friends."

"Maybe you thought wrong, Doctor Dolittle," Chloe snapped. "Still want to be in the clubhouse?"

"Chloe, come on," Horace said. "What is your problem?"

Chloe rounded on him, bristling furiously. "Are you kidding me?" she said, and then the wings of the Alvalaithen sprang to life. "You, of all people?" Without a look back at any of them, she marched from the room, passing right through Mr. Meister's closed door.

That sat in silence for a moment. Brian wore a look of guilty shock. "Oops," he mouthed at Horace. The raven croaked softly, his head bobbing up and down.

"Forgive me," Mr. Meister said to April, giving her a slight bow. "Chloe is prickly under even the best of circumstances, and the current circumstances are far from the best."

"She's Isabel's daughter," April said.

"Yes," said Mr. Meister. "Chloe has not seen her mother since she was a young child. Her life took a drastic and unforeseen turn on that riverbank last night."

"And it's my fault Isabel is even here."

"Isabel took advantage of the situation, yes," said Mr. Meister. "But you are not to blame. What matters is that *you* are here. *You* are safe."

April nodded, then smiled ruefully. "But will I be when I

450

leave? I have to go back home. Even if I did want to stay here and join you, I can't just run away."

"We do not accept runaways. And we cannot simply steal young Keepers away from their families without explanation."

Horace could almost hear the joke Chloe would have made had she still been here: *I'm sure that's very disappointing for you.* He wondered where she'd gone, what she was doing now.

"You saw the academy above the Warren," Mr. Meister continued. "It is there for a reason." He opened a drawer and pulled out a thick blue folder that said *Mazzoleni Academy* on the front. It was crammed with papers and pamphlets and forms. Horace listened, impressed, as the old man explained the plan to April—the offer of a scholarship, an actual education. "You would attend school right upstairs. Your family does not need to learn the whole truth, of course, but what we tell them is true enough to put a parent's mind at ease."

"My parents are dead," April said flatly.

Mr. Meister folded his hands politely. Horace looked down at his shoes, unsure what to say. Just when the silence was getting uncomfortably thick, Brian said cheerily, "Problem solved, then."

Mr. Meister's face turned into thunderclouds. But April turned to Brian calmly, apparently untroubled. "Exactly what do *you* do here, by the way?" she asked. "You weren't on the riverbank."

Her voice was so placid—and so laced with polite interest—that it clearly threw Brian. He grinned awkwardly and jiggled his skinny legs nervously. "I make . . . bad jokes," he said. He held out the front of his shirt as an example. It said:

MY OTHER SHIRT
MENTIONS THIS SHIRT

"I see," April said, reading. "How many shirts do you have that say that?"

"Um . . . just this one."

"That's less funny. You should have two."

Brian peered down at the shirt. "You're right," he said, clearly chastened.

April sat back and gazed up into the rounded dome of the office. Her raven was still directly overhead, immobile, but higher up, the little birds that lived here were flitting to and fro. She watched them thoughtfully, her eyes distant, and Horace got the distinct impression that she was listening to them with her Tan'ji.

"Anyway," April continued, "I guess it does help solve the problem a little bit—my parents being dead. My brother and I live with our Uncle Harrison, but he's more of a landlord than anything else. It's my brother who would raise a fuss about me being gone. He's the one who really looks after me. Well . . . besides myself, I mean."

"I see," said Mr. Meister. "And your brother—where does he think you are right now?"

"At a friend's house for a few days. I hope. I'm supposed

to be back home Friday night." She squinted in confusion. "Tomorrow?"

"Yes," Mr. Meister said. "And what if—hypothetically— we were able to fix your Tan'ji before you went home? Would you return? Would you join us?"

April seemed to be holding her breath, overwhelmed by the very notion. As if on cue, her raven slipped down from his perch, his wings unfolding massively, and dropped onto the couch beside Horace. He croaked at Horace sociably and then turned in April's direction, snapping his great thick bill. Horace had never been so close to a bird so large before. April pulled a chunk of something from her pocket—dog food?— and tossed it. Horace watched, fascinated, as the bird choked it down.

"This is Arthur," April said to Horace. "He likes you."

"How do you know?"

For an answer, April simply pointed to her Tan'ji. Arthur turned and cocked his head at Horace. His eyes were shining black, and his formidable beak was twice as thick as Horace's thumb.

"Look, I don't know if I want to join you," April said. "I don't really even understand who you are. Mostly I just know that every second my Tan'ji stays broken is one more second I stay broken too. So if you want to talk—fix me."

She fell silent, her pretty, crooked face sagging forlornly. Horace felt a peculiar pain in his chest at the sight, as if he too was breaking. Meanwhile, Brian looked at Mr. Meister expectantly, clearly asking for permission. Mr. Meister took a deep breath and gave him a subtle nod.

Brian leaned into April. "I might—maybe—be able to help you," he said quietly.

She lifted her head, her eyes wide. Horace could hear her breathing. "Explain, please."

"I can maybe fix your Tan'ji. Maybe." Brian gestured at the daktan. "Can I . . . may I?"

Without hesitation, April dropped the daktan into his hand. And then, shocking everyone, she pulled the Tan'ji from the tangle of her hair and thrust it at Brian. "Here. Please. Try."

Reluctantly, Brian took the delicate instrument, handling it as if it were hot. Despite himself, Horace winced at the sight. Most Keepers were loath to allow anyone else to touch their instruments, but April seemed not to have those reservations. Mr. Meister, watching, slipped his tiny notebook from a pocket of his vest and jotted down a hasty note.

Brian bent over the Tan'ji and its missing piece. The Tan'ji was lovely and wild, and from what Horace could tell, it seemed designed to hook directly around April's ear. He could see the broken stem clearly now, and it made him want to retch. How was April coping with such a ghastly wound? The sight, and the sickness oozing from it, brought Dr. Jericho's words unwanted once again to the surface of Horace's mind. *"Sickness . . . thrall-blight . . . a mistake."*

"The break is clean," said Brian, sounding professorial.

"But it's not just the structure. It's the Medium, the flow of operation, the input and output." With a steady hand he placed the daktan against the broken stem, holding it in place. The mere illusion of wholeness made April catch her breath. "I can reattach it physically," Brian said. "That's no problem. Weaving the flow again will be more difficult. The flower seems to be acting as some kind of vital sensor, or focal device. It would be like . . . reattaching a head."

"But can you do it?" said April.

"I don't know. Maybe."

Mr. Meister, his left eye looming large through the thick, shining glass of the oraculum, was watching intently. "It can be done," he pronounced.

"How?" April said. "Like, with what?"

Brian stood up, a reckless and uncertain grin growing on his face. "Come and see."

Brian handed April her Tan'ji and led her out of the office. The bird rode on April's shoulder, his massive talons digging into her flesh.

"And so the moment arrives," Mr. Meister said, standing to follow. When he noticed Horace wasn't moving, he stopped. "Are you coming, Keeper?"

Horace considered his words. "Yeah. Just, you know, wondering about some things. Things Dr. Jericho said last night."

Mr. Meister leaned back against his desk, his expression sour, but he gestured for Horace to proceed.

"Dr. Jericho said when I refuse the future the box

reveals—when I feel sick like that—my sickness affects the Medium itself. The Mothergates, too."

Mr. Meister crossed his arms. "He feeds you lies."

"He even had a name for it. Thrall-blight, he called it."

"I have heard the term before. I do not care for it."

"Blight is disease. And thrall—that's like . . . being a slave."

"Do you feel that you are a slave to the Fel'Daera?"

"Well, no, but—"

"You feel free to ignore the path indicated by the box, when the occasion warrants. Last night was a dramatic, if foolhardy, case in point. Neptune told me what you were doing."

Horace ignored the "foolhardy" comment. He had no plans to repeat last night's four-second stunt anytime soon. "But you've always told me not change the future the box shows me."

Mr. Meister held up a finger. "Correction. I have always told you to open the box with great care. I have explained that opening the box is the first step along the path to the future the box reveals. Take that step with your usual good sense, and this sickness—this thrall-blight—can be avoided."

"Okay, but—" Horace hardly knew how to say what came next. "It's dangerous, isn't it? The Fel'Daera is dangerous. *I'm* dangerous."

"Yes. But danger is relative. Speeding down the highway is dangerous, for example, but perhaps acceptable if you are fleeing from some great harm."

"In other words, the benefits of the Fel'Daera outweigh the risks—according to you."

"Just so. According to me."

"But meanwhile I don't even know what the risks are."

Mr. Meister shrugged. "That is because I do not wish you to know them," he said simply.

Dimly Horace knew that these words should have infuriated him, but instead he felt only a ripple of irritation. And he thought he understood why.

He didn't really *want* to know the risks. He wasn't sure he cared what the risks were—or maybe he was afraid he *would* care. Maybe he was afraid that the risks would turn out to be horrendous, and that even then he wouldn't stop himself from using the box.

"Okay," he said, refusing to let his thoughts wander down that road. "Okay, fine. But maybe at least reassure me about something. Dr. Jericho also said . . . he said that Sil'falo Teneves thinks the Fel'Daera was a mistake. Her greatest mistake, actually."

Mr. Meister didn't reply right away. He gazed at Horace for a long time, his huge left eye watery and soft, yet heavy as a hammer. "It is true that Sil'falo has proclaimed regret for the Fel'Daera in the past. When other Keepers held its reins."

"Oh."

"The last time we spoke, however, her views had changed."

"And when was that?"

Mr. Meister broke into a warm smile. He put an arm around Horace's shoulders. "Quite recently, my friend," he said. "Quite recently indeed." And then he ushered a suddenly blushing Horace through the door.

Outside, Brian and April were headed for the staircase that led to Brian's workshop. Horace, feeling a relief he wasn't quite sure he'd earned, cast about for Chloe. He spotted her back up the slope in the opposite direction, loitering outside an abandoned doba. He turned to Mr. Meister and said, "I'll catch up?"

Mr. Meister nodded. "She was strong last night."

"Maybe you should tell her that."

"I have. She disagreed—vehemently. But her stubbornness in resisting the despair sown by the Auditor allowed the others to fight back too." He sighed. "Tell her she can join us, if she wishes. If she promises not to sneer at the sanctity of what we are about to attempt."

"I can't guarantee no sneering."

"She lashes out. She feels lost. She doubts the motivations behind her mother's return."

"Don't you?"

Mr. Meister pushed his thick glasses up on his nose. "I have no doubt as to Isabel's motivations," he said gruffly, and then he spun on his heels and followed after the others.

Horace puzzled over that response for a moment, then went to Chloe. She watched him approach like an angry cat watches a neglectful owner.

"Party downstairs, I guess," she said. "What, am I not invited?"

"You are. Brian's going to try to repair April's Tan'ji."

Chloe's eyes lit up briefly with an unmistakable spark of interest, but then she scoffed. "Really pulling out all the stops for the new girl."

"Look, it's been a crazy day for you."

Chloe gasped indignantly. "What are you saying? Are you saying I did something wrong?"

"You were just . . . you know. Rude and scary."

"I'm always scary," Chloe said. "Meanwhile Mr. Meister is courting Bo Peep like she's some kind of all-star, but she's bad news. Isabel tricked her. Isabel used April to find the Warren. And April wasn't even smart enough to know she was being used."

"I wouldn't assume that. She seems plenty smart to me."

"Why, because she saw a TV show about elephants? Because she said *molecules*? Lots of people can say *molecules*, Horace."

"Chloe—"

"But maybe you just think she's smart because she wears pretty dresses."

Horace blushed. "Chloe, come on."

"Look, anybody can read a book, Horace. That's not the kind of smart I'm talking about. April is a dupe. It's her fault Isabel even came back."

"Yeah, that's pretty much exactly what April said, right after you left."

That threw Chloe for a second. "So she knew she was being used, and she still—"

"Yes!" Horace said. "Maybe she knew, and she did it anyway. All she wanted was to find her missing piece. Who cares what your mom was after?"

Chloe took a step back, her eyes blazing with rage and confusion and hurt. "*I* care, Horace," she said quietly, jabbing a finger into her own chest. "*I* care."

"That's not what I meant. I just meant I'm not sure it makes any sense to be mad at April for doing whatever she could to get the daktan. We'd both do the same, and you know it."

Chloe sighed. She kicked a loose pebble, watched it skitter away. "Fair," she said at last.

"Good. Thank you. So are you coming?"

"Maybe. I don't know. You go ahead."

Horace turned to go, wishing she'd come with but not sure there was anything left to say. After just a few steps, though, Chloe stopped him.

"Hey, Horace? If Brian really can fix April's Tan'ji, do you think maybe he actually *could* . . . you know?"

"Help your mom?"

Another shrug. Another kicked pebble. Horace's heart went out to her, so stubborn and brave and unshakably Chloe.

"We're Keepers," he told her. "Anything is possible."

CHAPTER TWENTY-FOUR

In the Light of Tunraden

HORACE CAUGHT UP TO MR. MEISTER, BRIAN, AND APRIL AT the top of the Perilous Stairs. They were watching Arthur the raven as he drifted in lazy circles out over the Maw, riding the currents that rose from below.

"He's having fun," April said with a faint smile, but the smile disappeared when she saw Horace, alone. "I take it Chloe's not coming," she said.

"I don't think so," Horace said.

"She doesn't like me."

At the same time, Horace and Brian both said, "She doesn't like anyone." They laughed and then Horace clarified: "She doesn't like anyone *at first*."

Mr. Meister stirred. "Come. There is work to do."

They descended deeper into the Warren, down the steep and winding staircase. April remarked that this was the most

461

lifeless place she'd ever been. Apparently, the only animal she could sense now was Arthur. "Usually there are bugs, at least," she explained. "Even in the city. But there's nothing living down here at all."

"No offense taken," said Brian.

They reached the oublimort, and Mr. Meister showed April how to use it. She made it through on her first try, Arthur riding on her shoulder. Silently—and somewhat shamefully—Horace thanked the stars that Chloe wasn't here to witness it.

Once in the workshop, April handed over her Tan'ji and the daktan to Brian again. He took them to a workbench cluttered with metalworking tools, large and small. "First the easy part," he said. Horace watched, fascinated, as Brian took a narrow strip of silver, hammered it thin, and then clipped off tiny flakes with a pair of dingy shears. His long, pale hands moved surely, with the ease of long hours of practice. April, who was keeping a respectful distance, oozed a fierce, maternal worry. Brian noticed her concern. "Do you want me to explain what I'm doing?" he asked.

"I know what soldering is," she said curtly.

Horace did too, vaguely—melting metal to metal—but he'd never seen it done before. Brian bent over the bench, focusing intently as he sanded the broken ends of both vine and flower. April grimaced. Brian then mixed a white, creamy substance in a dish and painted it onto the jagged ends of the broken stem. Then he casually lit a small blowtorch—making Arthur squawk in alarm—and delicately began melting the ends together with the tiny flakes of silver.

Slowly he bonded the flower to the vine. After just four minutes, he was done. He sanded the newly repaired break until it was smooth and all but invisible. After one last inspection, he held the Tan'ji out to April.

April made no move to take the vine. Mr. Meister bent in, clearly fascinated, his left eye staring hugely. Horace couldn't help but wonder what the old man was seeing—the flower had been reattached physically, but its power had not yet been restored. To Horace, the Tan'ji looked lovelier than ever, and the little black flower no longer hideous, but even he could tell it wasn't quite whole again.

"You're good at this," April said to Brian, her hazel eyes bright and wet.

"That's what I've been trying to tell everyone," Brian replied. "But don't thank me yet. The hard part comes next."

"Indeed," said Mr. Meister. "Are you prepared, April?"

"Yes, definitely, it . . ." April scrunched up her face. "It hurts now. Like a foot that's fallen asleep and is trying to wake up. Bad pins and needles."

This comment clearly interested the old man, who suddenly looked as though he had a thousand questions to ask. Horace could relate, but this was no time for experiment or examination. "We should hurry then," said Horace pointedly, catching the old man's eye.

Mr. Meister bowed. "Of course. Let us proceed."

Brian led them back to the small round chamber that held

Tunraden. Horace shivered again at the faint electric charge in the air, and at the daunting sight of Tunraden—so powerful and so obviously ancient. As April entered, Arthur croaked and leapt from her shoulder. He dropped heavily to the floor and strutted out of the chamber, chattering grumpily.

"What's his deal?" asked Brian.

"He's agitated for some reason," said April. "Not scared, but . . . I think maybe he doesn't like the smell." She came closer to Tunraden. "Wow. This is old, isn't it?"

"Ancient, actually," Brian said. "Her name is Tunraden."

April sniffed deeply. "I think she smells kind of nice— like rain. Why does your Tan'ji smell like rain?"

"It's not the Tan'ji making that smell, exactly. It's what I do with it."

"You fix things."

"Yes . . ." Brian glanced at Mr. Meister, clearly wanting to say more but unsure the old man would allow it.

"Correct," Mr. Meister said. "Brian is our repairman."

April peered at Tunraden, hands folded behind her back. "So you've done this before?"

Brian shook his head. "Never. Not even close." When April frowned, he quickly added, "I've imagined it, though. If that helps." He spoke casually, but Horace could see the doubt in his eyes.

"As I said before," Mr. Meister intoned, "it can be done."

A voice from behind startled them all. "That is the worst pep talk ever," said Chloe. They all turned as she continued, stalking into the room. "'It can be done.' What the heck is that? That's like a surgeon saying 'Survival is possible,' right before he cuts you open."

Brian threw up his arms. "I know, right? I mean, come on. Maybe I could get a 'You can do it, Brian,' or a 'Hey, Brian, we believe in you,' or a 'Gee, Brian, you sure are handsome and a good dancer.'"

"Gee, Brian, you sure are a good dancer," said Chloe.

Brian smiled goofily. "Close enough."

Chloe sidled up beside Horace. She nudged her foot against his, her signature private gesture—a greeting, a repentance, an embrace. Horace pressed his foot back against hers, letting her know everything was okay.

Chloe turned to April. She hesitated, seeming to consider her words carefully. "I saw your bird outside," Chloe said at last. "I'm pretty sure he talked to me."

"He does talk sometimes. What did he say?"

"He saw me and he went, *Uh-oh*."

"Ah," said April neutrally.

Chloe chewed her lip and then said, "I guess I don't blame him."

Horace suppressed a smile. This was as near to an apology as Chloe would get. April, to her credit, seemed to understand. "Well," she said. "He's just a bird. A smart bird, yeah—but just a bird."

Chloe nodded, shoving her hands deep into her pockets. "Right," she said. "So anyway . . . is this happening or what?"

Brian took a deep breath and let it out slow. He laid April's Tan'ji atop Tunraden and bent over it. Mr. Meister, who had been frowning faintly since Chloe's arrival, reached out and—to Horace's surprise—clasped Brian's shoulder. "You have done more difficult things, Keeper," he said warmly. "This is within your reach."

Brian tried to hide it, but he was clearly pleased. Then he shivered dramatically from head to toe, shaking out his limbs. He grew suddenly somber and laid his hands atop Tunraden. He looked up at April. "You sure you want to be here for this?"

"Unless you know a reason I shouldn't."

"I really don't," Brian said, and without warning he plunged his hands into the surface of Tunraden. At once, the room erupted painfully in a fountain of golden light.

Horace's skin prickled from head to toe as all his hairs stood on end. At his side, the Fel'Daera fumed with a wild and breathless untapped power. Chloe grasped Horace's shirt, sliding behind him, one hand on the Alvalaithen. Across the way, Mr. Meister took a calm step back, his shadow looming across the ceiling above. Meanwhile April—her own hair lifting stringily, as if she were falling—stumbled back against the wall, her eyes locked on Tunraden.

Above the blinding golden surface of the Loomdaughter, the vine hovered in the air, spinning slowly. Brian stared at it almost hungrily, his glasses shining in Tunraden's light. He looked more like a grown man than a boy of only thirteen. The tight bands around his wrists glowed intensely as he grasped the vine, holding it still, and delicately pinched the repaired stem of the little black flower.

"Brace yourself," Brian murmured, and he tugged. As he pulled, a complex golden webbing revealed itself, shimmering and liquid. It emerged from the vine's interior like a fisherman's net being pulled from the water. But this net, Horace knew, was made of the Medium. This was April's power made visible—or a part of it, at least. As for April herself, she had her eyes closed now, her hands balled into fists at her sides. Horace couldn't imagine what she was feeling.

The golden mesh pulsed and shimmered and slid, looking almost alive. Brian examined it for several long seconds, concentrating deeply. Horace stared too, thinking he might detect some flaw or deformity in the shining web. But he had no talent for that. Only Brian, of course, could truly see what needed to be seen. His face alone was lit with knowledge rather than wonder. Eventually he released the vine, letting it hang in the air again, the Medium still billowing from the repaired break like a tiny sail.

Brian sank his hands back into Tunraden and began to pull strands of the Medium up from its depths—great incoherent globs at first, dripping and messy, but then he brought his hands together and extracted smaller, neater threads. His fingers moved like a musician's, slowly weaving the glowing substance into a complicated shape, like a tiny bowtie. Horace knew minutes were passing, though it felt like only seconds.

Cautiously, Brian began attaching strands of this new structure to the webwork dangling from the vine. One strand, then two, then three. The old structure absorbed the new like one bead of water absorbing another. All at once April inhaled sharply, as if startled or stung. Her eyes flew open. Brian froze.

"Is this right?" he said.

"I don't know," April said through gritted teeth. "How would I know?"

"You would know better than me. I'm guessing here, filling in the blanks."

"Okay, well . . . what you just did—that last one—it felt wrong."

Brian frowned down at his work and then plucked apart two strands of the Medium. April gasped in relief.

"Better," she said.

Mr. Meister stepped forward. "I am not sure, Keepers, that this is the way. Perhaps it was a mistake to—"

"You're right," Brian said, interrupting him. "This isn't the way." He straightened and gestured for April to come forward. Reluctantly she approached the table where Tunraden sat fuming like a bottomless furnace. She stepped into its rippling yellow light. "You're here," Brian said. "You're here and you know best. Not me." He took the vine in his hands and held it out to her.

Eyes full of wonder, April took the vine. Tears began to pour silently down her face, like beads of molten gold. At a nod from Brian, she donned the vine, tucking it into place behind her ear. Her tears quickened, and abruptly strands of the Medium began to materialize in the air around her head.

468

"The veins," April sighed, as they formed a shape like a jagged golden crown around her hair.

As Horace watched, the branching tendrils grew—not so much spreading but swelling into existence from apparent nothingness. They grew thicker and more complex, until at last Horace realized they seemed to be encircling him, and Chloe and Mr. Meister too. As they grew closer, he held his breath, resisting the urge to flee. Mr. Meister covered his mouth with his hands in dismay, perhaps the most un-Meisterlike gesture Horace could imagine.

Brian stepped around the table, close by April's side. "You tell me," he said. "You guide me."

April swayed, looking sad and angry and noble all at once. She reached out toward Horace and Chloe, as if to yank the golden streams away from them. "I don't want to know what they're thinking."

Forbidden, Horace thought, watching the thin fingers of the Medium inching nearer, thickening. He felt Chloe's grip on his shirt tighten. She inhaled between her clenched teeth, a long slow hiss. Horace laid his hand atop the Fel'Daera.

"I can almost feel them," April said dreamily. She looked at Chloe. "I can feel you."

"I know," Brian said, reaching up into the incredible tangle of golden threads spreading from the vine. "And it would be easy to do it. . . ."

Mr. Meister reached into a pocket of his red vest, his face as sharp as a hawk's.

"But I won't," Brian finished. He leaned in close to April.

He plucked and wove and reconnected, his fingers grazing April's hair. The golden tendrils filling the room began to dwindle and vanish, like melting fingers of ice. Horace breathed again. Chloe loosened her grip on his shirt. "Better," Brian said. "Now reach out for Arthur instead. Tell me."

"I don't really reach out," April said. "I open up. Like this." Her gaze grew distant. Horace stepped back, bumping into Chloe, as a new and determined thread of the Medium sprang into existence beside them, coalescing through the wall of the chamber. "I feel him," April said a moment later. She smiled. "He's playing. He's got some wire or string or something—something shiny."

"How do you know it's shiny?" said Brian. "Can you see it?"

"No," April said quickly. "I just know how he is when he plays with shiny things."

"So you can't see what he can see. Smell, hear, feel—any of those things?"

April shook her head, her lips tight. "Sometimes I imagine I can, but when I try I get these headaches. These whiteouts. And I don't even know if I—"

"Try," Brian said. "Try now."

April nodded. Her eyes met Horace's briefly, scared and distant and full of need. And then they faded even further, focusing on nothing, green flecks in her irises fading to gray. Her brow furrowed and her jaw tightened, as if she was in pain. Suddenly the veins of the Medium around her head split, and split again, and again. The already intricate cloud became an impenetrable briar patch of flaxen threads, fine as hair. April squeezed her eyes shut, her fists trembling at her side.

As if it were water, Brian slowly ran his fingers through the strand of the Medium streaming through the wall. He let it grow thick in his hands, liquid light, gathering it into the fantastic tangle hovering around April's head. He worked with a fierce purpose now, stitching and weaving. April's mouth became a trembling O. The Medium assumed shape after shape, jagged and soft and rigid and round. Brian bared his teeth with the effort. Then suddenly, after a full minute, April gasped and shoved him hard in the chest.

Brian stumbled back, hands raised. April sank to her knees. Tunraden went dark, and the visible threads of the Medium winked out. For a moment Horace was blind in the new darkness, conscious only of the sharp electric sting in the air and the ragged sound of April's breathing. Slowly his eyes adjusted. April still knelt on the floor, head bowed, arms limp.

"What did you do?" Chloe insisted, glaring at Brian. "What did you do to her?"

"You don't understand," April mumured, her voice heavy with wonder. She raised her head. Her eyes were like a doll's, shining and new and utterly blank. "You couldn't possibly understand."

CHAPTER TWENTY-FIVE

Beyond the Rainbow

Everything.

For the first time, April's mind was wide open, letting every bit of Arthur's consciousness into her own, a torrent that poured through the beautiful black flower and into her brain, bringing her . . .

Everything.

His senses, yes, flooding and keen and immediate. April was blind to her immediate surroundings, but she didn't care. She could see what Arthur could see, and his sight was nothing short of astonishing. World altering. The colors! Shades her brain couldn't name, new hues beyond the rainbow.

Arthur stood atop a workbench in Brian's workshop, and through his eyes April had an extraordinary view, both panoramic and telescopic at once—the smallest details were drawn with a clarity she could hardly process. Across the room, on a box of cheesy crackers, she could read the ingredients: *whey protein, cheese cultures, salt.* At her feet—Arthur's feet— was a pair of pliers, and the textured grip on the handles was so vivid it looked like a geometrically precise mountain range.

But it was far more than vision—those feet, just for starters. Now April knew what it truly meant to be passerine. As Arthur walked, she could feel his feet mirrored inside her own, the way they curled up when he took a step and pressed flat again when they hit the floor. Her thighs and neck pulsed with purpose as he walked. She felt his beak as if it were her own, smooth and strong and terribly toothless. So convincing was the illusion that she actually had to run a finger through her mouth, to assure herself that her teeth were still there.

"It's incredible," she whispered.

"I fixed it," said Brian. "I did it."

April managed to stagger to her feet, remembering her own muscles. She fought to regain her sight, and discovered she could force Arthur's vision to fade until it was like a faint reflection on glass. Brian stood before her, gangly and dumb-founded.

"You did do it," she told him. "You more than fixed it. I can . . . see. I can feel. I can . . . everything." She laughed messily, snorting back her tears. "This is what I was missing. This is what was gone. All this time."

"If you could explain, please, Keeper," Mr. Meister said. "It happened so fast, I could not catch it all."

She tried to explain. "It was only emotions before," she

said. "I know that now. I mean . . . I think maybe I was good at it, figuring out what certain emotions meant. It was detective work. But now!" She hiccupped another sloppy laugh, and just then Arthur spotted a dirty scrap of canvas on the floor in the next room. She saw it, so keenly she could have counted the fibers, then felt the swell of curiosity from Arthur. A stab of intention. She leaned down—no, *he* leaned down; she was only feeling his movements in her muscles, a sensation she would have to learn to ignore. He plucked the canvas deftly from the ground. Oily bitterness between her toothless jaws. A pungent sting.

"Oh, god, that's terrible," she said, thankful that birds didn't have very many taste buds. "Why would you want that in your mouth?"

"You're sensing what Arthur senses," Horace said. "Right now. You can . . . taste what he tastes."

April nodded. "Yes, and I can see what he sees. Hear what he hears. He hears you, Horace. I can hear you twice." She broke into girlish laughter as her own voice echoed in her head. "I can hear myself! You probably think I'm crazy, don't you?" And then a new sensation crackled through the synapses of her brain, shocking and familiar, freezing her. She processed it, tears welling in her eyes, and then she whirled and wrapped Brian in a fierce embrace. "Thank you," she murmured sloppily into his shoulder.

"It's cool," Brian said. "It's good." He patted her awkwardly on the back, but she didn't care if it was awkward. She clung to him, sobbing and laughing, hardly able to believe it.

Because another new realm made itself known to her now too, one beyond senses, a realm she hadn't even thought to imagine.

Memory.

The sound of her own voice in Arthur's ears had triggered it. *"Don't you?"* And with those words a memory blossomed inside her—not her own memory, but Arthur's—a memory of the day she'd released him from the pen at Doc Durbin's house. The oppressive confines of the cage. Her own crooked face, leaning down, offering a delicious chunk of brown food. The wire mesh of the door. *Dontchoo?* Hope and gratitude. Glorious freedom. The scene flared bright and true, as real as any recollection of her own, and then faded. She tried to relive it again, but couldn't quite grab hold. It wasn't a video she could replay, but more like a messy collage, a shifting jumble of sensation and emotion. She understood that she couldn't force it, any more than she could force a cloud into a specific shape.

She let go of Brian. It was almost *too* much, all these new oceans of awareness. Her head throbbed dully—in a good way, not a bad way, but still she was glad Arthur was the only animal nearby. "Thank you," she said again, and again: "Thank you."

Mr. Meister cleared his throat. "I must thank you too, Keeper," he said to Brian. "With all the years I have on me, rarely do I witness something I have never seen before. But reconnecting a daktan—truly a remarkable accomplishment."

Brian untangled himself from April. "Wait . . . this was the first time you've seen someone do that?"

"Indeed."

"But you told me it could be done. I figured you were speaking from experience."

Mr. Meister nodded. "Yes. I was speaking from my experience with you." He stepped past Brian, leaving him open-mouthed, and leaned in close to April.

"My congratulations, Keeper," Mr. Meister said.

"Thank you," April replied vaguely. The old man was hazy, seen through the glass of Arthur's sight in the other room. She was finding it hard to resist the raven's magnificent vision.

Mr. Meister seemed to notice. "Your eyes," he said. "Am I right in thinking that you are concentrating on Arthur?"

"Partly, yes. He's on one of Brian's workbenches." April shifted her weight from foot to foot. "I can feel it under him— it's slippery. He's got a piece of wire and he's bending it. Just for fun." She frowned and spread her mouth wide, then ran a finger across the tops of her teeth again. "Beaks feel weird. I had no idea."

Abruptly Arthur let out a series of alien-sounding calls, like knocking on wood—*tok, tok, tok.* "Whoa!" April cried, clutching her throat, as the calls seemed to rattle inside her own voice box. Then she laughed. "I'm sorry, this is kind of overwhelming. I'm being ridiculous right now."

"Not ridiculous at all, under the circumstances," Mr. Meister said. "Your Tan'ji is whole again. At last you can take a deep breath, yes? You can open your eyes all the way, flex your muscles to the fullest. You are, if I may say it, your complete self."

"My complete self," April repeated. She pulled back from Arthur and focused on the old man's face. "I suppose I owe you one now."

Mr. Meister waved this off with a look of disgust. "A crude suggestion."

"You did me this favor, though. This . . . incredible favor."

"We do not do favors. We do what is best. If you want to repay us, repay us with silence about what has transpired here this evening. There are some secrets that must never see the light of day."

April looked at Brian. He shrugged, holding out his pale arms, and said, "Literally."

"I won't tell anyone," April said, wondering if this truly meant what she thought it meant. Did Brian really never leave the Warren? And maybe it was the heavy joy of the vine's power unleashed that made her say what she said next, or maybe it was a sense of belonging that she couldn't quite explain—or maybe it was the sight of pale, skinny Brian standing there, having just given her the greatest gift of her life, standing there making who knew what sacrifices in the name of this war she didn't fully understand. Where had he come from? What had he left behind? Isabel's words returned to her: *"You are Tan'ji now. Things can't be the way they were."*

"I'm going to join you," she blurted out. "If that's still okay."

Brian beamed. Mr. Meister took a deep breath and smiled and said, "Far more than okay."

April turned to Horace and Chloe. She knew Horace wanted her to stay—that was obvious—but Chloe was another story. "My brother is the only family I have, and I think I'm about to leave him," April said. She looked pointedly at Chloe. "It would help to know that I'm going somewhere I'll be welcome, at least."

Chloe rolled her eyes. "Look, it's fine," she growled. "We're all Tan'ji. We all have the same enemy. So just be here already."

"Thank you," April said. She stepped forward and held out her hand, not even sure why she was doing it, but knowing—for some strange reason—that it was this fierce girl's respect she wanted most of all.

Reluctantly, Chloe took the offered hand and gave it a single shake, muttering, "Sometimes I think I should just keep my mouth shut."

"I often feel the same," Mr. Meister said with an enigmatic twinkle, and then clapped his hands together before Chloe could react. "Excellent," he said. "Come, we have much to discuss. Tomorrow Beck will take April home so she can make arrangements with her family. I'll arrange for an escort." He swept past them, out into Brian's workshop, leaving them to follow.

As April entered the workshop, she got a shock that froze her in her tracks—the sight of herself, through Arthur's eyes. It was both unspeakably horrible and indescribably wonderful. The bad part was how glaring her flaws were. The pimples on her chin and high on her forehead looked *actually* like pizza. Her hair, unwashed for a few days now, looked as greasy as meat. But her eyes glowed, dazzling her, lit with flecks of color that didn't exist in the human world.

Arthur cooed at her, discordant and gargling. For a moment she thought maybe he could sense the change in the vine, but no—the connection remained a one-way street. She was a listener, not a talker, and that was just the way she liked it. She walked over to him where he stood on the workbench and knelt down close. She caught a glimpse of the vine, with the newly attached flower, gazing both into his eyes and through them at her own. Her irises were sculptures made of string and sand. Colors beyond the rainbow. Reflections within reflections. She stared so long she almost forgot it was herself she was looking at. "I wish you all could see yourselves this way," she murmured.

"By the Loom," Mr. Meister said, "very few will ever have the chance."

April stood, blinking the spectacle away. "What do you mean?"

Mr. Meister tugged at his vest. "Empaths are not uncommon. However, in my experience, most are quite weak and—at least from our perspective—not particularly useful. They are able to sense the location and basic disposition of living creatures, but little else. Historically speaking, in fact, most empaths used their power for hunting." He shook his head wonderingly. "Your instrument, however—if you'll allow me the pun—seems to be quite a different animal. I have never heard of anything like the sensory precision you're experiencing. Part of this is due to the instrument itself, no doubt. But part of it must be due to you."

"Well, I don't know about any of that," said April, feeling suddenly self-conscious. She let Arthur nip lightly at her fingertip, marveling at the sensation of toothlessly biting herself—which probably wasn't helping her self-consciousness much. She tucked her hands into her pockets. "I just wish it had a name. Everyone else's instruments have such cool names."

"Not all Tan'ji have names," said Mr. Meister. "Nonetheless, yours certainly deserves one. Who better to name it than yourself?"

"Me?" April said. "No, I can't name it. That would be like . . ."

"Naming your own hand," Chloe said.

"Exactly."

Arthur squawked amiably and fluffed out all his feathers, ballooning briefly to twice his size. April had to practically bite her tongue to keep from crying out—it was like the worst case of goose bumps ever. Arthur shuffled across the workbench and picked up a washer with his beak. After a brief burst of curious mischief, he tossed it over the edge, where it hit the floor and began to roll. Everyone's heads turned to follow it—everyone's but April's, that is.

"You guys would not believe how well I can see," she murmured, watching the washer flash and wobble and fall through Arthur's eyes. "How well *he* can see. It's like binoculars on steroids."

"The Ravenvine," Brian said suddenly. Now everybody turned to look at him. "What?" he said. "April doesn't want to name her Tan'ji. So who better than the guy who fixed it?"

"The Ravenvine," April murmured. "That's actually . . . pretty good."

Arthur opened his beak wide and bobbed his head, his throat pulsing. *"Purtygud,"* he cawed. *"Purtygud purtygud."*

"See?" Brian said. "Even the bird likes it. And since when did a bird ever steer a Warden wrong?"

CHAPTER TWENTY-SIX

Mothering

LATER THAT NIGHT, CHLOE STEPPED OUT OF BECK'S CAB IN front of Horace's house. Horace was with her, of course, and April too. April had brought her bird, Arthur, who had hopped into the cab as if he'd been doing it his whole life. Chloe loved animals, but had never had a pet herself—not even a fish. She wondered what it would be like to have a companion like Arthur, especially with a crazy power like April's.

It had been Chloe's idea for her and April to spend the night at Horace's house. She had expected Mr. Meister to say it was too dangerous, considering that the Riven had been pursuing April for days, but Mr. Meister seemed strangely unconcerned. According to him, the Riven had been interested in April and her broken Tan'ji for basically the same reasons Isabel had—they'd hoped that in pursuit of her missing piece, she would unwittingly lead them to the Warren.

482

And apparently empaths, even a powerful one like April, were hard to detect. Plus, as Mr. Meister pointed out, the very powerful leestone at Horace's house was more than enough to keep them all safe.

Of course, Mr. Meister no doubt understood the real reason for the sleepover: Chloe couldn't bear to stay in the academy tonight. Not with her father and Isabel right down the hall. They would want to talk to her, comfort her, convince her that everything could be okay again. As if anything they could say right now would be a comfort. No, Chloe was homeless. Placeless. She wanted to go to Aunt Lou's to see Madeline, but she wasn't sure she'd be able to bear it. That left only one place that felt remotely like home: Horace's house.

As for April, Chloe wanted her to come partly because April hadn't done or said anything really stupid yet, even though Chloe had been poking at her pretty hard. That was impressive. She also invited April partly because she *hung out with a freaking raven*, which was undeniably badass.

But also—very partly—Chloe wanted April to come because it was clear Horace liked the new girl, and Chloe didn't want to give him the wrong impression by kicking April to the curb every chance she got. God forbid he start thinking she was jealous or some horridly weak thing like that.

At Horace's house, though they arrived with no advance notice whatsoever, Horace's mom was gracious and smooth, unsurprisingly glad to let them stay. Horace's dad, also unsurprisingly, grunted and went along with it. He shook April's hand politely and gave Chloe a high five, their usual greeting. Horace's dad was the only person Chloe was willing to high five; he was a man of few words, with a dry and surly sense of humor. Chloe respected that.

Jessica, Horace's mom, seemed tremendously excited to meet April and Arthur. But then Loki the cat showed up in the hallway, practically skidding to a stop when he saw the raven on April's shoulder. All at once a tremendous commotion broke out—Arthur screamed bloody murder at the cat, spreading his huge wings astonishingly wide. Loki bristled and growled and spat like a fiend.

Grimacing in pain, April hustled the bird outside. Arthur took to the air—causing April to clutch her stomach and let out an involuntary "Woop!"—and flew up onto the roof. April said he'd be fine. But Chloe—maybe because she'd never had that pet—couldn't stop worrying that Arthur would fly away and never return. Once they were up in Horace's room, April gave Chloe a strip of beef jerky so she could take it up onto the roof, to encourage Arthur to stick around. Fascinated, Chloe lured him close and watched him for a minute as he tore at the tough meat with his thick beak. Back inside, April opened Horace's window so the bird could hear her voice.

Once they got settled, nobody said much. Chloe, feeling responsible for the get-together but not very hostessy, sat at Horace's desk and dug through his marbles. Horace flopped onto the bed and April tucked herself into a corner on the floor. Gradually they began to talk about the last few days—as if those days had been ordinary in any way.

April told them about taming Arthur, and recounted her trip to the city. They heard about the Riven showing up at her house, and Joshua, and Ethel the hedge witch. They talked about Auditors for a while, and agreed they were the worst. Remembering the feeling of the Auditor at the river invading their Tan'ji made them all shiver in disgust. April was somewhat relieved that Chloe and Horace hadn't seen one before. "Maybe there aren't that many of them," she said. "Maybe we won't have to face another."

Chloe assured her, with more confidence than she actually felt, that she and Horace were ready to take on another pack of Mordin, if it came to that. "Horace and I tracked down a Riven nest and destroyed it," she said. "We'll be ready if they come back, don't worry."

As they talked, April said very little about Isabel directly, apparently wanting to avoid a sore subject, but when Dr. Jericho came up, she let slip that Isabel seemed to know who he was.

"What, like they hang out?" Chloe demanded, alarmed.

"No, just like . . . she'd obviously had encounters with him before. She told me—if I remember right—not to believe anything he said about her."

Chloe couldn't understand what she was hearing. "So they know each other. It sounds like they've had conversations, even. This is bad news. Really bad."

"You're way overreacting," Horace said. "It doesn't mean anything. I mean, come on, we've all talked to Dr. Jericho. Heck, one time you even held—"

Chloe chucked a marble at him, shushing him. As a rule, she tried not to think too much about those two terrible nights, but sometimes she could still feel the horrible sensation of Dr. Jericho's skin against hers as he led her back to the nest hand in hand. "Point taken," she said.

Clearly confused, but not wanting to press, April asked about the missing piece—the daktan. Horace told her about how Brian had discovered it, and how Horace himself had sent it through the box. He described tracking her down and lying in wait for her at the riverbank. But when he began recounting the trip through the falkrete afterward, April stopped him. She asked him to describe the circle of stones inside the cloister. "I think I've seen one of those," she said. "Behind an abandoned barn by my house. There's even a stone shaped like a bird—but no wall, though."

"Maybe it's an old cloister," Horace said. "I doubt the falkrete circle works anymore, though. From what Mrs. Hapsteade said, it sounded like most of them were out of commission."

"Too bad," April said. "If only it worked—and if only I'd known—it would've saved me a lot of heartache these last few days."

"You and me both," Chloe said.

486

April looked at her. "Chloe, I want you to know that I never knew Isabel was your mom—that she was anybody's mom. She never mentioned it."

Chloe couldn't tell if that felt like good news or bad news. "No pictures of me in her wallet, huh?"

"She tried to make it seem like she was just helping me out. She didn't want me to know that she had her own reasons for finding the Wardens. I mean, I found out about the harp, and how she used to work for Mr. Meister, but—"

"No mention of any daughters, or a husband. Not a dropped clue or a shed tear. She never . . . I don't know . . . said something cryptic about loved ones, or an old life, or terrible regrets or anything like that?"

April considered it. "She had a nightmare once. I got the impression it was . . . personal."

An absurd shred of something like hope flickered to life inside Chloe. Maybe her mother truly did have regrets. But Chloe angrily snuffed out the thought, irritated with herself. Finding hope by imagining that Isabel had bad dreams about her past? Pathetic.

April's eyes suddenly went cloudy with that faraway dullness the Ravenvine gave her. A moment later, Loki trotted into the room, meowing loudly. April burst out laughing.

"What's so funny?" Horace said.

"Oh, nothing. He's feeling frisky. He just pooped. It was a good one, too."

Horace made a face. "I did not need to know that. How

about you stick to your bird, and my cat's life stays private, okay?"

April shrugged. "Sorry . . . this is like a whole new world for me."

Horace dug a yo-yo out of his drawer and dangled the string in front of Loki. The cat leapt onto the bed and rolled over, purring. He pawed furiously at the string, snagging it now and again on his claws and biting at it comically.

"Whoa," April said. "Cats aren't exactly my favorite, but that is . . . some super-impressive stuff." Her glassy eyes seemed to dance back and forth, as if following the string. "His reflexes are blowing my mind right now."

If nothing else, Chloe thought, April's abilities were a decent distraction from her current funk. "How come cats aren't your favorite?" she asked.

"Well, partly Arthur. He was attacked by one—that's how he got injured. Cats are kind of cruel. Not all that smart, either. Or actually, I guess that's not fair. They're smart in a creepy way—a selfish way." She startled and cried *"Whoa!"* as Loki unleashed a rapid flurry of paw swipes.

"Selfish how?" said Horace.

April considered it. "Like right now, Loki is enjoying your company, but he's not really thinking about you as a friend. More like an employee. He likes you, but mostly he thinks of you as some crazy ape that occasionally does nice stuff for him."

"Sounds about right," Chloe said.

"Hey," said Horace, objecting. He dropped the yo-yo and leaned into Loki. "Do you really think I'm a crazy ape?" he crooned. Then he reached out and scritched the cat between the ears.

"Yow," said April, slapping both hands atop her head. "Maybe let's not do that."

Horace yanked his hand back. "Right, sorry," he said, blushing beneath his shaggy hair. Chloe frowned. Horace always got red in the face when he was embarrassed, but around April his blushes seemed a lot . . . blushier.

"It's okay," said April. "I've got to learn not to be plugged in all the time. But see, that's what I mean—when I scratch my dog Baron's head, I feel total love from him. He's desperate for my approval. With Loki, though, he's mostly just satisfied that you're finally doing what you're supposed to do."

"And how about now that I've stopped?" said Horace. Loki stared up at him with lidded eyes that seemed—to Chloe, anyway—pretty lovey.

"He's disappointed in you, but not surprised," April said. "I don't know. It's hard to translate animal emotions into human ones. Let's just say—and no offense here, Horace— as far as Loki is concerned, you not scratching his head just proves again how dumb you are."

Chloe laughed. She liked cats just fine the way they were, and none of this was coming as much of a surprise. But Horace, despite being the most logical person Chloe had ever met, was still kind of a romantic at heart. He frowned at Loki with genuine hurt in his eyes. "Is this true?" he asked the cat. "Am I dumb?"

There was a knock at Horace's door, polite and crisp. His mom peeked in, holding a plate in her hands.

"Would it be way too mom of me to say I made cookies?" she asked.

Chloe hopped up and opened the door wide. Her list of favorite people wasn't very long, but Horace's mom was definitely on it. In fact, Chloe abruptly found herself very much wishing that Jessica would stay.

"We could probably use a little mom in here right now," Chloe told her, waving her in and closing the door behind her. Jessica gave her a curious glance but seemed to get the hint. She crossed the room and settled down on the floor beneath the window, putting the cookies before her. On the wall beside her head was the tiny note Chloe had written for Horace the first night they'd hung out. If Jessica had ever noticed it, she never mentioned it.

"I never baked cookies for three Tan'ji before," Jessica said lightly. "I feel strangely unimportant."

Watching her, Chloe was struck as always by just how *cool* Horace's mom was. Genuinely cool, the kind of person who always seemed to know where her foot was going to land several steps in advance. Jessica had to have known that her son had been out until all hours the night before, doing who knows what dangerous deed. But here she was, not even asking. Just making cookies and joking around like she was—well, not quite one of them, but still *with* them somehow.

Before Chloe even knew why she was doing it, she said, "My mom is back." Everyone stopped eating and stared at her. Chloe looked Jessica in the eye and tried not to stammer. "And you—it turns out you know her. You *knew* her."

"Oh," Jessica said, clearly at a loss for words. As far as Chloe was aware, all Jessica knew was that Chloe's mom wasn't in the picture. But now the door to everything was open, for better or worse. Chloe pushed onward.

"She was the girl you told us about. The Tuner. Her name is Isabel."

Jessica's brow furrowed in confusion for just a moment, then flew high in genuine, unmistakable shock. Chloe felt a flood of relief she couldn't quite explain—Jessica hadn't known, hadn't been keeping secrets. Jessica corralled her surprise, laying her half-eaten cookie on the carpet. "Isabel," she said. "Isabel Burke. She's your mother?"

Chloe nodded.

Jessica stared at her hard, studying her face. "That's . . . a shock, to put it *very* mildly. I'm hoping you can tell me more." Her voice was warm and encouraging.

So Chloe told her more. She told her everything. Well, not *everything*—not about her father's long lie. But everything else—the harp, the accident, her mother's return. Several times during the story, Jessica covered her face with her hands, wiping away thin tears in the most motherly way imaginable. At some point Chloe realized she was crying, too. But she didn't care. The doors were open. No one uttered a word until she was finished.

"Anyway," Chloe said when she was done. "She's back now. And I don't know what she wants."

Jessica took a long, slow breath. "I don't know for sure either," she said. "The last time I saw your mother, she was your age. People change."

"But she was like me, wasn't she? I'm guessing she hasn't changed much."

Jessica smiled. "You'll end up being surprised by what life does to a person, I think. But yes, Isabel was strong willed like you. Stubborn. Fierce."

"Did you like her?"

"No."

The immediacy of the response startled Chloe. Even Horace made a soft noise of surprise. "Why not?" he asked.

"She was selfish," Jessica said. "The Wardens could have treated her better, yes, and I felt bad for her. My sympathy ran deeper than you can know, in fact. Being a Tuner is . . . complicated."

"But?" Chloe prompted.

"At the time, Isabel was mostly only concerned about herself."

Chloe sat forward, craving the words even if she didn't want to hear them. "And do you think she's still that way? Do you believe it when she says she came back for me? For our family?"

"Oh, Chloe, I can't say. I'm not going to judge a woman I haven't met because of the girl she was twenty years ago."

God, she was smart. "I'm not asking you to judge. Just guess. Based on how she was back then."

"That wouldn't be fair. Like I said, we weren't friends. We . . . weren't close."

"You're lying," April said suddenly, and then slapped her hand back over her mouth again. "I'm sorry, Mrs. Andrews. You don't even know me, and that was madly rude. I'm so sorry."

"Why the hell would you say something like that?" Chloe demanded.

April gestured at the bed. "It's the cat. Loki. His hearing is crazy good. I can hear all your heartbeats." She turned to Jessica. "Just now after you said that—'We weren't close'—your heart pounded like a mile a minute. Loki twitched his ears at you, and even he thought . . . not like you were lying, exactly, because most animals don't understand that concept. But he was suspicious. You felt doubtful. Nervous." She looked around the room plaintively, cocking her mouth to one side and making her crooked nose even more crooked. "Maybe somebody could help me out here. Or maybe I should just go."

Jessica laid a hand on the girl's leg. "Don't go. You're not wrong."

Chloe couldn't quite grasp what was happening. "Wait, so you and my mom *were* friends?"

"No, we weren't. But it's wrong to say we weren't close."

She plucked her half-eaten cookie off the carpet. She scooped out the soft crown of a chocolate chip with her pinkie and sucked on it. Holding the cookie in her lap, she continued softly. "When I told you I was a Tuner, Horace, you never asked me how I became one."

Horace had the good sense not to respond. Chloe held her breath. This was it—this was what she needed to know. In the corner, April hugged her legs to her chest, trying to make herself small.

"You all bonded to your instruments," Jessica said. "You all went through the Find. But me? Any old harp will do. So the mystery of the Tuner is this: how do you become a Tuner in the first place?"

"So how did you?" Chloe asked.

"I was summoned, just like you. I was drawn to a kind of curiosity shop—a warehouse full of wondrous objects."

"The House of Answers," Horace muttered.

"No. It was called the Bent Ear. The sign said, 'Everything will be heard; nothing will be spoken.' I was intrigued, to say the least. None of my friends at the time—I was thirteen—wanted to talk about the things I really wanted to talk about. I kept my innermost self mostly to myself. But the sign seemed to promise . . . what I needed. Companionship. Shared secrets." She laughed. "Plus my face was on the sign— or so I thought. But when I got closer, I realized it wasn't me, just some older woman."

"Maybe it was you *now*," Horace said.

Jessica blinked several times, clearly startled by the idea. "I'm not sure I want to even imagine how such a thing might be possible," she said. "Anyway, I went inside. A young woman was there. She introduced herself as Mrs. Hapsteade."

Chloe scoffed. "Young?"

"Hey—this was twenty years ago, remember. I'm guessing she was younger then than I am now. Anyway, she had me write something with the Vora. You know the Vora, I'm guessing."

"What color was the ink?" Horace asked. "You're not Tan'ji, so it had to be black, right?"

"No, it was green."

"Green?" Horace said, clearly baffled. "Is that the color for Tuners?"

April lifted her head. "No, it was green for me, too. Mrs. Hapsteade had me and Joshua write our names and stuff earlier today."

"Yes, green is for empaths," said Jessica.

Horace shook his head. "But that doesn't make any sense. If you're a Tuner, how—"

"Horace," Chloe said, trying not to be pissy. This was his mom, after all. But it was *her* mom she was trying to learn about. "Plenty of time for questions later."

Horace closed his mouth, though he didn't look too happy about it.

"Let me tell you the part that matters most right now," Jessica said. "I was invited to return to the warehouse. I was told I might find something that interested me. Something that *belonged* to me. But when I came back the next day, Mr. Meister was there, and he looked me up and down, and he said, 'No. We have nothing for you today.'" She shook her head sadly. "I was devastated. I left empty-handed."

Loki leapt down from the bed, sniffed at the cookie in Jessica's lap, and then snuggled up against her hip. She started to pet him and then glanced at April, clearly thinking the better of it. "I came back again the day after that, but the sign was gone. The door was locked. I came back several more times. It was always the same—no sign, no one home. I tried to forget about it, but it wasn't easy. And then, about a year later, I felt the urge to return and I discovered that the sign was back—the Bent Ear. I went inside. The place was all but empty. All the merchandise had been cleared out. But Mrs. Hapsteade was there, and Mr. Meister too, and also a young girl with bushy red hair. Her name was Isabel. She was nine or ten. And she was *very* excited."

Chloe could scarcely breathe. "Why?"

"She'd been feeling the pull just like me. Today was going to be the day she found the thing she'd been looking for, and me too—but for her it had only been a few days since she'd first found the warehouse. They showed us over to this big Victorian-looking machine, kind of like a cast-iron stove but with two huge phonograph funnels coming out of it. They sat me down in front of one funnel, and Isabel in front of the other.

"Both of these funnel things led into a single black metal chamber. The middle of the chamber was ringed with a series of . . . I'm not sure what you'd call them. Gears? And then on each side of the chamber was a small, thick door, sealed shut. I sat there, waiting, wondering what was about to happen to me. I was excited too. I was slowly beginning to realize that on my end of the machine, behind that sealed door, I could feel something. A presence. A pull. I don't know how to describe it. I started thinking maybe it was the thing I was supposed to find. And then Mr. Meister started the machine, and those gears started to turn, and—" She swallowed and broke her cookie in half. She mashed the halves together again. "I'm not bitter. I didn't understand what was happening until later, but even when I did, I wasn't angry."

"What did they do to you?" Chloe said.

"They cleaved her, that's what," said Horace. He looked as angry as Chloe had ever seen him. "They cleaved you and made you into a Tuner, when you should have been Tan'ji."

Jessica tugged affectionately at the blanket beneath him. "Not exactly. I wasn't cleaved . . . but yes. I was supposed to be . . . could have been? Should have been? Might have become? . . . Tan'ji."

"What did your instrument look like?" he said.

"I don't know. I could feel it there inside that machine, for a little while, but I never saw it. But years later I was told—and I believe—that it was not an instrument of consequence." She gestured at the Ravenvine, peeking out from April's auburn hair. "Nothing nearly so powerful as this. Or the box or the dragonfly, of course."

Chloe didn't know whether to feel angry or sick or sad. As usual, she veered toward angry, even though there was no one here worth being angry at. "And my mom? I suppose it was the same for her?"

"Basically. Inside the machine on her end there was an instrument that she could have bonded to. A weak one. I couldn't tell you what its powers might have been. She wasn't an empath." She looked around at the group. "I want to be clear—had we been allowed to become Tan'ji, Isabel and I would have been the weakest sort of Keepers there are."

"Or so you were told," Chloe pointed out.

"True," Jessica replied. "But you know Mr. Meister. Whatever his . . . flaws . . . he's not going to miss an opportunity to recruit a powerful Tan'ji."

Chloe couldn't deny that. And as for Jessica, Mr. Meister had said that most empaths were relatively weak. But what about Isabel?

"So," Horace said, "you were more valuable to them as Tuners than you would have been as Tan'ji."

"That's right. They needed Tuners at the time."

"But why did they need two of you?"

Jessica tipped her head back, clearly choosing her words carefully. "That's how the kaitan works," she began.

"The kaitan—that's the machine?" asked Horace. Chloe grimaced, hating the name.

"Yes. The kaitan cuts the flow between each potential Keeper and her instrument. Permanently. It strips the instruments of their potential, leaving them powerless and Keeperless forever. And ordinarily, the Medium flowing from each individual would also wither away, but the kaitan stitches those two flows together. The end result is that the two individuals are bonded to each other, instead of being bonded to an instrument. We were fused—that's the word for it. There's no outward power when you're fused, though. Just a closed loop of energy. It was like . . . Isabel was my instrument, and I was hers, but we couldn't do anything with it."

Chloe stood up, unable to sit any longer. "So you and my mother are . . . bonded."

"We *were* bonded—very briefly. But a closed loop gets you nowhere, so there was one more step. The bond had to be pulled apart."

Chloe could hardly breathe. "And how did they do that?"

"They took us away from each other. Physically, I mean. I was taken south; Isabel was taken north. I don't want to upset you, but the experience was . . ." She fished for a word, her expression unreadable. "Uniquely painful? It hurt me in a way I've never been hurt before or since. From what I understand, it's similar to what you guys might feel if you moved very far away from your instruments—except for you, the limits are basically infinite." She rubbed her forehead, hiding her face for a moment, and then continued. "Our limits were not. Picture a thick bundle of rubber bands, stretched tight. Imagine that you just keep pulling, harder and harder, until they snap somewhere in the middle. The ends will be ragged and curled and . . . raw. That's what they did to us."

"But why?" Horace breathed.

"Those raw ends, that's why. That's what makes us sensitive to the Medium. Whereas Tan'ji like you can only feel the Medium through a single, highly specialized instrument, we Tuners can feel it across the entire spectrum. And then with the help of a harp, we can learn to manipulate the Medium in small ways. In fact, we were given our first harps the very next day. Mr. Meister led us to believe they were the objects we had been meant to find."

Chloe boiled furiously. Her mother had been so young— not much older than her sister Madeline was now. What Jessica was describing now sounded like torture, like the worst kind of deceit. She marveled at how the woman could stay so calm.

"Almost right away, Mr. Meister introduced us to the wicker harp," Jessica said. "I couldn't use it at all—it was way beyond my skills—but Isabel was sharper and it was no trouble for her." She laughed abruptly. "I think she got a bigger bundle of rubber bands than I did, if you know what I mean." She looked up at Chloe, and her face softened. "I'm sorry, I shouldn't be laughing about it. But it's been so many years, and I came to terms with it a long time ago."

"You did, maybe. But my mom didn't."

Jessica reached out and took Chloe's hand, a steely fist.

Chloe tried to unclench. "No," said Jessica. "She didn't. And I'm sorry for you both. I'm sorry for your family."

"The Wardens did this to her. They made her this way. She should've been Tan'ji."

"I'm not disagreeing with you, Chloe, but I like to be careful when assigning blame, especially when it comes to the Wardens. And there's no question that as a Tuner, Isabel became much more powerful—and needed—than she ever would have been as Tan'ji. Especially after the wicker harp."

Jessica was just about the hardest person in the world to argue with. "Miradel," Chloe said, trying not to sound sulky.

"What?"

"The wicker harp. That's what she calls it. Miradel."

"Okay," Jessica said slowly. Her tone suggested that harps weren't supposed to have names.

Chloe crossed her arms, unsure how to say what she wanted to say next. She wasn't particularly good at asking for favors. "I want you to meet my mom—to see her again."

April's mouth fell slightly open. Horace said, "Whoa." Chloe held up her hand to shush them both.

Jessica shook her head. "I can't say that sounds like a good idea."

"I'm asking you."

"But why? What would be the point?"

"I need to know why she's here. You know her better than anyone."

"Chloe, that's simply not true."

501

"My dad knows her, but he . . . I can't really trust him right now."

"Well, maybe you should try," Jessica said. "Maybe you should talk to him."

The very suggestion lit fires in Chloe's head. "No, that's—no. Listen to me." Her throat strained with the effort it took not to shout. "I. Need. Your. Help."

Jessica gazed at her for a long, silent moment, looking sad. She broke her cookie in half again. Chloe stood there, fighting off her doubts. Outside in the night, somewhere up above, Arthur croaked lazily. Loki growled and bristled, staring. Just as Chloe was about to call it all off, Jessica spoke.

"Fine," she said. "Tomorrow night. Dinner, here at the house. Invite your dad too, if you like."

Chloe's knees nearly buckled with relief. She locked them tight. "Thank you."

"I'm just doing for you what you would do for me," Jessica said. "What you're always doing for Horace."

"What's that?"

Jessica shoved the crumbled cookie into her mouth. "Being brave," she said.

———

CHAPTER TWENTY-SEVEN

Between Friends

By THE TIME DINNER ROLLED AROUND THE NEXT NIGHT, Horace's nerves—which had begun to simmer the moment Chloe suggested their mothers meet—were boiling over. He'd never seen his mom so anxious before, and if she was nervous, he was sure there was good reason to be.

April and Chloe—and Arthur, of course—had gone back to the academy early in the morning. April was headed back home tonight to talk to her family. Beck was driving her, with Gabriel as escort. With any luck, she'd be back by Sunday.

Horace's mom had spent the day cleaning the house and preparing the meal. She made both meat loaf *and* an enormous dish of macaroni and cheese, plus a veggie plate and a daunting pile of rolls. And a pie. Horace didn't get the sense that she was trying to impress anyone; the flurry of activity felt more like busywork than anything.

When the doorbell rang at 7:29, his mom smoothed her dress. "It's going to be fine," she said. Horace had the distinct feeling she wasn't talking to him.

They answered the door. Chloe came in like she lived there. Right behind her, to Horace's surprise, came Joshua—the mysterious little boy who had written with the Vora in blue. Isabel came in last, carrying a large patchwork bag. There was no sign of Chloe's dad. Isabel and Horace's mom exchanged muted greetings and then an awkward, one-armed hug, during which his mom's earring got tangled in Isabel's bushy red hair. Horace was shocked to hear his mother stammer nervously like a child, clearly flustered.

Technically, Horace hadn't been introduced to Isabel yet, but she shook his hand and then introduced Joshua in turn. She didn't explain his presence. The boy shook Horace's hand gravely, and then his mother's, saying to both of them in turn, "Thank you for welcoming me into your home."

"Quite the manners, I see," Horace's mother said, and then she turned to Chloe. "Where's your dad?"

Isabel answered for her. "He dropped us off, but we thought things might be better without him this time, all things considered. He sends his apologies."

"That's fine," said Horace's mom. "I gave my husband a pass, too. He's out with friends tonight."

Isabel clapped her hands together. "Perfect. Just us moms, then."

Chloe rolled her eyes at Horace. Now that he was seeing

her and Isabel side by side in the light, he could see just how much they resembled each other. They were clearly mother and daughter—same small frame, same fierce but pretty face, same dark, intelligent eyes.

While Horace's mom took Isabel and Joshua on a mini tour, Horace and Chloe set the table. In harsh whispers, Chloe complained about how she was sure Isabel had talked her dad into not coming.

Horace said, "Oh, I don't know. If I were him, I wouldn't want to be here either."

Chloe scowled. "Why is everyone dreading this so much?"

"Not everyone likes confrontation as much as you do, Chloe."

A few minutes later, the five of them sat down to dinner. It was clear from the start that nobody really knew what to say. The last time Horace had seen Isabel, she'd more or less saved his life, and it seemed strange not to acknowledge it now. But at the same time, she was the woman who'd nearly killed his best friend, and who'd abandoned her as a child—an opposite but equally awkward topic of conversation. And although his mother made a few game attempts at small talk with Isabel to get the evening started, they clearly had nothing small to talk about. The way Horace figured it, they were here to talk about big stuff anyway, so they might as well get to it. But he wasn't going to be the one to say so.

Only Joshua, with a kind of innocent, robotic formality, seemed oblivious to the tension around the table. He piled his plate high with food and dug into it with gusto while everyone else nibbled. Between bites, he recited a list of his twelve favorite foods, inspired by the fact that macaroni and cheese was number two—the box kind, not the homemade kind. He then launched into his own bizarre account of the journey he, Isabel, and April had made into the city, burying them with details about directions, distances, and landmarks, but saying almost nothing about what had actually *happened*.

Joshua was just describing the location and orientation of an ice-cream stand near the Chicago Botanical Gardens when Isabel interrupted him, pointing her fork at Horace. "You're the Keeper of the Fel'Daera," she said.

"Yes."

"Quite a coincidence, if you believe in that sort of thing. Who could've guessed the Fel'Daera would choose Jessica's son? I tuned the box, you know, back when I was with the Wardens."

Horace didn't really appreciate the reminder. "Yeah, that's what my mom said."

"She tried to tune it herself, if I remember right, but the box was a mess," said Isabel. "Isn't it spooky that your mother held your Tan'ji in her hands years before you even existed? A thing like that can't happen very often."

Possibly just another coincidence, Horace thought, but that hardly concerned him as much as the first thing she'd said. "The box was a mess?" he asked. "How?"

"Oh, the veins were clogged and tangled. Some of them

506

nearly torn. I don't know what happened to its last Keeper, but . . ." She shivered dramatically, scrunching up her face in fearful disgust.

"What's that supposed to mean?" asked Horace.

"Let's just say not every Keeper retires, if you follow me."

Horace's mom sat back, watching. She looked sharp all of a sudden—angry and impatient. "Can I ask you why you did it, Isabel? Why did you steal the harp?"

Isabel hesitated briefly before answering. "Miradel was mine."

Horace's mom frowned at the name, shaking her head in consternation. "You knew the harps weren't ours to keep."

Isabel laid down her fork. "Why are you attacking me? You know what *they* did to *us*."

"I'm not attacking you. I'm trying to understand the things you've done."

"We were supposed to be Tan'ji."

"I've never been crazy about that word."

"Tan'ji?"

"Supposed."

Isabel scoffed. "Semantics. You know as well as I do that our instruments were there that day. They were ours, and now they're lost."

"I'm the first to admit the Wardens should have told us what was happening."

Isabel rolled her eyes. "Very polite. You weren't nearly so polite about it back then."

507

"To be fair, I wasn't nearly as grown-up, either."

"We still could be Tan'ji," Isabel insisted. "The veins are still there. If they can snip them apart, they can sew them together again."

"And that's why you came back."

Horace had been frozen in his seat, overwhelmed by his mother's knifing tone and the rapid-fire exchange, but at these words he looked over at Chloe. Her face was a brewing storm.

Isabel seemed to remember herself too. "You got me sidetracked. I came back for my family. To ask forgiveness."

"Except you haven't," Chloe said abruptly. "Asked, I mean."

"Of course I have."

"No, you haven't." Chloe's expression turned thoughtful, remembering. "In fact, you haven't even said you were sorry."

Looking genuinely bewildered, Isabel began to sputter. "I . . . of course I am. I'm so sorry—sorrier than you can know. But even if I did beg for forgiveness, would you care? You're not going to forgive me—and you shouldn't. Not yet."

"No. I shouldn't. But you should still ask."

"It hurts too much to ask for something you won't give. You know what I want. I'm sorry for leaving you, Clover. A thousand times sorry."

Her words sounded sincere, but to Horace she looked anything but sorry. She and Chloe glared at each other across the table. Horace was struck again by how alike they were.

"Why is Isabel sorry?" Joshua said. He'd stopped eating and now sat wide-eyed, half a roll in his hand.

"Because she's a terrible person," said Chloe. Isabel shoved her chair back and shot to her feet, stalking out of the room.

No one spoke. Joshua looked as if he was about to cry. Chloe poked guiltily at her macaroni. "Well, that was exciting," she said after a while.

Jessica sighed and stood up. "I'll go get her."

Chloe stuck her fork upright in her meat loaf. "I think our dads had the right idea tonight," she said.

"You were the one who wanted this."

"I'm aware of that, Horace. Thanks."

"What were you hoping would happen?"

"I don't know. Your mom just seems to have the answers so much of the time. I thought she could help."

"Maybe she can. Maybe she is."

"Maybe." Chloe looked over her shoulder out the doorway. Horace took a bite of a roll. He could hear his mother and Isabel talking in low voices downstairs. Chloe said, "I went to see Mr. Meister today. To ask him about the kaitan."

"The Tuner machine? Wow. What did he say?"

"The usual. Drastic times. Drastic measures." She glanced down at the Fel'Daera. "It was because of the box that they turned our mothers into Tuners, you know. Not that that's your fault or anything."

Horace, mouth half full, stopped chewing. "What are you talking about?"

"According to Mr. Meister, he was expecting a delivery at the time. An Altari was coming, some kind of big shot, bringing a few very powerful Tan'layn. 'Instruments of great consequence,' he said."

Horace swallowed. Sil'falo Teneves. The Maker of the Fel'Daera. "And one of those instruments was the box," he said.

"That's what I gathered. Some of the instruments were in bad shape, like Isabel was just saying. The Wardens needed a Tuner if they had any chance of finding new Keepers for these powerful instruments, but they didn't have one. And so . . ."

"So the kaitan."

"Yup."

Horace slipped his fingers into the pouch and rubbed the lid of the box. So much history there, so many unknown deeds. It was hard not to feel connected to them all, hard not to feel responsible.

"I don't want you to feel guilty," Chloe said, reading his mood. "You had nothing to do with that. It was all Mr. Meister. And honestly, I think he told me that story today—about the Fel'Daera—so that I'd forgive him for turning my mom into a Tuner."

"And do you?"

"Not really. Especially since he wouldn't tell me what her

510

instrument was. But think about it—my mother had to tune the box so that the box could find its Keeper. And that Keeper turned out to be you. It's sort of . . . cosmically satisfying, I guess." She elbowed him. "Even though it took you like twenty years to show up."

He laughed. "To be fair, I had to be born and stuff first."

"Some excuse." She took a bite of meat loaf and chewed it slowly. "So . . . I've been thinking. About whether or not the Wardens could actually fix my mom—you know, make her Tan'ji again. I know she's kind of crazy, but what she said makes sense. If the Wardens can undo being Tan'ji, why can't they redo it? Like you said, anything is possible, right?"

Her tone was light, the way it always was when she floated an idea she wanted to believe in, but couldn't yet commit to. Whatever else she claimed she felt, it was clear Chloe hadn't totally given up on her mother. "It might be possible," Horace said. "But it sounds to me like her instrument—whatever it was—was destroyed by the kaitan. Or as good as destroyed anyway."

"I'm not talking about that. I'm talking about Miradel."

"The wicker harp? I don't see how. Surely you can't just create the bond with any old instrument. Especially a harp, I would think. A harp isn't Tan'ji."

"But you said it yourself—maybe Brian could do it. You saw what he did with the Ravenvine."

Joshua said, "What's the Ravenvine?"

511

Horace actually jumped—he'd forgotten the boy was even here.

"April's Tan'ji," Chloe explained.

Joshua looked deeply impressed. "So it's fixed now? Brian fixed it?"

Chloe just frowned at him, apparently realizing she'd said too much. "The point is," she told Horace, "maybe the reason Isabel can't control the wicker harp is because she's not Tan'ji. Maybe if she could be bonded to the harp, things would change."

"That's a lot of maybes."

Chloe bit her lip. "Maybe."

"Besides, even if Brian could do something like that, it's hard to imagine Mr. Meister would allow it."

A voice behind them spoke. "He does enjoy his rules."

Horace and Chloe spun around. Isabel stood in the doorway, looking especially wild. She couldn't have been there long, but she had obviously caught Horace's last words.

Isabel came in and took her seat. "Sorry I stormed off. Emotions got the better of me, as they sometimes do. But I suppose sometimes we all do things—and say things—we wish we hadn't." Isabel leaned forward, staring hard at Chloe. "So tell me," she said, her tone as light as her gaze was heavy. "Who is this Brian? I don't think I've had the pleasure."

Chloe shrugged, acting nonchalant as only Chloe could. "It's no pleasure, believe me. He's nobody special—T-shirt collector, girl chaser."

But Joshua piped up. "He fixed April's Tan'ji."

Isabel's dark eyes glittered. Her mouth fell open and she blinked several times before collecting herself. "So it's fixed! Incredible." She lifted her glass of water. "Cheers to our Brian." She took a sip, though no one else had so much as moved. Then she sat there for a full minute, apparently lost in thought. Horace could hear his mother banging around in the kitchen and he almost got up to help her, just to get away. Joshua continued to work on his meat loaf, and Chloe fiddled with the dragonfly.

At last Isabel broke the silence. "And tonight April is headed back home, yes? To tell her family she's been invited to join the Wardens?"

"That's right," Horace said.

"I'm surprised you two didn't go with her. Someone needs to keep her safe."

Chloe glowered at her. "She's got company. They can handle things."

"Oh, good," Isabel said, sounding genuinely relieved. She shook her head. "A lucky day for her, lucky for sure. I guess our trip was worthwhile after all." She gave Chloe a sad look. "Even if nothing else comes of it."

"What about me?" Joshua asked.

"You," Isabel said blankly, and then broke into a sudden smile. She grabbed him by the shoulder and gave him a jovial shake. "Yes, of course—you. You stick with me. You'll get what you came for, I promise."

Horace's mom returned, carrying the pie and a stack of plates. "It seems Joshua was the only one that had an appetite for dinner," she said. "Which means there ought to be room for dessert."

They each took a slice of pie. Raspberry, Horace's favorite. They ate in silence until Isabel said abruptly, "It's lucky you two found each other."

It took Horace a beat to realize she meant Chloe and him.

"Why?" asked Chloe.

"I'm assuming you look after Horace."

"We look after each other," Chloe corrected.

"But it's the Keeper of the Fel'Daera who really needs protection, isn't it?" Horace's mom shifted uneasily in her seat, looking sidelong at Isabel. Isabel said, "And my daughter is the one who's doing the protecting." She smiled at Chloe. "I'm glad. It's in your nature."

Chloe said, "I must've gotten that from Dad's side of the family."

Isabel laughed softly. "Yes, and you got your moxie from mine." She plucked a berry from her pie and ate it. "Jess, I never imagined that our kids would grow up to be friends. That they would look after each other. Support each other. Love each other."

Chloe sank down in her seat. Horace stared studiously at his pie.

"Well," said Horace's mom cautiously, "we're lucky to have Chloe around. She's practically—" She cut herself off, but everyone could hear the words she'd left unsaid. *Part of the family.* "It's like we've known her forever," she finished limply.

Isabel nodded, and then got to her feet. "I'm afraid I've got to use the restroom. Where was it again?"

Horace's mother pointed. "Upstairs, first door on the right."

"Feel free to talk about me while I'm gone," Isabel said, and left.

After she'd gone, Horace's mom pantomimed wiping sweat off her brow. "I cannot tell a lie," she said. "I've hosted better parties."

"I'm sorry," said Chloe. "This was a mistake."

"No, it's fine. I'm glad to see her face to face again."

"So what do you think about her?"

"She's definitely unpredictable."

"Yeah, but . . . what do you *think*?"

Jessica mulled it over. Then she turned to Joshua and said, "Joshua, would you excuse us for a moment? If you like, you can go downstairs and watch TV."

Joshua looked doubtful. "I don't watch TV."

"Okay then, I tell you what, there's a world atlas on the shelf down there—"

"Yes please, thank you," Joshua said, and he was up and gone, leaving his pie behind.

Horace's mother watched him go, then leaned over the table conspiratorially. "I'm not crazy about passing these

515

kinds of judgments, Chloe, but if you're asking me if you can trust your mother, my answer is no. You were right—she hasn't changed much since I saw her last. She's still too overwrought about the wicker harp, and about her status as a Tuner. I'm sure she surrendered the harp to Mr. Meister because she thought it would soften him up. That it would get him to help her in the long run. But that's not to say she doesn't love you, that she doesn't want to be back in your life. Honestly, I think she wants to reconcile with the Wardens *and* with her family."

Chloe squirmed uncomfortably but didn't disagree.

Horace's mother continued. "Now, if you're asking me if you should *help* her . . ." She reached out and took Chloe's hand, squeezing it. Chloe stared down at the hand and then squeezed back. "Chloe, she's your mother. In an ideal world, she's the one that should be helping you. But this world—our world—is rarely ideal."

"So what should I do?"

"Isabel has to prove herself to you. To everyone. And I think the least we can do—and possibly the *most* we can do— is to give her that chance."

"Cautiously," Chloe offered.

"That goes without saying. But I do believe she only wants good things for you."

Chloe nodded, swallowing. "Okay. Let me ask you this, then. What if . . . what do you think about the possibility that . . ."

She looked at Horace, pleading, and he stepped in. "We've

been talking about whether Isabel really could become Tan'ji. We're wondering if somebody with the right talents could help. If, for example, maybe someone who was the Keeper of a Loomdaughter could—"

His mother sat up straight, dropping Chloe's hand. "Hush," she hissed. "Don't say that word again."

"But—" Horace began.

"You shouldn't have spoken that word out loud, even to me. Not here." She leaned back and peeked out into the kitchen. "Some secrets need to stay buried. Isabel can't hear anything about this, do you understand?"

Horace and Chloe exchanged a look, but neither of them said a word. They went silently back to their pie. Horace's mother ate, too, but watched them both anxiously, clearly perturbed. At last, nearly in a whisper, she said, "For the record, what you're asking sounds impossible, but I've never—"

Suddenly she went stock-still, her face a mask of shock. She rocketed to her feet so fast her chair tipped over. She raced from the room.

Chloe bolted after her. Horace followed, bewildered. His mother ran up the stairs and burst into her own bedroom, the kids on her heels.

Isabel sat on the bed. An object lay in her lap—a boat with sails of shimmering string.

"Stop that," Horace's mom said through gritted teeth. It was her harp, of course. Isabel was looking down at it sweetly, and the strings vibrated on their own, as if an unseen hand

517

were plucking them. "Isabel, stop. That doesn't belong to you."

Isabel looked up, her expression dreamy, unconcerned. "Or you. You said so yourself." The strings continued to play. "But I suppose the old man let you keep it for services rendered, is that the idea?" She gestured at the mighty leestone on the bureau, the sculpture of the raven and tortoise. "And this too! I guess it's true what they say—what goes around comes around."

Horace had no clue what that meant. His mother didn't reply, seemingly transfixed by the shimmering harp in Isabel's lap. And now he realized there was something floating inside those strings—a clear crystal sphere the size of a large marble. A raven's eye, its power spent. Where had that come from?

"I don't know what you're doing," his mother demanded, "but you need to stop. That can be felt for miles."

"Oh, come on—you've got a leestone fit for the Warren. You know we're safe. Snug as bugs." Isabel bent her head over the harp. The raven's eye danced, and the strings glittered musically around it. "I surrendered Miradel, you know. To Mr. Meister. It was so hard."

Chloe opened her mouth to speak, but Horace's mom stopped her with a firm hand on her shoulder. "I'm sure it was," she told Isabel, sounding sincere.

"And then I came up here and I felt your little harp and I just . . . I couldn't resist. I'm sorry, but I—"

"I understand the urge, Isabel," Horace's mom said. "You

518

know I do. But we were just talking about regaining trust. Your own daughter wants to learn to trust you again. And from what you've said, I think you want that too. Do you think this helps? What you're doing right now?"

"What *is* she doing?" Horace said hoarsely, transfixed by the floating raven's eye.

His mother just shook her head. Apparently she couldn't follow whatever Isabel was doing.

"I told you," Isabel said petulantly. "I'm just toying. And that's all this harp is, anyway—a toy. No offense. I suppose that's why Mr. Meister let you keep it."

Now Chloe did speak, her voice like a blade. "It may be a toy, but you're the child. You say you want to be back in our lives. But what you're doing right now tells me that there's no place for you here."

Isabel visibly flinched. She sulked, unable to look Chloe in the face, and then focused on the floating raven's eye for a moment longer. Abruptly, the glittering strings of the harp went still. They faded from sight. The raven's eye fell and rolled across the floor. Chloe scooped it up, inspecting it closely. It looked unchanged.

"I told you, just playing," Isabel said, standing and holding out the harp. "Surely you understand, Jess. I mean no harm. I'm trying . . . I really am."

Horace's mom took the harp, folding it up again. "It's time for you to leave."

Isabel held up her hands as if surrendering. "I agree.

519

Matthew should be here any second. I called him ten minutes ago." When Horace's mom looked baffled, Isabel shrugged wryly. "I knew you'd feel me using your harp," she explained. "I knew it was the sort of transgression that would get me uninvited."

"But you did it anyway."

"Yes, I did it anyway." She pushed past them and headed downstairs. Halfway down, Horace's mother spoke to her.

"I might have let you use it, you know. If you'd asked."

Isabel paused. "Yes. You might have." She bustled on down the stairs, calling for Joshua.

Horace's mom thrust her hand out to Chloe. "The raven's eye. Quick."

Chloe hurriedly handed it over. Horace's mom peered into it as if she were a jeweler assessing a great spherical gem, turning it this way and that.

"What did she do to it?" Chloe asked.

"I don't know. She was running huge threads through the foramen, but all I can see now are traces."

"Foramen?" Horace asked.

"Yes. Every Tanu—even a simple Tan'kindi like a raven's eye—has a foramen, a permanent structure crafted out of the Medium by the device's Maker. It's sort of like . . . the eye of a needle. An anchor point, but also a passageway. It connects the Tanu to the Medium while also allowing the Medium to flow through. The foramen is the thing we Tuners feel for first when we're working—everything stems from there."

Despite the circumstances, Horace hung on her every word. There was so much he still had to learn—so much he might never truly understand. "But this raven's eye is all used up," he said.

"It's still Tanu. The foramen remains intact. And like I told you before, Horace, every Tuner craves a Tanu to work on." She unfolded her harp with a flick of the wrist and set it on the bed. She plucked lightly at the strings with one hand as she examined the raven's eye in the other, like a doctor diagnosing a patient.

"So did she do anything to it?" asked Chloe.

"Not that I can see."

"Could she be tricking you?"

"Yes," Horace's mom said immediately, continuing to gaze into the raven's eye. "Isabel is a hacker, of sorts. She could always string the Medium places you wouldn't expect, and no one is better at tying off flows. But nothing's coming in or out of here—that's for certain. And if there's anything here at all, it's delicate beyond anything I think even Isabel could do, even with the wicker harp. I'm guessing that she really was just playing, feeling the thrill of the Medium again. I won't pretend I don't understand that urge."

Swiftly, Chloe snatched up the raven's eye, slipping it into her own pocket. Horace's mom opened her mouth as if to argue, but Chloe said decisively, "I'm not leaving this here. Just in case." Horace's mom shut her mouth and gave Chloe a resolute nod.

The doorbell rang. Horace heard the front door open, and then the deep, friendly voice of Chloe's dad. But before they went down, there was something Horace needed to know. "Chloe, wasn't that your raven's eye? Why did Isabel have it?"

"I let her have it. I had my reasons at the time, but I guess she did too."

"Yes, and it might have been the simplest reason of all," Horace's mother said, herding them toward the door.

"What's that?" Horace asked.

"Need."

Downstairs, Chloe's dad filled the doorway. Huge but gentle, he apologized for not coming to dinner. Horace noticed that every time he so much as looked at Isabel, he seemed stupefied by her very existence. Meanwhile, he treated Chloe like a precious stick of dynamite. Seeing the three of them together—broken apart in so many ways and now shoved jaggedly back together—was unmistakably sad. Horace knew his mother could feel it, too.

Good-byes—maybe for the sake of Chloe's dad—were said calmly, though not quite warmly, as if the incident with the harp had occurred long ago but hadn't been totally forgotten. The only reminder was when Chloe held the raven's eye up to Isabel, like a challenge. "This is coming with us," she said.

Isabel's expression didn't change. She didn't say a word.

Joshua shook hands again and solemnly recited thank-yous, plus a long and technically incomprehensible compliment of their atlas.

With a polite rumble, Chloe's dad cleared his throat. "I'm ready when everyone else is," he said.

Isabel examined Horace's mother one last time. "I should have asked," she said simply, and then turned to go. Joshua fell in beside her, Chloe's father right behind.

Chloe was the last to actually leave. As she stepped over the threshold, Horace muttered under his breath, "You don't have to go."

"Someone has to," she whispered back. Horace understood at once—her dad. She was looking after him again. Still. Chloe leapt lightly out the door and trotted out into the growing dusk after the others.

And then they were gone. Horace's mother shut the door and blew out a long breath. "This is why we don't have more people over," she said.

"Really? *This* is why? How many Tuners do you know?"

Horace's mom rubbed her face and smiled at him apologetically. "Sorry. For a while there it was like junior high all over again." She shivered. "Chloe can handle this. She's got her dad, and Madeline, and you."

"And you," Horace said, feeling a surge of warmth and pride and gratitude for his own family. His mom was so awesome that . . . well, she had mom to spare.

"Yes, and me," she agreed. She wandered into the dining room. Horace followed. She shook her head at the table piled with uneaten food. "I can't cope with this right now," she said, and put her arm around him. "It's Friday night. We gonna play chess or what?"

Horace grinned. Nothing had ever sounded better. "Okay, but fair warning. It's going to be a rough end to a rough day. For you, I mean."

She grinned right back, his mother as he'd always known her. "Bring it, box boy," she said.

CHAPTER TWENTY—EIGHT

Fear Is the Stone

CHLOE SAT IN THE BACK OF THE BEAT-UP WAGON HER FATHER drove, watching Joshua watch the city slide by. She could practically see the miles—and the busy world that filled them—etching themselves onto his strange little mind. Chloe held the raven's eye in her hand, trying to remember its warmth from long ago, trying to imagine what Isabel might have done to it. But maybe she'd done nothing, just like she claimed. Maybe she'd only needed to feel that power again. Chloe could relate to that.

In the front seat, meanwhile, her father and Isabel weren't talking. He'd asked how the dinner had gone, and Isabel had only replied, "It's nice to know Chloe has such good friends." Her voice sounded sad.

Good friends, yes. And truth be told, it was because of Horace and his mom that Chloe had the raven's eye now. The most suspicious part of Chloe imagined that Isabel had been trying to plant some dangerous device in Horace's house, to do away with the Fel'Daera somehow, once and for all. And if there was even a chance that that was true, Chloe would take this danger with her instead.

Isabel and her father were murmuring now, discussing directions. Isabel was telling him not to take the Kennedy. Her father agreed without complaint. Joshua, meanwhile, looked confused. Chloe didn't know much about driving around the city, but hearing her father give in to Isabel so easily made her grind her teeth. She felt like she could practically crush the raven's eye in her hands. She gripped it so hard that after a while, it felt as warm as it had when it was working.

They crossed the river. Chloe caught a glimpse of it gleaming in the twilight, lined by trees, a surprising slice of wildness here in the city. She thought back to the riverbank two nights before, and that horrible Auditor. Despite everything, despite all of Chloe's power, what might have happened if Isabel hadn't shown up when she did? Her rage boiled higher. She hated the thought that she might've actually needed Isabel's help. She gripped the raven's eye until her fingers hurt, squeezing it harder and harder.

So hard it started to burn.

Chloe opened her hands. Her palms were warm—warmer than they should have been. And there between them, deep in the center of the raven's eye, she spied a speck of light. A golden spark, small and distant. She stared and stared, hardly daring to breathe, watching as the tiny glint of light grew brighter.

"What did you do?" she whispered.

Her dad looked at her in the rearview mirror. "Sorry, Clo, what did you say?"

She ignored him. She lifted the raven's eye up, cupping the tiny glow in both hands. Isabel turned, looking over the seat. When she spotted the yellow light, her face went slack with wonder—or was it dismay? "No," she breathed.

An icy finger of dread ran down Chloe's spine. "What did you do?" she said.

Isabel turned to Chloe's father. "Take us to the lakeshore. Hurry."

"No," Chloe said, her voice as thick as dirt. The glow of the raven's eye continued to grow in her hands, like a candle flame drifting slowly up from the deeps. "Stop the car. Stop the car, Dad."

"We can't stop," Isabel said. "They'll find us."

Chloe held her breath. She'd endured so much over the years—overcome so much, escaped from so much—that fear no longer came easy. But somehow these words chilled Chloe straight down to the marrow.

They'll find us.

"The Riven," Chloe said.

"Yes."

Chloe's dad looked over at Isabel but said nothing. Joshua, meanwhile, huddled against the driver's-side door, watching

Chloe fearfully. Chloe wrapped the raven's eye in her hands, trying to bury its blooming light. "What did you do?" she asked for a third time.

"It was an accident!" Isabel cried. "I told you, I was only playing, trying to see what Jess's harp could do. I was only peeling back the veins, pulling them inside out. There was no danger, not with that little harp, I never—"

"Danger," Chloe said. "Danger of what?"

Isabel hesitated. She looked at Chloe's dad, as if he had the answers, but he remained silent, gripping the steering wheel like he was strangling it. "Obversion," said Isabel.

Chloe had never heard that exact word before, but she knew that the obverse of something was its opposite. "A reversal, you mean."

"Yes."

"So instead of hiding us from the Riven, now this stone is revealing us. It's calling to them!" Chloe looked down at the orange-yellow light leaking from between her fingers. It grew slowly brighter by the second. She started rolling down the window, letting warm night air push into the car.

"No!" Isabel said. "You can't just get rid of it."

"The hell I can't."

Isabel reached over the seat and pressed the tip of her finger against the leestone. "It's warm. Don't you see? The light—it's already grown from nothing into something."

"What does that mean?"

"The light of an ordinary raven's eye shrinks for a reason.

And now, with the obversion . . . it *grows* for a reason."

Chloe knew all too well that the usual purple cloud of a raven's eye shrank whenever the Riven were focusing on the bearer of the stone. It shrank as the leestone absorbed that attention and eventually lost power. But now everything was backward. This burning yellow cloud was growing. "They already know we're here," Chloe said. "Is that what you're saying? They're already after us?"

"Yes," said Isabel. "And whatever security we've earned from the leestones at Horace's, or at the academy, it's gone now."

"Then I'll destroy the stone." She leaned toward the window.

"No!" Isabel said. "It won't matter—in fact, it might make it worse. You might bring every Riven in the city down on us."

"According to you," Chloe said.

"According to me, yes. I'm sorry, Clover. I never meant—"

"Stop it! Just stop it!" cut in Chloe, tired of excuses.

"It's okay, Belle," her father said soothingly—maddeningly. "It's okay." He looked in the rearview mirror anxiously, but not at Chloe. She realized he was checking to see if they were being followed. More than any of them, he knew what it was like to suffer at the hands of the Riven. And he was the one Chloe was worried about now.

Chloe cursed to herself, resisting the urge to look back. She didn't know what to believe. If only Horace were here— maybe he would be able to logic out what was happening, figure out what Isabel done, how this damn Tan'kindi was actually working. Or better yet!—he could send it through the Fel'Daera, erase it from existence for a while. But she couldn't risk taking it back there. She glanced over at Joshua. The boy was still cowering against the door, clearly afraid of the burning leestone.

"We need to get to the lake," Isabel said. "Someplace with a pier. We need to throw the stone into the water—the deeper, the better."

"Navy Pier," said Chloe's dad.

Isabel shook her head. "Too many people. We need someplace quieter."

That didn't make much sense to Chloe. Safety in numbers, right? Surely the Riven wouldn't dare to chase them down when there were crowds of people around—assuming any of this was true in the first place.

Joshua spoke. "There's a closer pier anyway."

"Where, Joshua?" asked Isabel. "Tell us where."

"Almost straight down the road we're on. Go all the way to Lake Shore Drive. Just a little bit north, there's a beach with lots of sand. A long pier, hooked like a clothes hanger. The water is deep."

"Perfect," said Isabel. She leaned into Chloe's dad, patting his arm. "Get us there. Fast as you can."

They drove on, gunning it between stoplights and sitting nervously when they were caught by a red. The leestone grew brighter and warmer in Chloe's hands. Time and again she almost chucked it out the window, Isabel's warnings be damned. How *did* a raven's eye work? And how had Isabel reversed that process? Chloe had heard Horace's tale about tossing a raven's eye into the street, shattering it, and how it had drawn Dr. Jericho away, saving him. Maybe with things in reverse right now, Isabel was right—maybe shattering the stone would be the worst thing she could do.

Or maybe this entire thing was a lie.

And then, as they were stopped at a red light, a flash of movement caught Chloe's eye. A strange, slashing flicker in the driver's-side mirror. Chloe twisted in her seat, staring out the rear window. A block back, she saw a towering figure just crossing the street. The figure turned and began sprinting up the sidewalk after them.

A Mordin.

"Dad, we've gotta move," Chloe said.

"I can't. The light's red. I'm boxed in."

Now Chloe spotted another Mordin behind them, farther back on the far sidewalk, swiftly closing in.

"We really need to move, Dad."

Chloe searched for the third Mordin that she knew had to be nearby. A little park off to the left was empty. Nothing up ahead. And then, just as she turned to the passenger side, the smell of brimstone drifted in through the open window, sharp and unmistakable. The same instant she caught the smell, she saw it—Mordin number three, hurtling down the cross street straight at them, all arms and legs and grinning teeth.

It was no more than thirty feet away—a mere three or four strides on those monstrous legs. Isabel saw it too and gasped.

Chloe fumbled with the button for her still-open window. "Now, Dad! Now!"

The words weren't even out before the engine roared. The wagon lurched into reverse, then surged forward. Chloe was thrown back in her seat. Tires squealed. Horns blared. And then a great gnarled hand reached in and caught the edge of the open window frame. The car actually heaved to the right under the force of the blow. The Mordin held on, loping alongside as they accelerated, glaring savagely in at them. It was particularly ugly, with a cruel nose and wideset eyes. It stank even worse than Dr. Jericho. It struggled to reach inside, but Chloe swung her fist as hard as she could against the long, bony fingers still gripping the door. Once, twice, three times. She might as well have been pounding on steel.

The Mordin growled and took a mighty leap, landing heavily on top of the wagon. The roof buckled. Joshua curled into a ball, keening.

Chloe went thin, so filled with rage that she barely heard the Alvalaithen's song. She shoved the raven's eye into her pocket and slipped out of her seat belt. She bent over the backseat, digging around in the hatch. It was heaped full of junk, and she didn't even know what she was looking for, but she had to do something. She *would* do something.

Her father sped down the street, weaving this way and that, but he couldn't shake the Mordin. The creature scratched at the roof with nails that sounded like they were made of steel.

Chloe's hand found something cold and hard, buried deep in the junk. She focused on the object, letting her fingers find purchase, knowing at once what it was—a crowbar. Holding it tight, she let her own lack of substance spread into it, turning it into a ghost. She pulled it easily from the pile and got up on her haunches.

Joshua stared. "What are you doing?"

"Chloe, no," said her dad, watching in the rearview mirror.

"Just keep driving," she told him. "Don't stop." And then she stood up.

Her top half emerged through the roof of the car. The wind whipped her hair. They were passing through a cemetery, dark rows of tombstones on either side of the street. The Mordin crouched overhead like a hulking, horrible marionette, clinging to the luggage rack with one powerful hand and raking at the roof with the other. When he saw Chloe, he reared back in surprise, but quickly recovered and reached for her neck.

She felt his ghastly fingers pass through her throat as his hand closed on nothing. The Mordin stared, shocked, and was nearly shaken loose as the wagon swayed violently, but he hung on and broke into a greedy grin. "You," he said, the word spilling musically from his ugly mouth like the strike of a bell.

"Me," Chloe said, and she laid the ghostly crowbar deep

across the meat of his thigh, and let go.

The Mordin shrieked in pain—a ghastly, trilling sound that split Chloe's ears. He clutched at the bar now melded in his flesh and toppled off the roof, spilling into the street like a bundle of lumber, rolling to a stop as they roared away.

Chloe sank back into the car and released the Alvalaithen. She looked out the back, watching as the Mordin staggered to his feet and limped toward the curb.

"What did you do?" said Joshua into his hands, his eyes wide.

"I took care of it."

Isabel's eyes were on her too. "That was smart," she said. "That was brave. If only I had my harp, I could have helped."

Chloe didn't reply. Truth be told, her heart was hammering over what she'd just done. She'd melded the crowbar inside the Mordin's body—something she'd never done to a living creature before. Even a creature like a Riven. She'd considered it on the riverbank, with the Auditor, yet hadn't actually had a chance to attempt it. But now it had just . . . happened.

"If I had my harp," Isabel was saying, "I could undo the obversion."

Chloe had heard enough. She pulled the raven's eye from her pocket and thrust it into Isabel's face. The raven's eye was so bright now that it blinded her, so warm that her leg felt sunburned. "Why the lake?" she demanded. "I don't need water to bury this. I can take it down into the ground and leave it where it'll never be found."

Isabel looked startled—frightened, even. "That's too dangerous."

"I can manage. I finally learned how to go underground, no thanks to you."

"It doesn't matter," Isabel said, turning away. "We're leaving a trail of smoke. Where there's smoke, there's fire. And how do you put out a fire?"

"Water," Joshua said.

"That's right. It's the only way."

The car rolled on, as fast as her father dared. Once, Chloe spotted another Mordin lunging from a dark alleyway, but they sped on past before it could reach them. Was it true that the raven's eye couldn't be buried? If her father hadn't been here—and Joshua too, she supposed—Chloe would have put Isabel's claim to the test. But she couldn't afford the risk that Isabel might be speaking the truth. She couldn't do that to her dad, not now.

"I don't blame you for not trusting me," Isabel said, not looking at anyone in particular but obviously speaking to Chloe.

"That's right," Chloe said. "I spectacularly don't."

"You think I did this on purpose."

"I think lots of things," Chloe replied.

Isabel twisted around again. "Then tell me: if I wanted the Riven to find us, why would I have warned you what was happening? Why wouldn't I just let the raven's eye burn, let the Riven come?"

Chloe hadn't considered that, but she didn't let an inch of doubt creep onto her face. "Maybe you're just extra sneaky."

"Or maybe I'm lost. Maybe I'm doing the best I can with the mess that's been handed to me."

"Like I said before," Chloe said, not budging an inch, "get in line."

Isabel held her gaze, steady and piercing. Chloe gave back as good as she got. Finally Isabel's eyes dropped onto the dragonfly. "You could leave the car at any time, I think," she said. "You could do with the raven's eye whatever you think is best. And yet here you still are." She flopped back into her seat, crossing her arms like a smugly satisfied child. Chloe had no answer for her.

They swung onto Lake Shore Drive. Off to the right, the dark waters of Lake Michigan stretched out to the horizon like an ocean. Joshua directed them to the beach. They passed a golf course and a marina, getting ever closer to the lake, but eventually they reached a point when Joshua was uncertain how to proceed any farther.

"There are no roads," he said. "But the lake is still a ways away."

"Which way is the pier?" Chloe's dad asked. Joshua pointed, and he wrenched the wheel, sending the car bouncing over the curb and down a wide, deserted sidewalk that cut through an area wooded with shrubs and scrubby little trees. Chloe caught a glimpse of a sign that said BIRD SANCTUARY.

"I'm going to get you close, Chloe," her dad said. "And

536

then you get out. You move fast. You get rid of that thing."

Cloe nodded. "Don't follow me. Everyone stay in the car."

"But—" Isabel began.

"Stay in the car," Chloe repeated. "Especially you. I'm handling this."

Far up ahead, they could see that the sidewalk ended in darkness. The lake lay somewhere beyond. Chloe leaned forward, gripping the raven's eye.

"Go faster," she told her dad.

"Chloe, it's a dead end, we can't—"

"Go as fast as you can for as far as you can. Wait until the last second. When you need to hit the brakes, tell me."

Her dad glanced at her in the mirror, then nodded. The car surged forward, the engine straining. Chloe loosed the song of the Alvalaithen, drinking from it deeply. Power coursed through her as she went thin. She moved to the center of the seat, crouching. She willed the seat to stay firm beneath her. She'd learned years before—after the accident, when the earth had nearly swallowed her up—that in order for matter to feel solid beneath her, she had to believe that it was solid. Until that terrible day, she'd always unthinkingly believed in the earth beneath her feet. And ever since, she'd learned to wrestle that belief into being, to hold on to it tenaciously whenever she went thin, and even—when she had to—to point that belief where she needed it.

The station wagon careened over the sidewalk, bouncing madly. In the headlights, a thick row of shrubs grew nearer and nearer. Chloe waited, ready to spring, sure they were past the point of no return now but trusting her father. The shrubs loomed ever larger.

"Matthew," said Isabel, bracing herself.

"Now!" her father shouted, and stomped on the brakes.

Chloe uncoiled, timing it almost perfectly. She leapt with all her might, diving between Isabel and her father. As she knifed through the cold plane of the windshield, she felt the distinctive warm hum of flesh streaking through her calf— someone's fingers. It was Isabel, trying to catch her. To stop her? Save her? But of course she couldn't be stopped, didn't need saving.

She sailed over the plunging hood of the wagon as it screeched toward a halt. She felt herself tumbling in mid-air and she curled into it, somersaulting, air rushing through her and not slowing her at all. She sliced through the line of shrubs. They were covered in thorns that couldn't touch her. Beyond: open air, darkness, the faint sound of water. A sandy beach, sloping gently away. Still thin, still clutching the raven's eye, she sailed far out over the sand, a hundred feet or more. She opened out of her slow spin and somehow found herself descending feetfirst. She touched down, sinking into sand up to her belly.

It was shockingly cold down deep, where her feet were, and she felt a flicker of panic. But by believing she would not sink, she pushed back steadily, coasting as if she were water skiing, holding out her hands for balance. Still sliding, she gradually willed herself out of the cold ground, letting the ground grow solid bit by bit beneath her—from fog to feather to water to earth. Gradually she lifted and slowed, until at last she popped free entirely. Airborne again just for a moment, she let the dragonfly go still and then hit the ground running, headed for the darkness ahead where the lakeshore lay waiting.

She laughed out loud, exhilarated. That was a stunt worthy of Neptune's cape. Sorry—*cloak*. But the thrill was short-lived. The sand was wet and soft and sprinkled with coarse vegetation. It was hard going. The wind off the lake blew straight into her face.

She ran for a hundred yards or so and then slowed to a trot, exhausted. She picked her way across the lumpy sand, almost like tiny dunes. She looked back once or twice but saw nothing—just the dark line of bushes and trees, and the city behind, with the bright lights of downtown far off to the south. She'd left her father back there without protection, and Joshua too. Even Isabel—without her harp, she was as vulnerable as any of them. But Chloe had the raven's eye. If the Riven were still in pursuit, surely they'd be coming after her, not them.

At last she reached the foot of the pier. She leapt over a ribbon of brackish water and onto the wide concrete surface. Relieved to be off the sand, she broke into a run again, the wind ripping at her. It was dark, and there were no railings— just a six-foot fall into the water on either side—but the light of the raven's eye lit the way now, gleaming like a torch. She set her sights on a small light tower shining far out on the hooked pier, a thousand feet from the shore.

She ran and ran, out onto the black water. She saw no one. The only sound was the soft slosh of waves against the pier and the slap of her tired feet. At last she arrived at the light tower, a latticed structure about thirty feet high with a platform at the top, like a miniature Eiffel Tower. A security fence surrounded the base. Chloe went thin and slipped inside, then mounted the ladder that led to the platform high above.

At the top, shielding her eyes against the bright green warning light that shone here, Chloe looked back to shore. She guessed she'd come nearly a half mile since bailing out of the car. Were the others following? Waiting? But it didn't matter. She'd come here for one reason, and one reason only. She turned toward the dark, windy expanse of Lake Michigan. She shifted the raven's eye from one hand to the other; it was so hot now she could barely stand to touch it. She reared back, ready to throw, and as she stepped into it, a single thought sliced across her mind.

Please be true.

She let the raven's eye fly. It soared like a comet out over the waves, so bright that its reflection shone like some luminescent underwater beast, racing to catch up. The leestone arced into the water, plunging into its reflection, still burning as it sank beneath the waves. Chloe watched it sinking slowly out of sight, stubbornly fading, until at last it was swallowed and the darkness of the deeps ate it up.

She stood there for another minute, breathing hard and waiting, until finally she realized she had no idea what she was waiting for. She descended the ladder, slipped out through the fence, and started slowly back down the long, curving pier.

She wasn't even halfway back to shore when she heard them. Footsteps, several sets, heavy and slow. And though she couldn't smell anything—she was well upwind—she knew immediately what it was.

Riven.

She found that she wasn't surprised. She didn't even feel a lick of fear—not for herself anyway. Just as long as they hadn't discovered her father's car.

Three huge shapes, eight or nine feet tall, marched down the pier toward her, backlit by the fading glow of twilight behind. Side by side, the Mordin completely blocked the pier—not that they could stop her, of course. But as they came closer, she saw they weren't alone. Another figure walked in front, smaller and feminine. For one crazy moment Chloe thought it was Isabel, but then she saw. Long, pale arms. A dangling white braid. The glint of a small red stone.

Chloe went thin immediately, swiftly drawing on the Alvalaithen's power. But no sooner had she done it than the Auditor was right there with her, inside the dragonfly. The Auditor yanked a thick ribbon of the Medium toward herself. Chloe wrestled with the invader briefly inside the

Tan'ji, feeling violated and infuriated—a silent tug-of-war, a struggle of wills.

In that first flush of rage, Chloe pushed the Auditor's presence down hard, feeling for a moment like she might be able to oust her from the dragonfly completely, as Horace had done along the riverbank. But she couldn't do it. Not alone. This time, all the Auditor's attention was on her, and the Riven surged back hard, staking her claim, easily snatching enough of the Alvalaithen's power to make herself every bit the ghost that Chloe was.

"Come now," the Auditor said silkily, coming closer, showing not the least hint of effort. The red stone on her forehead shone clearly now. "Surely there's enough for two."

Not wanting to look desperate, Chloe stopped fighting, but she held on hard to what she had and stayed thin. She'd learned the other night that the best the Auditor could do was fight her to a draw. Infuriating and humiliating, yes. Fatal, no. Chloe stood her ground as the Auditor and her escorts approached, stopping just ten feet away. She realized the Riven were breathing hard after their long chase. She eyed the Mordin, catching a faint whiff of their foul stench now. None of them was Dr. Jericho.

"Hello again," Chloe said to the Auditor. "Looks like you recovered from your little fainting spell on the riverbank the other night."

The Auditor narrowed her chillingly blue eyes and shook her head. *"Na'gali ji kothuk,"* she said, her words like the flickering blades of knives, her voice like a crackling fire. "Do not presume to know me. I am Quaasa—merely one of many."

Chloe nearly took a step back. Apparently this wasn't the same Auditor as before. And then Chloe remembered—the Auditor on the riverbank had had green eyes. "I see," said Chloe. "Must get pretty confusing at the Christmas party."

"Let us not waste time with jokes," the Auditor said. "I believe we have business to attend to."

"And what business is that?"

"Why don't you tell us?" sang one of the Mordin, his face particularly lean and skeletal. Chloe was surprised—she'd never heard any Mordin except Dr. Jericho speak English before. "You put out a beacon that was felt for miles. We are simply answering the call."

"That was an accident. A butt dial. My bad."

The Auditor smiled thinly. "More jokes," she said. She stepped aside, indicating one of the slouching Mordin behind her. With a start, Chloe realized it was the ugly Mordin who'd jumped onto the station wagon. He was favoring his right leg heavily, the flesh of his thigh still impaled by the crowbar. "It does seem you had some doubts, if indeed you meant to call us. But no matter. I'm still glad you did. I've very much wanted the chance to . . . get to know you."

The Auditor bent down in front of the ugly Mordin. Her poisonous presence thickened again inside the Alvalaithen. The Auditor took hold of the crowbar and considered it thoughtfully for several seconds. Chloe realized she was making the crowbar go thin. Sure enough, the Auditor lifted the crowbar out of the Mordin's flesh as if it were made of smoke. The Mordin grunted and buckled slightly, but stayed on his feet.

"My compliments to your Tan'ji," the Auditor said, examining the crowbar briefly. Then she lifted her blue eyes to stare hungrily at the Alvalaithen. "Truly, it is quite spectacular. Ja'raka Sevlo told me all about it—and you—but I had no idea it was this extraordinary."

"Who?"

"Ja'raka. You've met, dear—many times."

"*Ja'raka.*" Chloe whispered the word to herself. "You mean Dr. Jericho?"

"Yes," the Auditor said, frowning faintly. "Though the Quaasa don't care for blue-sky names."

"No, of course you don't. You're way hardcore. But if Dr. Jericho told you all about me, I don't suppose he included the part where we tricked him, back in the nest. He ended up looking pretty stupid."

"Oh, he told me—trapped in the dumin. Unlike you, we do not disguise our failures. And Ja'raka would be the first to admit that he should have sought our help sooner that night."

"He had your help on the riverbank the other day. That didn't turn out too well either."

The Auditor frowned. "Do not concern yourself. I will discuss those events with him."

"What, are you his boss or something?"

Another crystalline laugh. "I am Quaasa. The Mordin do not answer to me, and I do not answer to them—not even Ja'raka Sevlo." She spread her pale, graceful arms. "I am everyone's equal."

"Yeah, you just keep telling yourself that," Chloe said.

The Auditor hefted the crowbar thoughtfully, then slowly approached. Chloe stayed her ground. They were both formless, their bodies turned to phantoms by the Alvalaithen. Nowhere near as colossal as the Mordin, the Auditor nonetheless stood almost a foot taller than Chloe. The triangular red stone in her forehead seemed to glimmer rhythmically.

Without a word, without a sound, the Auditor plunged the tip of the crowbar into Chloe's chest. At first Chloe felt almost nothing at all, because the crowbar had no more substance than she did, but then a trembling bolt of cold took up residence right through the center of her heart. The Auditor had allowed the crowbar to resolidify inside Chloe's body. If Chloe herself were to become solid again with this inside her, she'd be dead in an instant.

Holding the crowbar in place, the Auditor leaned in, watching the flickering wings of the dragonfly. "I wonder how long you can last," she whispered.

Chloe didn't so much as blink. "Dr. Jericho wondered the same thing in the nest. It turned out to be longer than he liked." There *was* a limit to how long she could stay thin, of course—just over three minutes, give or take. She'd been thin for a minute or two already, but as far as she was concerned, the limit didn't exist until she hit it.

"You cannot do this forever," the Auditor said. "I know you cannot, because I cannot." Her voice was so lovely, so reasonable, so perfectly hateable. Her presence shimmered revoltingly along the taut strands of the Alvalaithen's song.

Her rage bubbling up high and hard, Chloe stepped in closer to the Auditor, impaling herself more deeply on the crowbar. She felt the tip emerge from her back. "Let's find out how long we can last, then," she said, lifting her scarred right arm. She reached up for the Auditor's neck, reached right inside and parked her rigid hand within the boneless flesh of that smooth white throat. "Let's find out together."

An unmistakable surge of fear flared briefly in the Auditor's eyes, but she didn't back down. Chloe could feel the creature's pulse thumping in her palm, keeping time with the rhythmic glinting of her bloodred stone. Neither of them spoke or moved. They stood there like that for a long time—twenty seconds? Forty? Waves slapped sloppily against the pier. The flat blast of a boat horn rolled across the water—once, twice. The Mordin shifted furtively, gesturing and muttering quietly among themselves. Chloe had the strange sense that they were making predictions.

Chloe's heart continued to pound around the crowbar. The flow of power from the Alvalaithen began to slow, growing tight, but she refused to panic. She purposefully clenched and unclenched her fist inside the Auditor's neck, and when the Auditor didn't flinch, Chloe broke the silence, making sure her voice showed no sign of effort. "I suppose you know this is how I destroyed the crucible. Maybe you've noticed my scars."

The Auditor nodded gingerly. Was that a hint of strain around her eyes? "I see your scars. And I *feel* them, too—all of them. The ghosts of knives and hammers under your skin. I'm beginning to understand what Ja'raka sees in you. Do you know, I rather think he admires you?"

Knives and hammers—that hit too close to home. And as much as Chloe tried to ignore it, staying thin was becoming more difficult by the second. She held on hard as the Alvalaithen's song was stretched toward the breaking point. Could the Auditor feel her struggles? How much longer could either of them last? For an instant, Chloe considered running. There was nothing stopping her. But no—she wouldn't run. She would outlast this creature, no matter what it took. She was the Keeper of the Alvalaithen, and the Auditor nothing but a filthy parasite. "So Dr. Jericho is a fan, is he?" Chloe said lightly. "Next time you see him, tell him the feeling is not mutual."

"Why not come with us, and tell him yourself?"

"Why not take a long swim with a big bag of rocks?"

The Auditor frowned, baring her teeth. Then she slid the cold, solid shaft of the crowbar slowly across Chloe's chest, letting it come to rest dead center through the flickering dragonfly.

Chloe nearly lost the fragile grip she still had on her

power. But then two of the Mordin stepped forward in alarm. The gaunt-faced Mordin barked what sounded like a curse. Chloe understood at once. "They're calling your bluff," she said. "You could never allow this instrument to be destroyed. No more than I can."

The Auditor's scowl turned into a rueful smile. "You are correct," she said, her voice cracking now with unmistakable strain. "I cannot destroy what is precious." And then she slid the cold metal up through Chloe's neck—her chin, her mouth, her nose—and brought it to a halt directly between Chloe's eyes. "There. Much better."

Chloe went rigid, clinging painfully to the last desperate threads of the Alvalaithen's song. It was like she'd been slowly inhaling a great breath and was still trying to pack more air into lungs that were close to bursting. She wondered if she might faint.

But the Auditor was grimacing openly now too, clearly at her own limits. She glared at Chloe, eyes alight with rage and disbelief. "You are close to the end, Tinker," the Auditor said. "Step back. You know you want to save yourself."

Chloe clenched her fist ever tighter inside the Auditor's throat. She forced her own lips to move. "Do not . . . presume . . . to know me," she snarled.

Without warning, a new voice cut through the windswept night, shrill but firm, coming from the shoreward end of the pier.

"Stop!"

548

The Mordin hissed and whirled around. The Auditor spun too, the crowbar slipping out of Chloe's skull, swift as an arrow. With a gasp of relief, Chloe released the Alvalaithen and staggered back, blinking hard. The gaunt-faced Mordin leapt and seized the small figure that stood out there in the darkness, curly hair bobbing in the breeze.

Isabel.

"Don't hurt her," Isabel said as the Mordin dragged her closer like a child. "Please don't hurt her."

The Auditor, sagging as much as Chloe, could only watch them approach. Chloe took a breath, recovering, and reached for the Alvalaithen again. She went thin, and a beat later she felt the Auditor do the same. This time they were both so exhausted that neither of them wrestled for control of the Tan'ji. Chloe let the Riven take what she would, seething, promising herself that someday the creature would get what was coming to her.

And now Isabel was here. Unarmed and helpless. Pleading for Chloe's safety. What was the woman thinking?

"You," the Auditor said, seeming to recognize Isabel. "Why are you here, Forsworn? And without your proxy, too."

Proxy—the harp, apparently.

"I'm not here to fight," Isabel replied. "I'm here to talk. To negotiate."

The Auditor considered her for a moment, and then turned to study Chloe's face. She looked back and forth between Chloe and Isabel, then started to laugh. "How exemplary.

You are here to negotiate. For your . . . daughter, if I'm not mistaken."

"That's ridiculous," Chloe said. "I'm not her d—"

"Yes, that's right," Isabel interrupted.

Chloe was filled with fire. What did Isabel think she was doing? "There's no negotiation necessary," Chloe said. "I'm not in any danger."

The Auditor ignored her, speaking to Isabel instead. "It was you that lit the beacon."

"Yes. By accident."

The Auditor nodded as if she understood. "Fumbling with powers you were never meant to understand," she murmured sadly. She sounded sincere. "And now you're here to make amends for your mistake. To save your daughter."

"I don't need saving," Chloe said. "You couldn't stop me from leaving if you tried, I—"

"Quiet," said the Auditor calmly, holding up a long, pale hand. Chloe was so infuriated that she lost her words entirely. The Auditor rounded on her and continued. "You do not yet understand the predicament you are in, Tinker. It is true I cannot stop you, but neither can you escape. I am Quaasa. I am everyone's equal." The Auditor sipped at the dragonfly and—to Chloe's astonishment—let herself sink briefly into the concrete pier, up over her ankles. Then she rose smoothly to the surface again and smiled. "There is nowhere you can go that I cannot follow."

The sight—and the very idea—sank into Chloe's bones

like bitterly cold air. This Auditor seemed much more skilled than the one at the riverbank. Between her astonishing mimicry and the presence of the Mordin, maybe it was true. Maybe Chloe couldn't escape. Even now she was exhausted from staying thin for so long; she was already starting to lose her grip on the Alvalaithen for a second time. But as her doubts rose higher, so did her outrage. She tried to crush her fears back down again. "You'd be surprised where I can go."

The Auditor simply shook her head. "Nothing surprises the Quaasa," she said, making Chloe practically quiver with fury. Then she smiled in a gruesomely friendly way and plucked at a thread of the Alvalaithen's waning song. "I grow tired. You do too. Let us not push each other to the edge again. Let us catch our breath, five seconds only—and then we will resume. Is this fair?"

Not fair, not at all, but Chloe had no choice but to accept the offer. She wouldn't last even another minute, and she didn't dare allow the Auditor to stay thin while she herself did not. She nodded, watching the Auditor warily, and then they both released the Alvalaithen at once. The Auditor silently counted off five seconds on her long, four-knuckled fingers, and they took the reins again, each to their corners. She gave Chloe an agreeable nod, as if to suggest that this poisonous stalemate was fine and dandy. Chloe wanted to rip out her braid by the roots.

The Auditor turned to Isabel. "You want to negotiate, Forsworn. But with what? You know we have no use for your . . .

talents. We cannot invite your kind into our nests."

"It's not my talents I'm offering. It's information."

Chloe felt dizzy. The mysterious remark about the Riven having no need for Tuners threw her, and suddenly here was Isabel, offering up information to this monster. What was she about to say? Chloe opened her mouth to stop her, but Isabel beat her to it. "I know where you can find easier quarry," said Isabel. "Another Keeper. A Warden."

The Auditor cocked her head, clearly intrigued. "What Warden? Where?"

"First, let my daughter go. Promise you won't follow her."

"No."

"Then I have nothing to tell you." Isabel's eyes flickered onto Chloe for a moment, still pleading. Chloe stared daggers back at her.

The Auditor hesitated, and then said, "Tell me what you have to tell me. If I believe you, your daughter will be free to lose herself in the city again."

"Swear it," Isabel said.

The Auditor shook her head. "The Quaasa take no oath but their own."

Isabel sighed in apparent frustration. She glanced at Chloe one last time and then spoke. "The girl I was traveling with—the empath. She's gone back home. She's there now. You know where she lives already."

Chloe surged forward. "Are you serious?" she fumed, storming up to Isabel. "What is wrong with you? You used her to find the Wardens again, and now you're betraying her?"

"I'm saving you," Isabel said calmly. "You are my daughter. April is not."

The Auditor watched Chloe with interest. "So the empath has gone home, you say. April, is it?"

"You tell me," said Chloe.

The third Mordin, silent so far, spoke. Shorter than the others, his voice was a deep and hearty wind chime. "The Wardens would never let her go back home by herself. If she's there, she's not alone."

"I don't know anything about that," Isabel said. "I only know she went home."

Chloe blinked, but said nothing. She herself had revealed to Isabel that April wasn't traveling alone. Was Isabel lying to the Riven now, or had she forgotten?

The Auditor stepped gracefully forward, the wind tugging at her hair. She walked a slow, thoughtful circle around Isabel, the crowbar still dangling from her hand. "I wonder," she said. "It would be foolish of me not to suspect that this entire endeavor is nothing more than a poorly conceived trap." Now she circled Chloe, coming so close that the tip of her long braid swung through Chloe's shoulder. "First, a beacon we could not ignore, borne by the one Tinker who has the least to fear from us. Next, the unexpected arrival of her Forsworn mother. And finally, this tale of a new recruit, conveniently alone outside the city, willingly offered up." She stepped back up to Isabel. "Tell me, Forsworn, where is your proxy?"

"In a safe place. I wouldn't dare bring it near an Auditor—not with my daughter present."

"I see. And why should we believe this tale you tell? Why should we not get what we want right now?"

Chloe could not help herself. The fool of a Riven actually believed this whole setup had been planned. "And just what *do* you want, exactly?" she said.

The Auditor shrugged. "The same thing we want from every Tinker. Acquiesence. Cooperation. Fellowship, if we find you worthy. But failing that?" She drew hard on the Alvalaithen, forcing Chloe to heave desperately back against her. Laughing softly, the Auditor eased up at once. "Surrender."

The Auditor lifted the crowbar and ran Isabel through, straight into her belly. Isabel flinched violently and slapped her hands over the spot, only to find that the crowbar had no substance. She was unharmed—for now. She blinked at it for a second or two, then lifted her face to the sky.

The Auditor cocked her head at Chloe. "You have a weakness for family, I think. Your father was worth risking your life—and the lives of your fellow Wardens—that night in the nest. How much, I wonder, is your mother worth to you now?"

Chloe didn't hesitate even for a second, not sure whether she was driven by anger or bravery or bitterness or fear. Or something worse—something she wasn't sure she wanted to name. "Nothing," she said. As soon as the word was out, she felt a knot tighten in her throat. She summoned up a fresh jolt of rage—*the harp, the accident, her father, April*—and swallowed it down. "She's worth nothing at all."

The Auditor raised her perfect eyebrows. "Explain."

Chloe forced herself to look at her mother. "Explain, *Mom*."

Isabel still held her head high. She didn't flinch. "I chose my harp over my family," she said, her voice thin but clear. "I nearly killed my daughter, and then I abandoned her. I left my family without so much as a good-bye, and I never came back." Now she turned her head, looking Chloe straight in the eye. "She is my daughter, but I am no mother of hers."

The knot leapt painfully back into Chloe's throat. She gritted her teeth, willing her face not to move. The Auditor took a deep breath. She stood there looking lost in thought for several long seconds, and then at last pulled the crowbar from Isabel's belly. She tossed it over the edge of the pier. It disappeared into the dark water with a gulp.

"There are many abominations the Wardens would foist upon the world," the Auditor said softly, "but none are more regrettable than the Forsworn." She turned to the little pack of Mordin, and the four of them began talking quietly in their own tongue, their words crawling through the air like insects.

Isabel had her face turned to the heavens again. Chloe tried to imagine something to say to her. She was so infuriated with her, but whenever her anger threatened to spill over into words, she remembered Jessica's terrible tale, and the pain Isabel must have suffered the day the Wardens made her a Tuner.

Overhead, out across the lake, stars were creeping in upon the fading twilight. Chloe didn't know any of their names. How she wished Horace were here right now, to help guide her, keep her true, help her understand what came next.

The Auditor interrupted her thoughts. "We leave you now. Remember this day."

Chloe tried not to act surprised. "What, like you're doing us a favor? Letting one Warden go only to chase down another?"

"We do not do favors. We do what is necessary." Chloe frowned. Why did those words sound so familiar? "We will pay a visit to April's home, and we will see what we shall see." She waved a long finger in the air, scolding. "Do not attempt to follow us, Forsworn. Do not intervene."

"I won't," said Isabel.

The Auditor turned to Chloe. "Tell the Wardens not to bother contemplating a rescue," she said, but Chloe was already making plans. It must be 9:30 by now. It would take an hour or so to get Horace and arrive back at the Warren. And then they would set out for April's house—all of them. She didn't know where April lived, but they would have to make it on time. "I will have my sisters with me," the Auditor continued. "And Ja'raka too. You slipped away from us on the riverbank, but only because your mother saved you. She saved you again tonight. I do not think she means to save you a third time."

"I don't even need—" Chloe began, but before she could

spit back her reply, the Auditor's presence slid from the Alva-laithen like a shadow chased by the sun. Despite herself, despite her fury and dread, Chloe gasped and greedily pulled every inch of its power into herself. It was clean again, hers alone. Her knees almost buckled beneath her.

"Need is a funny thing," the Auditor murmured. She glanced over at Isabel. She looked back at Chloe one last time. Her eyes were earnest and strangely sad. "Maybe you can forgive her your scars," she said, and then she turned to go, sprinting nimbly up the pier, the shadows of the Mordin falling swiftly in behind her.

Orphans' Oath

APRIL COULDN'T GET CLOSE TO SLEEP. SHE LAY ON HER BED, IN her own room, in her own home. Everything was just as it was when she'd left.

Everything but her.

It wasn't late—not even ten o'clock—and she'd only been back for an hour or so. The Warden's mysterious cab driver, Beck, had driven her home, with Gabriel as an escort. April had envisioned this trip home as a kind of good-bye, a chance to spend time with Derek and mold things into the right shape before leaving to join the Wardens. She'd imagined over and over again how the conversation with her brother would go, but when the actual moment arrived, with Derek actually in front of her at the kitchen table tonight, she couldn't re-create any of the clever or compelling things she'd thought to say.

"Too tired to talk about it" was all she'd said, when Derek

asked about her visit with Maggie. And then she'd fled awkwardly upstairs.

Once in her room, she'd placed the leestone Mr. Meister had given her—a beautiful green-and-golden stone carved into the shape of a bird's skull—atop her bookshelf. It would protect the house and anyone living in it from the Riven. And there was another protective leestone in her pocket, just for her, as warm as a sun-baked rock—a raven's eye. A very appropriate name, all things considered. On the drive up in Beck's cab, Gabriel had repeatedly asked her to check the color of the raven's eye, which was worrisome, but he seemed satisfied every time she reported that it was still black.

Mr. Meister thought there was little danger of the Riven showing up here. The Riven knew where she lived, of course, but it seemed the leestones would take care of that, in time. Meanwhile April—vine repaired—was no longer the target she had been a couple of days ago, when the Riven hoped to follow her bloody trail straight to the Warren.

Or at least, that's what Mr. Meister seemed to think. What his logic amounted to, strangely, was this: now that April was whole again, she wasn't nearly so valuable. It was kind of insulting, in a way, but April took it in stride. It made sense. And after all, she firmly believed it was better to be small and safe than big and in danger.

No, there was no real reason to think the Riven would show up tonight. Nonetheless, precautions were always necessary, and so Mr. Meister had not only sent the leestone and the raven's eye, but Gabriel too. Gabriel, in fact, was outside somewhere right now, staking out the house in secret, keeping watch. He didn't talk much, but April liked him. He seemed like a person who only spoke when he had something worth saying, which was a quality April herself aspired to. However, now that she was here, now that there were things she *had* to say to Derek, she had absolutely no idea how to go about it.

It didn't help that the newly repaired Ravenvine continued to bring her oceans full of wonder. Arthur was doing his half-brain dozing thing on the roof. She basked in the sensation of the night breeze ruffling his feathers, the rise and fall of his powerful chest muscles as he breathed.

Her senses wide open, she startled as a bat fluttered into range higher up, echolocating like mad. Her own throat and tongue seemed to vibrate as the bat fired a rapid series of chirping clicks, like the chattering teeth of some tiny, rusty robot. The sounds rose and fell as the bat zeroed in on flying insects. She did her best to ignore the sensation of bugs squishing juicily in her mouth, the taste of their guts on her tongue. She tried to catch a glimpse of Gabriel through the bat's sharp night eyes, but never saw him.

A little past ten, Uncle Harrison creaked heavily up the stairs for bed, just like always. Not long after, Derek followed. As April lay there—hiding, to be honest—a singular and unfamiliar urge grew in her belly. Escape. She would go outside and find Gabriel, and then Beck would drive them back to the Warren. The urge shocked her. She couldn't do that. She wouldn't. She would try talking to Derek again tomorrow, keeping it simple. She had Mr. Meister's folder, packed with brochures and letters and applications to fill out and forms to sign. She would show it all to Derek in the morning and she would . . .

She would lie.

She imagined all the lies she'd have to tell, tomorrow and the day after, and on and on, until her stomach churned with doubt and her head buzzed with angry contradictions and her legs ached to run and before she knew it she was out of bed. She eased her door open into the dark hallway and slipped down the hall to Derek's room. She knocked twice, heard nothing, and let herself in.

She groped her way toward Derek's bed and fumbled for his lamp. When she turned it on, he slurred out a mumbled question:

"Whosit?"

"It's me. Wake up."

"I just fell asleep," he said, opening his eyes. "What's going on? You okay?"

"Not really. I mean yes. Yes, I'm fine. It's just . . . I have something big to ask you. And you're going to say no, but I need you to say yes."

Derek sat up straight, crossing his legs. He rubbed his eyes and looked at her hard. "What is it?"

"I need to go. Away." She laid the folder for the Mazzoleni Academy on the bed.

Derek eyed the folder warily. "What are you talking about? Go away where?"

"There's a school in the city. I've been invited to attend—to live there—for free. But the thing is—"

"No," Derek said, not even opening the folder.

"—there's more to it than just school, I—"

"Absolutely not. What do you mean you 'got invited'? You're thirteen years old! You just mysteriously got invited to go to school in Chicago for free. In the summer. For no reason." He flipped the folder open and slapped it shut again without really looking.

"No. Not for no reason. Something's . . . happened."

Derek pressed one hand against his forehead, his thoughts clearly racing. His face turned stern. After several deep breaths, he said, "Pill, tell me you were at Maggie's house the last few days."

April took a deep breath of her own. "I was not at Maggie's house."

The muscles in Derek's jaw clenched and unclenched. His eyes were steely but sad. "You swore," he said at last. "I made you swear you weren't lying to me, and you swore. Orphans' oath."

"I know. I'm so sorry. I *had* to lie."

"Why? Where did you go—to this school of yours?" Derek turned away, tugging at his hair. "I can't even look at you. I can't understand what you're even telling me."

"Then listen. Forget the school. The school is just an

excuse for what's really going on with me. And I'm trying to tell you—it's important. I need you to listen."

"I'm listening."

This was the moment. She knew that the school story wouldn't be enough. It would be enough for Uncle Harrison, but not for Derek. She would have to tell him more.

She would have to *show* him more. And she could do that. Yes, she could.

The thought of stepping out from under these lies and into her newly found power emboldened her, made her stand up tall. "There's a reason I lied to you—you know I wouldn't break the oath without a reason." Wordlessly, heart pounding, April turned her head and pulled back her hair, revealing the vine.

Derek leaned in, squinting. "Jewelry," he said, his voice dripping with skepticism.

April let her hair fall. "Not jewelry. It's an instrument."

"What's that supposed to mean?"

"It belongs to me. It's called a . . . Tan'ji. It's magic, I guess you could say, except it's more like science, but it'll *seem* like magic. To you."

Now Derek sat back. "I have . . . nothing to say to that. Nothing at all."

"You won't believe me unless I show you." She grabbed him by the wrist and pulled him out of bed. She knew what she had to do.

She led him through the kitchen and outside. The night

was hot and moonless and still. They passed beneath a spider, and for a moment April swooned as her vision blurred and multiplied. A vast spray of white filaments appeared before her—the spider's own web, as seen from the center. But she pushed the spider's sight away, grateful for the new control she had over the vine.

Arthur stirred and strutted across the roof to perch on the gutter directly overhead. Out in the darkness of the backyard, April could feel First Baron, edging fitfully up from sleep. She'd been avoiding the dog so far, both in person and through the vine—the last time she'd seen him, she'd cried, and she wasn't sure she wouldn't do it again. The dog got slowly to his feet as the porch light came on, his sleep dissipating in a polite swell of happy excitement. He came toward them, tail wagging.

And as he approached, she realized she needn't have worried about crying. The moment she opened herself to the dog with the newly repaired vine, she was overwhelmed with a flood of sensation that swept everything else from her mind, a thick and complicated stew that drowned her mouth and nose. It was his sense of smell, even more rich and astonishing than Arthur's razor-sharp sight. She'd known that dogs' noses were incredibly keen—she'd researched it—but she'd never really realized just how dominant Baron's sense of smell was, how much of his brain was devoted to it. For him, smell *far* outstripped sight and even sound. With some difficulty, she groped her way through the busy cloud, clearing her head.

April grabbed the dog by his jowls and gave his head a friendly shake. He sniffed and licked her face, a bizarre sensation through the newly attuned vine. She smelled like salt and dirt and girl, and fast-food grease and cheap chocolate shake, and—undescribably but undeniably—worry and hope and sadness. In other words, exactly like herself in exactly this moment. Again she struggled not to let it engulf her. How strange to think that emotions had a scent.

"Is this the magic part?" Derek said.

If you only knew, she thought as she rose and faced him. "Here's what's going to happen. I'm going to read Baron's mind."

Derek paused, then laughed out loud. "Hell, *I* can read his mind. *Food food food, bark bark stranger, food food food, wag wag poop.* Oh, and then *food.*"

"That's about half right," April said, staying calm. "But to be fair—from what I can tell—every animal thinks mostly about food."

Derek stopped laughing. "From what you can tell? What does that mean?"

"Like I said." She pulled back her hair, revealing the vine again. "With this, I can read the minds of animals. I can . . . hear what they're thinking. What they're feeling, and sensing."

"You're serious."

"I'll prove it." She began backing away, the crisp night grass crinkling under her bare feet. "Just wait. Stay here with

Baron." She crossed the lawn. As she moved deeper into the shadowed woods ahead, she began to feel the usual assortment of nocturnal animals out there among the trees. Rodents, mostly, and a solitary sentinel hidden in the branches up high—an owl, patient and predatory. Cautiously, unable to resist, she took in the owl's eyes for a moment, and its ears. The forest lit up like day. Her own footsteps sounded like a dinosaur's. A moment later, the owl flew away on powerful, soundless wings, but not before she lost her breath at the sight of a figure on the edge of the owl's keen vision, crouched motionless twenty yards out among the trees.

Gabriel.

April sighed with relief. At the yard's edge, she stepped behind a large hackberry tree, leaning back against the rough bark, hidden from Derek's sight. She pulled her attention away from the woods and back toward the dog. "Okay," she called out, "Now . . . do something."

"Like what?"

"Anything. Move around or something. Just make sure Baron sees you."

"You're telling me you're going to see what the dog sees?"

"That's what I'm telling you, yes." Defocusing on the dimly illuminated trees before her, April let the dog's vision become her own. She saw her brother's face through Baron's eyes, the colors strangely muted. He looked deeply doubtful. "Stop shaking your head and just do something," she said.

Derek leaned down to the dog, his face full of consternation. He held up his hand.

"Four fingers," April said.

Through Baron, she saw Derek's surprise. He glanced over in her direction—her *actual* direction—then turned his back to her and bent down again. This time he made a circle with his left hand and brought it to his right eye, staring hard into Baron's face.

April felt a little catch in her throat. "The oath," she tried to say, but even Baron could hardly hear her. With effort, she found her voice. "The oath. You're doing the orphans' oath. And I swear I'm telling you the truth this time."

Derek dropped his hand. He looked back once more at the shadows where April was hidden, then up at the porch and the house. "You've got me on camera or something. You must. Why are you doing this?"

April practically boiled with frustration. "There's no camera. This is real."

"Oh, yeah? Then prove it."

Gritting her teeth, April opened herself more fully to the vine, to the torrent of information pouring from the dog. He was content, happy for the attention he was getting, but confused about why April was so far away. With his ears, she could hear a complicated blanket of sounds—far-off cars and Uncle Harrison's air conditioner and the steady *buh-thump*, *buh-thump* of Derek's pulse. It occurred to her that Derek was much more unsettled than he was letting on.

She could discern the aftertaste of dog food in Baron's

mouth, earthy and oddly spicy. She could feel the grass beneath his rough paws. But above all, she was awash in that ocean of smells, rich and overpowering and for the most part unidentifiable, like colors that had no names. A few of the scents were recognizable, but even these took shapes she could never have imagined. She could smell the night trees, and somehow she knew that morning trees had a different scent than this, and that morning trees in June were different yet again from morning trees in September. She could detect smoke from some distant fire, acrid and chemical, and realized she could even tell what direction it came from, as if the dog were smelling in stereo. There was also a deeply pungent odor that was very distracting, and vaguely unpleasant, drifting in from the woods to the north. It took April a moment to realize that it was the smell of something dead, and that to Baron the stench wasn't unpleasant at all—just another rich note in this omnipresent swarm of odors.

As she struggled to make sense of it all, she slowly became aware of an extra dimension Baron's nose opened up—specifically, the dimension of time. She grasped that this dead thing, for example, was nothing new to Baron; he'd been smelling it for days or weeks, tuned in to the evolving states of decay. He could smell April's recent passage through the grass, fading slowly from house to tree in the direction she had walked. Because of his sense of smell, Baron wasn't locked into the here and now . . . almost like Horace. And of course—sights and sounds disappeared at once, but smells lingered. Every object in Baron's world, April realized, oozed with history, telling a story.

And that included Derek.

April stepped out from behind the tree. "Did you know a dog's sense of smell is tens of thousands of times stronger than ours?" she said. "If you translated that into sight, it would mean that whatever humans could see from three hundred feet away, dogs could see from eight hundred *miles* away. From here to New York City."

"Why are you telling me this?"

April closed her eyes and started walking toward him, homing in on First Baron's location like a beacon. "You haven't showered since yesterday," she said firmly. "And when you did, you used my strawberry shampoo." She watched herself through Baron's eyes, tall and willowy and gray. The porchlight threw the dog's and Derek's shadows across the lawn at her feet. "You ate something with peanuts today. And you were around people who were smoking cigarettes, but you didn't smoke one yourself."

"None of that is news," Derek said unsteadily. "I have peanut butter sandwiches a couple of times a week. Half the guys I work with smoke." He hesitated and then said, "And I'm out of shampoo."

April dug deeper, hardly listening to him, coming closer still. She caught new smells, and identified them. Blood. Plastic. She opened her eyes. "You cut yourself somewhere," she said, gesturing along her left side. "You had a Band-Aid on, but I think it's gone now. You didn't put any medicine on it."

Derek glanced down at his left elbow, silent.

"You were out with a girl. Last night, I think." April focused hard, trying to separate and translate the scents that were thick in Baron's mind. Butter and salt. Flowers and fruit. "You went to the movies. You had popcorn. The girl was wearing perfume or lotion or something . . . it smells like peaches. She has a cat—no, not a cat." April stopped just in front of Derek and the dog, trying to ignore her own powerful scent in Baron's nostrils, concentrating instead on this foreign animal odor. Musk and wildness. Meat and mischief. At last she thought she had it. "A ferret? You're dating a ferret owner?"

Derek slowly sank to the ground, his eyes ablaze with confusion. "How did you . . . ? And anyway we're not dating, we're just—"

"Friends, I know. But . . ." Just then Baron sniffed amiably at Derek's face, and the peachy scent April had been catching blossomed wondrously, unmistakably. "She kissed you," April said, and pointed to her right cheek, just below the corner of her eye. "Right here."

Derek reached for the same spot on his own face, his mouth open in amazement. "No one saw that," he murmured.

April cleared Baron's thoughts from her mind and sat down in the grass beside them. A moth fluttered by unseen overhead, headed for the bright beacon of the porchlight, where a mindless swarm of insects already droned dizzily.

Baron lay down and put his head in her lap, exhaling noisily, his jowls flapping.

"This is real," Derek said.

"Yes." April watched her brother, knowing she'd done enough.

After a few minutes Derek spoke again, softly. "Tell me," he said.

So she told him. She held nothing back—or at least, almost nothing. She told him about Isabel and Joshua and the daktan, about Morla and the Riven, about Horace and Chloe and Mr. Meister. And Arthur, of course. She gave him a vague account of the vine being repaired, so caught up in her story that before she knew what she was doing she mentioned Brian and Tunraden. These were secrets she knew she shouldn't share, even with Derek. From inside the house, the grandfather clock suddenly began to chime, as if to warn her off. April ended her story awkwardly. "Anyway, that's what happened," she said lamely. "And now here I am." She counted the rest of the clock's chimes as they sounded. It was eleven o'clock.

Derek took a deep breath and let it out, but didn't speak. He watched the night sky. They sat there for a few minutes, April knowing she had to let him absorb everything. She'd had days to absorb it—weeks, really. He'd had scarcely half an hour.

Suddenly, a jolt of alarm shot through the vine. Baron sat up straight, ears perked, staring out into the dark yard. A thin, whining growl leaked out of him, and his nose pulled at the air, twitching. April opened herself up to the dog's senses. Her hand fell involuntarily onto the raven's eye in her pocket.

"What is it, boy?" Derek asked lightly, clearly unconcerned.

A stinging scent. A memory of a bad shadow in the woods. Anger. Fear. Foulness. That cruel stench, sulfurous and vile, filling April's head—brimstone. It was faint and far away, even for Baron, but unmistakable.

She rocketed to her feet. "Gabriel," she called, and then, louder: "Gabriel!"

Derek stood. "What are you doing? Who's Gabriel?"

Then the sound of footsteps, sprinting across the yard. Baron's protective rage exploded. The dog lunged and barked ferociously, powerful motors churning in April's legs and chest. Derek took a step forward as he spotted Gabriel running toward them. "Whoa, whoa!" he called. "Who the hell are you?"

"It's okay," April said, to dog and brother alike. She grabbed Baron by the collar, feeling the worn leather digging into her own throat. "It's okay—he's a friend," she said, quieting the dog and reassuring her brother.

Gabriel came to a stop twenty feet away. He held the staff like a weapon. "What is it?" he said.

"Brimstone."

Gabriel lifted his chin and sniffed the air. "I don't smell it."

"I do," she said. "The dog does. But we have the raven's eye. Shouldn't we be—"

"Check it."

April yanked the still-warm stone from her pocket, holding it up in the light. No longer solid black, the raven's eye was now clear around the outer edges, with a spiky cloud of violet in the center. The cloud pulsed faintly, contracting, almost seeming to shrink as she watched.

"What's going on, Pill?" Derek insisted. "What is that thing?"

"Well, I'm no expert," she said, "but I'm pretty sure it's bad news."

CHAPTER THIRTY

A New Journey

MR. MEISTER SAT BACK IN HIS CHAIR, HIS LEFT EYE AS BIG AS A silver dollar. Horace didn't blame him for staring. In fact, everyone—Brian, Neptune, Mrs. Hapsteade, Horace himself—had been staring at Chloe as she told her astonishing story. They were packed into Mr. Meister's office, listening to every incredible detail about what had just happened. The raven's eye. Mordin. The pier. The Auditor. Isabel. Even Joshua, who had witnessed part of it and was with them now, listened with wide, fearful eyes, particularly to what Chloe revealed in the end.

April and Gabriel were apparently in danger.

Horace could hardly believe it. For the first hour after Chloe had left his house, taking the raven's eye with her, he'd fretted. His mother too. They'd stumbled through a bad game of chess in which neither one of them was able to focus.

But then they'd both relaxed, starting a second game. Ten moves in, however, Chloe had returned. She'd stalked right through the bedroom door without notice, looking grim and smelling of brimstone. She didn't say a word—she didn't have to. Obviously something had gone terribly wrong. Horace followed her down to the waiting car, her parents and Joshua still inside. There was no sign of the raven's eye.

The ride back to the academy had passed in painful near-silence. Horace itched to know what was going on, but Chloe had refused to say, insisting she would only tell the story once. She had uttered just two words on the way downtown, when Isabel had twice tried to talk to her, pleading. Chloe interrupted her both times, adamantly: "No."

Mrs. Hapsteade had been waiting for them in the entryway of the Mazzoleni Academy, somehow anticipating their arrival. "Go upstairs," Chloe had ordered her parents. "Stay there."

But Mrs. Hapsteade, looking confused and concerned, had pulled Chloe's parents aside. Horace only heard one scrap of the murmured conversation that followed, when Isabel whispered earnestly, "It's all my fault." She'd then retreated to the upstairs dormitory, her husband in tow.

Now down in the Great Burrow, her story told, Chloe was sulkily avoiding everyone's eye. "Anyway," she said. "Here we are again, having an emergency meeting because of one of my parents. It's turning into a super-fun tradition for me."

Mr. Meister's chair croaked alarmingly as the old man

leaned as far back as it would go. For a long moment he seemed to contemplate Isabel's wicker harp and the spitestone that sat beside it, the little cyclops owl. But then his gaze shifted even higher, straight up through the ceiling of his office—as if he could see up through hundreds of feet of wood and stone and concrete to the Mazzoleni Academy, where Isabel was. Horace couldn't help but wonder if he was thinking back across the years to what he'd done to Isabel, and Horace's mother. Even though Horace's mother didn't seem to be harboring any grudges, still Horace found himself hoping the old man felt responsible for what was happening now. Guilty.

When at last Mr. Meister spoke, he seemed to be talking to himself. His voice was almost inaudible. "Her powers are unique, yes," he murmured. "Quite astounding. But even so, I cannot—" Suddenly he stopped as if something had occurred to him and sat up abruptly. "No more talk. Our friends are in danger, and we must get to them as quickly as we can. Chloe, when did your encounter with the Auditor end?"

"A little over an hour ago, I guess. We got here as fast as we could."

"An hour! What is the time, please, Horace?"

"Ten forty-five."

"With haste, the Riven could reach April's house as early as eleven o'clock. Meanwhile, we could not hope to arrive until nearly midnight—even if Beck were here to drive us. And I'm afraid we have no other means of travel that would get us to April and Gabriel in time." He sank into thought,

his brow knitted once again.

Horace shrank into his seat. But something in the words Mr. Meister had just spoken ignited a spark of memory in him. *"Other means of travel . . ."*

"Wait a minute," he said. "Last night we were talking about falkrete circles, and April said she thought there was one by her house."

Mr. Meister shook his head dubiously. "Very few cloisters remain that far outside the city."

"Well, from what April said, it sounds like the cloister *is* gone," Horace said. "But the stones are still there—some of them, anyway."

Neptune was already drifting overhead. She grabbed the rolled-up parchment Mr. Meister had been examining the other day and handed it down. "Check the map," she said.

Mrs. Hapsteade, also alert now, took the scroll and unrolled it across Mr. Meister's desk. Joshua pushed through the others to get a closer look at it. Two feet wide and four feet high, the wrinkled parchment was covered in a patchwork jumble of colorful circles connected by a dizzying network of lines. It looked more like a diagram than a map. But then Horace noticed the faint outlines of streets and waterways— and the lakeshore itself—beneath the array of circles. And now he saw that each circle was a ring of crudely drawn, distinctive shapes, and that within each ring was a small bird. Each was labeled with a word in a flowing script he couldn't quite decipher. The map was covered in notes and scribbles and additions. Most of the circles were slashed through with a red X.

"Cloisters," Horace said. "Falkrete circles."

"Yes," Mr. Meister said. "What's left of them. If there truly is a cloister near April's house, it should be on the map."

Joshua stretched onto his toes and stabbed a finger at the top left corner of the map. "April lives right *here*," he said firmly. His fingertip touched the edge of a falkrete circle. The bird there was a jay—blue, but with a black head and a taller crest. "I saw a rock that looked like this bird," said Joshua. "And there were other rocks, too, like part of a circle—April was jumping on them."

But no sooner had Horace's hopes risen than they fell again. "There's a red X through the circle, though," he said. "That seems bad."

"Not always," Neptune replied. "Sometimes even after the cloister is gone, the falkrete stones do still work."

"We must try," Mr. Meister said. "Track it back, please. Find the route, and we will go."

Neptune and Mrs. Hapsteade bent over the map. They were clearly the experts. Pointing and tracing lines from the black-headed jay in toward the city, they recited the strange names of the cloisters like a chant. Each time they reached a dead end, they started over. At last Neptune raised her hand.

"Got it. There's a way—assuming the final stone is working, of course. Tharwen, it's called. And the third stop is a question mark."

"How many jumps in total?" Mr. Meister asked.

"Six."

"Six!" The old man's eyebrows leapt high over his glasses, but then he regained his composure. "No matter. It will have to be done."

"Why so many jumps?" Horace asked. "Why can't we just go straight there?"

"Leaps between falkrete stones are limited to a dozen miles or so. If the stones are any farther apart than that, the trip becomes . . ." He shrugged, as if he did not want—or need—to explain more.

Brian nudged Horace's elbow. He pantomimed his brain exploding, and then let his eyes roll back in his head. The shirt he was wearing said *BEWARE OF DANGER*.

"Yes, thank you, Brian," said Mr. Meister. "Your subtlety is most appreciated." He examined the map for a moment. "Very well. Let us waste no more time. Have we committed the route to memory?"

"Yes," Neptune said.

Mr. Meister glanced at Mrs. Hapsteade. The woman shook her head. "I'm staying here. With Joshua and Brian."

Mr. Meister was clearly taken aback. He studied Mrs. Hapsteade's face and then said, almost scoldingly, "There is no cause for that, Dorothy. The spitestone still burns. The Warren is quite safe."

Horace and Chloe exchanged a look. They were talking about Isabel.

"So you say, and so it might be," Mrs. Hapsteade replied breezily. "But your opinion is your own, Henry, just as mine is mine. This won't be the last time we go our separate ways."

"We may need your help at April's house tonight."

"Let Horace take the phalanx."

"Horace has other duties."

"What, like dodging about with the breach set to mere seconds again?"

"Wait, you did *what*?" Brian said, staring at Horace.

Nobody answered him. The two adults stood in silence, locked in a stubborn, unspoken battle.

"Very well," Mr. Meister said at last. "Neptune, Horace, Chloe—meet me at the home cloister in ten minutes. As for the rest, may yours be light." It was hard to tell whether his eyes lingered on Mrs. Hapsteade a little longer than the others with these words. And then he swept from the room.

"Trouble in paradise, I guess," said Chloe.

Mrs. Hapsteade snorted. "If this is paradise, where's my apple? Now let's go—time for you three to get moving."

They headed up to Vithra's Eye. Joshua seemed very worried about April. He walked hand in hand with Neptune, describing in great detail how to get to April's house from the nearby falkrete circle.

At Vithra's Eye, Brian and Joshua stayed behind, an odd pairing—one of them awkwardly formal and the other awkwardly not, but both of them with furrowed, anxious brows. Mrs. Hapsteade crossed with Horace and the others. As they walked through the tunnels on the far side, their path lit by the collective purple light of their jithandras—blue, red, black, violet—Neptune and Mrs. Hapsteade quietly discussed the uncertainties of the coming trip.

Six jumps. And with each jump, the side effects that always came with falkrete travel would increase. Horace was nervous. Not because of the side effects—a brief case of dreamy confusion—but because of the jumps themselves. The other night, leaving the riverbank, he'd secretly struggled to will himself through from the forest cloister to the home cloister. As he'd squatted there with the Fel'Daera pressed against the falkrete stone, he'd found it all too easy to be in both places at once. He suspected that perhaps his talents were the cause. After all, as Keeper of the Fel'Daera, it was his job to consider all paths, to imagine every possibility. But when traveling by falkrete, there could be only one possibility—forward.

At last they arrived at the doorway that led up into San'ska, the home cloister. Mrs. Hapsteade gave Neptune a hug and Horace and Chloe a surprisingly warm look. "As you travel, remember why you are going—your friends need your help."

"I'm sorry," Chloe said suddenly, surprising them all. "For . . . my mom."

Mrs. Hapsteade's brow wrinkled in sadness. "I am sorry for her too," she said softly, looking for a moment as young as the woman she must have been all those years ago. But then she straightened, and gave them a terse nod. "Fear is the stone we push. May yours be light."

"And yours," they all murmured, and she turned to go. Horace hauled the doors open, and they emerged into the cloister.

Mr. Meister was already there, of course. "Excellent," he said crisply. "Let us begin. Neptune will go first. We'll each follow separately, with thirty-second gaps between us so that our jumps remain unobserved. Neptune, if you will mark the trail for us, please?"

"Can do," Neptune said. She approached the falkrete circle and quickly found the stone she was looking for. "Here's our start. In each cloister along the route, I'll mark the correct falkrete stone with a marker of some kind—a pebble or a twig or something like that."

Chloe shook her head. "Uh . . . no. After just one jump the other night, I could barely find my own face. Let's use something more attention getting." She fished half a roll of wintergreen mints out of her pocket, used her thumbnail to count the mints that were left, and then popped one into her mouth. She handed the remainder of the roll to Neptune. "Here, use these instead. There are seven mints in there."

Neptune blinked down at the mints as if they were a memento of another time. Her face was sad but steely. The she plucked out a mint and laid it atop the falkrete stone. It shone there bright and obvious, a perfect marker. "Mints," Neptune said, looking thoughtfully at the roll again. "I think I might have one."

Chloe smiled crookedly. "Sure. Fine. If you think you can handle it, tiger."

Neptune put a mint between her front teeth and squatted down beside the stone, her tourminda in hand. "Shirty sec-cunsh," she said.

Horace and the others slipped out of the cloister, out onto the sheltered sidewalk, leaving her alone. Horace counted. Chloe noisily chomped her mint. After seventeen seconds, Chloe produced a fresh roll and took another. She devoured the second mint even faster than the first. Once it was gone, Chloe backed against the cloister wall, her face comically grave. "Don't forget to remember me," she said. And then she too vanished.

"You'll go next, Horace," said Mr. Meister. "I'll bring up the rear."

Horace nodded, glad not to be going last. As they stood there waiting, he did the math. Four people, thirty seconds between them, six jumps in all . . . he estimated that they would arrive at April's house—if the route was intact—in no more than three or four minutes. Incredible. It was now two minutes to eleven, which meant they might beat the Riven to April's house after all.

He should probably readjust the breach now. At the moment, it was set to a full day again; he had let it swing open wide after coming home from the riverbank, exhausted, and it had been there ever since. Where to put it now? Four seconds was out of the question, but then again, twenty-four hours wasn't going to do him much good either. In fact, he wasn't sure how much good he was going to be tonight at all.

As if reading his mind, Mr. Meister reached into a pocket

of his vest and pulled out a pale baton laced with black, as thick as a thumb and about seven inches long. "Here," he said, handing it to Horace. "The phalanx."

Horace took it, gripping it firmly but cautiously. It was yellowish white and unpleasantly smooth—was it made of bone?—except for three separate zigzagging metal bands that ran down the length of it. "How do I use it?"

"I'll explain when we arrive. I'm only giving it to you now because we'll be too far away for me to retrieve it later. Had I known Mrs. Hapsteade would not be joining us tonight, I would have taught you how to use it sooner."

"She's staying because of Isabel, isn't she?"

Mr. Meister sighed. "Yes," he said reluctantly. "But as I assured her, while the spitestone burns, Isabel cannot hope to find her way into the Warren. Now, correct me if I'm wrong, but I believe it has been thirty seconds?"

"Thirty-four, actually," Horace said. "But one more thing." He looked the old man in the eye. "If you'd known then what you know now, would you have fused Isabel and my mother? Would you have turned them into Tuners?"

Mr. Meister stiffened visibly. "No one can see twenty years into the future, Horace. Not even you."

"But if you could have?"

Another sigh, weary and resigned and as thick as a novel, pulled deep from some dark pool Horace suddenly did not want to imagine. He lowered his eyes as the old man spoke. "Regret is a doubt that has found its way home, Horace. And

584

when you've fathered as many doubts as I have, you cannot afford to give them all a place to stay." Mr. Meister put a hand on Horace's shoulder and pushed him firmly forward. "Go now. Help your friends. I will be with you."

Horace turned away. Numbly he reached up for the passkey and slipped through the cold brick of the cloister, remembering—rightly or wrongly—something Mr. Meister had said on the riverbank: *"Let us hope for no new regrets."* That Horace could do. He approached the falkrete stone with the mint on top and hunkered down beside it. He unholstered the Fel'Daera, slipping the phalanx into the pouch in its place. Steeling himself, he took a deep breath and touched the box to the stone.

The world divided in two. To his surprise, the new cloister that he opened into was familiar—quiet, with trees overhead, and a brown, blue-winged bird for a leestone. This was the cloister by the riverbank. He hovered for a moment, indecisive, half in the city and half in the forest. He scanned the falkrete circle in the forest and spotted the mint, halfway around, atop a stone that looked like a human tooth. He tried to push himself through, but as he feared, he got snagged, unable to escape the sensation that by choosing the path forward, he was abandoning another path altogether. A path that belonged to this Horace, here in the city.

But seconds were passing. He focused on the mint in the forest cloister and tried to imagine himself approaching it. He would be there. He *was* there—and maybe after all this wasn't so different from looking through the Fel'Daera. He had to be open-minded, yes, but he also had to commit. To believe. And he did believe. He was there.

Suddenly, with a bone-squeezing spasm, he was through. The city lights and sounds vanished—or did they? Had they even been real? For that matter, how real was this new place? Horace shook his head and hurried around to the next stone, box still in hand.

Again and again he jumped to the next cloister, forcing himself forward. Another forest cloister, then another with loud highway traffic roaring outside. The mints helped; each time he crouched and felt his consciousness splitting in two, he could look into the new cloister and spot the bright mint indicating the next jump. He would focus on that mint, thinking of Chloe, and those thoughts led him to Neptune, and Gabriel, and April, and the whole reason for this mission in the first place.

But even so, he grew more and more disoriented. It was like waking from a dream-filled sleep, except that the cobwebs of his dreams clung stickily, stubbornly, insiting that they were real. There was this Horace, yes, but also another who had gone a different way, was choosing a different path. And it was not always easy to tell which Horace was which. Still he kept pushing. Forward. This way, and not the others. The cloister walls stayed high around him, changing shape but never falling. Jump after jump. Mint after mint.

Horace—this Horace—knelt before a stone shaped like

a jagged sleeping bear. There was a leestone here, too—an orange bird with a gray head. He reached out for the falkrete stone with box in hand, trying to summon up a new round of belief, ready to commit to whatever this next stop would turn out to be—stop number four? Number twenty? But this time, the moment the Fel'Daera touched the stone, he was jolted hard, muscle and bone and nerve and neuron, as if a heavy slap of cold water had doused him from head to foot, yanking him violently into a new dream, heaving him into the deep dark of a wide-open space beneath a sunless sky. In his fractured mind's eye, he watched himself—some version of himself—playing the role of Horace, walking a stark stage while a dozen other Horaces waited their turn. Stars littered the black.

"Sorry about that. It was hard not to notice you, of course."

A girl—for a moment Horace thought he would try to redirect the dream away from her. But she kept talking.

"You'll be okay. Just give it a second. Chloe's only just coming around herself."

"I'm around." Chloe. This was her voice. "But god, that last one . . . my brain feels like a rubber ball on a chopping block."

In his dream, Horace understood that he'd been seen from the far side as he straddled the falkrete stone. Neptune had seen him, and her observation had yanked him through into the next cloister. And now Horace saw stars, stars he knew—not just the dreamish idea of stars but actual, chartable, knowable stars. Vega shone almost directly overhead, and off to its side, the bright smudgy sweep of the Milky Way, a deep flat plane of sun beyond sun, out to the tip of the galaxy. You couldn't see that in the city, not a chance.

Horace sat up. He was in a meadow, beside a dilapidated barn—here and nowhere else. As his eyes adjusted, he saw Chloe rubbing her temples, looking foul. Neptune was a silhouette hovering against the dim shine of the sky. "Like I said, sorry about that last one," she said. "I saw you arrive, and that yanked you through."

"We're here," Horace said. "We made it." He wasn't quite sure yet what that meant, but it was good.

"Yes. Welcome to Tharwen—or what's left of it. But you'll want to move aside, of course."

Horace saw at his feet a crude but purposeful arc of chunky stones, and farther on, a flat slab in the shape of a bird. "April," he said. "We're here for April."

"And Gabriel," Chloe said. "Now you better move or you're about to become part of a Meister smoothie."

Horace lurched to his feet and stumbled awkwardly away. Four seconds later, Mr. Meister appeared, crouched down in the grass, his hand atop the falkrete stone. He went rigid, grimacing, but didn't topple over. He squeezed the bridge of his nose and took a deep breath.

They waited in silence for thirty seconds. Slowly Horace began to feel like himself again. This process of recovery—minus the vomiting caused by the thrall-blight—reminded

Horace of what happened whenever he defied the future revealed by the Fel'Daera. Committing to a new path took time, and action. Belief in the now.

"Just so," Mr. Meister said at last. He stood, slipping a small, unseen object into his vest. "We have arrived. Some of the forgotten paths still remain after all." He looked around, searching. "But we are not quite there yet, it seems."

"No," Neptune said, and then pointed. "According to Joshua, April's house is about a half mile that way."

"Any sign of the Riven?" Mr. Meister asked.

"Nothing in the meadow. I haven't been farther than that. But I caught a whiff of brimstone earlier."

"Show us the way," Mr. Meister said.

Neptune turned and began to bound effortlessly over the meadow, leaving them to follow. Quickly Horace pulled the phalanx from the Fel'Daera's pouch, tucking the box away tight in its place, and hurried to catch up to the others. They jogged after Neptune in the dark, insects buzzing and snapping all around them. Tall weeds whipped at Horace's legs and arms, and he marveled at how easily Chloe, just in front and much shorter, moved through the grass. But then he realized—she'd gone thin. Must be nice.

Mr. Meister kept pace with Horace, unassisted by Tanu but moving smoothly nonetheless, and breathing more easily than Horace himself. As they ran, Horace—clutching the phalanx but still having no idea how to use it—reached out for the breach. He closed it down with a firm squeeze. He was more confident now, learning its limits, and swiftly the breach shrank to below an hour. He kept closing it down, eventually getting it under five minutes before pinning it in place and releasing his hold on the silver sun. Four minutes and thirty-four seconds—better too wide than too narrow. He could always close it more if need be. He glanced over at Mr. Meister to see if he'd noticed anything, but the old man seemed unaware.

They left the meadow, entering a thick stand of trees. The stink of brimstone was obvious now. At last Neptune slowed to a stop. Horace bent over, breathing hard. "We're getting close," said Neptune. "April's house is maybe two hundred yards ahead, through the trees."

"Scout ahead for us," Mr. Meister said, apparently not at all out of breath. "Be cautious."

Neptune nodded and launched herself into the dark trees. Horace thought he heard someone's voice calling out far off in the distance, toward April's house.

Mr. Meister turned to Horace. "The time, please, Keeper?"

"Eleven . . . oh four," Horace said, puffing. A far-off dog began to bark furiously, but no sooner had the barking begun than it was cut off.

"Let us hope we are not too late," said Mr. Meister, and turned to Horace. "You have the phalanx. Good. I suspect it will be more helpful to you now than the Fel'Daera. I'll spare you the detail, but the phalanx fires a bolt of energy that will temporarily immobilize any instrument it hits. And because the Riven are physically bound to their instruments—"

"They can't move."

"Just so."

"For how long?"

"In your hands? A minute or two, perhaps longer. The power of the phalanx is proportional to your Tan'ji. In fact, you must draw on your instrument's power to fire the phalanx."

Chloe, listening, piped up. "So explain to me why we aren't using these things all the time?"

"They are . . . hard to come by," Mr. Meister replied. "And there is a downside. A phalanx works by funneling power away from its wielder's Tan'ji."

"So wait—after Horace fires the phalanx, he won't be able to use the box?"

"Until the rift collapses and fades away, yes."

"Never mind, then." Chloe flashed Horace a thumbs-up. "Better you than me."

"But how do I fire it?"

"You must draw on the power of the Fel'Daera and then channel that energy into the phalanx. Touching the phalanx to the box isn't necessary, but it might help you make the transfer. Releasing the energy is another act of will—hard to describe but easy enough to do. Again, a little flick of the phalanx might help you find the right state of mind."

"Sure sounds like a wand to me," Chloe said.

Just then the dog started to bark again, more savagely than ever. How strange to think that it must be April's dog—Baron, that was his name. And now from the distant house, the furious cry of a raven reached them. That could only be Arthur, of course. April had to be there. Was Gabriel with her, protecting her?

"What happened to Neptune?" Chloe said. "This is usually about the time she drops in with more bad news."

As if in answer, a shriek of surprise cut through the night, nearby and high in the air. Neptune. All three spun toward the sound. Branches snapped and leaves rustled violently—Neptune was falling. She dropped out of the canopy thirty feet up. They stood there, frozen, as she plummeted unchecked toward the ground, her cloak trailing like a plume of smoke.

—∿∿—

CHAPTER THIRTY–ONE

Battlefield

"WE MUST GET AWAY," SAID GABRIEL. HE COCKED HIS HEAD sharply toward the woods behind April's house, as if he heard something.

Derek scoffed nervously. "What, because of a marble? Because the dog smells something out in the woods?"

April squeezed the fading raven's eye. She still couldn't smell the brimstone, but to Baron's nose, the smell seemed to be getting stronger. The Riven were coming closer. "What about inside? Maybe the leestone in the house will protect us."

Gabriel shook his head. "I do not think so. The Riven knew where you lived before you had a leestone, and it takes time to rebury secrets that are already revealed. Plus, they are apparently aware that we're here now."

"Is that my fault? Because I was using the vine?"

"No, they came too quickly. They must have had some

other reason for showing up here tonight."

Derek held up his hands. April could smell his fear. "Sorry," said Derek, "but somebody needs to explain to me what's going on. These bad guys you were talking about— these Riven—they're here?"

"They will be here soon," Gabriel said.

Derek dragged a hand down his face, clearly struggling to absorb it all. "And it's April they want."

"It's April we must protect," Gabriel said, not bothering to mention that he himself was also in danger.

Baron surged to his feet again. He broke into great, bounding barks. Rage and fear poured off him as the faint smell of brimstone suddenly blossomed in his nose, piercingly over-powering. And now distant footsteps too, stealthy and slow, moving through the woods out back. April spun, staring, her eyes straining to the see the source of the noises Baron heard.

Her memory doubled over on her, remembering the night just a handful of days before—how she'd sat on the roof star-ing into these same woods over the head of this same barking dog. Only this time, she knew what she was looking for. A moment later, she realized she was smelling the brimstone herself now.

Baron bounded across the yard stiff legged, still barking his savage challenge. And now from the rooftop, Arthur stood and let out a raucous complaint of his own, gobbling and hiss-ing, puffing out his feathers and bringing an instant crop of goose bumps to the surface of April's skin.

Derek stared up at the bird. "That is . . . freaking me out."

As if in response, from somewhere in the woods on the opposite side of the house, a faint, far-off shriek cut through the darkness. Gabriel cocked his head sharply, clearly hearing it. Human, or Riven?

Gabriel frowned and stepped in close, the worry apparent on his face. "Get down," he murmured.

April hunkered down at once. She grabbed Derek's hand and pulled him down beside her. His brow was wrinkled with consternation, but small fires of fear burned deep in his eyes. April's heart broke a little—her big brother, always her protector, the closest thing she'd had to a father for most of her life. Yet here he was, confused and helpless, unable to protect her from the greatest dangers she'd ever faced. "It's okay," she told him. "Everything's going to be okay."

He nodded hastily, not even objecting, and for some reason this tiny surrender made tears bolt up in her eyes.

"I must keep it small," said Gabriel. "Do not move. Do not try to get out." He held his staff perfectly vertical, its silver tip just in front of April's face. Three claws, drawn into a point. Smoky tendrils began to drift from the gaps between them.

Derek looked up at him, bewildered. "Get out of what?"

April, who had not forgotten the senseless confusion of the humour back on the riverbank, knew what was coming. She squeezed Derek's hand. "Close your eyes," she said. "Trust me."

595

Derek nodded again, and shut his eyes.

"Stay together," Gabriel said gently, and then the world deleted itself.

Derek cried out as the gray nothing of the humour consumed them, his voice blurring as if he were underwater. He reared back, but April clung to him, refusing to let go, knowing that her touch was one of the few sensations he had in this void. "It's okay," she told him, her voice like liquid. "It's okay."

She herself felt stunningly calm. She knew what Derek was experiencing—she'd been in the humour back on the riverbank, and it had been horrible, a total loss of senses. A kind of prison that had no walls, no nothing.

But not anymore. Not for April.

With the Ravenvine at full power, the humour couldn't hold her.

She could see. She could hear. Not inside the humour, of course, but outside. From the roof of the house, Arthur gazed down into the yard, and April was out there with him, sipping cautiously at his vision, escaping from this impenetrable fog. She kept her power to a trickle, hoping Isabel had been right when she'd said empaths were hard to detect, hoping that the raven's eye would help mask her still. She had to see what was happening beyond this blindness. Baron was out there. The Riven were coming.

In the middle of the yard Arthur's sharp eyes revealed a faint shimmer, a sliver of lawn that resisted being seen.

The humour. Gabriel was indeed keeping it small, an invisible cloak wrapped tightly around their huddled forms. How phenomenal to think that she was in there—and Derek and Gabriel, too. April had no idea what the humour was made of, or how it worked, but it was a fiendish trick. Even Arthur, curious and keen, could not truly lay his eyes on it. He crowed experimentally, questing, calling for April. Meanwhile at the edge of the yard, Baron was still standing his ground, barking wildly. She didn't reach out for the dog, mindful not to draw attention to herself. She tried to focus solely on Arthur's eyesight, keeping the Ravenvine at a low throttle, just like the humour was now.

Suddenly Gabriel's voice filled April, coming from everywhere, regal and calm. "Hold out the raven's eye."

For a second April thought he meant Arthur, and she had no idea what he was asking for. Then she remembered the leestone in her hand, still warm. She held it out. Gabriel wrapped her hand in his, sandwiching the raven's eye between their two palms.

"It won't last long," he said.

And then, suddenly, through Arthur's eyes she saw towering shadows, knifing forward from the forest. Baron's barks took on a round, fearful shape, and then he lost his nerve completely. He skittered away, whining and yelping, and—after seeming to look around for April and Derek—ran down the path toward Doc's house and out of sight.

April watched as the Mordin stepped out of the woods

and onto the lawn, first one and then another, and then a third, tallest of all. "They're here," April said. "Three Mordin, including Dr. Jericho."

Gabriel's hand went slack atop hers. "You can see outside," he said, his voice dreamy with surprise. And of course—Gabriel had no way of seeing beyond the boundaries of the humour. April was giving him sight he could never hope to have on his own.

"Through Arthur, yes," she said. "Just a trickle."

"This is . . . very good," Gabriel said with a warm rumble. "One raven's eye inside, two raven's eyes outside. Watch the Mordin, then. Once they've gone past us, we'll slip away. Warn me if they get too close, if they seem too curious."

Derek's voice rang out in the void. "I can't hear what you're saying," he said. "What's happening?"

April just squeezed his hand again, understanding that Gabriel didn't want him to hear what was happening.

Out in the yard, the Mordin were coming closer, moving very slowly toward the house. Arthur was burning with rage, shifting uneasily along the gutter and occasionally cutting loose with a shrill cry of warning. Although the bird's eyesight was acute, the view sometimes disoriented April—he kept flicking his head from side to side, and his field of vision was much wider than April was accustomed to. Nonetheless, she could see the Mordin clearly. She could still see the humour too, slippery and all but invisible, lying in the Mordin's path. The first Mordin passed by without so much as a glance. The second, just a few feet away, looked straight at the humour and seemed to briefly do a double take. April opened her mouth, but the Mordin kept walking.

"Breathe," Gabriel said from everywhere.

April hadn't realized she wasn't. She forced her lungs to work as Dr. Jericho approached. He was coming closer than the others. The humour was practically at his feet now, but still he didn't see. Instead, his beady black eyes were locked on Arthur. It felt as though he were staring straight at April. How strange it was to be seen and unseen at the same time. April joined Arthur in glaring back at the Mordin, feeling the bird's hatred, letting it become her own, letting her fear slowly evaporate.

But then Dr. Jericho stopped just beside the humour. He stood so close that he could have bent down and touched April's hair, had he only known she was there. Arthur squawked at him and strutted up the slope of the roof as the other two Mordin began to mount the porch steps. Dr. Jericho continued to watch the raven with apparent interest. "Who's a pretty bird, then?" he crooned pensively.

"He's right beside us," April whispered. "He's staring at Arthur. I think he's figuring it out." Between her and Gabriel's clasped hands, she was sure she could feel the warmth of the raven's eye fading away.

"Be ready," said Gabriel. "Move when I say move. Go where I tell you."

April thought she knew what Gabriel planned to do. He

was going to spread the humour wide, burying the Mordin in it, blinding them. But that would announce their presence to every Riven in the area, wouldn't it?

Slowly Dr. Jericho turned his head. He peered suspiciously down at his side, straight down at the humour. April squeezed Gabriel's hand.

A huge sharp *crack!*—almost like a gunshot—ripped through the silence outside the humour. Arthur startled, squawking, and April jumped too. Despite herself, she released Derek and Gabriel and slapped her hands over her ears. The raven's eye fell free.

"What is it?" said Gabriel.

"Something happened. A sound."

"What kind of sound?"

April kept herself open to Arthur, bringing the outside world into this lonely fog. Dr. Jericho was standing up straight now, staring alertly off toward the woods on the north side of the house. The other two Mordin spoke to each other quietly, clearly alarmed. Then Dr. Jericho issued a few curt words of command, and the two Mordin sprang into action. One leapt off the steps and slunk around the corner of the house toward the sound they'd all heard. The other, frighteningly, ducked his head and continued up onto the porch, out of sight.

No sooner had Arthur lost sight of the two Mordin than the sound came again, again making April jump. *Thak!*

"There it was again," she said. "One of the Mordin is

chasing after it. It's like a . . . gunshot, or something. But not like that. What is it?"

"It is the cavalry," Gabriel said, his voice swelling with satisfaction. "The Wardens have come for us."

April laughed, sagging with relief. The Wardens were here. Horace and Chloe and the rest.

She reached out through the fog for Derek, trying to find him again, to reassure him. Her finger grazed his skin, and he let out a cry. She felt him recoil violently, heard Gabriel's warning shout.

And through Arthur's eyes, horrified, she saw Derek tumble suddenly into existence right at Dr. Jericho's feet.

HORACE WATCHED AS Neptune dropped like a stone. His first thought was that Isabel had severed her again—but that was impossible, wasn't it? And then a second before Neptune hit the ground, her acceleration slowed. She got her feet beneath her and landed hard, her powerful legs bending deeply. She sprang lightly back into the air, clearly recovering, pinwheeling her arms for balance. She hit the ground again running and sprinted toward them.

"Auditor," she said breathlessly, turning to search the shadows back the way she'd come.

"You let an Auditor evict you?" Mr. Meister asked sharply, also scanning the shadows now.

"She caught me by surprise, okay?" Neptune said, sounding chagrined. "I came across three Mordin along the driveway, in front of the house. Then that dog started barking around back. And that bird! I got distracted. The Auditor ambushed me. She hit me hard and pushed me right out—just for a second." She craned her neck, still trying to see.

Apparently the Auditor had pushed Nepture's presence out of the tourminda. Horace hadn't even considered that such a thing was possible. The dog went on barking, unnerving him. He stared into the night, looking for any hint of movement among the trees.

"I believe I may have underestimated the Riven's interest in April," Mr. Meister said softly. Then he straightened and began barking out orders. "Split up. Auditors are at their most powerful when we're together. Chloe, you head for the house—"

A voice cut through the night air, a voice made of silk and sand. "Oh, please, no. Let all of us remain. I do like a party."

Horace gripped the phalanx at his side, wishing he were more sure how to use it. As for the Auditor, she remained unseen in the darkness, but he could hear furtive footsteps out in the gloom up ahead.

Chloe stepped up close to Horace. "I'm leaving," she muttered. "It's me she wants most—my power."

Baron's angry barking stopped at last. What was happening up at the house?

"I'm coming with you," Horace said low.

Chloe shook her head, adamant. "No. You stay with Mr. Meister."

"I hear your whispers," the Auditor said, still unseen and seeming to circle to the right. "But you cannot escape. *Ji'karo mufali*—I am everywhere."

Abruptly—horrifyingly—another voice broke out, nearly identical to the first. But now it came from behind them: *"Ji'karo mufali. I am everywhere."* And then off to the left, closer still, a tinkle of gritty laughter that faded and became words: *"Ji'karo mufali Quaasa."*

Three Auditors. The Riven were *definitely* interested in April. Horace shook the phalanx, desperate to have it do anything. What had Mr. Meister said? It would channel energy from the box?

"Do not fear," Mr. Meister said quietly. "Remember, whether it's one Auditor or eleven, they can never be stronger than we are. Split up—that way they won't be able to leech multiple powers at once like they did on the riverbank." Neptune nodded and launched into the air.

A beat later, Arthur's hoarse warning call rang out. Chloe turned toward the sound, the Alvalaithen seeming to glow in the darkness, its wings already a blur. "I'm going under."

"Chloe, no!" Horace said. Arthur crowed again.

"Don't worry. I won't let go. I'll find Gabriel and April."

"Whispers, whispers," one of the Auditors crooned creepily, somewhere out in the night, and then the others took up the chant, circling them—*whispers, whispers, whispers.* Off to the right, one of them laughed and said, "Tinkers love their secrets. Want to hear one of ours?"

Heavy footsteps seemed to shake the earth. A huge dark shape slashed through the air. A Mordin, leaping into their midst, reaching for Horace.

With a speed that seemed impossible for his years, Mr. Meister spun and raised his hand, pointing it at the Mordin. A chest-slapping crack split the forest—*thack!*—and a blast of air rushed past Horace, ruffling his hair. But the Mordin, struck dead-on, was blown back forty feet. He smashed against a tree and crumpled, grimacing.

"Split up, I said!" the old man cried. "Go!"

Chloe tugged at the chain of her jithandra. "Look for my light."

Horace could only nod. The next instant, Chloe vanished, falling into the earth like a trapdoor had opened beneath her.

A moment after she disappeared, a pale figure streaked by, legs pumping and braid swinging. Mr. Meister again raised his hand—he held something small and black—but apparently he could not get a bead on the Auditor. The Auditor glanced over with a wild grin, her eyes as black as coals. She sprinted on past, and Horace thought he knew why.

She was after Chloe.

But Horace hardly had time to worry. Another Mordin barreled into their midst—short for a Mordin. Mr. Meister spun and fired a second shot with his mysterious weapon. A second crack ripped through the night. But the short Mordin spun and stumbled, dodging it. A tree twenty feet on trembled as if struck by an invisible car.

"Pin him, Horace!" the old man cried. "Pin him!" Even as he spoke, another Mordin lurched into view behind him.

Horace had no idea what to do. He lifted the phalanx, pointing it, but nothing happened. The first Mordin lunged and wrapped a huge, hideous hand around Horace's shoulder, grasping him under the armpit and beginning to lift him. The Mordin grinned, reaching for the Fel'Daera.

"I'll just hold this, shall I?" he croaked. And then a rotten log the size of a park bench dropped out of the sky and crushed the creature into the ground with a nauseating *crunch* and an explosion of splintered wood. Horace fell back, freed. The Mordin groaned and stirred but did not rise. In a patch of clear sky overhead, a hovering Neptune saluted down at Horace. But as he watched, a gleaming white figure, also airborne, streaked in silently and tackled her. Neptune and the Auditor floated out of sight over the treetops, tussling.

Meanwhile, down below, the second Mordin was still on his feet, circling Mr. Meister warily. He seemed to be moving with a limp, favoring his right leg. "Any other tricks in your pockets, Tinker?" the Mordin sneered. His face was monstrously ugly, even for a Mordin.

"Remember, draw on the power that belongs to you," Mr. Meister said, his eyes never leaving the Mordin's hideous face. "And then exert your will."

It took Horace a moment to realize that the old man was talking to him. He looked down at the phalanx. *The power that belongs to you.* Horace reached out for the Fel'Daera, summoning its strength. He placed the tip of the phalanx against the box. He squeezed, almost as if trying to adjust the breach, and miraculously began to feel power seeping into the phalanx. He could swear the phalanx grew heavy in his hand.

The Mordin with the limp, still circling, was watching the phalanx with a look of wary disgust. As he did so, Mr. Meister caught Horace's eye and—ever so faintly, eyebrows raised high—he demonstrated swinging his left hand with a smart flick of the wrist. But no sooner had Horace absorbed the gesture than another Mordin hurtled into their midst. He ran straight at Horace, not slowing in the least.

Horace practically groaned with exasperation. How many Mordin could there be? Barely aware of what he was doing— out of anger and frustration more than anything else—Horace flicked the phalanx at the newcomer. "No!" he shouted.

A brief pulse of light lit the forest, yellow and cloudy, as a churning golden ring emerged from the tip of the phalanx with an almost silent *whump!* The light faded instantly, but a rippling cloud of distortion raced through the air like a spirit. It struck the approaching Mordin in the chest, and the Mordin slammed to a halt, midstride. He hung in the air, one foot off the ground, arms flailing, his tiny eyes wide with shock. He gasped for breath as if he'd had the wind knocked out of him.

Across the way, Mr. Meister casually lifted his hand, pointing it at the ugly, wide-eyed Mordin in front of him. But before he could fire his mysterious weapon, the Mordin reached up into the tree above and hoisted himself into the branches like some great, gangly ape. He melted quickly into the darkness overhead.

Mr. Meister watched him go and then walked over to Horace. The Mordin who was miraculously pinned in mid-air watched him approach with wary, angry eyes. He threw a ferocious swipe at Mr. Meister, but the old man, standing just beyond the creature's long reach, barely flinched.

"The Mordin carry their Tan'ji—one for disguise, one for tracking Tanu—embedded in the flesh along their spines," Mr. Meister explained calmly, as if this weren't at all horrific. "It makes them easy targets for the phalanx, but they can still put up a fight when pinned." He turned to the Mordin. "How many are you?" he asked pleasantly, sounding like he was taking dinner reservations.

"More than enough. We'll take home a prize tonight, don't you worry."

"I am not worried." As if on cue, a loud, crunching *thump* rang out from back behind them in the darkness, accompanied by a rasping cry of pain—unmistakably the voice of an Auditor. "Ah," said Mr. Meister thoughtfully. "One of the Quaasa is down, it seems."

Horace strained to see. That must have been Neptune—it seemed she'd won her wrestling match. But now another Auditor materialized from the woods, approaching with hands up. Horace filled the phalanx again, readying himself.

"Peace," the Auditor said. "Peace."

"One of your sisters has had a nasty fall."

The Auditor's shining face split into a mirthless smile. Her blue eyes shone. "I am quite aware. I feel her pain."

Mr. Meister gestured to the two wounded Mordin, and the third still trapped by the phalanx. "You are losing this battle."

"You brought the battle to us," the Auditor said plainly, sounding so reasonable that for a moment Horace had to stop and wonder if that was true. "As you usually do. Under the circumstances, I see no reason why we cannot—"

The Auditor flinched as if shot. She threw her head back, rigid, hands frozen into claws. What was happening? Mr. Meister took a step back, clearly as confused as Horace was. Then the Auditor opened her mouth and let loose a piercing scream of agony and fury, like a rake across a chalkboard. It seemed to shake the very stars. Then she turned and raced through the trees toward the house, looking for all the world as though she meant to tear it to the ground.

CHLOE LET HERSELF slip into the cold flesh of the earth, into the dark and quiet. She went down five feet, or ten—she had no real way of knowing. She gauged her depth by the temperature, and by the density of the earth. She slowed her fall, finding buoyancy, trying not to think about the unfathomable deeps that yawned beneath her, all the way to the molten core of the planet, four thousand miles down. She was the Keeper of the Alvalaithen. The Earthwing. Down here, she would decide where she would and would not go. And while she couldn't quite fly through the dirt and stone—not yet—still she was getting better. She was getting faster.

The first trick, of course, was to be brave. If there was one good thing about her mother's return—and Chloe wasn't sure there was—it was discovering the truth about that long-ago accident, that horror that had haunted her for so long. She now knew she hadn't done anything wrong that day. Going underground wasn't some scary side effect of her powers, meant to be avoided at all costs. In fact, she was starting to think maybe it was the *heart* of her powers.

The Earthwing, right?

But even if so, the second trick was learning how to move underground. Ordinarily when she went thin, she moved around by thinking of surfaces and planes, the borders between objects. When she was thin and standing on the floor, or sitting in a chair, she kept herself from sinking in by telling certain parts of her body—her feet, her rump—that they couldn't be *there*. They couldn't enter *that*. And her body obeyed without question. But down here, there were no easy borders. Nothing to push against or resist.

And yet on that terrible night when her house had burned down, she'd discovered that the thought process underground wasn't so different from the one above ground. It was telling parts of herself where they couldn't be. Except that here, the telling had to be gentle—a suggestion instead of a command—and it had to ripple down the atoms of her body from head to toe. *Let's not be here.* And when she did it right, the result was movement. Propulsion.

Earthwing.

Of course, working through all the mechanics like that didn't feel ideal. It was not very swashbuckling. Six months ago, she'd have barfed at the thought. But apparently she was getting older. More mature, more methodical.

She blamed Horace for that.

She set herself into motion now, rejecting the space she was in inch by inch. It was so silent here, so utterly dark—the humour had nothing on this. She slid through the ground at the speed of a slow jog. Almost immediately, two Auditors stuck their noses into the Alvalaithen alongside her, greedy and grasping and unwanted. But Chloe was ready for it—as ready as a Keeper could be—and she pushed back hard against them.

She managed to oust one of them immediately, bullying her presence clean out of the dragonfly. The other lingered, actively fighting Chloe for control. Chloe held fast. As she cruised away from the scene, hoping she was headed toward the house, she could hear swift footsteps on the ground over-head—the Auditor, trotting along at the surface. Chloe was pretty sure that the Auditor who had done most of the talking earlier was the one from the pier. But this Auditor was differ-ent, possibly the one who had been giggling. Chloe frowned on giggling.

Chloe soared through a veiny net of tree roots, and a smooth submerged boulder. She willed herself to go faster, and faster, but it was like pushing a brick through mud. Through the Alvalaithen, she almost felt like she could sense the Auditor's astonishment at what she was doing, a devilish curiosity. The Auditor probed at the threads of power Chloe wove. And then, suddenly, the footsteps overhead ceased. Had she given up?

No sooner had Chloe asked the question than she felt a wondrous and horrible tingle all up and down her body—the distinct sensation of flesh within flesh. The Auditor was underground with her, swimming alongside her. Moving through her.

Chloe burned with rage. She knew the Auditor was only imitating, but still this was insult on top of injury. It had taken Chloe seven years to learn this particular trick, a trick she still hadn't even mastered, and the Auditor was duplicating the feat with no practice at all. And part of Chloe's rage, she knew, was born out of admiration for the bravery involved—if the Auditor somehow lost her grip on the Alvalaithen down here, she was dead.

Then again, so was Chloe.

Chloe tried to surge ahead, to leave the Auditor behind. But if she sped up at all, it was only a tiny bit, and the Auditor kept up easily, weaving back and forth, in and out of Chloe's body. Frustrated, Chloe willed herself upward, thinking wildly that she might be able to catch air and lose the Auditor. She barely broke the surface, like a dolphin coming up to breathe. She was shocked to catch a glimpse of a Mordin loping toward her, headed toward Horace and the others. It stopped, seeming to spot her, but Chloe kept moving and let gravity take her back under.

She went deeper instead, daring the Auditor to follow her. She went deeper than she'd ever gone, into chillier, rockier ground. She still had plenty of breath—both with her lungs and with the Alvalaithen—and she meant to use it. Her heart hammered inside her chest. Inside the dragonfly, meanwhile, the Auditor's presence still burned. Chloe went deeper still, to depths she'd only had nightmares about, pushing the limits of her own bravery, hoping the Auditor wouldn't be able to stomach it. Down and down she went.

But then she hit wetness, shockingly cold, and realized she'd gone so deep she'd hit the level where the ground was saturated with water. How deep was that—fifty feet? One hundred? Two hundred? She had no idea. She panicked and pulled up, and as she pulled up the Auditor sliced through her again.

Seething, Chloe went completely vertical. She sped upward, not just pushing but pulling now, straining for the surface. She thought perhaps she'd never gone faster. The Auditor swiped at her feet—was Chloe leaving her behind? She rose out of the water-soaked ground, into warmer earth. Up and up. She entered the looser soil that told her she was almost to the surface, and she reached up over her head with both hands. When they touched air, she grabbed at the surface of the earth and pulled, hard, as if she was hoisting herself up out of a swimming pool.

Chloe pulled so hard that she launched herself three feet into the air, into the blessedly warm night air. When she was completely clear, still aloft, she released the Alvalaithen, surrendering its power completely, letting the still-buried Auditor have it all. And then an instant later, as she came back down to the ground, Chloe went thin again, hard as she could, wrenching every bit of the Alvalaithen's power back toward herself, calling on all her anger, all her fear, all her bitter sadness. The Alvalaithen was hers and no one else's. This was the one thing she knew for sure, and armed with that sureness, she ripped the Alvalaithen's power away from the Auditor. The Auditor, still underground, struggled to hold on but could not. Chloe swept over her, banishing her completely from the Alvalaithen once and for all.

"Mine!" Chloe bellowed, landing firm on solid ground again, her hands balled into fists, staring down into the earth at her feet.

And from that ground, a muted, muffled *thump*.

The forest went quiet, and she was alone.

Chloe breathed. She staggered back, releasing the Alvalaithen again. She fell against a tree, still staring at the ground. She'd cut the Auditor off—ousted her from the Alvalaithen—while she was still buried.

The Auditor was dead. Melded with the earth.

Chloe had killed her.

From farther back in the woods behind her, a long, high

wail broke out, a keening cry that sounded like a siren filled with sand. One of the other Auditors, no doubt sensing what had just happened. But there was light spilling through the trees just ahead. April's house. Chloe headed for it, running almost blind. She tripped over a tree root and tumbled painfully to the ground, skinning her knee. She got to her feet again and kept running. Blood trickled down her leg. It felt good.

A commotion broke out on the far side of the house. The dog was barking furiously, and then April shouted. Chloe raced on. She would go straight through the house and find them, and then—

It had been stupid of the Auditor to follow Chloe underground, to take that risk. The worst could have happened . . . and it did. Not Chloe's fault. Not really. What did Brian's shirt say today? *BEWARE OF DANGER.* It was hard to argue with that advice. Chloe was here to rescue her friends, and if the Riven wanted to stand in her way, then they were standing in a bad place. They were putting themselves in the path of danger, and they had only themselves to blame. It was as simple as that.

"Simple," Chloe muttered, still running, nearly at the house now. "Not. My. Fault."

WHEN DEREK TUMBLED out of the humour at Dr. Jericho's feet, the Mordin struck like a snake, as if he'd been expecting it. He reached down and snatched Derek off the ground by the wrist, letting him dangle. April saw it all from Arthur's vantage point atop the roof.

A split second later, the horrible sight was swept away. A wave of pressure briefly crushed her, head to toe, and then released. April understood at once what it was—the humour, blossoming instantaneously to full size. Through Arthur's eyes, the entire backyard disappeared, like a drawing folded abruptly in two. Confusion. Disorientation. Arthur's head darted to and fro, dizzying April.

Gabriel grabbed April's hand and yanked her to her feet. "Move!" he shouted, tugging her through the humour so hard she thought her arm would come out of its socket. "We must get away."

"Derek!" April cried, stumbling through the gray gloom. She struggled with Gabriel and at last broke free.

She heard a distant, watery voice. Not Derek. This voice was both thin and cruel, both musical and sinister. Dr. Jericho. She couldn't make out the words, though. "What is he saying?" she asked.

Gabriel spoke reluctantly from the void. "He wants me to take down the humour. He says he—"

"Do it," April said.

After a hesitation, the humour evaporated with a great tearing sound. Sights and sounds flooded over her—her own senses, all but forgotten. Dr. Jericho stood thirty feet away, still holding Derek aloft. He brother looked so small, so helpless. He grimaced in pain and shock.

The Mordin smiled. "Much better," he said, locking eyes with April. Then his smile deepened to a savage grin. "Here we are, face-to-face again, but it seems you've changed. You've changed a great deal."

Her missing piece. April was no longer broken, and the Mordin knew it. "That's right," she said. "Whatever you hoped to get from me before, it's gone. I'm useless now."

The Mordin laughed. "Far from useless," he said. "More valuable than you know."

A desperate scream cut through the night, a far-off wail of angry despair—the unmistakable voice of an Auditor. Dr. Jericho barely seemed to notice.

"Come with us," the Mordin said to April, "and I'll let your brother go. Come with us, and help us save the Tanu. We have much to learn from each other."

Save the Tanu? April thought, and then a red-hot barrel of rage exploded in her head. *Kill. Bite. Tear.* A yellow streak tore across the yard, headed for Dr. Jericho, snapping and snarling.

Baron. April felt him leap from the ground, full of loyalty and rage, felt the deep satisfaction of sharp teeth sinking into foul flesh. She tasted blood in her mouth, coppery and warm.

The dog had Dr. Jericho by the arm. Derek, struggling, managed to wrench himself free. He fell to the ground and ran.

Dr. Jericho shook the furious dog off. "Baron, no!" April cried, as the dog rounded for another attack. This time as he leapt, the Mordin unleashed a furious backhanded swing with his mighty four-knuckled fist. The blow caught Baron across the ribs. April heard them crack through the dog's ears, even as a lightning bolt of pain ripped across her own torso. *Agony. Fear. Shame.* The dog yelped and tumbled across the grass like he'd been shot.

Derek reached her and took her by the hand, his eyes wild with fear. Dr. Jericho turned toward them, a tower of rage. He took a long step—

And then the humour swallowed them all again.

"Follow me," said Gabriel, taking April's free hand once more. "I won't let him find us." This time April didn't resist, dragging Derek with her through the void. She left herself open to Baron, basking in every inch of his pain, not wanting to spare herself the least bit. He was alive, struggling to get up, but the humour was making him mad, robbing him of all his precious senses—even smell.

"Use your Tan'ji only sparingly," Gabriel said. "Dr. Jericho is trying to find us, and the raven's eye has worn down."

Reluctantly, April tried to pull herself away. She told herself Baron would be okay. *Such a good dog. Such a brave dog.*

"If you're going to use your power, use it to guide us back to the driveway," Gabriel said. "I haven't had a chance to learn the lay of the land here, and Beck is coming. Beck will get us away."

April was already looking. Arthur was aloft now, high over the house. The incredible rush of flight was like a universe of sensation compared to the unfeeling fog of the humour.

She realized that the range of the Ravenvine had grown since it was repaired—Arthur was a hundred feet up, at least, and she now had a literal bird's-eye view of the house and its surroundings.

She spotted the unseeable wrinkle in the yard that indicated the humour, sliding slowly. "Turn right," she said. "Go between the house and the trees." They moved on. The wrinkle shifted direction. And then, abruptly, Baron popped into view. He was limping away. Through the vine she felt a burst of relief from the dog, but she couldn't risk trying to hear more. She wasn't up in the sky; she was here in the humour with Gabriel and Derek, and Dr. Jericho was with them, searching for them. She could hear his sinister voice, calling to them, but Gabriel was keeping it muted.

She stumbled on. It was hard work moving your body when your eyes belonged to someone else. Through those airborne eyes, meanwhile, one side of the farmhouse was simply absent, swallowed by the humour as they moved toward the driveway. But now on the opposite side, she caught sight of a sprinting figure, streaking toward the house—an Auditor, running fast. With a shock, April watched as the Auditor plunged straight through the wall of the house like a ghost.

"Chloe is here," she said, understanding at once. "In the house, I think—but an Auditor is after her."

"Chloe can take care of herself," said Gabriel. "Keep moving. Dr. Jericho is behind us."

"Uncle Harrison is in the house," Derek said. "Will he be safe?"

April stumbled again. Uncle Harrison—she'd forgotten him. "No," she said thickly. "Not safe, no more than you were." The Riven would use her family to get to April. And then she remembered the third Mordin, creeping up onto the back porch. They had to get Uncle Harrison out of there. Now.

Arthur wheeled about on a thermal, rising higher. April's view shifted. "Oh," she cried as a jab of recognition hit the bird, a familiar knot of puzzlement. Neptune was floating above the house. She was descending toward the humour, obviously knowing it was there. And beyond her, down the long driveway, a sight April could never have seen with her own eyes. A rising plume of dust, moving toward the house. A car was barreling down the driveway.

"Beck," she said. "Beck is coming."

CHLOE BROKE OUT of the woods and angled across the front lawn at a full run, headed for the boxy old farmhouse where April lived.

She didn't hesitate. She didn't even slow. She leapt up and went thin in midair, ghosting through the front corner of the house. She emerged into a dimly lit room, and when she landed—her feet already primed to refuse the wooden floor— she hit a loose rug and slipped, upending. She fell backward into the ashy pit of a fireplace for a moment before springing back out and righting herself. She let go of the Alvalaithen's song. She went still. She listened.

The house stank of brimstone.

And then something grabbed her by the leg, hoisting her

roughly into the air. She swung upside down for a moment, captive—petrified and gasping. Her jithandra dangled, and a Mordin's cruel face leaned in to leer at her in the red glow. "Looking for someone?" he sang. She recognized him, a long neck, high cheekbones, barely any eyebrows at all. This was one of the Mordin who traveled with Dr. Jericho, one of the Mordin who'd been there the night Chloe's house burned down.

Chloe didn't hesitate. She went thin, dropping free. The Mordin growled and swiped at her uselessly, his fingers knifing through her flesh as she fell. She let herself hit the floor and reached for the rack of tools on the fireplace. She grabbed a wrought-iron poker in one hand and a pair of tongs in the other. Making them go thin as she spun, she plunged the tongs through the Mordin's massive foot, deep into the floor and the concrete below. She let go.

The Mordin roared in pain, falling forward awkwardly. One of his great hands fell flat onto the floor, and Chloe pierced it with the poker, melding the poker in place. Another roar. The Mordin struggled, glaring at her, but he couldn't get leverage, couldn't break loose. Chloe skirted by him, headed through the house.

"What's going on? Who are you?"

A fat man stood on the stairs in an enormous red bathrobe. Chloe started to say she was a friend of April's, but she wasn't sure that would be doing April any favors. "I'm just leaving," she said. "You should too."

"Stay right there!" the man thundered. He craned his neck, trying to look over to where the Mordin was still roaring. "What the hell is that?"

"That is . . . a very good reason for you to leave. It's not safe here."

"Leave?" the man shouted. "I'm not—"

Suddenly, a car horn bleated madly. Chloe heard the roar of an engine and the clatter of loose gravel. *Beck!*

And then, all at once, she was severed. No—not severed. She was ousted from the Alvalaithen, forced out by a furious invading presence. Against her will, she went thick. Her stomach dropped. The draonfly's wings were still fluttering, but she wasn't the one doing it.

She turned and saw an Auditor materializing through the far wall, leaping like a lion. The creature's eyes blazed blue—it was the Auditor from the pier. She hurtled through the downed Mordin, face contorted with rage and long fingers extended like claws, barrelling straight at Chloe.

At the last possible second, Chloe regained a fingerhold on the Alvalaithen. She went thin again just as the Auditor tore at her—but not quite thin enough. The Auditor's nails ripped gashes in Chloe's sweatshirt, leaving deep furrows in her skin. Chloe toppled back into the dining room but quickly found her feet. The fat man, meanwhile, rumbled down the stairs and out the front door.

"I told you not to come here," the Auditor seethed, her icy coolness gone. "We made a bargain."

"You made a bargain with my mother," Chloe said. "Not me."

Inside the dragonfly, the Auditor's poisonous presence balled up and then unclenched savagely, pushing with a ferocity that took Chloe's breath away. Again she was evicted from her Tan'ji, and again the Auditor leapt. Chloe stumbled back, this time regaining possession of the dragonfly just as a whistling swing of the Auditor's long arm swept through her, a blow that would have broken her arm had she not been thin. Chloe retreated into the kitchen, unwilling to slip out through the walls or the floor while her hold on the dragonfly was so tenuous. Dimly she realized that she couldn't find even a drop of her usual rage. What was wrong with her?

"Afraid to go underground now, are we?" the Auditor taunted from the kitchen door. "Afraid I'll do to you what you just did to my sister?"

Not my fault, Chloe thought, trying not to imagine what it must have felt like. Buried deep and dark forever, eaten by the earth. Unbidden, the memory of that horrible day so many years ago floated back to her. The ground like black bottomless water, with no shore in sight. Her legs sinking beneath the surface. "The dragonfly is mine," Chloe said. "Your sister had no right to it, and neither do you."

"It's you who have no right, Tinker. Even so, we came for the empath, not you. I had no quarrel with you until now."

"I wish I could say the same," Chloe replied. Mustering up what anger she could, she tried to thrust the Auditor out of the Alvalaithen. But the Auditor held fast like a seawall in a storm, and countered with a mighty surge of her own. Chloe was swept away, evicted for a third time. And this time, when Chloe tried to reach for the Alvalaithen again, she found herself utterly blocked. Impossible. Unthinkable. The Auditor had hold of her Tan'ji, not granting an inch. Again Chloe tried to find her rage, but instead found something much worse, something that couldn't help her now.

Fear.

Still Chloe kept reaching for the dragonfly, backing away to the far end of the kitchen. The Auditor crept closer, her blue eyes glinting madly and the red stone pulsing fast. "This is the end for you, Tinker," she said, her words like blades. *"Dolu ji'tatha, na'dola ji'daenu.* You have my sympathy, but not my mercy."

An ear-bursting *crack!* slapped the air. Chloe flinched even as she went thin—the Alvalaithen was hers again, the Auditor's presence yanked loose completely. And now the Auditor was hurtling toward her through the air, not leaping but thrown, her beautiful cruel face rippling with pain. Chloe didn't even have time to get out of the way. The Auditor flashed through her, hot and swift, crashing into the wall behind and crumpling in a silent heap.

Chest heaving, Chloe turned to find Mr. Meister standing in the kitchen doorway, his hand raised. Horace was at his side. She straightened, trying to find her spine, drinking deeply from the Alvalaithen and trying to forget that for a brief moment, it hadn't been hers. She shoved her hands into her pockets and forced a scowl onto her face.

"What took you so long?" she said.

As Horace and Mr. Meister ran through the woods toward April's house, Horace heard a car engine approaching. Then the spit of gravel and the honk of a horn. When they emerged from the trees, they found Beck's cab was sitting out front in a cloud of dust. The driver emerged and nodded at them. A moment later, Neptune dropped out of the sky onto the hood. "They're coming," she said, pointing. "April and Gabriel—they're nearly here."

As if on cue, April emerged from the darkness at the far corner of the house, seeming to appear from nowhere. An older boy was at her side, about Gabriel's age. Her brother, no doubt. Beyond them, he could just make out a slippery patch of air that indicated the humour. But where was Gabriel?

"Dr. Jericho's inside the humour," April explained. "Gabriel's keeping him busy."

A moment later, a huge man stumbled out of the house, looking bewildered. He staggered to a halt, staring around in confusion.

"Uncle Harrison!" April cried.

"April, get your family into the cab," Mr. Meister ordered. "Neptune, go to Gabriel. Tell him to bring the humour to the front of the house. Hide the cab. Once everyone is inside, we'll take the humour down and deal with Dr. Jericho."

Neptune nodded and sprang away. A few seconds later, she vanished into the humour.

Mr. Meister looked at Horace, at the phalanx in his hand. "Ready?"

But Horace wasn't ready. Not remotely. "What about Chloe? Where is she?"

April's uncle, who was reluctantly being led toward the cab, turned and called out, "I don't know what you all are doing, or who you are, but there's a girl in my house with a woman after her. If that girl's your friend, you better get after her. Last I saw, she was getting cut up."

Cut up? That was impossible. Horace sprinted toward the front door, Mr. Meister close behind.

A Mordin lay in the front room, apparently wounded. He seemed unable to move, and Horace saw why—his hand was pinned to the floor, right through the flesh. "You're too late," he sang when he saw them. Without thinking, Horace fired the phalanx at him, pressing him against the ground as if a couch had landed on him. The Mordin struggled for breath.

They heard the Auditor from farther back in the house. Mr. Meister scampered through the dining room, raising his hand. From the next doorway, he fired his mysterious weapon, making the house tremble. Horace joined him just in time to see the Auditor crashing into the far kitchen wall. Chloe stood there cringing, looking as frightened and as small as he'd ever seen her. Then she saw them, straightened, and scowled.

"What took you so long?" she said.

625

"Overconfidence," Mr. Meister said. "Come, we found April. It's time to go."

They returned to the front door, only to find that it opened into nothing. Literally nothing. Horace's eyes refused to see outside, as if the world did not exist. Gabriel had brought the humour into the front driveway, as Mr. Meister had asked.

"Follow me into the humour," said Mr. Meister. "Dr. Jericho is still out there. I'll give Gabriel the word, and he'll take the humour down so we can deal with the Mordin. Horace, have the phalanx at the ready." Then he stepped forward and vanished from sight.

Horace refilled the phalanx, watching Chloe from the corner of her eye. Her face was ashen. "You okay?"

She tugged her hood up over her head. "Why wouldn't I be?"

"Tough night."

"Not for me."

He noticed that her sweatshirt was torn, three ragged slices. He thought he saw blood. However that had happened, she wasn't ready to talk about it. "Let's go then," he said, and turned toward the door to nowhere.

But then something terrible happened. A hand emerged from the nothingness of the doorway, with fingers like tent stakes. Then a leg—long and thin and black. Finally a head, stooping through the doorway, black hair and beady eyes and a wide grin filled with tiny sharp teeth.

Dr. Jericho's small black eyes widened when he saw them.

"My dear Keepers!" he cried smoothly. "I'm so surprised to find you home."

Without a word, without a thought, Horace whipped the phalanx forward, willing the power out the tip. The yellow light lit the Mordin's face as he recoiled in shock, lurching back into the humour. The shot struck Dr. Jericho in the chest just as he vanished from sight.

"Whoa," Chloe said. "Did you get him?"

"I got him," Horace said. "I think he's right—"

One of Dr. Jericho's horrible hands groped suddenly out of the void, grasping the doorframe. His hideous, four-knuckled fingers curled and strained, digging furrows into the wood. But he clearly could come no closer.

"I got him," said Horace. "But we're definitely not going this way."

"Why isn't the humour coming down? Gabriel must be seeing this. It's safe now."

"Unless it isn't."

"Come on," said Chloe. "Out the back."

They ran through the house, burst out the back door, and hurtled down the steps. Just as they rounded the corner, though, Neptune suddenly alighted on the grass in front of them. "Not this way," she said. "Come on." She ran past them, across the backyard, toward the woods, explaining as she went. "The others just left. Four more Mordin showed up, and we couldn't wait. Gabriel's driving, if you can imagine that, with the cab in the humour."

That explained why Gabriel hadn't brought the humour down. "So what do we do?" Horace asked.

"Second verse, same as the first. The Riven will be distracted by their wounded, but we need to get away. We'll head for the falkrete circle and go back home the way we came."

"But everyone else is safe, right?" asked Horace. "Everyone got away."

Neptune nodded. "Everyone but us," she said merrily.

CHAPTER THIRTY-TWO

What Lies Ahead

HORACE, CHLOE, AND NEPTUNE BROKE OUT OF THE WOODS AND hurried through the meadow, not quite running. Horace was exhausted, and hauling his big frame as fast as he could. He wasn't sure how long Dr. Jericho would remain pinned, but Horace hoped to be long gone before he had a chance to find out.

Chloe ran in front, not daring to go thin. Neptune, whose tourminda was all but undetectable, was taking full advantage of her instrument, loping slowly at Horace's side. Nonetheless, he noticed she seemed to be limping faintly, and the pinkie on her left hand was bent sideways, sticking out at an impossible angle. "Oh my god," Horace blurted. "What happened to your finger?"

Neptune blinked at him with those big, innocent eyes. She spread her hands as she ran, letting her crooked pinkie

629

stick out grotesquely. "What finger?"

"Uh . . . ," Horace said.

"I'm kidding, of course." Neptune glanced at her hand. "Don't worry. It's only dislocated. Mrs. Hapsteade will pop it back in."

At last they arrived at the barn. They took out their jithandras and huddled around the falkrete circle. Neptune pointed to a stone that looked like the hump of a sea serpent. "Here's our starting stone. I'll have to go first, to re-mark the trail. We need to go faster than last time, so we can get out of here. Fifteen seconds between jumps?"

"That might be too fast for me," Horace said. "I'm slow through the falkretes. But I'll just go last."

"No way," Chloe said. "No one's letting you go last. It should be me, and everyone knows it."

"I'll just slow you down."

"You say that like it's a new thing."

"Chloe goes last," Neptune said. "Look for the mints, and go as fast as you can. Now get inside the barn so I can have my privacy."

Horace and Chloe hurried into the barn, their jithandras casting swaying shadows as they ducked beneath the tilting doorway. Horace took a cobweb to the face and swiped it away, spitting. They moved out of sight and stood there, waiting. Horace began counting automatically.

"You okay?" he asked Chloe quietly.

"Some ways yes, some ways . . . probably not."

"You're hurt," he said, pointing to her torn sweatshirt.

"Just a scratch. That blue-eyed Auditor evicted me, and I couldn't stay thin. She was so angry, and I just couldn't . . ." She trailed off. "She deserved to be angry. I didn't."

"Because of what happened to the first Auditor, you mean," Horace said gently. "She went underground with you, didn't she? But she didn't come up."

"Has it been fifteen seconds yet?"

"Okay," Horace said. "We'll talk later."

Chloe nodded, avoiding his gaze. But as he turned to go, she said, "That would be good."

Horace went out to the falkrete circle. Neptune was gone. He unholstered the box and found the falkrete stone that looked like a sea serpent. Bracing himself, ready to force himself through, he laid the box against the stone.

Nothing happened.

Frowning, he lifted the box, then touched it to the stone again. And again.

Still nothing. No doubling, no other cloister.

"It's not working!" he called out.

"Not with you shouting like that," Chloe called back. "You're very obviously here, and not there."

"Very funny."

"Are you sure it's the right stone?"

"Come and see."

Chloe came out of the barn and over to him. She squatted down beside him. "It's the right stone, all right. Let me try."

631

She unhooked the dragonfly. Horace just sat there beside her, waiting, until finally she said, "Privacy please?"

"Oh, right. Duh." Horace wandered over to the barn and slipped inside, somehow stumbling into another cobweb. As he swiped it away, a terrible thought occurred to him—maybe the falkrete stone wasn't working because someone was watching. Maybe the Riven were out in the darkness, observing them, preventing them from leaving. His heart started to pound.

A moment later, though, Chloe spoke. "It's working now—*whoop!* Okay, it was working until I said that, and you heard me. That is so super weird."

"But it's working for you."

"Yes." A silent pause, while she apparently tried again, and then: "Yes."

"Go ahead and go, then."

"Nope, you first."

"Chloe, just go. I'll come right after, okay? Like ten seconds after."

He heard her sigh. "Fine. But ten seconds. I'll go super fast, so don't be all gentlemanly and give me extra time."

"Okay."

"I'm serious, Horace."

"I got it. Just go already."

"I'll wait for you in the tunnels under the home cloister."

Silence. Horace counted to five. "Chloe?" he called. No response. He was alone.

He hurried out of the barn and over to the falkrete circle, box still in hand. He crouched down beside the stone and—precisely at ten seconds—laid the box against it.

Nothing happened.

"Come on, come on," he muttered to himself, and tried again.

Still nothing.

Horace went cold. There was only one logical explanation for this.

Someone *was* watching him.

He stood up slowly. He spun in a circle, searching the wide darkness that surrounded him, but between the twenty-foot circle of light cast by his jithandra and the star-filled dome of the night sky overhead, there was only a wide expanse of utter black, sprinkled with fireflies. Anything could be out there. He strained his ears, listening hard.

He heard nothing but the buzz and swell of insects. He tucked his jithandra away, knowing his eyes would eventually adjust—starlight was actually decently bright, if you gave your eyes enough time to adapt. But Horace feared he didn't have that time.

"Time," he murmured. Of course—the Fel'Daera wasn't hindered by darkness. He raised it to his eyes, preparing himself. It was 11:17, and the breach was still set to four minutes and thirty-four seconds. He opened the lid. Through the blue glass, a figure, startlingly close—*Horace himself, just a couple of feet away, the phalanx in his hand, and twenty feet beyond,*

Dr. Jericho, tall and mutating; now, his long arms spreading wide as if in greeting, the lips of his many merging faces peeled back into a smile.

Horace slammed the box closed, his mind racing. He stared out into the darkness with his own eyes, seeing nothing yet. But there could be no doubt—the thin man was out there somewhere right now, perhaps even far away across the flat meadow, stalking through the impenetrable darkness and watching Horace from his great height with his keen night eyes. He could see Horace, right now. Dr. Jericho might be a thousand feet away, but because he was watching, Horace could not escape through the falkrete.

And what was worse, Horace suspected that the Mordin had seen Chloe, too, but had chosen to let her go. It would have been easy—a simple matter of closing his eyes until she was gone.

Dr. Jericho wanted Horace all to himself.

"I know you're out there!" Horace shouted, loud as he could. His words rolled across the open meadow. A few seconds later, a faint and shivery tinkle of laughter returned to him on the night breeze, chilling him even further.

"Patience, Tinker," Dr. Jericho called, clearly still a very long ways off. His voice sliced through the night like a knife. "I'll arrive when I arrive—as you're no doubt aware."

Horace started to panic. He was well and truly alone out here, and the thin man was coming. Yes, Horace still had the phalanx, but even if he used it to immobilize the Mordin,

634

it seemed likely that Dr. Jericho would still be able to see him, preventing his escape. Meanwhile, seventeen seconds had already passed since closing the box. How much time did Horace have?

Horace yanked the box open again. He didn't look inside—not yet. He didn't even know what, exactly, he hoped to see. But he knew that the Mordin would sense that the Fel'Daera was open. He wanted Dr. Jericho to fear Horace's knowledge of the future. The question was, how could Horace use that knowledge to make his escape?

"Ah, there it is," Dr. Jericho called out from the distant darkness, clearly sensing the box. "Good news, I hope? Tell me, how far into the future are we looking today?"

So it seemed Dr. Jericho couldn't sense how wide the breach was. That was good news. But Horace could smell the brimstone now. He tried to calm himself. He was going to have to outsmart the Mordin somehow, which meant that this approaching future was a puzzle he was going to have to solve. And the first step in the solving—as always—was to see truly. He lifted the open box to his eyes.

But through the blue glass, a horrifying sight—*the clear meadow marred with blurring shapes, one small and one tall, first here and then there; the thin man—stooping, running, fallen, standing, absent altogether; Horace himself—dodging, crawling, backing away, the blue light of his jithandra flashing.*

None of it was clear. None of it was decipherable. The future was a mash of a dozen different possibilities, and

Horace couldn't make sense of any of it.

His panic grew. He'd opened the box too quickly. If he couldn't see the future clearly, his greatest weapon against the Mordin was lost. He couldn't threaten Dr. Jericho with the future if he couldn't even see it! He started to close the box, to reset himself, when suddenly a memory drifted to the surface of his mind: Horace in the Riven's nest, telling Dr. Jericho what his own future would be. And the Mordin had asked the obvious questions:

Why on earth would Horace tell Dr. Jericho his future?

And was that future true?

If Dr. Jericho knew what his future was, he could then work to avoid it. The logical assumption, of course, was that Horace might be lying, trying to steer Dr. Jericho into any dangers—or away from any successes—that the box had foreseen. In that particular instance, in the nest, Horace hadn't been lying.

But why couldn't he lie? Why shouldn't he?

Horace looked into the still-open box. More blurring, more uncertainty. And then for a moment, the entire scene went utterly black. Horace held his breath, but then the meadow returned, the uncertain futures of Horace and Dr. Jericho blurring to and fro across it.

Horace knew what that blackness was. He'd seen it before at the river. The box in the present was occupying the same space as either himself or Dr. Jericho in the future, the glass opening up inside one of their bodies. It was a gruesome notion, but one he'd become accustomed to. In fact—somewhat morbidly—he had often wondered what would happen if he were to send something forward at just that moment, into that future body. He was pretty sure the result would be something like what happened when Chloe used the dragonfly to meld—

Horace's mouth fell open. "Oh, holy cow," he said. He knew what he had to do.

He moved quickly, unsure how much time he had until Dr. Jericho arrived. He pulled his jithandra out of his shirt and returned to the ruins of the barn, to the hard-packed dirt floor. Leaving the box open, he got on his knees and pried a pebble the size of a grape out of the ground. He crawled around, scanning and scraping, until he'd found six more stones of decent size, and then he went back outside to the falkrete circle.

He could hear the thin man's footsteps now, faint but steady, perhaps two hundred feet away. Horace knew the thin man could still see him, but it didn't matter. Let him watch. Let him sense the Fel'Daera. Let him wonder.

Horace picked a spot at random a few feet away from the sea serpent stone and made a show of looking through the box without actually looking. He took note of the time—just a handful of seconds before 11:20. He dropped a single rock inside and then closed the lid, sending the rock four minutes and thirty-four seconds into the future. No sooner had the familiar tingle wormed up his arms than Dr. Jericho spoke again from the darkness, much closer now. "What's this? What are we up to, Tinker?"

Horace ignored him. He opened the box again and hurried to a new spot near the falkrete circle. He sent another stone, fast as he could. He continued this way methodically, picking a new spot each time, sending stone after stone. Just as he reached the sixth stone, Dr. Jericho at last appeared in the flesh, looking taller than ever in the flat expanse of the meadow, faintly lit by the jithandra's blue glow and the white light of stars overhead.

Horace looked into the box as if taking careful aim and dropped the sixth rock inside. Barely twenty seconds had passed since he began. Then he met the thin man's eye and closed the lid, slowly and deliberately. The stone vanished with a tingle. Still gripping the seventh and final stone in his other hand, he then slipped the Fel'Daera back into its pouch and pulled the phalanx from his pocket. Swiftly he filled the phalanx with the Fel'Daera's power.

"My, but you've been busy, Tinker," Dr. Jericho said. "What have you been up to, I wonder?"

"Stick around and you'll find out."

"Such confidence." The thin man began to circle him slowly, looking predatory even with his gruesome hands folded behind his back.

"The Fel'Daera tends to do that to a person," said Horace. "Maybe you'd like to hear what I saw through the glass just now."

"Once again, you're so eager to share," Dr. Jericho sneered. "Just like you were on the riverbank."

"When I saved your life, you mean."

The Mordin let out a low growl and took a half step toward Horace.

"Yes," Horace said sweetly. "Keep moving. Just like that."

Dr. Jericho froze. His eyes dropped to the Fel'Daera. "Tell me what you saw."

Horace would tell him, yes—but not the truth. "I saw you, on your hands and knees. You were immobilized." He indicated the phalanx.

"How fascinating," said Dr. Jericho, frowning deeply at the ivory-colored wand.

"It gets better," Horace said. "You seem to know a lot about the Fel'Daera. So maybe you know what happens when the Keeper of the box looks forward through time and finds his view of the future obstructed by an object that has moved—"

"Juxtaposition," the Mordin said.

Horace nodded as though he'd heard the word before. Again the Mordin's familiarity with the Fel'Daera was like a blade of doubt between Horace's ribs. He was sweating now. "Juxtaposition," Horace repeated confidently. "Right. Like I said, the box showed you on your hands and knees. You were pinned—you *will be* pinned. You will be struggling. I came in for a closer look. Very close. In fact, I put the open box into the space where your chest will be. It was black, obviously—no light—and so I only approximated. But I'm pretty sure I got close enough."

Dr. Jericho crossed his long arms, considering it. "Close enough for what?"

For an answer, Horace tossed him the seventh and final stone. The thin man snatched it out of the air deftly, quick as a snake. He examined it and smiled gruesomely.

"You sent a stone forward into my heart."

"Yes," Horace lied. "I sent six altogether—I'm sure you felt them. But I sent them to six different times."

"Playing with the breach again, oh my."

"Six different times, and also six different places, somewhere in a twenty-foot radius of where I'm standing now. Five of the stones were decoys, but one was not. Good luck figuring out which one was the one that mattered."

Dr. Jericho chucked the rock into the weeds. "Such a big promise from such a clever boy," he sang. "I wonder if you will deliver."

"Wonder all you like. But good luck deciding what to *do*."

Horace went on meeting the Mordin's gaze, determined not to back down. Everything depended on this bluff, on convincing the Mordin to avoid the false future Horace had invented. Horace kept his strength going by putting himself in Dr. Jericho's shoes, by realizing that—just as Horace had hoped—he'd presented the Mordin with a difficult proposition. Dr. Jericho had to at least *suspect* that Horace's version of the future was true. And if it was true, how could Dr. Jericho possibly know how to avoid it? Two steps this way, three steps that way, a sudden charge—any of these things might lead to his death. As the Fel'Daera had supposedly seen.

There was one problem, of course. Time was passing. Any moment now, Dr. Jericho would feel the Fel'Daera opening in the past, right after Horace's last failed attempt with the falkrete stone. And roughly two minutes and ten seconds after that, the first of Horace's six pebbles would arrive. The rest would follow quickly after, and his fragile threat would fall apart.

Right on cue, Dr. Jericho smiled and spread his arms wide, just as Horace had foreseen when he first opened the box four minutes and thirty-four seconds ago. "Ah, there it is. The Fel'Daera is open in the past. Watching this very scene, no doubt."

"Yes."

"And as for the stones, you claim that I won't know when or where they'll arrive."

"That's right."

Dr. Jericho went on watching him thoughtfully. Abruptly he feinted a step to the left, making Horace's heart skip a beat. Now he feinted to the right. Horace held the phalanx at the ready but didn't so much as blink. Dr. Jericho shook his head ruefully. "This way, that way," he muttered, echoing Horace's own hopeful thoughts. "Whatever I do now, there's a chance I'll be starting a chain of events that ends with you killing me."

"No," Horace said. "You'd be killing yourself."

"Perhaps so, perhaps so." Dr. Jericho grinned viciously. "But what if I said I did not believe a bit of this tale?"

"It doesn't matter whether you believe it or not," Horace said. "It's still true."

After a beat, Dr. Jericho broke into laughter. He went on laughing, his musical cackles filling the night air. He bent forward toward Horace. *"Delicious,"* he said through a toothy, foot-wide smile, and then straightened to his full, towering height. "So delicious, in fact, that perhaps I will yield to you. Perhaps I will let you go, Horace."

Horace tried not to grimace, hearing the sound of his own name on the Mordin's lips for the first time. "You say that like you have a choice."

"And I do. You of all people should know that there is always a choice." He laughed again and then sighed. "But I cannot risk my life on a suspicion. You win."

Relief flooded through Horace. He didn't dare show it. In one more minute, the first stone would arrive. "Yes," he said. "I win, again." He stepped back and knelt beside the falkrete stone that would take him away, unholstering the Fel'Daera with one hand while clinging to the phalanx with the other. "Now close your eyes."

Dr. Jericho's smile abruptly faded. He bent his neck like a coiled snake. "First, a question," he said. "By convincing me not to risk my life, haven't you changed the future the box supposedly promised you? I'm curious whether you're feeling ill yet. You've disobeyed the Fel'Daera, after all."

Thrall-blight. Horace hadn't thought of that. He reasoned it out quickly—if he said he felt sick, that would mean the pretend future where Dr. Jericho died had been lost, right? "I feel fine," he said, a stab in the dark.

"Interesting," said Dr. Jericho, with a flat tone that suggested Horace had guessed right. But the Mordin went on. "Thrall-blight is a pernicious condition, you know—it does its damage slowly, unseen. I'm sure Mr. Meister told you all about it."

"I'm sure he did," Horace said, refusing to take the bait. Twenty-five seconds until the arrival of the first stone.

Dr. Jericho bent down from his great height until his eyes were level with Horace's. "Then he also told you—I'm sure—that the Mothergates are dying."

Horace froze. Precious seconds ticked past, but the Mordin's words stunned him so deeply he stopped counting.

"As I suspected," the Mordin said quietly, straightening again. "Go then. Ask your master. See what he has to say." He took a step back and closed his eyes.

Horace still couldn't speak. The Mothergates, the source of the energy that powered all Tanu . . . dying? Impossible. "You're a terrible liar," he managed at last.

"Am I?" Dr. Jericho murmured, his voice like a sad violin. "Ask him to take you there. Lay your eyes upon the Veil. Take the empath with you, and see what she learns. And then when we next meet, perhaps we will speak more about the truth."

He turned his back on Horace. "Go now, before I change my mind. Before the others come. My eyes are closed, so go—go and find your answers."

His mind in a spin, with mere seconds before the arrival of the first rock, Horace touched the box against the falkrete stone—gently, *gently*, without the slightest sound. Immediately he was yanked out of himself, torn in two. The open sky overhead disappeared. The smell of brimstone vanished. Horace toppled onto the ground in some new place, gasping and struggling to rid himself of the remnants of a dream he hadn't had—a dream in which he'd died, in which the Mothergates died with him. He blinked, trying to get his bearings. There was a stone in the ground in front of him. It looked like a mother bear sleeping.

"Horace."

Horace struggled to sit up. High cloister walls surrounded him. "Chloe?"

"Horace. Am I dreaming this?"

He spotted her. She was on her hands and knees in the dirt, the dragonfly shining in her hand. And somehow the sight of her Tan'ji cleared Horace's mind, made him remember himself. He'd escaped from Dr. Jericho and his terrible tales. He'd come through the falkrete stone. Chloe must have been here in the next cloister, and her presence had yanked him through.

"Chloe," he said again, her name on his lips helping him shed the horrors that clung to him. "Have you been waiting here this whole time?"

"No. Not waiting. Been breaking and breaking and breaking in two."

Horace understood at once. She'd gone all the way back to San'ska, the home cloister. But when Horace hadn't followed, she had eventually come back for him. Six jumps home, then five jumps back—on top of the six they'd made to get to April's in the first place. He could scarcely imagine it.

He found his feet. He holstered the box and shoved the phalanx into his pocket. He went over and sat down beside her. Chloe rolled onto her back, arms thrown out to her sides.

"Tell me I'm here," she said. "Tell me this is it."

"You're here. This is it. You came back for me—you shouldn't have."

"I almost didn't. Lots of me didn't. Part of me with every jump. I need to gather myself for a minute." Her eyes found his. "Tell me again."

"You're here. We're here. This is it."

She nodded and looked up into the sky. The soft broad branches of a ginkgo hovered overhead. "You were late," she said. "So late. I waited forever—didn't I?"

Horace did the math. "Seven minutes. I'm sorry."

"Are you going to tell me what happened?"

No, he almost blurted out, and then said simply, "Dr. Jericho."

She nodded. "God, I hate that guy. How did you get away?"

"I . . . outsmarted him. I think."

Another nod. "You were always the smartest." She lay

there breathing and gazing up into the leaves above. "I need to lie here awhile. I can't go back yet."

"Of course not. There's no hurry. We're safe here." He lay down beside her, looking up into the tree. He tried to open his mouth to tell Chloe what Dr. Jericho had said about the Mothergates, but he couldn't bring himself to repeat that terrible lie.

Chloe spoke instead. "That Auditor," she began.

Horace nudged her foot with his, urging her silently on.

"She died," said Chloe.

"I know," he said gently.

"I mean I killed her."

Horace swallowed. "I know."

After that, they both let it be. Overhead, the leaves of the ginkgo shifted and rustled like a flock of whispering birds. The Alvalaithen shone in Chloe's hand, a captive star. Slowly the urgency and horror of the last half-hour lifted. The night's hard deeds began to become memories, remote and pliable. After a while, a solitary lightning bug flashed its way through the night air above them.

Chloe pointed. "Hey," she said. "Remember Rip?"

"Never forget him," Horace said with a smile. "Rip Van Twinkle, time-travel pioneer."

"I wonder . . . do you wonder if, after we let him go, he went and told his friends about his adventures?"

Horace didn't bother to tell her that there was a good chance Rip had already died of old age. Instead he told her,

"He's the most famous firefly now. He's a legend."

But Chloe shook her head. "No," she said. "He's locked up, because of all the crazy things he says. No one believes a word. And I don't blame them." She looked over at Horace. "Do you?"

Horace tried to think what to say. He shrugged. The lightning bug drifted out of sight over the cloister wall. "It's crazy," he agreed at last. "It's crazy what we do."

CHAPTER THIRTY-THREE

How Long Nothing Lasts

UNSURPRISINGLY—ALTHOUGH HER ARRIVAL STARTLED THEM both half to death—Neptune came looking for Horace and Chloe. She popped into the orange bird cloister with a crabby groan, yanked through in the instant Horace spotted her. She fell back onto her cloak, clutching her head, and said, "This is the real me, of course. Right?"

"Of course," said Horace. "Who else would you be?"

"Fallen angel," Neptune said dreamily. "I've been falling a lot lately. It's not optimal."

The three of them sat in the cloister and talked, slowly finding themselves, finding their faith in the now. Eventually they would have to start back through the falkretes toward the Warren, but none of them was ready, least of all Neptune and Chloe. They'd made the journey three times already. Strangely, despite the fact that Neptune was far more experienced with falkrete travel than Horace and Chloe, she seemed the loopiest of the three. They kept her talking for a while, discussing the deeds of the night and the fates of the other Wardens—Mr. Meister, Gabriel, April. Not to mention Beck. Neptune seemed not at all concerned, convinced that Gabriel had gotten them all away safely.

"Why do they try so hard?" Chloe said.

"Who?" asked Horace.

"The Riven. Why can't they just leave us be? Is it really so awful if a few humans here and there are Tan'ji?"

"You've got it all wrong," said Neptune. "All wrong." She took a great breath and let it out slow. "How much do you even know about the Riven?"

Chloe shrugged. "The basics. They were the Makers. They want the Tanu because they think they're the rightful owners."

"And do you think they are? Rightful, I mean?"

The question startled Horace. "Do you?" he asked.

"Not totally," Neptune replied. "I can't—I'm a legacy. My mom was the Keeper of the Devlin tourminda before me, and her dad before her, and so on. If anything, I'm proof the Tanu don't all belong only to the Riven. Not totally."

The way Neptune talked, it sounded as if she felt the Riven had a rightful claim to at least some of the Tanu. "What do you mean, *not totally?*" Chloe demanded.

"It's not a simple matter of the Riven possessing the Tanu, you know," Neptune explained. "Humans and the

Riven—and the Altari, for that matter—have lived side by side for centuries without the kinds of conflicts we have now." She shrugged. "Or so I'm told."

Horace was confused. "That's not exactly how Mr. Meister described it."

"Yeah, well."

"Yeah, well, what?" Chloe said.

"There are secrets you haven't earned yet." She pointed her horrid pinkie at Horace. "Especially you."

"Me? Why me?"

Neptune propped herself up on one arm, looking straight at Horace. Her normally blank eyes were full of dark mischief. "Have you heard of the Mothergates?"

Horace's breath caught in his chest. "They're the source of the Medium," he said. "That's where the power for our Tan'ji comes from."

"Close enough," Neptune replied. "There are three of them, spread out around the world. But one of them is practically in our backyard. Would you be surprised if I told you I'd seen it? Up close and in person?"

Horace remembered his mom saying that one of the Mothergates was only a couple hundred miles away. "What did it look like?" he asked.

"I couldn't tell you. Not one thing. You can't see through the Veil."

The Veil. Horace's mother had mentioned that too.

And so had Dr. Jericho.

"What is the Veil, exactly?" Chloe asked.

"The Veil of Lura," Neptune breathed. "It keeps the Mothergates hidden. It's so beautiful, you guys. You have no idea." She slid her hand through the air, wiggling her fingers. "It's so beautiful that if you didn't know better you'd never suspect—" Neptune stopped midgesture, staring at her hand. She balled it into a fist over and over again, watching her crooked pinkie carefully. "Hey. A few cloisters back, I was sure my finger had fallen off. It's sort of a surprise to see it here now." She paused and furrowed her brow. "It is here, isn't it?"

Chloe looked over at Horace. He refused to meet her gaze. What was Neptune saying? *"You'd never suspect"* . . . what? Had Dr. Jericho been telling the truth about the Mothergates? If the Mothergates were dying, surely that meant the Tanu would die too. But that couldn't be. The thought was impossible. Not even Mr. Meister would keep a secret like that.

"I'm sorry," Neptune said. "I shouldn't be saying these things. I haven't found my head yet. Seventeen jumps in one night! It's funny though—I suppose that means that there's a different path upon which I told you everything." She looked Horace firmly in the eye again and smiled disconcertingly. *"Everything."*

Horace held up his hands. Were they shaking? "I think you've said plenty for now. I don't really want to hear any more. If Mr. Meister hasn't told us, then . . ." He trailed off, unable find the right excuses. Again he felt Chloe's eyes on him. The Alvalaithen gleamed at her throat. So pure and white and bursting with power.

"You don't want to hear more," Neptune said. "That's fine. Also dandy, of course. But you know how it goes, Keeper—tick tock, tick tock. And if Mr. Meister has a flaw, it's an excess of patience. He practices patience on a geological scale."

"Okay, so don't tell Horace," Chloe said suddenly. "Tell me."

"Chloe—" Horace began, but Neptune interrupted him with a laugh.

"You're kidding, right?" she said. "You guys are like two halves of the same bun. I'd be willing to take a kick to the face for every secret you two keep from each other."

"You might be surprised by how much you get kicked, then," Chloe said stubbornly.

"I tell you what," Neptune said. She grasped her tourminda in her good hand and began to hover a few inches in the air. She paddled at the ground and drifted toward them, crossing her legs while airborne, a wide-eyed genie. "No secrets, just a riddle. Surely Mr. Meister wouldn't object to that. Everyone likes riddles. Don't you?"

"We like riddles, yes," said Chloe, before Horace could stop her. "Heck, Horace eats riddles for breakfast."

Horace held his breath.

"Okay then, here goes," Neptune said, still floating. She

leaned over them conspiratorially. "Do you know how long nothing lasts?"

Chloe shook her head, transfixed. "How long?"

Neptune spread herself wide—her arms, her eyes, her smile. Her tourminda glinted darkly between the fingers of her fist. "Forever," she whispered gleefully. And then she dropped to the ground, fell back laughing, and promptly— shockingly—went to sleep.

Horace still couldn't take a breath. Chloe whirled around to glare at him, the dragonfly swinging wide on its cord as if it were alive. "Nothing lasts forever," she said. "What kind of riddle is that?"

Horace shook his head to say he didn't know—but he did know. He knew it with a certainty he could scarcely stomach. He reached down and cradled the Fel'Daera in his hand as if it were his own racing heart, his own drowning hope.

There were no riddles here. Only secrets buried deep underground, miserable truths hidden beneath lie upon lie.

The Mothergates were dying.

And Mr. Meister knew it.

GLOSSARY

Altari (all-TAR-ee)
: the Makers of the Tanu, and the ancestors of the Riven

Alvalaithen (al-vuh-LAYTH-en)
: Chloe's Tan'ji, the dragonfly, the Earthwing; with it, she can become incorporeal

Auditor
: a type of Riven; though not Tan'ji, they can imitate the powers of nearby instruments

breach
: the gap in time across which the Fel'Daera sees into the future

cleave
: to forcibly and permanently rip apart the bond between a Keeper and his or her Tan'ji

cloister
: one of the small safe havens of the Wardens, usually a walled

654

	garden containing a leestone and a falkrete circle
daktan (dock-TAHN)	a piece broken off a Tan'ji, usually through deliberate sabotage
dispossessed	term for a Keeper who is permanently cut off from his or her instrument, usually by cleaving or being severed for too long
doba	small stone buildings in the Great Burrow; living quarters
dumin (DOO-min)	a spherical shield of force through which almost nothing can pass; a dumin is created by crushing a small glass ball called a *dumindar*
empath	a Keeper who can read the minds of nonhuman animals
falkrete	the strangely shaped stones found in cloisters; usually arranged in a circle, only a few of these stones possess the power they once did
Fel'Daera (fel-DARE-ah)	Horace's Tan'ji, the Box of Promises; with it, he can see a short distance into the future
Find, the	the solitary period during which

	a new Keeper masters his or her instrument
Great Burrow	the uppermost chamber of the Warren
harp	an instrument used by Tuners; only Tuners can use a harp, but harps are not Tan'ji
jithandra (jih-THAHN-drah)	a small, personalized Tan'kindi used by the Wardens for illumination, identification, and entry into the Warren
Keeper	one who has bonded with an instrument, thus becoming Tan'ji
Kesh'kiri (kesh-KEER-ee)	the name the Riven use for themselves (see "Riven")
Laithe of Teneves (TEN-eevs)	a mysterious Tanu, a spinning globe, in Mr. Meister's possession
leestone	a Tan'kindi that provides some protection against the Riven
Loomdaughters	the first Tan'ji made with the Starlit Loom; there were nine in total
Maw	the great chasm at the back of the Great Burrow
Mazzoleni Academy	the boarding school beneath which the Warren lies
Medium, the	the energy that powers all Tanu

Mordin	Riven who are particularly skilled at hunting down Tan'ji
Mothergates	mysterious in nature, the three Mothergates are the structures through which the Medium flows before reaching out to power all Tanu in the world
Nevren	a field of influence that temporarily severs the bond between a Keeper and his Tan'ji; Nevrens protect the Wardens' strongholds
oublimort	a Tanu within the Warren meant to confound unprepared visitors
oraculum	a Tan'ji belonging to Mr. Meister, a lens that allows him to see the Medium
passkey	a Tan'kindi that allows passage through certain walls
Perilous Stairs	the cliffside staircase that leads down into the Maw in the Warren
raven's eye	a weak and portable kind of leestone, a Tan'kindi
Riven	the secretive race of beings who hunger to claim all the Tanu for their own; they call themselves the Kesh'kiri

San'ska (sahn-SKA)	the home cloister, the haven nearest to the Warren; its leestone is a magpie
sever	to temporarily cut a Keeper off from his or her Tan'ji
Staff of Obro	Gabriel's Tan'ji, a wooden staff with a silver tip; it releases the humour, which blinds others but gives him an acute awareness of his surroundings
Starlit Loom	the very first Tanu; a Tan'ji that gives its Keeper the power to make new Tanu
Tanu (TAH-noo)	the universal term for all of the mysterious devices created by the Makers; the function of these instruments is all but unknown to most (two main kinds of Tanu are Tan'ji and Tan'kindi)
Tan'ji (tahn-JEE)	a special class of Tanu that will only work when bonded with a Keeper who has a specific talent; "Tan'ji" also describes the Keeper himself or herself, as well as the state of that bond—a kind of belonging or being
Tan'kindi (tahn-KIN-dee)	a simpler category of Tanu (raven's eye, dumindar, etc.) that

	will work for anyone; unlike Tan'ji, Tan'kindi do not require a special talent or a bond
Tan'layn (tahn-LAIN)	the term for Tan'ji that do not currently have a Keeper; the unspoken
Tinker	a Kesh'kiri word for ordinary humans
tourminda (tour-MIN-dah)	a fairly common kind of Tan'ji that allows its Keeper to defy gravity; such Keepers—like Neptune—are called *tourmindala*
Tuner	though not Tan'ji, Tuners can use instruments called harps to cleanse and tune other Tanu
Tunraden (toon-RAH-den)	Brian's Tan'ji, a Loomdaughter
Vithra's Eye	the name of the Nevren that guards the Warren; very powerful
Vora	Mrs. Hapsteade's Tan'ji, the quill and ink; it is used to determine the abilitites of potential new Keepers
Wardens	the secret group of Keepers devoted to protecting the Tanu from the Riven
Warren	the Wardens' headquarters beneath the city, deep underground

Acknowledgments

Once again, there are so many people to thank for making this book a reality.

A big thank-you to all the folks at HarperCollins for all their patience and support, especially to my editor, Toni Markiet, who probably had more than one vacation ruined on my behalf. Much gratitude to you for all your great insights. You say the things that have to be said.

To Miriam Altshuler, for your generosity and guidance, and for tirelessly advocating for The Keepers.

Thanks also to Abbe Goldberg, Reiko Davis, Gina Rizzo, for everything you do.

Thanks to all who responded so positively to the first book in the series, and who gave it so much support, including Matt Mulholland, Becky Anderson, Michele Whisenhunt, Ksenya Kouzminova, Jeff and Rosita Durbin, Jason Mierek,

Mathew Green, Brian Delambre, and Randy Lynn.

To Matt Minicucci, for making me leave the house once in a while.

To Laura Koritz, for keeping still. I have you to thank for April.

Thank you to my son, Rowan, for getting better at proving me wrong, and to my stepdaughter, Bridget, for helping to keep me young. I need more of both of those things in my life.

And finally, above all, to my wife, Jodee. More than ever, so much would not have happened without you. Thank you for almost never saying no when I said, "Can I ask you a book question?" Thank you for all the reading, and talking, and arguing, and for helping this project find a way to betterness. Thank you for being the sane one, and for sometimes not. Thank you above all for our family. I love you.